WORLDS
TOGETHER
WORLDS
APART

WORLDS
TOGETHER
WORLDS
APART

David Brown

Lights On

www.worldstogetherworldsapart.com

Published by Lights On Press
lightsonpress@gmail.com
www.worldstogetherworldsapart.com

ISBN 978-9-6592-2110-3 (print)
ISBN 978-9-6592-2111-0 (eBook)

Printed by CreateSpace

This book is dedicated to my wife,
who is truly my life

PROLOGUE

Sunday, June 1, 2014
Old City, Jerusalem

Y OU'VE REACHED BRAHIM Surin. Please leave a short message, and I'll return your call as soon as possible."

"*Salam*, Mr. Surin, this is Yousef Abu Saeed of the PLO. *Shukran*, the fifty million dollars has been confirmed. It reached our bank today. You can be assured, Mr. Surin, it will be put to good use. Our Palestinian homeland desperately needs your gifts. On behalf of the PLO, I wish to thank you personally for your generous support of our work."

Abu Saeed looked out of his window onto the Old City of Jerusalem. The Dome of the Rock glistened. When he made the call, it was 6:45 a.m. He'd already been up for two hours, busy working on the PLO's books.

Outside, the sun was rising. The Old City had a special feeling at that time of morning. It felt as if time stood still, like thousands of years had passed but you were still walking among the prophets. The narrow alleys were filled with homes made of Jerusalem stone. Each house had been rebuilt multiple times. Whenever the old occupiers were driven out by war, new dreamers of peace moved in.

Now some of the merchants were preparing to open their stores.

Bakers had already been at work for hours. You could smell the aroma of the hot pitas fresh from the ovens. Soon tourists and locals alike would be crowding each other in line to purchase their wares. Young Arab boys wearing torn sneakers wove through the freshly washed cobblestone streets with carts full of goods yelling, "Pitas! Hot pitas!" They knew that in this world there are no free lunches.

At the Western Wall the Jews had already started to gather, looking for a tenth man to complete their *minyan*. Morning prayers would commence momentarily. Suddenly the tenth man would appear as if sent from heaven, and the service could begin.

It was known that the Western Wall was a place where prayers were answered directly by the Creator. Millions of visitors placed millions of notes into the crevices between the stones every year. Presidents, kings, and popes had all delighted in ascending the mountain where King Solomon and the Holy Temple once stood.

The Old City had been sliced into pieces like a pie, the Armenians, Christians, Muslims, and Jews each getting a slice of an area totaling only 0.9 square kilometers. Bells from the church steeples rang, the Muslims' minarets groaned five times a day, while the Jews wailed at the Wall.

This was the center of the world and everyone knew it. Everyone prayed for peace, but wars had already destroyed the Holy Temple twice. At midnight, standing on this holy mountain, you could have a conversation with the Creator like nothing else you would ever experience in your life.

Abu Saeed knew the quiet was deceiving. Beneath the surface, things were already boiling over. With a bow toward the Al Aqsa mosque, he prepared to leave for morning prayers. The minarets sounded, calling the faithful to prayer. Abu Saeed had every intention of being one of them. But this morning that would not be the case.

A rapid banging at the door diverted his concentration. Two men with black hooded masks rushed into the room yelling, "*Allahu

Akbar! Allahu Akbar!" Eighteen bullets from their AK-47 automatic weapons penetrated Saeed's body. As he fell to the floor, the Persian carpet beneath him started to fill with his blood. The masked men rolled Saeed into the rug.

A copy of the holy Koran sat next to the telephone. One of the gunmen gently placed it on his chest with a note—"A *thief who stole from our people"*—then turned and left.

As if the minarets knew someone had died suddenly, they fell silent. Life in the Old City kept moving forward, but not for Abu Saeed.

The assassins ran out of the building, guns in hand. They jumped into a 1986 Mercedes Benz with a license plate that read HAMAS in green bold letters. They were gone before anyone knew what had happened. Outside, a crowd of people had gathered. The Old City was getting hotter.

CHAPTER
1

Monday, June 2, 2014
New York City

S AMMI, PULL OVER so I can get some reception on this lousy PDA."

"As soon as I can, boss. Everybody must be driving in today. The traffic is crazy."

"I'm gonna throw this thing out the window."

"Wait a minute, boss. I see a space over there."

"It keeps trying to receive a message."

Sammi pressed the 2014 black Tesla Mandarin limousine's advanced parking guidance system. "Boss, this okay?"

"Sit here for a minute while I try to get the whole message. It's finally working. Okay, they received the wire transfer. Abra will be thrilled. Let's get going."

Sammi Boaz had been driving Brahim Surin for over fifteen years. Brahim had realized that the commute from Jersey was beginning to take a toll on him. One day, as he pulled into his Manhattan Racquetball Club, he decided he needed a driver and fast.

Brahim had looked at John, the club's manager. John always

knew who was coming and who was going and how to get done whatever needed attending to. They were old friends by now, and he'd solved more than a few problems for Brahim in the past.

"Hey, John. How's it going?"

"Fine, Mr. Surin. And you?"

"Good, John. Question for you, though. I need a driver. You know of anyone?"

"Actually, Mr. Surin, I do. He'd be perfect for you. He's even Persian, speaks Farsi and everything. This guy is a good one, came in here looking for work. I liked him, wanted to hire him, but I just didn't have a position available. Maybe you can help him out."

John had handed Brahim a number, and the interview was set for the next day.

As soon as Sammi sat down, Brahim had started in on him. "Talk to me in Farsi."

"*Salam, shoma chetur hastin? Mitoonam ke komaketoon konam?*"

"Alright, now tell me about yourself."

"I was born in a small village in 1960. My parents and the rest of family still live there. It's not far from the Iraqi border. My family has been there for generations."

Brahim noticed that Sammi's face filled with anxiety, and then suddenly his expression had turned into a painful one. Brahim stopped him.

"Enough. You got the job."

"When can I start?"

"Next Monday. I'm leaving for California tonight and will be back Sunday."

Sammi's demeanor changed, and his eyes dropped.

"What's wrong?"

"Mr. Surin, I'm embarrassed to tell you this, but my rent is due Friday, and I don't have the money."

"How much do you need?"

Sammi paused for a moment, his face reddened, and then he whispered, "Four hundred dollars."

Brahim took out his wallet, counted out ten hundred-dollar bills, and placed the money into Sammi's hand. "You owe me nothing except your loyalty."

Sammi's eyes filled with tears. "Thank you, Mr. Surin, thank you so much. This would never have happened in Iran. You have my loyalty until my dying day. *BarakAllahu feekum.* May Allah bless you."

"I'll let you know when I'm due to arrive Sunday at JFK airport. Give my best wishes to your wife and children."

"Have a safe flight. If you need anything done while you are away, please don't hesitate to call."

Brahim turned and left the club. Sammi stood still as he watched him walk out the door.

Sammi was still shocked by what had just happened. John walked over to Sammi. "You got the best boss you're ever going to have."

"I can see that. *Subhaanallah.* Praise to Allah."

SAMMI HAD WORKED for Brahim ever since. Every morning Brahim stood looking out his window, waiting for Sammi to drive through the electronic gates of his Morristown, New Jersey, property. He used the time to think about the blessings Allah had given him. There was so much to be grateful for.

The house had taken two years to build on a one-hundred-acre estate of wooded land set back from the road. The business world added more than enough pressure to Brahim's life, and the house afforded him the calm he needed.

He lived there with his wife, Abra, and their adult children when they were home. Brahim had been a lucky man not only in business but in love as well. His family had made him a good match, as was the custom of the time in Iran. Abra was from a prominent and respected family, but she came with much more than a good name. To both their good fortunes, what had started as an arranged marriage quickly turned into a deep love for one another. It was clear to both of them that they were soul mates from the beginning.

Brahim and Abra loved autumn on the estate. They enjoyed taking pictures of the leaves changing colors when walking in the woods early in the morning. Their two sons, Nasim and Raji, and their daughter, Ghayda, were the pride of their life. The children loved riding their Arabian horses on trails around the estate.

Nasim, the oldest, worked hard in Brahim's business, knowing that one day he would be a partner. Brahim's second son, Raji, had graduated summa cum laude from Harvard Law School and was now working for the election of the first Muslim governor in the United States, planning for the day a Muslim would be president. Ghayda was engaged to a doctor and wasn't interested in much else these days.

Family was everything to Brahim. Nothing was more important.

CHAPTER
2

SAMMI TOOK THE same route every day, over the George Washington Bridge, down Park Avenue to Forty-Ninth Street, arriving in the city as close to 7 a.m. as possible, depending on traffic. He always parked the car in front of the Waldorf Astoria, where they stopped for breakfast.

The black Tesla Mandarin was a special-edition luxury limousine, all electric, completely eco-friendly, requiring only one hour of charge in an electrical socket to yield five hundred miles of travel. Brahim loved that car. His order had special requirements: bullet-proof windows and complete voice automation. When Brahim got the delivery, the final cost was five hundred thousand dollars. Money he felt was well spent.

Joe Madino, the Waldorf's front door attendant, always reserved a parking space for the Tesla Mandarin. Joe was a fixture at the Waldorf. He'd spent almost twenty years holding spots for limos, helping patrons out of their cars, and whistling for cabs.

"Morning, Joe."

"Morning, Sammi."

"What will I do when you retire, Joe?"

"Nothing to worry about. My son Dominic is gonna take over.

And who said anything about me retiring?" He bent down and touched the sidewalk with his hand. "I own this piece of property, Sammi. This is mine."

"You're the best, Joe."

Sammi reached into his pocket and slipped him a twenty-dollar bill before walking inside. The hotel's restaurant, Oscar's, was a famous landmark. Breakfast for Brahim was at the same table every day. As soon as Brahim sat down, the maître d' served him a cup of Turkish coffee.

"How can you drink that without sugar?" Sammi asked.

"I love it." *This is a man's coffee.*

The maître d', accompanied by a waiter, placed before each of them a plate with a large toasted bagel, cream cheese, and smoked salmon. He always served them separate bowls filled with extra-large black and green Greek olives.

He poured Brahim a fresh cup of coffee. Brahim had already finished reading the Arabic daily *Al Hayat* on the way into the city and was about to begin on the *Times*.

Sammi finished eating. "You know, boss, my Persian friends call bagels 'Jew food.' I try to tell them that one of my bosses is a Jew, but they aren't impressed."

"Did you tell them bagels are what make the Jews so smart? Before my partner Isaac eats a bagel, he washes his hands and says a blessing. You know, the Jews weren't affected in the bubonic plague. Most people say it's because they always washed their hands before they ate bread. Saved a lot of lives, that custom. You can tell your friends I said their brains are like the hole in the bagel. Empty."

Sammi laughed. Brahim's phone rang.

"Hello, Dov."

"Brahim, you were asking for me?"

"Good. You received the message from Susan. Where are you anyway?"

"I'm in Paris."

"Wonderful. I'm planning to be there this week."

"I'm hoping to meet with you when you come. We have to start planning how we'll handle the individual sessions with the business leaders at the symposium."

"Of course, Dov. Call Susan. She can set up the meeting."

"And you need to give me at least two hours to go over your speech."

"Okay, have Susan block out as much time as you need. How is everybody at home?"

"Sara and the children are great. Maybe you can see them this time."

"I would love to. I have to go. I have another call."

Dov Kanoui was the top PR man in the world. He'd met Isaac Green, Brahim's Jewish partner, in St. Moritz, at the hotel bar. Isaac was so delighted to see someone drinking Macallan he offered to buy Dov another drink and asked if he could join him. From that day on, Dov became one of Isaac's closest friends. Isaac was the one who convinced him to leave his packaging business and do all the public relations for World.

With World as his first client, Dov's firm, DKC SA Public Relations, soon became the number one firm in Europe. He and his creative team made unique corporate presentations and helped build World into the most followed company by governments and business leaders.

They finished eating, and Sammi got up and signed the check at exactly eight thirty. Sammi knew how Brahim ran his life, like an expensive Swiss watch. He never lost a minute.

Outside, Joe opened the door to the car and handed Sammi the keys. Brahim got into the back seat. Sammi shook Joe's hand. "I'll see you tomorrow."

CHAPTER
3

SAMMI GOT INTO the limo and headed toward East River Drive down to the Battery and the World corporate offices. Brahim was busy reading the *Wall Street Journal*.

"Sammi, turn on the radio. I want to hear the news."

Sammi turned the radio to his favorite station, WINS 1010. They had news 24/7 all year. *Give us twenty-two minutes and we'll give you the world.*

He turned up the volume.

"The chancellor of Germany, Fritz Hummel, has been assassinated. The group claiming responsibility calls itself the Guardians of the Holy Islamic Koran. Neo-Nazis are now rioting in Hamburg, handing out swastikas and yelling, 'Muslims go home.' One person has been killed and the fighting continues. Please stay tuned for more news and the weather."

Sammi turned off the radio. "And have a great day. You know, they're planning to close Guantanamo prison in 2014 and let out terrorists so they could go on and kill more innocent people. Boss, I think they should kill them before they ever make it to prison."

"It's about education, Sammi. I keep urging our Muslim leaders to take action to eradicate them."

"Yes, but how?"

"They must start by reeducating the imams and mullahs. Someone has to start preaching the true Koran. They teach them to hate the West and its culture. It doesn't have to be like this."

Sammi was accustomed to torrents of curses from Brahim, so when Brahim launched into one of his rants, it was no surprise.

"They're like deadly rats carrying a virus trying to escape the holes in the sewers where they breed. Terrorists hide in caves. Their goal is to turn the world back to the Dark Ages."

Sammi nodded. "Here we are in 2014 and what's been accomplished? The situation is getting worse by the day. They're disgracing all Muslims. Now every Muslim is seen as a terrorist."

"I know. I get it all the time."

Brahim's voice began to rise. Sammi could feel his anger building.

"No U.S. president has ever won a war since World War Two. They've just dragged us into them."

Sammi nodded his head in agreement.

"Korea, Vietnam, Iraq. And we're still stuck in Afghanistan. Talk and more talk. In North Korea the blockade did nothing. They still went ahead and developed a nuclear bomb. Their missiles can reach Los Angeles now. Look at Iran with nuclear weapons. Only Israel has done something by sabotaging their reactors to slow them down. Look at them now. They're moving ahead again with the help of Russia and China."

Sammi nodded again.

"Lebanon and Syria, civil war, Muslims killing Muslims, Europe is afraid of its own shadow. Turn on the TV. People blown apart while going to pray. I mean, what the hell happened in India last week? Hindus and Muslims killing each other. Africa a basket case, nobody gives a damn. The rest of the world demanding a new world system to be developed, but talk is all they do." Brahim paused for a second. "Winston Churchill—"

Sammi glanced at Brahim in the rearview mirror. "Winston Churchill?"

"Right. You should read his works. He was the greatest leader the world ever had."

"I know, boss. You quote him all the time."

"So here's the quote for today: 'What's our aim? Victory at all cost, victory in spite of terror, victory however long and hard the road may be, for without victory there is no survival.'"

"When'd he say that, boss?"

"In the House of Commons, England, May 1940. We need a Churchill today. I'll be speaking about this in Paris at the symposium."

"I've been meaning to ask, do you want me to come with you?"

"Maybe. I'm in the middle of working out the scheduling with Susan."

"Okay."

The PDA started ringing.

"Hello. Hello. Damn. No one there."

"Don't worry, boss. I'm sure they'll call back."

"Damn! Sammi, remind me to tell Isaac and Jim about this piece of junk."

"Yes, sir.

Why the hell did I agree to pay fifteen billion dollars for a wireless system that is a piece of junk for World's communication network?

"Sammi, I must have been out of my mind the day I signed that contract. We must be losing customers every time someone drives behind a tall building."

"Hate to say it, boss, but you're right. Half the time when I try to contact you or one of the other partners I can't get a signal."

"Isaac told me we needed our own satellite for security reasons. He assured me that with our new chip the reception problems would be gone. It's so damn frustrating."

Many things frustrated Brahim these days, the chip being the least of his problems. The situation the world was in, the constant reports of terror attacks on the news. This was not the future he'd envisioned as a young boy in Iran. This was not the America he'd dreamed of.

Brahim closed his eyes. *The world has changed. The world governments are weak, and the United States flag is no longer respected. Each of its fifty stars has gone dim.*

Brahim opened his eyes and said, "We're all praying that with this president and the Congress behind him, the U.S. is going to make a big push for clean energy."

"They better do it now, boss."

"Right. World's investing heavily in clean energy, mainly wind, solar, and some new technologies."

"What about Canada?"

"Better than we expected. We made the right move. The Canadian government gave us every incentive we asked for to encourage us to invest. They eliminated our corporation tax for the next twenty years. We're working closely with all their government offices."

"What a deal."

"Nothing compared to the land concessions we got."

"Land concessions?"

"Less than fifty thousand people live in the northwest of the country. The area has over one million square kilometers with natural resources like gold, oil, and other minerals. World will be the largest landowner in Canada. We plan is to use some of the land to build cogeneration wind and solar farms."

"Last week I heard an interview with a *Wall Street* journalist about tax incentives," Sammi said. "He said Germany was producing more than twenty percent of its electricity with wind power."

"Now it's our turn. Susan introduced us to a longtime friend of hers, Mindy Zinger in Israel. She's the chairman of a renewable energy company. Isaac arranged a meeting with her for when he's there. We're going to try and acquire her company. He's already had some preliminary conversations with her. She needs financing to expand her business in Europe."

"How's Isaac doing in Hong Kong?" Sammi asked.

"He's tying up manufacturing contracts to produce silicon wafers for solar energy and robotics to build the solar panels. He and Jim are coordinating our company's plan to invest fifty billion dollars around the world into green energy over the next five years. Three billion for starters in Europe alone."

"Wow, that's a lot of money."

"Energy is the trigger. It's already happening. The resource of oil and natural gases that exist today will severely diminish with time. Whatever resources exist in a country today, they'll want to fight to protect them, to keep them for their own people. If governments won't be able to provide fuel for their citizens, civil wars will erupt and the world will be in a state of constant chaos."

"Everything I read agrees with you, boss."

"The economics and philosophy we live by today will end up in the garbage bin of history. We've always been aware of that. It's been a priority of World since its inception that our chips will set the standard for the world in efficiency, economics, and innovation. Ordinary people will wake up one day, and they'll be better off because our chips will be in their homes and in their lives."

"I noticed the other day they closed the forty-seventh floor to all employees except the partners and certain personnel. What's going on?" Sammi asked.

"We've been working on some top-secret projects for the United States government."

"Isaac won't talk about any of the research on that floor. Is that what's been keeping him so happy?"

"He had a hard time containing himself. We're close to a breakthrough in capturing and storing electricity with the use of our chips and a new nanobattery technology. We partnered up last year with

NASA's Glen Research Center in Ohio to further develop technology in the semiconductor industry. Before he left for the Orient, Jim and I had a meeting. Isaac was ready to hold a press conference and make an announcement, but Jim and I convinced him to wait, not to make any press releases until we receive the results on the new chip."

"When do you expect to make the announcement?"

"On our twenty-fourth anniversary. New Year's Eve. In the first trading week of the new year, our stock will go through the roof."

"What a way to start the new year. That will be something to celebrate."

"Wait a second, Sammi. I just got an SMS from Jacob, Isaac's brother. We finally closed the deal with the government of Canada on concessions for the Abacus tar sands. He's just received the signed documents."

"Congratulations."

"Jacob's law firm did a fantastic job lobbying the Canadian government. Our teams of geologists with our newly patented nanochip geo-scanning sensors determined there were twenty billion barrels of shale oil in the desolate region of the Northwest Territory."

"So what's next, boss?"

"We're going to turn Canada into the next Saudi Arabia, kaffiyehs and all."

CHAPTER
4

SAMMI DROVE INTO a narrow street and entered a private tunnel leading to World's headquarters at the tip of Battery Park. As a multi-international conglomerate focusing on technology, World consulted the FBI, NSA, and special agents from the CIA for its security needs. There was always something sensitive being developed in the building; thus the need for the constant security. Most recently, World had won the contract for the development of an ultralow-temperature system for U.S. Navy missiles.

Together, the multiple agencies unanimously approved World for top-secret clearance. In Washington, D.C., the NSA had given it the code name "Three Bulls from Wall Street." The bulls were a Jew, Isaac Green, a Muslim, Brahim Surin, and a Catholic, Jim Murphy, who knew how to appreciate each other's differences and create magic when it came to business, technology, and making money.

Anyone entering the lobby of the World building could see immediately that it was a unique edifice, a work of art as much as a building in itself. Designed by an international team of world-class designers and architects integrating the most advanced technologies in clean energy, the three diverse cultures of the partners were present throughout the building.

Every visitor, private or government, marveled at the security system. Former members of the Cape Canaveral space agency had designed and implemented it. At the core was a thermal redirecting electronic system, the first of its kind, which eliminated the need for a lot of security personnel. An array of screening cameras embedded in the walls scanned everything and everyone that entered the building.

No one entered the building without clearance from the key people in the company: ten individuals, including the three founders. Upon admittance to World's offices, one received a printed photograph and a code word to speak into a microphone. If the voice recognition system recognized the voice, a special card made from a newly patented form of silicon was presented to the visitor. The card had a limited time of use based upon the time of the appointment.

"We've had ten good years in this building," Brahim said.

Sammi nodded. "Happy years."

"Isaac and Jim made a fantastic deal for us. The Bank of Dubai purchased it from us for nine hundred million dollars."

"Yup, good deal."

"That's not all. We pay only one dollar a year for ten years to rent the building, including the roof and our heliport."

Sammi turned into the underground garage. Each partner had his own car elevator. The steel doors closed quickly behind them as Sammi drove into the one marked "Brahim." A red light flashed, indicating the car was being scanned for explosives. After a moment it turned green, and they were able to proceed to the forty-eighth floor and the offices of the partners.

Brahim was tired. He closed his eyes for a moment. He thought back to the beginning of World Corporation. The partners had formed the company twenty-four years ago. December 31, 1990. Their lawyers had formed a Delaware corporation. Brahim, Jim, and Isaac had met in the lawyers' offices to sign the documents, so they would be able to receive their stock certificates and the corporate book.

Brahim remembered that day like it was yesterday.

THE LAW OFFICE was on Fiftieth Street, off of Third Avenue. New Year's Eve was on everyone's mind. The partners sat in the conference room. They signed the issued stock certificates, one hundred common shares of World Corporation. None of them could have dreamed that twenty-four years later the shares that had cost them one dollar per share would make them multibillionaires.

Each one folded the certificate into an envelope, and put it into their pocket.

"We should make a toast," Jim suggested.

"With what?" Brahim asked.

"The secretary left us some bottles of Coke. They'll do," Isaac said with a smile.

Brahim and Jim raised their glasses.

Isaac raised his glass too. "To my brothers from a different mother. Today's my birthday, and you guys as friends and partners are the best birthday gift I've ever received. With God's help, we'll build a business that we'll all be proud of."

They each took a swallow of the Coke and hugged.

So many years had passed since that night, but they always agreed it was the greatest New Year's any of them had ever experienced, until that moment or since.

The partners' friendship started on Fifty-Sixth Street in Manhattan, at the Racquetball Club. Jim and Isaac had served together in the U.S. Army Special Forces in Vietnam. Both agreed 'Nam had been hell, and they were pretty sure they were the gatekeepers. After they both received honorable discharges, they talked on the phone weekly and met at the club once a month.

Even between them, there were certain things they didn't discuss, like the time Jim had been captured and tortured by the Viet Cong. Or that it was Isaac's heroic actions that saved Jim's life. After being shot in both the leg and the arm, Isaac still managed to pull the pin from a grenade and throw it into a bunker, eliminating the enemy and facilitating their unit's rescue of Jim. The medals they both received spoke for themselves. Only a few people really knew what had gone on there, and they liked it that way.

Jimmy Murphy was born in the Red Hook section of Brooklyn. The youngest son of John and Elizabeth Murphy, he had three older brothers, John Jr., William, and Frank. Jim was the youngest in the family, and his brothers felt the need to protect him. Not that he needed protecting. By his seventeenth birthday, Jimmy was six feet tall and one hundred and seventy-five pounds of muscle. He loved to work out and was still growing. With his flaming red hair and freckles, he could have played Huckleberry Finn in the movies. His brothers called him "Little Jimmy." Their father worked on the floor of the New York Stock exchange as a trader and made sure to mention his son Jim to his associates whenever appropriate. It was no secret that Jim was his father's favorite.

Excelling in high school, Jim was a star player on the basketball team and graduated early. For his graduation gift, his father took him to a Knicks game against the Boston Celtics. It was after the game that Jim told his father he was going to enlist. He would be eighteen in a few weeks, and the army was waiting for his call. His father was proud when Jim told him that he'd decided to join the army to defend America. While Jim went to the enlistment office, his mother went to church to pray.

The enlistment office was in New York City's Times Square. Jim walked into the office and sat down. Next to him, Isaac Green was sitting there waiting for his turn to enlist.

"Where are you from?" Jim asked.

"Brooklyn, near the Brighton Beach Baths. You know it?

"Sure. We used to sneak in there all the time as kids. Practically every Sunday after church."

"Yeah, us too, hold the church. Where're you from?"

"The Red Hook section of Brooklyn."

They shook hands. They immediately had a connection, one that would serve them well, in war and far beyond.

There were three desks in the enlistment office. Each one was occupied by a noncommissioned officer (NCO) who resembled the poster on the billboards outside. Medals covered most of their chests. Navy, Air Force, and Army recruiters each eyed the new recruit as if his next medal depended on signing him up.

"I'm signing with the Army," Isaac announced.

"Why?"

"I want to see if I can get into a Special Forces unit. A friend of mine just finished his first tour of duty and he's reenlisting. He loves it."

"I'm with you. The Army's the way to go."

Isaac Green was born in the Brooklyn Jewish Hospital to Hannah and Joseph Green. His parents had met after the war ended in a DP camp in Poland. Joseph had a cousin in New York, and soon they were on their way there to find a new life.

Joseph went into the diamond business, eventually taking over when his cousin died. He soon became the largest buyer of raw diamonds in the world. In those days you could purchase raw diamonds in Russia with nothing more than a handshake and walk out of the country with millions of dollars of rare stones in your pocket. On the wall of his office read a sign: "A good name is all you can take with you to the next world."

Joseph wanted Isaac to be a rabbi, but Isaac wanted to serve his country. He appreciated what America had done for his family, and he wanted to give back. His enlistment caused a lot of tension in the house. The day he came home and told his parents that he had joined the army the room was silent. Nobody moved for five minutes. Hannah and Joseph looked at the floorboards as if a rare diamond had fallen in a crack. Without a word, his father suddenly rose from his chair, put his hands on Isaac's head, and blessed him. His mother put her arms around him and kissed him. Years later, at family reunions, Isaac would tell his children about those five minutes with teary eyes.

When Isaac came back from Vietnam, he started wearing a black skullcap. Isaac's attitude toward Judaism had changed. Before the war he had heard of God, knew his parents were believers. But after what he'd been through, he'd seen God on enough occasions to know he was real. Isaac started practicing the Jewish laws more strictly and keeping the Jewish Sabbath. By now people referred to him as Orthodox, and he didn't feel a need to correct them.

Brahim Surin was born on August 15, in Tehran, Iran, in the year 1953. As his mother struggled to give him life, the world outside her bedroom door was preoccupied with something very different. A coup d'etat was in motion. The prime minister, Mohammad Mosaddeq, was being ousted by the Iranian military, backed by the British and American intelligence agencies.

Staged by the CIA, riots had broken out on the streets of Tehran. Had his mother gone into labor a few hours earlier the midwife would not have been able to reach her. By the time Brahim was three days old Mosaddeq was deposed and arrested.

In 1951 Mosaddeq had made a move to nationalize Iran's oil industry, which had been controlled until then by the British-owned Anglo-Persian Oil Company. His efforts were not well received and led to a national boycott of Iranian oil. It was then the plan to push him out of office was first born. Perhaps it was due to the unusual circumstances of his birth that Brahim Surin cared so much about the world he lived in.

Most of Brahim's family was in the oil business. When the Shah was overthrown in 1979, his parents felt even more fortunate that they'd sent him to the United States to receive a college education in 1974. He was accepted to the University of Southern California and graduated in1978 with a business degree in economics. After college, his family backed him financially when he started to trade in the oil and gas business. His family had managed to thrive in spite of the political climate. Early on, when he traveled for business, Brahim proudly joked that he had so many relatives in the Middle East he never needed a hotel.

Every day he went to the Racquetball Club in Manhattan. One day Brahim sat with a towel around his neck watching Jim and Isaac as they finished their game.

"Any chance either one of you care to play another?"

Isaac looked at Jim. "Okay."

Jim arranged for the court to be reserved from noon to two o'clock every day after that. All fiercely competitive, most the time they played one-on-one. None of them could stand to lose. When the games were over, they all showered and went for a quick lunch at the Citicorp Center on Fifty-Third and Lexington Avenue.

Usually, after eating his favorite sandwich, corned beef on club bread with pickles, and a large draft beer, Jim would head downtown to Wall Street by taxi. He worked as the head bond trader for Goldman Sachs. Isaac had a tuna fish with tomato and mayo on rye and a can of cream soda. He walked to his father's diamond business on Forty-Seventh Street. Brahim had a salad, only greens, and a large black coffee. As soon as he finished, he hurried to his office at 9 West Fifty-Seventh Street. He had six employees, all dealing in buying and selling oil from the United Arab Emirates.

It didn't take long for them to become a strange sort of the three musketeers. They all liked basketball and the New York Knickerbockers. Jim had season tickets that placed them right behind the Knicks bench through his firm on Wall Street.

One day, as they were about to order, Brahim put down his menu. "Isaac, you're not talking. Is anything wrong?

"I quit my father's business."

"Why?" Jim asked with a confused expression.

Brahim looked at Isaac in disbelief. "What do you plan to do?"

"Guys, I love my dad, I make good money, but I want more. I want to build a major world-class high-tech company. I can't do it while working for my dad. After Jim and I came out of the army, it took almost a year to get my head together. I spent four years at the University of Albany studying nanoscale science and engineering. I have a degree hanging on my wall at home, and what do I do? I hustle diamonds my father bought in Antwerp or Tel Aviv and sell them to the Chinese in Hong Kong."

Brahim smiled at Jim, then turned to Isaac. "How much do you need to start?"

"Ten to fifteen million. Maybe I could do it for a little less."

"Seed money, right?" Jim said.

"Right."

The waiter stood listening to the conversation. "Very interesting, gentlemen, but can you please place your order? We're busy with the lunch rush, and we have people waiting for the table."

They placed their orders. The waiter took their menus, smiled, and left.

Brahim looked at the date on his watch. July 3, 1990. "I need a few days."

Isaac looked at him, stunned. "You serious, Brahim?"

"When I talk about money, I'm always serious. Jim and I have been discussing the idea of forming a new company. Last week we decided to go ahead. We were going to ask you to join us anyway. We were just waiting for the right moment. I guess the moment is here."

Jim chuckled.

After taking a bite of his salad, Brahim spoke. "Jim knows Wall Street inside and out. I have connections in the oil and gas markets in the Arab world. You have the London connections to the Diamond Syndicate, De Beers, and the Oppenheimer family, plus all of your clients around the world."

"How do we split it?" Isaac asked.

They stared at each other. Then, as if they had one brain with one thought, they all blurted out, "One-third for each."

Isaac put out his hand first, then Jim and Brahim put out their hands. One on top of the other like you'd stack pancakes for break-fast.

"We're gonna make history. A Jew, a Muslim, and a Catholic as business partners. The world will never be the same."

"You got it, Isaac," said Jim. "One for all and all for one. We're gonna change the world."

CHAPTER
5

BRAHIM WAS STARTLED by the sudden stop of the elevator. He looked at his watch. Nine fifteen. He already anticipated the busy day ahead of him. As the elevator doors opened, Sammi grabbed the attaché case from the front seat next to him and started walking to Brahim's office.

At World's headquarters, all the walls were made of special bulletproof glass. Each window was designed with the latest solar technology. The large battery banks in the sub-basement had the capacity to capture electricity and release it, making independent electricity for the company a reality.

The partners' offices divided thirty thousand square feet between Brahim, Jim, and Isaac. The space was open so they could see each other from their desks. Susan, their COO, had an office with glass walls next to the reception area. All secured communication systems had been designed by the National Security Agency.

When the partners met business leaders or heads of governments, the forty-ninth floor was the place. The floor had three apartments with a full-service staff in addition to two state-of-the-art conference rooms. The fiftieth floor had a swimming pool, personal gym, and a shareholders conference room. They'd also built a separate kosher kitchen for Isaac.

Oil and commodity trading operated on five floors; they directly connected to the Chicago Mercantile Exchange. World's Private Wealth Funds division had ten floors, while Equity and Hedge Funds had five floors of their own. World had built one of the most sophisticated electronic stock-trading systems in the world. The other floors hosted the corporate headquarters for each of their companies.

The heart of World's financial and business empire revolved around this building. Over two thousand employees entered the building's doors every day. Looking at the building from the outside at night, the lights on random floors looked like a checkerboard. The entrance doors to the building had a massive globe on them. The golden rule for all their companies was no clocks on any walls in the offices. It reminded the employees of Las Vegas: open for business at all times.

Brahim walked into the reception area.

"Susan, any calls?"

"Jenny called wanting to know how I'm holding up acting as secretary while she's taking care of her mother."

"How's her mother?"

"Not well."

"You sure about doing this?"

"Positive. I've got someone coming in, but she can't start till tomorrow. It's not worth it to train somebody just for the day. I'll manage. Just tell me what you need."

"Okay."

"By the way, your wife called. She needs to speak to you. Isaac and Jim called too."

"Where're they?"

"Jim's in London at the Churchill. Isaac's on his approach to Hong Kong International Airport."

"What's the time in Hong Kong?"

"Nine fifteen p.m."

"Please ask them to be available on the secure lines for a video call in one hour. But first get me Abra on the line."

"OK. Do you need anything else before I get into my own work?"

"Please call Tiffany's and check if they sent the package I purchased the other day."

"Will do."

Susan Kais was World's first and most important employee. By now she was an integral part of the company.

Isaac had called several executive head hunting firms for a COO. He reviewed over one hundred CVs and interviewed a dozen or more candidates, but none could get the unanimous vote of the partners.

A friend of Jim's who worked at a bond house on Wall Street had referred Susan to the partners. He'd known Susan for years and recommended her highly. Jim had set up an interview with her and the partners at the Waldorf Astoria. Due to a sudden summer rain shower, the streets were slick and the traffic was horrible. Running late as it was, they decided to jump out of the taxi and walk the last three blocks. Jim had prearranged the meeting place, common to anyone familiar with the Waldorf Astoria: the clock. By the time the partners arrived, Susan was already there waiting. She had arrived early and stood there holding a small dog.

"That's her with the dog," Jim said as they approached her.

"How can you be sure?" Isaac asked.

"My friend told me that she has the demeanor of an executive and she's a sharp dresser."

"She does look like she's a model for Brooks Brothers."

Brahim laughed. "If we want her, does the dog get a paycheck too?"

They introduced themselves. The clock struck four thirty, and the dog started growling at them. Susan patted him on the head and said, "It's okay."

"Would you like something to eat?" Jim asked.

"A cup of coffee would be nice."

Isaac began the interview. "So, Susan, tell us about yourself."

"I've been the COO of the Northeast Investment Fund, and its assets totaled over ten billion dollars while I was on board. There was a sudden change in the management, and I decided to leave. I believe things happen for a reason. By leaving that position I'm available for this one. I'm ready for the right opportunity."

One hour later the interview finished. They had covered her with a blanket of questions anyone would find hard to breathe through.

After a short pause, Susan asked, "Would you mind if I had another cup of coffee?"

Jim ordered a second round of cappuccinos. The partners kept glancing at one another. Their eyes gave them away. By the end of the meeting they all agreed to hire Susan as their COO.

"So who do I report to?"

They looked at each other. No one answered.

"For one thing, I think all legal documents should pass by me. I'm the only one at this table with a law degree, correct?"

Jim had her CV in his attaché case. At Harvard, she'd finished in the top ten of her class. Recruiters immediately pursued her for top law firms. Early on she had already decided to continue her education. She enrolled at the Wharton School of Business at the University of Pennsylvania. She earned a doctoral degree in applied economics, then met a fellow student and got married. The marriage ended after two years. After the divorce, N. M. Rothschild offered her a position in London in the investment-banking field. After six months she was head of a team of bankers. Together they closed a two billion dollar merger of a Romanian bank and an Israeli holding company. After two years of nonstop work, she took a well-deserved vacation. She was sitting on Waikiki Beach when a friend called her about the position at Northeast. She liked the chairperson; it was a no-stress situation—nine to five—not like her investment banking position. But now she was ready for more.

Brahim took the lead. "When will you be able to start?"

"I just did."

Whenever the partners met with their lawyers, Susan attended. She earned their respect immediately, and their affection for her grew daily. Always organized and professional, Susan was in the loop on any major decision involving World. Nobody had better intuition than her. She knew how to smell out the bad apples hoping to get on the inside track with the partners, and her brain absorbed information like World's latest chip. "The boys," as she called them, became her family.

Susan loved two things: music and her employers. On the anniversary of her first year at the firm, World bought her a penthouse apartment across the street from the Lincoln Center and season tickets. The "boys" loved her too.

CHAPTER
6

Monday, June 2, 2014
Long Beach, California

THAT SAME DAY across the country, at California State University Long Beach, the cafeteria filled with excited students preparing to leave for their summer vacations. The dining hall buzzed with conversation, everyone looking for a familiar face. SMSs flew this way and that; robotic thumbs abounded. Wrinkled Levi's, worn Crocs practically ready to be recycled into shopping bags, and hair that looked like it hadn't been brushed in days seemed to be the style on the campus. The fashion was set and students held on to it like a dress code. Most of the young men had one earring; someone else must have had the other.

The cafeteria line was long. Burgers and french fries were out of style. Salads of mixed vegetables, with lots of greens, fresh fruit smoothies, or sushi was now the fare of choice. Giant soy lattés the preferred drink. The sign over the door read MAXIMUM ONE HUNDRED AND FIFTY PERSONS. Looking around the room, you'd think there was double the amount.

Lo Chi Xi sat alone at a table for two underneath the exit sign.

She had convinced anyone looking to share the table that she was holding it for her boyfriend. But boys were not on Lo Chi Xi's mind.

She'd entered her first year at Cal State as an exchange student from the Fujian province of southern China, scoring 1580 on the SAT. She was an absolute genius at the development of cutting-edge nanotechnology and a designer of computer programs for advanced medical research. She published articles in math theory and was a potential Olympic runner in the women's one hundred meter.

Though MIT had offered her a full scholarship, she turned it down to be in California. Silicon Valley called to her. In the Valley, there were companies who hired the best brains in the world, and she planned on being one of them.

In China, the family was there at the beginning of the great revolution with Mao Tse-tung. Her father was the most distinguished professor at Beijing University. Lo Chi loved him and missed spending time with him. As a founder of advanced research, Dr. Hoc Yu Xi was a nominee for a Nobel Prize for his work in the molecular growth of underwater agricultural plants.

Her older brother, Wei Long, was the director in charge of the Chinese Space and Research Center. He had accepted an invitation to the U.S. to visit the Kennedy Space Center in Florida. While in the United States, a special dinner was held at the White House in his honor. Senators and some of the top business leaders from Boeing, General Motors, and General Electric were in attendance.

The day he planned on returning to Beijing, he asked the vice president of the United States to facilitate Lo Chi studying in America. A short time later, she became an exchange student. She was extraordinary not only in math and science, but in language too. She spoke Mandarin, English, and Arabic fluently.

Lo Chi sat at her table sipping her fruit smoothie, her eyes focused on the entrance. It was 8:30 a.m. The meeting had been called for exactly eight o'clock. She'd planned to finish the meeting by eight fifteen.

She had started to grow concerned, looking down at her watch every few seconds. Just then, Mohamed Halabi entered through the double doors she'd been staring at. She waved him over. Mohamed maneuvered himself across the room, stepping over legs and weaving between the tables.

"*Salam, Mohamed. Kif halah.*"

"*Chamdu Allahu.* Thank you, Lo Chi."

Several months had passed without them seeing each other. "I trust all is well," Lo Chi inquired.

"Fine. Let's get down to it." Mohamed looked into her eyes. "Fifty million. That's the deal, right?" He handed her a copy of a coded wire transfer.

She took it. "Thank you."

"Check your account."

"I am in process."

Lo Chi punched seven numbers into her iPhone. A voice answered in Chinese, "The transfer has arrived."

"It's done."

She felt relieved. As she got up, she slipped a microchip from under her plate to Mohamed.

He put the computer chip in his inside jacket pocket, then reached across the table and took hold of her hand.

"Lo Chi, stay. Eat something with me."

"Thanks, not today. I'm dieting."

"You're beautiful. Come on, let me get you something. Just sit with me for a while. It's been too long."

"Thanks again, but I'm in a rush. Some other time."

Lo Chi took the envelope with the wire information and stuffed it into her bag. As she headed toward the cafeteria exit, she paused for a second, looking back at Mohamed. He had no idea who was really going to gain from this transaction.

Outside, she picked up her cell phone. This time she dialed thirteen digits. Her voice was strong. "It's done."

MOHAMED HAD JUST finished his coffee when a hand touched his shoulder. He turned his head to see who it was.

"*As salamu aleiykum.*"

"*Waleiykum assalam.*"

"You ready?"

"Yes, Fahd, let's go."

They moved slowly toward the exit doors, out to the parking lot. They stood by a sign that read TOW AWAY ZONE, both anxious to get going.

"I see Asim coming," Fahd said.

A red Ferrari 599 GTB Fiorano pulled up. Mohamed opened the door and eased into the front seat.

Fahd crouched down, leaning into the car through the window. "I will meet you in one hour at the office."

Mohamed nodded, then looked straight ahead as Asim drove away. "Take the streets instead of the freeway."

Mohamed's office was located at 92 Sunset Boulevard, down the street from the famous Beverly Hills Hotel. Mohamed had leased the office two years ago. The name in the lobby read "Intelligence Information International."

Asim drove the Ferrari into the underground garage. Two spaces were reserved for the company. A Mercedes already occupied a space. The license plate read HAKIM.

Mohamed entered the elevator with Asim. He pushed the button for the seventh floor. They walked off the elevator. Right in front of them was the office. Asim turned the key in the lock and they entered. The lights off, Mohamed yelled, "Hakim!"

In the ceiling, a hidden video camera observed everything. A voice shouted back through a voice box. "I'm back in the transmission center."

The steel door to the transmissions room had an eyehole; from inside you could scan the waiting room. Mounted on the side of the door was a box into which one had to punch a secret code: your birthday and your mother's birthday. A thumbprint on the electronic pad, and finally the door would open.

The small room had four chairs, no desks, and electronic monitoring systems wall to wall, the most sophisticated decoding equipment used in the intelligence-gathering business. Only the United States, China, and Israel had this level of top-secret decoders. Israel had spent several years developing them with the NSA. China had obtained the same plans for the decoders through a defector from the NSA now living in China.

Intelligence Information International agreed to pay the Chinese millions of dollars to get their hands on it, and they did. Wireless transmitters, state-of-the-art listening devices, and four plasma television screens hung on the walls. On one screen, the Al Jazeera TV station broadcasted from Qatar giving the news in Arabic. CNN, CNBC, and Al-Manar broadcasting from Lebanon played on the other sets.

On one of the chairs sat Hakim.

Mohamed reached into his inside pocket and removed the envelope with the chip. "Hakim, you load the decoder box with the chip."

Hakim took the chip from Mohamed and loaded it. Mohamed typed "Abud Al-Hakim"—servant of the Almighty—and their eyes fixed immediately on the computer screen. It started to roll out thousands of letters, line after line. Suddenly, the screen went dark.

"Hakim, what happened?"

No one spoke for a moment. Fear had grabbed their hearts and choked off their oxygen.

"One minute," said Hakim. "It's started to print words and numbers. It's working!"

"*Subhaanallah!* Allah is great," each one shouted as they grabbed each other's hands.

Mohamed smiled. "I knew Lo Chi would deliver."

After ten minutes, the computer finally stopped feeding information. Individual names, telephone numbers, credit card pin numbers, banks' computer wire and transfer codes were being printed out, as well as Swiss Bank numbered accounts and other secret interbank transfer numbers. Nothing was sacred anymore. With this chip, you could find the most secret information of a country or a business if you knew what you were doing.

Mohamed's mobile rang. Mohamed spoke into the phone.

"Yes, Fahd."

"Something came up. I can't come to the office like we said. I'll meet you tonight at the usual place. In the meantime, send the chip to Beirut as planned."

CHAPTER
7

Monday, June 2, 2014
World Corporation offices, New York City

THE PEOPLE AND the streets were partners, everyone rushing to get somewhere. High above the commotion below, Susan waved her hand to Brahim.

"Your wife is on Skype."

He'd been looking out of his office window at the Statue of Liberty, something he liked to do often. The statue represented freedom. Brahim loved freedom.

His thumb pressed the video button on his phone, and a seventy-two-inch Sony screen came up from the floor, his wife's face on the display.

"Brahim, how are you?"

"Great. I've been staring at the green lady. After you she is one of the most beautiful women in the world."

"Brahim, you're so kind."

"How are the children, Abra?"

"I spoke to them a short while ago. They're all busy and doing fine, praise be to Allah."

"Have you finalized your plans for your trip to Mecca?"

"Yes, I want to be there by Friday. You said you would join me. Brahim, please don't tell me you're—"

"Abra, my love, you have nothing to worry about. My suitcase is already packed. It's in my closet. But I forgot one important thing. Could you please make sure you take my dishdashas? They're hanging with my suits. I don't know how I forgot them."

"Do you need anything else?"

"No, Sammi will pick you up tonight at ten o'clock to take you to the airport. We can sleep on the plane. Susan already gave the pilot our itinerary."

"What itinerary?" Her smile disappeared.

"We're going to London, Paris, and Bahrain. We'll be arriving at Heathrow Airport at around six a.m. Eleven a.m. London time. We should be at the Churchill Hotel by twelve thirty at the latest. And one more thing. Our suite. Don't be surprised if it looks like there's someone there. I asked your sister Fatima to sleep there last evening."

"You didn't tell me."

"I also haven't told you I invited her to spend the next two weeks with us. She's all set to go to Paris, and next Wednesday night she'll go on to Mecca with you. I'll join you on Friday, after the symposium."

"What wonderful news. Thank you, Brahim."

"For you anything, my love."

Brahim signed off, and the video slipped slowly back into the floor.

Susan was waiting for him to finish his call. She motioned by placing her hand on her head that Isaac was on the line.

Brahim picked up the receiver. "Isaac, how are you?"

"A bit tired. Other than that, I'm fine. How are you?" "I'm okay. I'm leaving for London tonight with Abra. We'll be staying at the Churchill. Jim's already there. We plan to have a working meeting with some of our staff in London. Peter and Carl told Jim they're excited about the new offices in Mayfair."

"What's on the agenda?" Isaac asked.

"We want to review the second quarter's results."

"What does Jim think?"

"He gave it the thumbs up. But he thinks it's important to show our faces. After that, we fly to Paris. The symposium is next Thursday at the George V. Everyone one will be there. I promised Abra I'd go with her to Mecca afterward."

"Ask Susan to send me your entire schedule later today."

Brahim texted Susan as their conversation continued.

"Let me call you back after I receive the schedule," Isaac said.

"Wait. One more thing."

"Go ahead."

"Jim believes the U.S. dollar is going to crash. I think we need to make some decisions. Jim, you, and I should sit down to discuss what we should do. We should meet as soon as possible."

"Good idea. Maybe I'll make a stop in London before Paris. Call you later. *Shalom*."

CHAPTER
8

THE PILOT STARTED the engines of the helicopter and Brahim boarded. Susan stood watching the liftoff. As they waved to each other, a strange premonition came over her. She had a feeling this trip was going to be different. She waited until the helicopter was out of view and then returned to her office.

"We'll be arriving in twenty-five minutes, sir," the pilot announced.

The sky was clear as they headed across the Hudson River. Seeing the lights reflected from the buildings of Manhattan at night gave him a special feeling. He loved the city. This is where it had all happened for him.

The touchdown at Teterboro Airport was to the minute. The helicopter taxied within fifty feet of the Gulfstream. As Brahim disembarked and was about to greet the pilots, his cell phone buzzed.

"Sammi, how close are you?"

"I'll be with you in fifteen minutes, boss."

"Fine, see you then."

Brahim began checking with the crew about last-minute details.

"Can I get you a drink, Mr. Surin?" the flight attendant asked.

"No, thank you. Did the package arrive? I sent it by messenger."

"Yes, sir. It's locked up in your private compartment, as you instructed."

Sammi arrived and parked the limo five feet from the plane. A few minutes later he entered the plane. "I loaded your luggage, boss. Anything else you want me to do?"

"Stay in touch with Susan. She'll give you instructions."

"Okay, have a good trip."

By eleven p.m. Abra and Brahim had settled into their seats. The plane started taxiing to the runway.

"This is your pilot speaking. Just like to let you know that we are fourth in line for takeoff. We should be in the air within ten minutes. Relax and enjoy the flight."

Brahim closed his eyes for a moment, but this night he would get no sleep. Abra had a lot on her mind, and she started in on Brahim immediately.

"Did you send the donation to the PLO?"

Brahim knew this question would be coming. "Yes. I also told my accountants to put tracers on the last donation you convinced me to send to the Popular Palestinian Front. Of the fifty million we gave, twenty-five million went to President Abu Kesef and fifteen million to a Swiss numbered account. The orphans received only ten."

"You know it takes money to run an organization, Brahim. I am sure the funds you gave them was used to further the cause." She stared into his eyes. "You know the only reason we have this wealth is that Allah blessed us with it. He gave it to us, Brahim, because he knew we would be wise in how we used it. There is no greater way of spending our wealth than in assisting the Muslims' battle to win back Palestine. You see where the money didn't go. I see the good it did. We helped children, Brahim. That donation made the world a better place. You and I don't see the world the same anymore. So much has changed. Nothing in this world, jewelry, vacations, fancy yachts, none of it means anything to me anymore. I am filled with a holy fire. It drives my life now. Allah is here, with me, guiding me."

"Abra, I want to understand your feelings, but this fire that you say drives you has taken you somewhere I cannot go. You are so far from me now. Do you remember our honeymoon? Do you remember that burning look in your eyes that you had only for me? It has diminished, my love, and I miss it. Allah blessed us beyond the dreams of our youth. Not only with wealth, but with children and grandchildren. We've had so many good times together. Now I feel that your connection to these groups is dragging you away from me."

"You just do not understand. My life has no meaning without this connection to Allah, Brahim. Money and power have no importance to me. They are just a means to reach the end, and now I am wondering about that end more and more."

"What end?" Brahim paused. "You know, you're starting to sound like Isaac's son who studies in Jerusalem. When he talks about the Messiah's coming, he doesn't sound so different than you."

"How can you compare me to some lowly Jew?"

"Do you hear yourself? You talk only of the spirit of Allah, yet you speak like this. He also prays and serves God."

Abra's eyes filled with anger. "He's our enemy, he's Allah's enemy. He does not believe in Muhammad the prophet."

"I don't understand you. Are we not from the same father, Abraham? We have the same blood as Isaac. He's my best friend. You've been friends with his wife, Chava, for years. I would trust him with my life.

"Abra, you know all of this. What has gotten into you? The leaders throughout history have used the Jews as an excuse for all of the world problems, and now you too? I'm asking you to stop this. Please don't talk this way anymore."

CHAPTER
9

Tuesday, June 3, 2014
Over the Atlantic

EXCUSE ME, MR. Surin."

"Yes, Gail, what is it?"

"It's Paul Britt from Washington."

"Okay." Brahim looked at Abra for a moment. *Was I too harsh?*

"Please excuse me, Abra. I'm sorry I was so short with you. I have to take this call. We'll speak more when I return."

Brahim walked to the front of the plane and sat down at his desk to compose himself.

"Hello, Brahim, can you hold for a minute? I want to patch you into our embassy in Paris and introduce you to Mike O'Shea. He's on a special task force assignment for the NSA. Hello, Mike, you on? I have Brahim on the phone. He's flying over the Atlantic in his private plane."

"Mr. Surin, are you on a secure line?" Mike asked.

"Yes, go ahead, and please call me Brahim."

"Thank you. We've been picking up a great deal of chatter from terrorist organizations about your symposium in Paris."

"What are they saying?"

"Words like 'big arrival,' 'dispose of the package.' Nothing good."

"Is there anything else?"

"Yes. But I think we should finish this conversation in person. In London perhaps."

Paul interrupted. "Brahim, we want to assign some of our security people to you. Look, it could be nothing at all, but let's be cautious."

"Okay."

"I'll meet you at the airport." Mike hung up.

"Paul, are you still there?"

"Yes, Brahim."

"This Mike O'Shea. He can be trusted?"

"Don't worry about a thing. Mike's the best." Paul filled him in a little on Mike's background.

Mike O'Shea was the number one agent in the Secret Service. Respected by his peers in the intelligent agencies around the world, he was considered the most trustworthy in his field. That trust is what got him the nickname "Captain America," like the comic book character. Completely devoted to God, country, and the Secret Service. For Mike O'Shea, the three were one.

Brahim thanked Paul and hung up. His mind tried to digest the conversation. On the desk in front of him was his attaché case. He opened it and took out a folder. Inside were pages upon pages on the participants for the symposium they were organizing in Paris on June 12, 2014. Less than two weeks away.

The list was confined to those who could influence world opinion. Government, religious, and business leaders, all with some connection to the partners on a personal level as well as in business. These were the most powerful people in the world. They were uniquely positioned to change attitudes within their countries to encourage peace. This was a long-held dream of Brahim's, and he felt that he and his partners, at the pinnacle of success, could finally achieve it.

The George V in Paris was among the finest hotels in the world. Reservations had to be made one year in advance. Over two hundred guests were expected, and all the hotel suites had been assigned. The Salon Vendome ballroom was being outfitted with digital screens for the event. The international media was going to be present.

Brahim had finished reviewing the list and was about to get up when his phone light blinked on.

"Hello, Isaac, is everything alright?"

"Fine. I just wanted to tell you we finished the meetings with the government in Hong Kong. The lawyers are finishing the paperwork. They've agreed that all the silicon factories will be owned jointly. The six plants planned for producing silicon wafers for solar energy will have the capacity to supply our projected needs for the next ten years."

"When can they start shipping?" Brahim asked.

"In six months."

"Is there anything else?"

"Yes. I spoke to Chava. She's okay with me stopping in London. She'll join me in Paris for Shabbos. We have close friends there. After Paris, we plan to go to Jerusalem to be with our children and grandchildren. Care to join us?"

"Wonderful idea. Let me check my schedule. We planned to go to Mecca after Paris, but Abra has always wanted to visit the Al Aksa mosque."

"Great, I'll send you my flight details."

Brahim placed the phone down. Gail saw he'd finished his call. "Can I get you anything?"

"Black coffee and a bottle of Perrier, please. And, Gail, can you check with the pilot if we're on time?"

"I already have, sir. We are on schedule."

Brahim looked at his watch. It was 2 a.m. He stood up and

slowly walked to the back where Abra was lying down. Her overhead reading light was still on, the Koran resting on her chest, while she slept soundly. He lifted the Koran gently and placed it on the table next to her and shut off the light. He knew he too should get some sleep.

He motioned to Gail. "Please make sure I'm up thirty minutes before we land. Have a good night," Brahim said softly as he pulled the blanket over his head.

CHAPTER
10

Tuesday, June 3, 2014
Mandarin Oriental Hotel, Hong Kong

THE MANAGEMENT OF the Mandarin Oriental Hotel in Hong Kong was familiar with all of World's personnel and their needs, including kosher meals for Isaac. Isaac was in his room packing his bags when the phone rang.

"Good morning, Mr. Green, this is the front desk. You have two visitors waiting for you in the lobby."

"Tell them I'm on my way down."

Isaac took a quick glance at his watch. Nine thirty. It was getting late. The chauffeured limo service was already outside. He had checked everything—closet, drawers—and made sure copies of the agreement were in his attaché case before he left the room. In the lobby, his attorneys Lee Henry and Robert Lewis were waiting. Their firm, Simmons and Williams, was recognized as the best commercial law firm in the Far East. They had negotiated more megacontracts with the Chinese than any other firm.

Isaac stepped out of the elevator.

"Good morning, Isaac," Lee said with a big smile on his face.

"Good morning, Lee. How are you, Robert?"

Robert was already shaking Isaac's hand. "Couldn't be better."

Lee pulled an envelope from his attaché. "Isaac, this envelope is for you. Inside there are three original contracts with the government seal."

He opened his attaché case and put the papers inside. "You guys did one hell of a job, thank you."

Robert reached forward. "Let me help you with your bag."

All of a sudden, Isaac's face turned pale. "Wait a minute. I forgot something in my room."

Isaac hurried to the elevator and left Lee and Robert waiting. A few minutes later, Isaac disembarked from the elevator with a grin on his face.

"What did you forget?" Lee asked.

"My *tefillin*. I need them every morning to pray. Let's go."

"Where are you heading?" Lee asked.

"My first stop is London, then on to Paris and finally Jerusalem. Ride with me to the airport. I have something I want to discuss."

When they were settled in the limo, Isaac asked, "What's going on in China?"

"Our office in Beijing reported that the Chinese government has been in secret meetings all day."

"Any thoughts?"

"One of our lawyers, Kim Li, has a boyfriend in the currency office. He told her they're going to drop the United States dollar as a preferred currency."

"Is it final? Does she have any idea when?"

"It looks like sometime in July," Robert responded.

Isaac opened his PDA and punched in a number. "Are you at the airport, Charlie?"

"I'm at the special security desk like you told me, Isaac."

"I'll be with you in twenty minutes."

Isaac closed his PDA and turned to Lee. "Contact Kim Li. Tell her it's very important to get the latest data from her boyfriend."

"As soon as I get back to my office, I will, Isaac."

"No, call her now."

Isaac looked at Lee and Robert. He knew what they were thinking. "Let me tell both of you, if the Chinese do this, it will make 2008–2009 financial crises look like a birthday party."

Robert agreed. "This could easily lead to a world depression, even a war."

Lee turned to Isaac. "The line is busy. I'll keep redialing."

"Try Kim Li's private line," Robert suggested.

Lee punched in the number and put it on speaker. "Hello, Kim Li. This is Lee. Can you hear me?"

"Yes, how can I help you?"

Lee looked at Isaac for a second. "This is completely confidential. I need you to meet with your boyfriend outside his office. We must have the latest information today on the currency issue you mentioned to me."

"Lee, he wasn't even supposed to tell me the little he did. If I push for more, he could lose his job, or worse."

"Hold on a minute, Kim Li." Lee put her on mute and turned to Isaac and Robert. "What do you think?"

"Tell her he won't lose his job," said Isaac, "and if he does, we'll give him a better one. Tell her he'll be rewarded, and we'll make sure nothing happens to him."

Lee turned back on the speaker. "I promise, nothing bad will happen to him."

Robert took the phone. "Kim Li, this is Robert. Listen carefully to me. As managing partner, I'm telling you the firm needs this information." Then he said something in Chinese and hung up the phone.

Lee smiled. He understood Chinese.

"What did you say?" Isaac asked.

"I just told her that if she got the information today, she would be a partner by tomorrow."

The limo pulled into the airport. Isaac looked at his watch. "We made good time."

"I'll call you as soon as I hear back from Kim Li," Lee said.

Robert shook Isaac's hand. "Isaac, have a safe flight. We appreciate you firm's business, and anything you need, just ask."

The limo stopped in front of the special entrance to the private plane departure terminal. Lee and Robert jumped out. Lee grabbed Isaac's bag. Isaac gave them each a hug, taking them by surprise.

"Anything, anytime just call us," Robert repeated.

Isaac walked away with a smile and said under his breath, "Come on, Kim Li. Let's see what you've got."

CHAPTER
11

Tuesday, June 3, 2014
Hong Kong International Airport

CHARLIE WAS WAITING next to his bag. "*Shalom.* How are you, Isaac?"

"Tired, Charlie, but okay. Let's go to the plane. We should be taking off shortly."

They put their bags onto the conveyor belt and walked through an X-ray machine that blew cool air at them.

Mark Brenner, their personal flight attendant stood at attention. "How are you today, Mr. Green, Mr. Goldman? This is a great day for flying."

"When we land in London, I hope the weather is as good as it's been here in Hong Kong," Isaac said.

Mark took their bags, and they followed him up the stairs. As they entered the Gulfstream G650, the copilot greeted them. Ed Black had been flying them around for years. The pilot, who was busy as usual, looked out of the open cockpit door and waved. Isaac understood that he was getting his last-minute instructions from the tower.

"Can I get you anything?" Mark asked.

"Thanks," said Charlie. "Can I please have a Diet Coke?"

Mark turned to Isaac. "Anything for you, sir?"

"Yes, a double espresso and a Perrier, thank you."

An announcement came over the loudspeaker. "This is William Jones, your pilot. Good afternoon. We are beginning our taxi to the runway. Please fasten your seat belts. The flight time to London Heathrow airport is eleven hours and forty minutes. We will be flying over six thousand air miles and will be arriving at approximately 1:40 p.m. London time. Have a comfortable flight."

Too bad I can't get air miles on my American Express card, thought Charlie. He turned to Isaac. "If it's okay with you, maybe I can get some sleep before we discuss things."

Isaac nodded and asked, "Did you pray the morning service?"

"Yes, I was lucky to find a *minyan*. How about you?"

"We have the same group of businessmen and some local people at the hotel every day."

"Excuse me," Mark interrupted, "I just finished speaking to the pilot. We're next in line for takeoff. If you need anything, just pick up the phone on the side of your seat and press one. I'll be in the back."

Isaac closed his eyes. Charlie busied himself with the *Wall Street Journal*. The headline read, **STOCKS SURGE IN BROAD RALLY.** Isaac could feel the runway under him as the plane started to accelerate. Soon they were off the ground. Isaac closed his eyes and dozed. Charlie laid down the paper and quickly fell asleep.

Isaac felt restless, his mind mulling over his last conversation with Lee and Robert. He pressed the flight attendant button.

"Yes, Mr. Green," Mark answered over the intercom.

"How long have we been flying?"

"It's been three hours, twenty minutes. Eight hours and twenty minutes more."

Isaac stood up and walked to the back of the plane.

"Is everything alright?" Mark asked.

"Yes, I just want to wash my hands. I have to pray."

Isaac removed his prayer book from his bag and started praying. The plane started to shake.

Mark came over. "Mr. Green," he said, "you better hold on."

Isaac sat down. Charlie was awakened by the sudden turbulence to find Isaac immersed in his prayer book. Charlie glanced at his watch, still half-asleep, then sat up for a moment and looked out the window. It was cloudy, and he could only just make out the plane's wing. He opened his own prayer book, deciding to join Isaac in praying the afternoon service from his seat.

When they were done, Mark approached them. "Can I get you something to eat?"

"No, just a cappuccino please," said Charlie.

"The same, thank you," Isaac said.

"You ready to go over the report, Isaac?"

Working and traveling around the globe over the years, they'd had countless discussions about sensitive projects. Everyone in World knew that outside of "the Boys," Charlie Goldman was Isaac's closest confidant.

Charlie had earned his law degree at Harvard and went to work for a small firm in New York. Then he applied for a job in the Justice Department. His specialty was cases involving defrauding the Environmental Protection Agency. At the same time, Isaac was looking for someone to assist him in World's law department. They two had seen each other at different religious functions in their community in New Jersey. One day over drinks Isaac casually asked Charlie, "You know any attorneys in the community looking for a job?"

"To be honest, I was thinking of leaving the Justice Department. It's been eight years. Time to move on."

"What do you know about my company?" Isaac asked.

"I know you are the forerunners in microchip technology. I also know that you work with various U.S. government agencies, including the NSA and the military."

Isaac nodded. Charlie was well informed. "What can you tell me about your work with the Justice Department?"

"To tell you the truth," answered Charlie, "not much. I signed a nondisclosure agreement."

That was the decisive factor for Isaac. He was going to make Charlie an offer he couldn't refuse. A week later Isaac made the offer and Charlie accepted.

Isaac was shaken out of his reverie with another bout of turbulence. "I'm ready for your report," he said.

"I visited the South China Agricultural University, as you requested. They've been involved in controlled experiments on infectious diseases for several years. Swine flu is one of them."

"Did they discover something?"

"Yes. AHCC."

"What's that?"

Charlie explained. "Active hexose correlated compound. Added to a dietary supplement, it will fight the swine virus and a new, more deadly virus they believe to be coming shortly."

"Back in 2009 the world was going crazy fighting the flu virus H1N1. Some estimated three billion were infected."

"This new virus could be worse. Millions will die if we don't start producing an antidote now. It could cause an economic meltdown around the world."

"Did they finish the laboratory testing?"

"Yes."

"What about the human trials? Are they completed?"

"Yes, and your information was right on the money. The Commission for Science, Technology, and Industry for National Defense in China classified the information top secret, as you thought. My contact, Xu Ming, was involved in developing the antidote. He wants to defect to the United States. He wants to work for us."

"When Xu Ming contacted you, I had a hunch that he was look-ing to defect."

"He asked me if the World Fund would consider building a virus research center outside China."

"You think he'll be able to produce the antidote to fight the virus?" Isaac asked.

"Xu Ming is brilliant. Someday he'll win a Nobel Prize for his research. All of his data has been stored on a chip and he's ready to give it to you."

"What are we waiting for?"

"There's more. He also has information that the Chinese govern-ment is going to use the antidote as a power play to surpass America as the number one world power."

"Did he tell you when and how?"

"We've got less than a year. If they don't release the chemical formula for the antidote, you can bet there's going to be a massive epidemic."

Isaac paused. "What's the time in London? We need time to fig-ure out what to do about this situation."

Charlie picked up the phone. "Mark, can you please check the exact time in London."

"Of course, sir."

After a minute, Mark walked up to Charlie. "Mr. Goldman, it's five a.m. in London. We'll be arriving in less than nine hours."

Isaac picked up his PDA and pressed five digits. They spelled IRISH. The phone rang once and Jim answered.

"Isaac, where're you? You alright?"

"I'm well. We're over the Atlantic heading your way."

"I heard from Brahim earlier about you and Charlie coming to London. That's great. How's the family?"

"They're fine. How about you? The kids all well?"

"Mary has a cold. Nothing serious, thank God."

"Jim, Charlie has obtained some important information. The

three of us should meet right away."

"What's he got?"

"Not even on the secure line. Much too sensitive. We have to discuss this in person."

"Got it.

Do you need anything from me before you arrive?"

"We're going to need the latest breakdown of all our corporate assets, including our current cash positions in our banks."

"No problem, I'll get on it."

"Speak to Susan. Most important is a list of all our traded securities."

"I'll take care of it right away. Have a safe flight, Isaac. I'll see you at the Churchill."

"Yeah, see you."

Isaac hung up. His thoughts were moving fast. He knew this was a game changer for the world. If the Chinese didn't release the antidote, the epidemic could cause worldwide social and economic collapse. Everything the partners had built could disappear overnight. His life, his family, all the people he loved, now their lives were on the line.

Isaac looked at Charlie. "What else have you found out?"

"My investigation tells me something big is going on with the Arabs and the Chinese."

"What do you mean?"

"I'm getting bits of information."

"Who's it coming from?"

"Moa Li."

"What do you know about him?"

"I met him when I was with the Justice Department. We had a case where a United States business and its principles tried to swindle a Chinese manufacturer of wind turbines with fraudulent bank documents. The Secretary of State asked the Justice Department to get involved. Moa Li was the attorney representing the manufacturer. I went to China several times, and Moa Li and I became friends. Over the last few years, we've kept in touch."

"What did he say?"

"I sent him an e-mail that I was going to be in China. We met for dinner. He booked a room for me at the Renaissance in Beijing. He was already checked in and waiting for me in the lobby when I arrived. The bellhop took my bags to my room.

"Moa Li suggested we have a drink. After a quick drink, where he said nothing except 'Please follow my lead,' we proceeded to a car waiting outside. He had instructed his driver to take us to the Beijing Panda Zoo.

"He was unusually quiet during the ride, most of the time looking straight ahead. Occasionally he would turn his head and look at me. His eyes sent me the message not to say anything. We drove down an enormous boulevard.

"Looking out my window, all I could see was literally thousands of people on bicycles, old and young, everyone just pedaling. It was a miracle we didn't hit someone. I always wanted to visit the pandas, but I never thought I'd see them this way. The driver dropped us off at the entrance. I was surprised there were no crowds and we walked right in. I said to myself, *Something big is happening*, and as my thought finished, Moa Li turned to me and said in a low voice, 'Please smile a lot when I talk to you.' I did."

Isaac listened with great interest.

"We went in to see the giant pandas. Moa Li told me that the CIA planted a mole inside the Chinese Embassy in Beirut. I asked him why he was telling me this, and he told me the mole is his younger brother and he's a double agent working for the Chinese. Somehow the CIA caught on and they're planning to kill him."

"What does he need?

"He needs assurance of a safe sanctuary. He has information about a certain terrorist group. Something big. He'll give it to me if we save his brother's life."

"How much time do we have?"

"Thirty days, maybe sixty, but I doubt it."

"Why does he think we can help his brother?"

"First of all, Moa Li knows how influential World is. Second, he has lots of information about World's business dealings and some of the partners' private activities. It's leverage."

"What does he have on us?"

"He says he has a personal dossier on you and Jim from when you served in Vietnam. He says it's marked top secret."

"Did he tell you what's in it?"

"No, he only said the files were from the president's office."

"Do you believe him?" Isaac asked.

"I do."

"How did he get such classified information?"

"I'm working on finding that out."

Isaac closed his eyes. He pushed a button to put the seat into a reclining position.

"Is there anything else, Charlie?"

"That's it for now."

Isaac pressed the button to summon Mark. Mark walked over. "Can I get you something?"

"I need a double scotch. Macallan or Glenfiddich if you have either one. Straight up with water on the side, thanks."

"Mr. Goldman, do you want anything?"

"The same, please."

A few moments later Mark returned with the drinks. As Isaac reached for his glass, his PDA buzzed.

"Hello. Yes, within the hour? Wonderful. I'm waiting for your call, thank you."

He closed the PDA and lifted the glass. "Charlie, Lee got the information I requested. He'll call back as soon as he knows more."

"That's good, Isaac."

"Let's get some more sleep. We have a busy day ahead of us."

Isaac pressed the button for Mark. "Mark, can you wake us up two hours before we land?"

"Yes, sir."

Isaac washed up and then went to lay down. He looked over at Charlie who was already sound asleep. *I got the right person when I hired him.*

CHAPTER
12

ISAAC TURNED HIS PDA to vibrate and placed it in his shirt pocket. He was almost asleep when he felt the vibration near his heart. Half-conscious, he pulled out the PDA and said in a low voice, "Susan, how are you?"

"Outside of missing all of you, great. Jim told me what you wanted. I've sent him the whole file with our new encryption algorithms."

"What's happening in the office?"

"It's quiet when you're all out of the country at the same time. I get a chance to catch up on my paperwork."

"Everything well in Canada?"

"I received my daily report about an hour ago. Jay Russo said the runway is behind schedule. It's going to be thirteen thousand feet long, the longest runway in the world. The short story, it's not finished yet. Nevertheless, he promised me they would be ready on time. Think they'll make it? If he's not on time, they pay us a lot of money per day according to our agreement."

"You and Brahim handled the contract. How much was the penalty?"

"Two hundred thousand U.S. dollars per day."

"He'll make it. With today's rate, it's costing him even more. We hedged against the Canadian dollar. You can bet Jay will finish on time. What about the office buildings and the high-security command center?"

"Everything's finished. We received the go-ahead from the National Security Agency. All the federal departments in Washington signed on."

"Did we get any feedback from NORAD?"

"Bryan Robert, the air director, gave the green light on the subterranean vault."

"Susan, my other line is flashing. Call me later." Isaac picked up the other line. "Hello, Lee. Go ahead."

"Kim Li came to my house with her boyfriend. They're in the garden room."

"They're in your house? What happened in Beijing?"

"I got a call from Kim Li at the Hong Kong airport. She said she needed to meet me. I told her to come to my house. When I answered the door, I was shocked when I saw she'd showed up with her boyfriend, Hui Ying."

"Wait a minute." Isaac reached across the aisle and prodded Charlie. "Wake up. I want you to listen to this."

Charlie sat up. Isaac turned on the speaker. "Lee, Charlie is listening. I want him to hear this."

"Hello, Charlie."

"Lee, repeat what you just told me."

"Okay. Kim Li and her boyfriend arrived at my house a short while ago. They caught the last flight out of Beijing today. The Chinese secret police tapped Hui Ying's phone. He told me he received a call from a friend who tipped him off. They planned to arrest him for spying for the United States. Kim Li told him to avoid his house, take whatever he had on him, and meet her at the airport."

"Then what?" Isaacs sounded concerned.

"Kim Li's sister, Daiyu, is the director of airport security. Kim

Li told Daiyu her situation and that she was afraid for her life. She felt if they suspected Hui Ying, they must also suspect her of spying. Her sister had them meet her at her office. She escorted them past security and boarded the plane with them. She seated them up front with a special VIP pass.

"Daiyu told her that when she disembarked from the plane in Hong Kong someone would meet her with a sign that said 'Dragon Fire.' She told them to follow him until they were outside the terminal and not to talk to anyone, even on the plane.

"When Kim Li asked Daiyu why, she explained that the planes' headrests were wired with hidden microphones to record all conversations. Isaac, you still on?"

"Yes, I'm still here."

"Kim Li and Hui Ying managed to make their way to me without trouble, but they can't stay. They have to get out of Hong Kong."

"What should we do?" Charlie asked.

"Lee, call the United States consulate. Ask for Allan Peters. Use my name to get through."

"If he's not in, what should I do?"

"Try his voice recording. Press 1613777 and hang up. Unless he's dead, you'll get a call from him within the hour."

"What's the message?"

"After you reach him, tell him that you spoke to me and that you need to meet immediately. Either way, get back to me in thirty minutes. Now put Kim Li on the phone."

"Hello, Isaac."

"Don't talk. Listen and do exactly what Lee tells you. You and your boyfriend will be fine. We'll make sure of it. Please put Lee back on the phone."

Lee took the phone.

"Lee, the minute we hang up, make the call."

"I'll do it right away."

"Charlie, I need you to go get our pilot."

William appeared a moment later. "Mr. Green, you look tired. Did you get any sleep this evening?" he inquired.

"Short naps. Please sit down. Something very important has come up. You're under no obligation to do what I'm about to ask of you." After pausing for a moment, Isaac said, "How fast can you do a turnaround flight back to Hong Kong after you refuel in London?"

"About three hours, sir."

"Two Chinese nationals must leave Hong Kong immediately. We believe they're in trouble. I want to use our plane to bring them to England. I'm sure you realize the danger. If the Chinese secret police catch you, it won't be pretty. Our company will deny any knowledge of your actions."

Charlie was watching William. "Very dangerous. The Chinese could lock you up. They may even kill you."

"But if you can do it, I'll considerate it a personal favor."

William reached over to shake Isaac's hand. "Mr. Green, you got yourself a pilot."

"Please call me Isaac."

"Thank you, Mr. Green—I mean Isaac. It's an honor."

Isaac opened his computer and started typing.

"What can I do?" Charlie asked.

"You're going to fly back with William to Hong Kong. Are you up for this?"

Charlie smiled. "I wouldn't miss it for anything."

"Tell William to give you all the information. Make sure he allows enough time for delays." Isaac pressed the button connecting the phone to the pilot.

"William, how long do we have until touchdown at Heathrow?"

"About four hours depending on air traffic."

Isaac started reaching for some nuts on the table. His PDA rang.

"Hello, Isaac, Allan Peters here."

Allan was in charge of covert operations at the U.S. Embassy in Hong Kong. They would need his help to get Kim Li and her boyfriend out of Hong Kong alive.

"Allan, how are you doing?"

"I'm having a bad day. I was just on the phone with the State Department. They've been consistently screwing up since the North Korean missile crisis, and now Iran. It's a headache."

"I completely agree. I hope the president takes some military action instead of just talking." Isaac paused. "Are you on a secure line?"

"Yes, the algorithm automatically changed this morning and will change again in four hours. This is the one your people installed for us."

"Did Lee fill you in?"

"Yes, what do you need?"

"Charlie Goldman will be heading this operation for me. Our pilot is working on the flight time from London back to Hong Kong."

"Okay, what else?"

"Charlie will give you further information after we land in London."

"Is he aware of the danger?"

"He's in on everything. I need him for this job. I'll keep you in the loop. This has to be a success. There's too much riding on it for it not to be."

"Consider it done."

"Okay, Allan, you'll be hearing from Lee and Charlie. Any problem you reach me."

"You bet."

Isaac looked tired.

"We still have a little time left until we land, Isaac. We should get some shut-eye."

"Charlie, how can you sleep at a time like this?"

Charlie was about to answer, but William interrupted. "I've got it, Mr. Green."

"Fill us in."

"I'll fly out of London early Wednesday morning and leave Hong Kong Thursday night nine p.m. This allows for a window if the weather is bad or we need more time on the ground."

"Sounds right. Let's go with it."

"Yes, sir, and I've already briefed the crew. All signed on. We're gonna get this job done."

As William turned to head back to the cockpit, Isaac motioned to him. "Thank everybody for me."

"This is big trouble, right, Isaac?" Charlie asked when William was out of earshot.

"Well, it could turn into an international incident. One of the reasons we have to be so careful."

But Charlie's eyes were already closed. Most likely he hadn't heard Isaac's answer. Isaac turned out his overhead reading light, laid his glasses next to him, and fell asleep.

CHAPTER
13

Tuesday, June 3, 2014
Heathrow Airport

BRAHIM WAS IN a deep sleep when the plane reached its final approach to Heathrow Airport. Gail eyed her watch. Five thirty a.m. Ten thirty London time. She put up a fresh pot of coffee, then walked over to Brahim and touched his shoulder to wake him up.

"Mr. Surin."

Brahim rubbed his eyes. "What time is it?"

"Five thirty in the morning. We'll be landing in thirty minutes, sir."

Brahim stood up and walked to the back of the plane. He looked over at a sleeping Abra starting to wake up.

"Good morning, Abra. Some coffee?"

"Yes, please, Brahim. Thank you."

"Gail, please bring Abra a cup of coffee."

"Do you want anything for breakfast, sir?

"No, only coffee. And please bring me my package."

Brahim went to the washroom. Gail proceeded to serve Abra her coffee.

"Did my husband sleep at all?"

"Not really."

"Thank you, Gail."

Gail returned to the compartment, and as Brahim came past, she handed him the package. Brahim sat down across from Abra. "I bought you a little present. I'm sorry about last night. We still have to talk. Let's wait until we are together in Mecca."

"You're right. Now is not the time." Abra reached for the box in his hand.

Brahim watched her face as she opened Tiffany's signature turquoise box. There was a card with Brahim's handwriting: *May Allah keep you safe on your journeys through this life. And may we always be at each other's side.*

In the box, there was a necklace with three hearts made of rubies, emeralds, and sapphires. Abra's eyes filled with tears. She took his hand in hers.

"Thank you, Brahim, I love it."

"And I love you, Abra, I always have."

She glanced down at the necklace again. "We'll make this journey with the help of Allah. Help me put it on." She lifted her hair up so he could fasten the necklace around her neck.

A sense of relief washed over Brahim. At that moment came the announcement, "Please fasten your seat belts. We'll be landing in five minutes."

The plane landed and started to taxi to a private arrival area. Brahim stared out the window. Something was happening on the runway. Two SUVs were driving beside the plane, blue and red siren lights flashing. The plane stopped, and the vehicles pulled up alongside. As the staircase was lowered, Brahim remembered that Mike O'Shea was meeting him at the airport. He wondered who else had come to greet them.

Brahim turned toward the pilot. "Thomas, I'll be in touch, thanks."

"The plane will be ready whenever you need it, sir."

Abra and Brahim's feet had barely touched the ground when Brahim spotted who he now realized must be Mike O'Shea walking toward the plane.

"Glad to meet you in person, Mike."

"My pleasure, Mr. Surin. Everything okay?"

"Yes, fine."

A few meters behind, he noticed Jim and Dov Kanoui walking toward them.

"Let's get into the SUVs," Mike muttered.

Jim was all smiles as he shook Brahim's hand and gave him a big hug. Dov leaned over to shake hands, then kissed him on both cheeks.

"I'll explain everything to you on the way," Mike told Brahim.

Abra stood by, listening attentively.

"Abra! Abra!" She turned and saw her older sister Fatima walking toward her waving.

"What're you doing here, Fatima?"

"My dear sister, I couldn't wait at the hotel to greet you. Let's go. We'll catch up in the car."

Mike turned to Abra. "Would you and Fatima mind getting into the other SUV? There's something I need to discuss with Brahim. This way you ladies can talk without any distractions."

Abra and Fatima looked at Brahim. "Is everything alright, Brahim?" Abra asked.

"Everything's fine. I'll see you at the hotel in a short while. We have some business to discuss. It would bore you. Get settled and I'll meet you two for breakfast. I love you."

"Please excuse us, ladies, we have to go." Mike led Brahim to the car, hurrying him along.

Jim and Dov were already seated in the back. Mike and Brahim slid into the seats behind the driver. A security agent Brahim didn't recognize sat in the front seat next to the driver.

Mike looked back over his shoulder. "Please say hello to Ben Swift. He'll be assisting us with security."

"Hello," Ben said without turning around.

"Ben and I are both from the NSA. They've assigned us to protect you."

"Is all of this really necessary?" Brahim asked.

"Yes. You'll be meeting some of my other associates shortly at the hotel, where we'll all be briefed."

"Brahim, are you okay?" Jim asked.

"I'm fine. I just need some sleep."

"Mike, what's with all this security?" Jim asked.

"I promise you all of your questions will be answered. I can tell you this much: the threat is real and the security warranted."

Brahim nodded. "If you're here, that says a lot."

"I'll fill you in a bit on the way to the hotel."

Jim interrupted. "I asked Dov to come over from Paris when I heard about the security threat. We thought he could be helpful in case we need to put out a press release."

"Good thinking. Dov and I needed to discuss the symposium anyway."

"He can also join our meeting at our new offices."

"That's perfect," Dov said. "I need some new information for our corporate brochure."

Mike continued the briefing. "Our director's put us all on high alert."

"Can you give us some more specifics about what we're up against?" Jim asked.

"PE-4, DEMEX, C-4, SEMTEX. They showed up on the chatter through our satellite pickups. Over this past week, it's been heavy. In October 2000, terrorists used C-4 to attack the U.S.S. *Cole*. We lost seventeen sailors. Do any of you remember Khobar Towers in Saudi Arabia?"

"I sure do," Jim answered. "A good friend of my family lost a son there. He was in the Air Force, stationed in Building 131, the one that was blown apart."

"We're still hunting down suspects in Hezbollah. Al-Hejaz is still number one. We believe he's planning to attack us."

"Do you have any idea where they're operating from?"

"We're pretty sure Beirut. When Israel left Lebanon in 2000, they had many Lebanese friends, including top officials and high-ranking officers in the Lebanese army. They've been supplying both Israel and us with electronic intelligence information ever since."

"It seems like you're getting close," Dov said.

"Can't tell you all the details, but we've infiltrated almost to the top of Hezbollah. We're gonna get every single terrorist and kill them one by one if we have to."

Dov's smile changed with his tone. "We all have to face the reality of 9/11. This September it will be thirteen years since the Twin Towers were destroyed. We all know things have been degenerating, and the nations of the world still refuse to address this as a religious issue."

"What do you mean?" Mike asked.

"We've been hiding our faces in the sand for almost a decade. But we are at war. We just forgot to mention it to the public. But it doesn't have to be like this. We need powerful people to show the world there are other options. That religion doesn't have to divide us. That we can learn to appreciate our differences, that they can be seen as strengths, not weaknesses." Dov took a breath. "That's what we'll be addressing at the symposium in Paris."

"I was going to ask about that," Mike said. "Tell me about the symposium."

"It's going to be the biggest public relations campaign ever seen," Dov replied. "But instead of slim-fit jeans, we'll be selling peace."

"How're you going to pull that off?"

"World Corporation: Brahim, Jim, and Isaac. They could do it. They could help bring about the type of change I'm talking about.

The way they run their company, how they can live and work not only in peace but at this level of financial prosperity. They're the poster boys for how this can work, for why this can work. Who could look at them and not want a piece of what they have?"

CHAPTER
14

Tuesday, June 3, 2014
On the M4, London

BEN FELT HIS BlackBerry vibrating. He checked the screen. "Mike, HQ's trying to reach you. Your system must be off and they say it's important."

Mike flipped open his mobile and punched in a code. "This is Mike. Connect me to HQ1."

"Mike, where are you?"

"Alcott, I'm on the M4. I should be at the Churchill in twenty minutes."

"We've doubled the security on your group."

"Why? What's happening?"

"Our guards discovered three men at the London Eye planting bombs. There was gunfire. Two of the terrorist were killed, and one escaped by boat on the Thames."

"What about the threat on Brahim? Any updates?"

"No, but you should know we asked the BBC and other news outlets to hold off announcing the story about the Eye until one o'clock."

"I'll call you after my briefing." Mike hung up the phone. To the others in the car, he said, "Terrorists tried to blow up the Millennium Wheel."

"When did it happen?" Jim asked.

"About eleven a.m. Two of them were killed, one got away."

Brahim pointed to Dov. "We have to talk."

Ben turned on the radio, tuning into the BBC 94.9.

"You're listening to news hour from the BBC in London. I'm Dan Fergusson. There's been an attempt to blow up the London Eye. Authorities reported security guards prevented terrorist from setting off plastic explosives. Two terrorist have been killed. The authorities continue searching for the third one. Stay tuned for more information."

Ben turned off the radio.

"Mike, when's the meeting at the hotel?" Jim asked.

"As soon as we get you all safely to the hotel and I can be in contact with Isaac and Charlie. I've decided to move the meeting to my suite at the Connaught Hotel. Even with all the security we've posted at the Churchill, it's too big, too many people. Security will be tighter at the Connaught, less ears listening in."

Brahim spotted Harrods Department Store as they drove past. "We should be at the Churchill in ten minutes."

"I hope so, but the traffic's heavy at this hour," Ben replied. "Could take thirty minutes, maybe more."

Mike took out a Motorola CLS1410 two-way radio and called the other SUV following right behind.

"Joe, everybody okay?"

Joe, another member of the NSA team, replied, "We're alright. What about you?"

"We're trying to get through this traffic," Mike said.

"Me too."

Ben opened the glove compartment in front of him and pulled out a blue light. He stuck it on top of the roof. The siren started screeching. The flashing light on the roof commanded the traffic to move, and it did.

Jim and Dov looked at each other, trying not to show their fear as the SUV wove between the other cars. Mike was on his two-way radio talking to his staff at the hotel.

"Seven minutes," Ben said. "We're crossing Oxford Street and Marble Arch. Two minutes to touchdown."

As they approached the hotel, they could see several security vehicles with flashing lights parked at the curb. The SUVs pulled into the circular driveway of the Churchill Hyatt Regency. Ben got out of the car first. Four uniformed police officers immediately positioned themselves near the doors, and four others surrounded Abra and Fatima. Two plainclothes officers walked up to Mike, Brahim, Jim, and Dov. One of them said, "Good morning, gentlemen. Mike, good to work with you again. How's Paris?"

"Paris is Paris," Mike said, shaking hands and smiling. He introduced the man to the others. "This is Peter Dunlap."

Peter turned his head and said, "This is my colleague, Sean Watts. He's on our special team."

Sean nodded a greeting. "Nice to meet you all."

"We're here to assist NSA personnel for as long as you are in the UK," Peter said. "We're in charge of the counterterrorism unit, a division of the Metropolitan Police. We're headquartered at the New Scotland Yard. You'll all have security twenty-four/seven."

Mike encouraged everyone to keep moving. "I think we should go inside, so everyone can settle in."

CHAPTER
15

Tuesday, June 3, 2014
Churchill Hotel, London

BRAHIM ALWAYS STAYED at the Churchill when in London. Churchill was his favorite world leader, and he'd once been a patron of the hotel. The hotel's library was filled with his books. And at night, when the staff turned down the bedding, they placed a chocolate and a quote from Churchill on the pillow.

George, the door attendant, and three porters were waiting to greet Brahim and Abra. George smiled. "Hello, welcome back." He shook Brahim's hand and gave him a hug. "I missed you. Don't stay away so long."

"Thanks, it's good to be here."

Mr. Blake, the general manager, and several of his staff were waiting to greet them in the lobby. "Welcome back, Mr. Surin. It's a pleasure to have you with us again."

The concierge walked over to the ladies and presented them with a bouquet of flowers.

Abra nodded her head. "Thank you."

Mike checked his watch. "I'm sure you're all tired after the flight. Take some time to get settled in, and if you agree, we'll meet in the lobby at three o'clock. I'll have cars waiting to transport us to the Connaught."

"We've taken over the eighth floor, and we've arranged to have meals served there too," Peter informed Mike. "We scanned the seventh, eighth, and ninth floors for bombs. They're all clear."

Jim's phone rang. "Isaac, where are you? Okay, I'll see you soon." Jim turned to Brahim. "Isaac's plane is landing in a little over an hour."

Brahim spoke to the ladies. "Abra, Fatima, I suggest we go to our rooms and get some rest. It's going to be a busy afternoon." They headed for the elevators. Jim followed. Mike got a call on his cell phone. He turned away to answer it.

Dov turned to Ben. "Ben, what's really going on? In the car, Mike said something about a threat to Brahim."

"Dov, all I can tell you is that Brahim's life is in danger."

"What do you mean danger?"

"Sorry, friend, I have to go and make some calls." And Ben walked off.

Dov went after Mike. "Mike, I just had a few words with Ben."

"What did he say?"

"He told me Brahim's life is in danger."

"That's right. A lot's going on. I'll brief you at three."

Mike walked away, talking on his two-way to Isaac.

"Everything okay at the hotel?" Isaac asked after Mike had introduced himself.

"Yes, but it's important we talk right away. Isaac, we've assigned you a security guard by the name of Robert Butler. He'll be waiting for you when you land. Tell him to take you straight to the Connaught in Mayfair. Have the concierge show you to my suite. Number 502. I'll be there to greet you."

"Okay. Anything else I should do?"

"No, I'll see you soon."

CHAPTER
16

JIM'S MOBILE STARTED to beep before he could step onto the elevator.

"Hello, Susan."

"Jim, call your wife as soon as you can."

"Did she say there was problem?

"She didn't say."

"What's the news from Canada?"

"I'll be there next week to sign off on the work they completed. With any luck, we'll be on time for the grand opening."

"Good. I'll talk to you later today after our meetings."

Jim walked across the lobby to find a quiet place to call Mary. Before he could, an incoming call popped up on the screen. *Frank Murphy 312-685-1224.* He picked it up.

"Frank, how're you and Joan and the rest of the family doing?"

"We're all fine."

"What's on your mind?"

"When are you due back in the States?"

"End of next week if all goes well. Why what's up?"

"I need to talk to you. I'll come to your office in the city."

"Do you need money?"

"No, it's about our brothers."

"Tell me what's going on."

"I think they're in trouble. John Jr. and William got involved with some right-wing whack jobs. A local group of neo-Nazis."

"Neo-Nazis? What the hell is wrong with them? They know better than that. You tell them to be in touch with me right away."

"Jim, easy. I'm sure you can get them back on the straight and narrow."

"The last thing I need is my brothers getting arrested by the FBI."

"I'll meet you in your office when you get back and we'll talk about it."

"No, you'll get to both of them today, no excuses."

"I hear you."

"If I'm in a meeting and my phone is off, just let it ring through. I'll see your number and call you as soon as I finish."

Jim spotted Dov looking toward him and motioned for him to come over. Dov sat down.

"Is anything new?"

"Actually there is. We have a problem and it could affect our campaign."

"Go ahead."

"I just got off the phone with my brother Frank in Chicago. He informed me our other brothers John Jr. and William are involved with some right-wing radical groups. I'm waiting for some more information, but for the moment that's all I have."

"Okay, let's not press the panic button. Are they speaking to you?"

"Yes."

"Good, when you speak to them, calmly tell them you want to meet them in New York next week."

"Then what?"

"I'll be in the city putting together all the media buys for the blitz following the symposium. You'll introduce me as your firm's public relations expert. I want to understand their motives and what they stand for. Tell them if I'm impressed with their cause, I'll help them get their message out through the press and TV."

"I don't know. What if they catch on it's a phony story?"

"They won't. Jim, trust me, all of the radicals in the world, the right wing, left wing, anyone with a gripe about any issue, need to get publicized. Listen to me, I have years of experience. Everybody wants publicity. The media can make or break a cause like theirs."

"Maybe you're right. I just can't understand what's gotten into them."

"Everybody wants to belong these days. These groups can be very accepting. They can make you feel like family."

"My brothers have a family."

"Then maybe it's something else they're looking to gain. Honor? Prestige? Ego can make men do pretty stupid things." He patted Jim's shoulder. "Trust me. This is gonna work. You'll see. Hamas recruits more suicide bombers when CNN and BBC show the destruction they've caused. It's a known thing."

"Okay, I'll try it."

"You gonna be alright, Jim?" Dov looked concerned.

"Yeah, I'll be fine as soon as I speak to them. I just don't like it. Not knowing what's really going on or how deep they're into it."

"Keep cool. See you later."

Dov headed for the elevators. One of the doors opened. Brahim came out with a security guard next to him.

"Dov, everything okay?" Brahim asked.

"Yes."

"Have you seen Jim?"

"I just left him. He's sitting in the corner, near the restaurant."

Dov entered the elevator and pressed number nine as the door closed. "We'll meet up later, Brahim."

Brahim walked over to Jim and sat down next to him. He sensed trouble.

"What's wrong?" Brahim asked.

"Nothing. Everything's okay."

"Come on. How many years have we known each other? Tell it to me straight."

"I received a call from Frank. He told me my brothers are in some kind of jam."

"Did he say anything else?"

"Not enough to do much with."

"Anything I can do?"

"Not at the moment. I'm waiting for Frank to get back to me."

"I saw Dov at the elevators. He said he just left you."

"Yeah, we set up a plan on how to deal with my brothers' situation, but without more information, there's nothing else we can do. I'll keep you in the loop as soon as anything develops."

Brahim's phone started to ring. He answered it. "Okay, I'll be up in a minute." He turned to his partner. "Jim, let's talk about this again later. I'm going back up to talk with Abra for a minute. I'll catch up with you soon."

CHAPTER
17

BRAHIM WALKED TO the elevators, his mind now preoccupied with Jim's new problems. He stepped into the elevator.

"What floor?" asked the security guard, who had followed him into the elevator.

"Eighth floor, please."

Entering the suite, Brahim called, "Abra where are you?"

"I'm in the bedroom getting dressed. I'll be with you in two minutes."

"Take your time." Brahim took a bottle of cola and some ice from the credenza and sat down. Abra walked in. "You look beautiful," he said.

"Where's Fatima?"

"She's getting dressed. We decided to do some shopping in Harrods while you're in your meeting, okay?"

"Of course, what time do you plan to be back?"

"In about two hours. We may go to Selfridges too. They have some special items. I want to buy gifts to take home with me for some of our friends."

"What about lunch?"

"Fatima and I were planning lunch in Selfridges. Tonight, if you're free, we can all have dinner together."

"What time?"

"Eight o'clock?"

"Sounds all right. Do you mind if I invite Jim and Isaac?"

Fatima walked in. "Brahim, the security guards will be going shopping with us?"

"Seems so. I don't like this either, but there are people out there looking to harm us."

Abra interrupted. "I would prefer a quiet dinner with just the three of us."

"Fine, I understand. Please listen to your security people. I have to get to a meeting. Call me when you're on your way back to the hotel. I pray you enjoy the day."

Once Brahim left, Fatima turned to Abra. "What's going on with you and Brahim?"

"Nothing's going on."

"I'm your sister. I feel the tension when you are together. Tell me it's not true."

"Please, let's get going."

Fatima wouldn't let it go. "Tell me, Abra, what's going on between you and your husband?"

Abra sat down. Her eyes filled with tears. "Fatima, my life is worth nothing."

"What are you talking about? You have everything you could possibly want."

"You see the money, the private jets. This isn't what I need anymore. I need to enrich my soul. This life I am living, it's so empty. The children are all out of the house. There's nothing left for me to do."

"Brahim loves you, gives you everything. He'd kill for you. What's the matter with you, Abra?"

"I need to be with my people."

"What are you talking about? Everyone in the Muslim world loves you and respects you, Brahim, and the children."

"It's not enough. I need more. Try to understand me, Fatima."

"Listen to me carefully. You'll get through this. We'll get through it together. I've been taking care of you since you were a little girl. Here you are crying on my shoulder once again. Only this time your problems are a little larger than which doll to play with or getting the attention of the boy you love who doesn't know your name."

"You are a good sister, Fatima. Thank you."

"We're going to handle this, I promise you. You'll be fine."

Tears poured down Abra's face. Fatima put her arms around her. "I promise you."

BRAHIM WAS BACK in the elevator with his security guard.

"Where are we going, sir?"

"The Connaught Hotel. My partner and Mike are waiting for me there."

"Yes, sir."

Brahim stepped out of the elevator. Jim and Ben were waiting.

"Did you reach Mary?" Brahim asked as they headed for the SUV.

"No, I kept trying, but nothing. In the end I left her a voice mail."

"Let's go," Ben said.

"Ben, it looks like there's more personnel here than when we arrived."

"Yeah, they'll be here until this thing gets resolved."

In the SUV Brahim said, "Jim, I'm having dinner with Abra and Fatima tonight. I hope you don't mind if I'm not with you and Isaac."

"No problem. Isaac. Charlie, Dov, and I will go over to Reubens Kosher Deli on Baker Street. I love the salt beef and pickles."

"I'd love to join you, but I need to spend time with my wife."

"The schedule's tight today. I hope we can still go to the new offices. And we have to talk about the markets and the information that Isaac had Susan put together."

"Let's improvise," Brahim said.

"What do you mean?"

"When we first started, if we had a lot to discuss we even met at midnight."

Jim smiled. "I remember working all night and then I'd start trading at the opening bell of the Exchange. Not a wink of sleep. That takes me back. Okay, let's run it by Isaac. If we need the time, we'll meet again after dinner."

As they drove by the United States Embassy, Brahim asked, "When did they put up all the concrete barriers, Ben?"

"They've been up for a few years. We live in a crazy world today." He checked his watch. "We'll be at the hotel shortly."

Pulling up to the hotel, Jim noticed the absence of police cars. Only the door attendant was there, standing at attention. Mike was right. This was more discreet. The car stopped in front of the entrance and everyone got out. Ben spoke to the attendant, while Brahim and Jim walked into the lobby. An unmarked police car pulled up behind the SUV. Ben walked over and leaned into the car.

"How are you guys? Anything new at HQ1?"

"Monitoring calls from Newham," the officer answered. "Translators listening to chatter believe another attack will happen in the next twenty-four hours."

"Thanks, I have to go."

As Ben walked in, he looked to his right and spotted two plain-clothes officers sitting in the waiting area. They spotted Ben in the same moment and immediately came over and introduced themselves.

"I'm Officer Tom McCain and this is my partner, Harry Pickard. We're here from the Internal Security Division to assist you in any way you need."

Ben nodded. "Thanks."

"By the way, Mike told us you should wait with us. He and the others went up to the suite."

"Fine, can I buy you guys a coffee?"

"Thank you," Harry replied. "That would be great."

CHAPTER
18

Tuesday, June 3, 2014
Connaught Hotel, London

THE CONNAUGHT WAS a traditional, old-style English Hotel. It had the feel of upper-class English nobility, including a butler on each floor waiting to fulfill your requests. Suite 502 was at the end of the hall. The concierge walked them to the door and pressed a button. A moment later, the door opened.

"Brahim, Jim, come on in," Mike said.

Isaac and Charlie stood just behind Mike. Isaac gave Jim a hug.

"You look like you're putting on weight. How many Guinnesses did you have this week?"

"I stopped counting at ten." Jim laughed.

Isaac grabbed Brahim by the arm. "How are you and Abra?"

"Good."

"I hope both of you are coming to meet Chava and me in Israel."

"I'm planning on it. I'll firm up the plans with Abra tonight."

Mike interrupted. "Sorry, fellows we have to move on. I know you're uncomfortable with all of this security, but it's necessary. The chips World Corporation produces are major contributors to the security of the United States. Our government is committed to doing everything in its power to protect you."

"Thank you," said Isaac. "Let's start the meeting."

"Why are we meeting here in this suite?" Jim questioned Mike.

"After the attack at the London Eye, I realized the Churchill is too public. This suite was set up as a special security center for our staff. The bedroom is now being used for communications. All the rooms have been soundproofed, and security camera monitors watch everyone who enters the hotel. Our own security guards have been strategically positioned on both ends of the fifth floor, and they will be there twenty-four/ seven. With the push of a button, the elevator will be locked down and the suite will be sealed."

Everyone was seated around the conference table. Mike scanned the room before he spoke.

"Brahim, we have credible information that an attempt on your life will be made in the coming week."

Brahim's face turned pale, but he said nothing.

"Who gains from killing Brahim?" Isaac asked.

"Someone who wants to make it very clear that Muslims shouldn't try to make peace with Jews," Mike said. "It's because of the symposium."

"Where did this information originate?" Charlie added.

"Beirut. Our source from the Chinese Embassy has information that Iran and China are involved."

"So what should I do?" Brahim asked.

"What about all the preparations for the symposium in Paris. Should we proceed as planned?" Jim asked.

"Could we postpone it, or should we cancel it indefinitely?"

Brahim slammed his fist down on the table. "And what if that's what they want, that everyone who has the power to create change sits in fear instead of acting on what needs to be done? No one will make any attempts toward a lasting peace because they know a death threat will be taped to their door."

"Brahim's right. We go on as planned," Isaac said forcefully.

"Gentlemen," Mike said, "let's think about this for a minute. Isaac, forgive me, but if you were going to kill Brahim, how would you do it? I want to know where, when, and with what?"

Isaac stood up and began to pace back and forth. "Not in London. In Paris."

You're right. At the symposium. Even with all the security, somebody could slip through. Sometimes it's easiest to be invisible in an enormous crowd." Jim looked straight at Mike.

"I agree."

"That's why we should cancel," Charlie said.

Isaac looked at Charlie. "No, there's a solution. We just have to find it."

"Is that final?" Mike looked toward Brahim for a decision.

"It certainly is."

"Okay, then I'd better go make some calls ."

"Thanks for all your help, Mike." Isaac nodded his approval.

"If you need me, I'm in the communications room." Mike got up and walked out the door.

"Brahim, you're gonna be fine," said Isaac. "We'll all be with you in Paris, and we'll have the finest security in the world guarding you."

Brahim exhaled deeply and smiled an unconvincing smile at Isaac.

"Let's take this time to go over some business," Isaac said.

"I've briefed Isaac on all I know," Charlie added.

Brahim motioned to Isaac to go on.

"We have credible information that the Chinese are planning to try to move away from the dollar. We're just waiting for the confirmation when they plan to do it."

"Our people in the Forex currency department in New York, and our gold traders here in London, are seeing signs that things are already underway," Jim remarked.

"Charlie has some information that might shed light on all this," said Isaac.

"What have you got?" Brahim asked.

"I had a very interesting meeting with a Chinese official who I've done business with before. He has information about a certain terrorist group in Beirut planning something big."

"How do we know he's telling the truth?" Brahim asked.

Charlie shrugged his shoulders and continued. "His brother is a double agent who's working for the Chinese in Beirut. "

"Go on."

"The brother is willing to trade information if we help him."

"With what?" Jim asked.

"His brother's life is in danger. He's stuck in Beirut."

"Okay," said Brahim. "What else have you got?"

"One of my contacts in China obtained the Chinese plan to counteract a new and deadly virus. He has the formula for the flu antidote on a chip. Needless to say, this virus will devastate the economies of the world and that's what China wants."

"What do you mean?" Jim asked.

"Listen carefully. China has been scheming since before the financial meltdown in the end of 2008. It has penetrated Africa, acquiring a significant amount of their natural resources. It's controlling the United States by having the largest investment in U.S. Treasury bonds. Every country in the world is looking to gain favor with them politically. That situation matured when the British gave them back Hong Kong."

Isaac stopped for a moment to take a sip of water. "The Muslim world has started looking to China for their future security, not to the U.S., and that's a big problem."

"What about North Korea? Not to mention Venezuela and most of South America," Brahim added. "They're all coming under China's sphere of influence."

"You still don't get it. In your minds, you see China operating as part of the world system. Connect the dots and a new picture appears: a King Kong–sized gorilla ready to destroy everything in its path just to survive."

Jim raised an eyebrow. "Nice people."

"My gut feeling is that at the top of their government a handful of people are involved in planning a global strategy to control the world. The dollar, Beirut, the virus, it's all connected."

Brahim looked at Jim. "Jim, you have all the information that Susan sent you. Let's go over everything when we get back to the Churchill, and when we meet again tomorrow, hopefully we'll have a plan."

"We'll need two hours in the morning," Jim said.

"Okay, seven a.m., my suite. We can have breakfast. The ladies will still be sleeping. Charlie, what's your plan?"

"I'm expecting a call momentarily from our lawyers in Hong Kong. Isaac asked me to fly to Hong Kong with William and I agreed."

"This is one of those things," Isaac said. "It's one of the dots that keep appearing."

Before he could explain more, Mike walked in looking upset.

"What's wrong?" Brahim asked.

"I received word that a bomb has gone off on Oxford Street near the Marks and Spencer Department Store."

"I must get in touch with Abra. She could be hurt."

"Brahim, she's safe. My security people put them in a car immediately and got her back to the hotel."

"*Subhaanallah*. Thank Allah, thank Allah. And thank you, Mike."

Jim's phone rang. "Hello, Mary."

"I've been trying to reach you. Did you hear the news about the bombing?"

"Yes, don't worry. I'm fine."

"I have to talk to you. It's about your brothers."

"Okay, let me get a handle on things here first. Can I talk to you in a little while?"

"Please, as soon as you're free."

"I have to go now. I'll call you later. If you need me, I'm at the Churchill. Room 803."

"I love you."

Jim slid his mobile into his side pocket. "Mary was watching CNN when her program was interrupted to announce the bombing. Ten people were reported dead and many critically injured."

"I received an SMS," Mike said. "The suicide bomber blew himself up on his motorcycle. We're finished here. Are we ready to go? Ben and the rest of the security detail are in front with vehicles."

"Abra and Fatima must be all shaken up," Brahim said. "I must get there right away."

"I'm going to call Peter and Carl at the office and cancel the meeting," Jim said.

"Wait a minute," Mike interrupted. "My people can pick them up. Just tell me where and when."

"Thanks. As soon as I can reach them, I'll let you know."

Mike started to leave when his phone rang. "Hello, yes, when did it happen? Okay. I will be at the HQ in one hour."

He turned to the three partners and said, "There's been another suicide bomber, this time at Piccadilly Circus. The report just came into HQ."

"Did they say how many are dead?" Isaac inquired.

"Not at this time. They'll update me shortly with more information. We've got to move."

"We're going to do whatever it takes to stop this," Isaac said, looking at his partners.

With a nod of their heads, they all agreed.

CHAPTER
19

IN THE LOBBY Ben was on his two-way radio. Mike got off the elevator. Ben motioned for him to come over. "You should hear this."

Mike took the two-way and listened. He spoke into it. "How many?" He was already anticipating just how bad it was going to be. "So far twenty-five dead and six in critical condition," he repeated to Ben.

They exited the hotel in silence. The streets were blocked with unmarked cars with blue lights flashing on their roofs, several Metropolitan patrol cars, and police on motorcycles. In the distance, where the bomb had exploded, sirens blasted. Everyone was on edge; quiet was no longer on the schedule today.

When the three partners emerged, Tom McCain stood by his car with the door open. His partner, Harry Pickard, was speaking to Ben. Ben motioned for Brahim and Isaac to get into the first unmarked car. Tom closed the door after them.

"Isaac, what gives them permission to blow up innocent people in the streets?" Brahim murmured. "The Arab authorities do nothing concrete to stop the terrorists. Innocent Muslims suffer because of their lack of courage. They think we are all the same." He shook his head in disgust.

Tom jumped into the front seat and locked all the doors with the push of a button. "We may have to wait a few minutes," he said. "There are ambulances blocking the road." Five minutes later, on the two-way radio, he was told the traffic was moving.

"Okay, we're all set. Let's move it," he said to the driver.

As they pulled out, Tom said to Brahim and Isaac, "Charlie, Jim, and Mike are in the car right behind us."

As the cars started moving, motorcycles drove along each side of the car. The sound of sirens was deafening. In the other car, Jim was busy on the phone dialing Mary.

"Hello, Mary. I'm in a car with Charlie and Mike. I'm safe. We have more security than we need. Nothing to worry about."

"Jim, Frank's been trying to reach you."

"Tell him to call me later, about five p.m. London time."

"Where will you be?"

"I'll try my best to be in my room. If for any reason he misses me, tell him to call back at nine. I'm fine. I'll call you before I go to sleep."

"I love and miss you. Please be careful, honey." She clicked off.

Charlie was on the phone with Hong Kong. Jim looked out the window. In the streets people were running with cell phones stuck to their ears. Buses and cars stopped dead in their tracks, and traffic was at a standstill, gridlock everywhere. *All this in less than twelve hours. What's next?*

"It's definite," said Charlie. "I'm going to Hong Kong."

"When are you leaving?"

"Sometime tomorrow. I have to check with William."

"Who else is going?"

"As far as I know, just me and the crew."

In the street, the policemen on motorcycles yelled at drivers, telling them to move over. Horns blew like a brass band at the Proms in the Royal Albert Hall just ten minutes away. Mike yelled on the blow horn, commanding everyone he could to move aside. A bomb squad appeared out of nowhere with a special vehicle. Suddenly they started moving.

As they drove past the United States Embassy and the statue of General Eisenhower, Brahim asked Isaac, "What would Ike do in this situation?"

"I don't know, but I can tell you one thing: we had better do something or else the democracy we all love is going to be a thing of the past. Time after time history has proved that appeasement with radicals led to human suffering and the collapse of democracy." He checked his watch. "We should be in the hotel in a couple of minutes. We can finish our meeting over lunch. There are still several corporate matters that can't wait."

CHAPTER
20

Tuesday, June 3, 2014
Churchill Hotel, London

THE STREETS WERE returning to normal as the SUVs pulled into the driveway of the hotel. Mike jumped out of his car first. He approached Isaac and Brahim.

"I need to go to HQ right away. Please ask everyone to excuse me. Let's see if we can get together later if possible."

Brahim nodded. "We understand."

"One more thing. No one is to leave the hotel for any reason without checking with me or Ben."

Brahim nodded. "Understood."

Charlie and Jim were talking in the lobby. Brahim and Isaac walked over to them. Two security guards stood at each side of the elevator doors. One entered with them. "What floor?"

"We need the eighth floor," said Jim.

Exiting the elevator, they saw two officers wearing blue bullet-proof vests and machine guns slung across their chests. The lounge and conference room was to the right. A buffet table had been set up for a late lunch.

As they looked over the selection, Dov walked in. "I hope everything is satisfactory."

"Fantastic," Jim said. "I need a beer. What about you guys?"

"I'll take one," Isaac answered.

"Coke for me," Brahim said.

"I'm on it," said Dov.

Charlie followed Dov to the buffet table. "I'm leaving tomorrow for Hong Kong. The situation is getting worse by the hour. Did Isaac brief you on what's at stake?"

"No."

"I'm sure he will. Let's get back inside and see what Isaac has to say about the trip."

Dov grabbed a tray and placed a few bottles of Coke and beers on it. He picked up a bowl of mixed nuts and another with some olives. He spotted a tray of sandwiches with stickers that said KOSHER.

"Charlie, there's plenty of kosher food, at least seven platters."

They grabbed a few sandwiches and brought them over to the table.

"Any hot pastrami or salt beef?" Brahim asked.

Isaac started to tear off all the wrappings, like a kid opening his birthday presents. Then he noticed a tray marked desserts and got up to grab a slice of pie. Everyone stared at Isaac.

"What?" Isaac looked down at the piece of pie he was holding. "If any one of you tells Chava that I ate this, you're gonna get it." Everyone laughed.

"Isaac, you're not afraid of your wife, are you?"

"Of course not. I promised her I wouldn't eat cake, but this is pie, and lemon meringue, it's my favorite."

Soon everyone was sitting with plates of food in front of them. Brahim rubbed his eyes. "Isaac, this has been one heck of a day."

"We're all tired, but let's start."

"I just got off the phone with Peter and Carl," Jim said. "I told them to stand by, and I would call them as soon as I had any idea about our timing for meeting up."

"Fine, let's step back and analyze some of the facts. We've obtained information that the Chinese are doing something big in the currency area. Lee and Robert are hiding two Chinese nationals in Hong Kong who gave us this information at the risk of their lives. The information about the details of the Chinese financial scheme is extremely valuable to us.

"Next, Charlie has found out that the Chinese have a new virus that's about to destroy the free world. They have the only antidote, of course. We also have a Chinese double agent in Beirut who can prove connections between the Arabs and the Chinese. The NSA is going to kill him, so we'd better get to him first." Isaac took a sip of his drink.

"Anything else?" Jim asked.

"Yeah, the most important fact to us. Someone is targeting Brahim and we don't know who it is. Our biggest problem is the unknown. We have no idea what's on their agenda or who are the masterminds behind this." Isaac turned and looked at Charlie. "Charlie, you want to add anything?"

"Yes, Isaac. Whatever the plan of action, I strongly suggest that Mike should be in the loop."

"I agree."

"There's a real chance we may be breaking some laws along the way," Isaac added. "He can smooth it over with the different federal agencies." Everyone nodded in agreement.

"Jim, my gut tells me that starting today, whatever markets are open, we need to start getting out of our positions in all the different time zones—Hong Kong, London, and New York. I want to sell all our stock portfolios. Get the managers on our secured video conference network. Tell them if they do this right and we succeed, they'll receive the biggest year-end bonus of their lives."

"I'll try to keep you posted every hour."

"Nobody but you can make it work, Jim. You were the best trader in the business when you were on the Exchange floor. When we started our company, it was your skills in the market that made us the profits to do what we've done."

Jim smiled modestly. "You and Brahim were the drivers. All I did was execute your plans."

"Our chip companies needed to fund their research-and-development departments, and as we all know, cash is king. On Wall Street they feared you because of your success, and then they followed your every move. Everyone who's working in World's financial area studies your books on charting and the analysis of the derivative markets. Nobody has the instincts day in and day out to make the right call on any segment of the world financial markets like you do."

"Keep going," Jim said. "I need my ego massaged, you know, and a bigger bonus this year." He laughed.

Everyone laughed along with him.

"My brother," said Isaac, "we've been to hell and back a few times. And I'm afraid we're in for it again. Politically things are going to get hot. As our positions are closed out, I want you to buy gold and silver contracts, as many as you can within a specific range."

"What's next?"

"Eventually we want to take possession of the actual gold bars. Do this as soon as possible. Buy platinum, palladium, and Canadian Silver Maple Leaf coins. Get rid of all of the U.S. dollars in our accounts and buy Canadian dollars. The last summit the Chinese attended with the United States they were already looking for a way out of the dollar. Now it's been confirmed. They want to create a basket of currencies. They're talking about special drawdown rights issued by the International Monetary Fund. Under pressure from them, everybody will cave in."

"No question the balance of power is on their side," Dov added.

"It's like you say, Isaac," said Jim. "The gorilla is on the move."

Jim reached for his computer. He pulled up the paperwork Susan sent. "Isaac, these transactions will be in the area of three and a half trillion dollars."

"Go on."

"If the markets turn down on the metals, World would be in serious trouble. All that we worked for could disappear overnight. Our investors would lose everything."

"Wait a minute," said Isaac. "Twenty-four years ago *we* started this company. We're the investors. Well, except for the ten million dollars seed money Brahim got for us."

All eyes were on Brahim.

"Isaac, you needed ten million to start a high-tech business, I offered you the seed money. It took me a few days, but I got it." Brahim nodded his head. "Yes, and I never told you how I got it."

"That's right, you never did," Jim said, "only that in two years we would have to pay it back with no interest. Which we did, thank God. The rest is history."

"You're bringing up old memories," Isaac added.

"This is the moment. The right time to tell you what I did."

"Go ahead."

"When I left that meeting, I called my uncle in Cyprus."

"We wondered where you'd disappeared to," Jim said.

"He was one of the founders of the Arab Bank in the 1930s. A special man, soft spoken and modest though very wealthy. I flew to meet him in Cyprus. I explained to him that I was going into business with some partners. He asked questions about the market and the product, and I gave him a short overview on the future of nanochips.

"He said, 'French fries? I've never heard of that brand.' We both started laughing, and then with a serious tone he asked, 'How much do you need?'

"'Ten million dollars,' I told him.

"'For how long?' he asked me.

"'Two years,' I said, 'and I'll sign on the loan personally.'

"Then he asked me about my partners. I told him that one was a Catholic and the other a Jew, both good men.

"'Is the Jew religious?' my uncle asked. I thought it a strange question. I told him, 'Yes, he's religious.'

"He told me that in 1929, during the great Depression, when he was living in Palestine, times were very difficult for our family. The only thing he had was a dream to get a job or start a business so he could support his family. Cyprus was close by, so he hired a fishing boat to take him to the island. He had three close friends in Jerusalem. All were religious Jews. They knew he wanted to leave, but he had no money. So they went and borrowed from their relatives and friends. They raised eighteen hundred dollars and gave it to him as a gift.

"When my uncle finished telling his story, he handed me his business card and said, 'Go to my bank. You'll have the money.'"

For a moment, Isaac was motionless. He was about to speak when Brahim held up his hand. "Wait. I'm not finished. I go to the bank and the manager hands me a check made out to my name for the ten million dollars. I asked him about the paperwork so I could sign. He told me that my uncle had taken care of everything and that there's nothing to sign. 'Your uncle told me to tell you, "May Allah bless you and your partners."'

"Jim, do you remember what you said twenty-four years ago? All for one and one for all."

"I sure do."

"Isaac, you call this shot. I'm with you, my brother. All for one, as usual."

Jim stood up and put out his hand. Brahim did the same, placing his on top, then Isaac.

Dov looked at Charlie and asked, "Can we join in?"

"You bet," Isaac replied.

One hand on top of the other, they shouted like kids on a playground, "All for one and one for all!"

When they sat back down, Jim said, "I need another beer and then I got work to do."

"Charlie and I have to discuss the situation in Hong Kong," said Isaac. "Dov, you should be in on this meeting."

"Do you need me, Isaac, or can you fill me in later?" Brahim asked. "I want to check on Abra and her sister."

"No problem. Give them my best. I'll catch up with you and Jim later."

"I'm in my room if you need me. I'll be ready to meet up with Peter and Carl as soon as Mike picks them up."

BRAHIM ENTERED HIS suite as the telephone on the desk started to ring. From the bedroom he heard, "I'll get it."

Abra came running. For a moment, she was startled to see Brahim closing the door. She had expected to see Fatima.

She lifted up the phone and pressed 1. "Hello." Then, after a long pause, Abra said, "Hold on for just a moment, please." She looked at Brahim. "Brahim, is everything alright?"

"Yes, I came up to see if you and Fatima were okay after what happened today."

"We're fine, thanks to Allah." She put the phone to her ear. "I will call you back later."

"No, please continue," Brahim told her.

"It's fine. It's just a friend calling to make sure I'm safe."

"Please go on. I'm going to wash up."

When Brahim left the room, Abra returned to her phone conversation. "I am looking forward to visiting you in Riyadh. Fatima and I will arrive tomorrow."

Fatima walked in and sat down slowly on a straight-backed chair. "I'm having some back trouble. Do you have any painkillers?" She noticed that Abra was on the phone. Who are you talking to?"

"A friend. One minute and I will be finished."

"Please make it fast. I need your advice."

"I will call you later," Abra said into the phone. "Make sure everything is in order." She hung up.

"Abra, I should take something for the pain."

Brahim came in. "Is it your back again, Fatima? What can I do for you?"

"I'll be alright. My back's been giving me trouble. Abra, please get me some pills." Abra left to get the medication.

"Let me call a doctor or a chiropractor to come examine you," Brahim said.

"Don't be silly. It will pass in a short while."

"Are you sure you're going to be okay for dinner tonight? Maybe we should just eat in the suite."

Abra returned and handed Fatima a glass of water and two pills. "Here, take these."

"Thank you Abra."

Brahim checked his watch. Five o'clock. "Fatima, you are sure about going out?"

"Yes, I am sure. I want to tell you both how much I care for you."

Brahim noticed that there was a distant look in Abra's eyes. Abra said nothing and left.

"Fatima, we both love you too. I have to go." Brahim stood up to leave the room. First he turned to Fatima. "When I have a minute, we need to talk. I think there is something very wrong with Abra."

CHAPTER
21

IN THE LOUNGE on the eighth floor, Isaac, Charlie, and Dov were finishing up details about the move to Canada.

"I need two minutes to call my wife and tell her I won't be home this week," Charlie said before they moved on to his trip to Hong Kong.

"Good idea. Let's all take a break for ten minutes, get our personal calls out of the way."

Charlie started to dial, wondering what he should tell his wife. The phone rang and a voice said, "Hello."

"Debbie, how are you?"

"Charlie, where are you now?"

"I'm at the Churchill with Isaac, Brahim, and Jim."

"When are you coming home?"

"That's what I'm calling you about. Something important came up. I have to return to Hong Kong tomorrow and then shoot right back to London."

"I understand, but you still haven't told me when you're coming home."

"I'll have a better idea by Thursday."

"Everything alright? Is there a problem?"

"You know how it is. Something came up and I'm the only one available. Why don't you take a trip to Long Island and visit with your sister for the weekend?"

"Charlie, something's wrong. I can hear it in your voice."

"Nothing's wrong, Debbie. The kids love visiting your sister. I'll call you tomorrow from Hong Kong."

"Okay. Please be careful. Make sure you call me when you land."

"Give the kids a kiss for me and tell them I'll bringing them a special gift. Debbie, I love you."

Charlie hung up the phone and walked over to where Isaac and Dov were sitting.

"Anything new, Isaac?" Charlie inquired.

"No, let's go over the plans for your trip."

"Okay, we fly tomorrow, weather permitting. William will be calling me at any moment to update me with the exact time of departure."

"How long do you expect to be on the ground?" Dov asked.

"Not long. My guess, with refueling, two hours."

"Check the weather forecast through the weekend."

"William's on top of it."

"Let's call Allan Peters," Isaac suggested. "See if he has an update."

Charlie dialed and the phone started to ring. After four rings someone picked up.

"Charlie, what's up?" Allan asked.

"Isaac's right here with me and needs to speak to you." Charlie handed his phone to Isaac.

"Isaac, I understand all hell is breaking loose in London. Is everyone okay?"

"We're fine. We're about ready to give the green light on the assignment."

"I'm ready to go from here. I cleared all the documents. I was just on the phone with our chief of security. The Chinese put out a coded alert for Kim Li and Hui Ying."

"When did you last speak to Lee or Robert?"

"I met with Robert at the Yung Kee Restaurant earlier today and discussed the situation."

"What about Lee?"

"Lee, Hui Ying, and Kim Li are in a safe house. Everyone will be moved soon as the plane is on the ground. It's going to get very hot."

"We decided to bring Mike O'Shea on board. He's an agent with the NSA. He can run interference for us in D.C."

"We're going to need all the support we can get. Anything else you need, Isaac?"

"No, Charlie or I will call you as soon as William calls back with the final information."

Isaac handed the phone to Charlie. "Now's your chance to back out. This could turn into a real mess. Think it through."

"Nothing to think about. I made up my mind on the plane."

Isaac looked at Dov. "Dov, sorry, can you give me a few minutes alone with Charlie?"

"No problem, Isaac. I've got to talk to Jim anyway. Call me when you need me."

Dov left. Isaac started talking. Charlie held up his hand.

"Isaac, there's one thing. If I don't come back, I need to know my wife and children will be taken care of financially."

"You're not getting off that easy. You're coming back. But if, God forbid, it ever came to that, I promise you I will take care of them personally."

"Good enough for me."

Isaac's phone rang. He glanced at his caller ID. "It's Allan. Hello, Allan, everything set?" He turned grim as he listened. "Okay, Allan, I'll tell Charlie and see to it that our pilot gets the information immediately."

Isaac hung up the phone. He looked at Charlie. "Allan said the Hong Kong International Airport is swarming with regular police and plainclothes agents."

"What else?"

"Allan received information from one of his people that Wen Tian's in charge. He's heading the operation. We've been told by the NSA to be extremely careful."

"I heard about him when I was with the Justice Department. He had informants everywhere. You wouldn't believe the file our agency's got on him. His reputation for getting information out of prisoners, well, let's just say his tactics are terrifying. He broke the triads of Hong Kong, then became the head of the secret police."

"He has orders to arrest anyone he suspects may have a connection to Kim Li."

"Smells like trouble."

"Get William on the phone. We have to adjust our plan."

Charlie dialed a number and then handed Isaac the phone.

"William," said Isaac, "can you switch your flight plan?

"Yes, but why?"

"HKI airport is locked down with security."

"What do you have in mind?"

"Kai Tak Airport. What do you think?"

"When they built Hong Kong International, they basically closed it down. As far as I understand, it's only used for freight carriers and for emergency situations. The runway is dangerous. You have to fly in through the mountains, and then you have to contend with the skyscrapers. I've done it a couple of times over the years, but it's no joyride."

"What about today? Can you do it today?"

"Yes, if we have no other choice."

Isaac paused to think for a moment. "Okay, call Charlie as soon as you've nailed everything down. I want to give Allan the final go-ahead by midnight. It'll be around eight a.m. over there."

"You'll have it in two hours."

"Thanks." Isaac hung up the phone. He turned back to Charlie.

"Charlie, I need you to locate Brahim. Ask him if he can meet me in fifteen minutes for a short meeting."

"Okay."

"Ask Dov and Jim if they can join us. In the meantime, I need to call Chava."

As Charlie left, Isaac's PDA rang. His wife, Chava, showed up on the screen.

"How are you?" Chava asked.

"Fine, I'm just very busy."

"I can imagine, I'm glued to the TV. So many people have been killed or injured in the attacks. It's terrible. Isaac, are you safe?"

"We're okay."

"Maybe you should come home, and we'll do the Paris-Israel trip another time."

"No, I want to keep to the plan. Please join me in Paris as we planned. Besides, we promised the children we were coming to Jerusalem. I want to visit with the grandchildren, and we could both use a break. We need to spend some time together too. "

"You sure we'll be able to spend some time alone?"

"Yes, I promise. We can do whatever you want."

"Did you take your blood pressure pills?"

"Yes, of course."

"Are you eating right?"

"Yes, Chava, I'm fine."

"I spoke to Susan. She booked me on a flight with Air France."

"What's the flight number? I'm punching the information into my PDA as we speak."

"AF2035. I leave tonight at eleven thirty p.m. and I'll be arriving in Charles de Gaulle Airport at ten a.m. Wednesday."

"Someone will be at the airport to pick you up and take you to the George V. I would pick you up myself, but I'm not sure what time we'll be cleared for takeoff from Heathrow."

"It's fine, Isaac. Please be careful. I'm bringing your extra medicine. Anything else I can bring you?"

"Only you. I love you. Brahim just walked in. I need to go."

"I love you too."

"If you need anything, call Susan before you take off. She'll get me the message. We'll speak soon."

CHAPTER
22

EVERYTHING OKAY WITH Abra and Fatima?" Isaac asked Brahim.

"Fatima is having a little back trouble, nothing serious."

"What about Abra?"

"I don't understand her lately."

"You want to talk?"

Brahim hesitated. "Thank you, Isaac, but it's painful for me."

"I'm your brother. I'm here to listen whenever you want to talk."

"Thank you, I'll keep it in mind."

"Where's Jim? Weren't you meeting Peter and Carl?"

"Yes, we just finished. Jim's coming up in a few minutes." Brahim looked at his watch as Dov walked in with Mike. It was already six o'clock.

"Isaac," asked Dov, "do you want me to call Jim? Wait, I see him coming this way."

Isaac waited until Jim sat down. "How'd it go?" he asked.

"I just finished my conversation with Peter and Carl. They're going to control the first liquidation of one billion dollars in equities from our new office here in London. Brahim, sorry about Paris, but I need to fly back to New York."

"When?"

"I'll fly out tonight and take charge of the tracking and further selling from World headquarters. We expect to be executing the first trades in New York in about an hour from now. By then there'll be two hours of trading left before the market closes at four p.m. This will give us some indication of the momentum our selling is having on the markets. I plan to be on the floor trading tomorrow when the markets open at nine thirty. We'll work Hong Kong and Europe as they open and close."

"What about the private equity funds?" Brahim asked.

"Jerry Clarke, our top Asia-Pacific fund manager, will be in charge of all that from Hong Kong."

"Any questions?" Isaac addressed everyone.

Dov spoke. "Only my recommendation, but nobody should discuss this with anyone, not even your wives. The Security Exchange Commission should be informed, of course. Our market makers should be issued notifications too."

Mike's two-way started to buzz. Everyone's eyes focused on him. He stood up and shouted, "We got him." He closed the two-way and said, "We just captured the third terrorist who tried to blow up the Eye. He was hiding near the Tower of London."

"Did they say what his name was or his motive?" Brahim asked.

"Abu al-Mousavi. They haven't had a chance to question him yet."

Brahim's eyes dropped. His voice now angry, he said, "Another Muslim terrorist. We must stop this insanity, I'm going to meet with King Faisal and demand they jail anyone who preaches hate or killing in the schools and the mosques. Today, World Corporation declares war on the enemies of peace."

Isaac patted Brahim's shoulder. "We're all in this together."

Mike spoke up. "If there's anyone who can bring about change, it's you guys. What you've accomplished building the largest business in the world stands as an example. People will follow if you'll lead."

"You know, Mike," said Jim softly, "when we got together it was to make money. As things developed, we all knew there was a bigger purpose to our coming together."

"As our success grew, we started to understand we could affect the way people thought about people from different religious backgrounds working together," Brahim added.

"Enough of our idealism," said Isaac. "Let's put our words into action. First order of business, we're helping two Chinese nationals defect from China," he informed Mike. "They're hiding in a safe house in Hong Kong. Charlie is leaving momentarily with my pilot. I informed Brahim's pilot, Thomas Boyd, about our plan and he's on board."

"What do you need from me?" Mike asked.

"We have Gulfstreams waiting at Heathrow, and we're going to send them both to Hong Kong. Both will file the same flight plan within a few minutes' difference. I'd like you to instruct your people to leak certain information to the Chinese within five hours of the jets' arrival at the airport."

"What information?"

"That two high-level Chinese citizens plan to defect to the United States with the help of the NSA. They're hiding in Hong Kong and will be put into coffins as a cover and brought to the airport. They'll be picked up by a private jet the NSA borrowed from World.

"World will deny any knowledge of anything. We'll say only that we were informed that the bodies of two American soldiers were discovered and need to be returned immediately to the U.S. They're to be picked up by an undertaker's limousine hired by the U.S. consul and taken to HKI airport. They will then be flown to Arlington Cemetery in Washington, D.C."

Mike nodded. "Okay, what else do you need?"

"I believe mainland China will notify Hong Kong and Wen Tian, head of the secret police. He'll be waiting for the arrival of the plane and the coffins at the airport. Mike, your security people need to get two unclaimed American bodies from the mortuary and put them into the coffins. I've confirmation from the State Department that several are waiting to be claimed. As soon as your people secure the bodies, they take the next step."

"I think I can see where this is going," said Mike.

"Right. Two hours before the planes land, they notify the airport they have two coffins to be loaded on a private plane landing at HKI and the bodies need to be flown to Washington, D.C., for burial. Brahim's plane will be the one landing at HKI. Your people have to give Hong Kong the flight information and ask them not to inform anyone, since the families of the deceased and the State Department want to keep this as low profile as possible. Ask them to reserve a spot for landing away from the main terminal."

"Which plane do I fly on?" Charlie asked.

"You're on my plane. William will call Kai Tak Airport as soon as Brahim's plane is on its final approach and ready to set down on the runway. He'll tell them he had to make an emergency landing and he had no time to divert to HKI. As soon as William sends his message, he'll break off communications with the tower, faking a transmissions glitch. His radar will tell him if the runway's clear so he can land.

"Allan will be with Lee, Kim Li, and Hui Ying. He'll only inform them he has to move them to another safe house. When they're near the airport, the car will stop off the road. Allan has arranged for them to be transported in the back of a FedEx freight truck making its regular delivery to the FedEx plane. The truck's allowed to drive directly onto the airport runways. On our signal, he'll stop in front of the plane. Allan will open the door on the side of the truck from the inside. The truck's size will block any view the tower has of the plane. Kim Li and Hui Ying will jump out of the truck and board our plane.

"William will notify the tower that he fixed his communications problem and is ready for takeoff. Our multiple satellite transponders on our private channel will be tuned in to all their conversation from the moment he leaves England."

"What could possibly go wrong?" Brahim joked.

"We have no other option. If the Chinese make this move on the dollar, we might lose everything. Kim Li and her boyfriend are holding all the information. Let me be candid. Success will be based upon the precision with which we will execute every move of this operation."

Everyone nodded their heads in agreement.

"I'm going to call Mary and tell her I'm heading home," said Jim. "I'll check with you later about dinner."

"Brahim," said Isaac, "I want to go over some things with Charlie before he takes off. Dov, let's get together in an hour."

"Okay." Dov nodded in agreement and headed for the elevator. Mike excused himself so he could set his part of the plan in motion.

Brahim said to Charlie, "Can you give us a minute? I want to talk to Isaac in private."

"Of course. I'll come back in fifteen minutes." Charlie got up and left the room.

Brahim looked at Isaac. "Isaac, you got a lot on your plate. I'm worried about you."

"I'm fine, this has to be done. The three of us can make a difference. This is not about our company and it's not about money. God blessed the three of us with more money than we or our children's children will ever need. Freedom, the right to choose our own way of life, that's what this is about. Churchill said, 'Courage is rightly esteemed the first of human qualities because it is said it's a quality that guarantees all others.'"

Brahim was motionless. "Isaac, can I talk to you about something else?"

"Of course."

"It's Abra. She's become so distant. Since the last Ramadan and the hajj, something's different about her. Please don't be upset about what I'm going to say, but she's turned against Israel because of the Palestine situation. She said she has no respect for Jews because they don't believe in Muhammad. I don't want to even repeat all the crazy things she's been saying. Needless to say, I haven't mentioned your suggestion of stopping in Jerusalem after the symposium."

"Our families all face difficulties because of the condition of the world today. My children question my being in business with you."

"What do you tell them?"

"I tell them we're all from one God. Everyone must look inside himself and ask, 'What can I do for my Creator today?' That we all have free choice, that we can go out and spread hatred and destruction or set out to do kindness and build a better world. A few moments ago, Mike said we could make a difference. I believe we can make a difference even if it starts with our own families." Isaac paused. "Listen, let me talk to her. I think I can help."

Brahim's brow furrowed. "Alright, but it won't be easy getting her to sit down with you."

Isaac put a hand on Brahim's shoulder. "Brahim, my brother, we'll win this war together."

Isaac and Brahim stood up and embraced.

Charlie walked in with Mike and Jim. "Excuse me, Isaac," said Charlie, "sorry to interrupt. Our pilot called. HKI's been cleared. He's been talking to Brahim's pilot. They're on the same page, and the weather's on our side, so we're good to go."

"Any new developments?" Isaac asked Mike.

"No, I finished my call with D.C. They said I should do whatever I need to for this operation, that I have a green light."

Brahim asked the question no one else had thought yet to ask. "What about Paris?" Brahim asked. "We're supposed to be leaving tomorrow, but our jets have been diverted to Hong Kong. What do I tell Abra and Fatima?"

Mike smiled. "I checked into that. We're in luck. Two jets from the agency arrived yesterday with some congressmen on a fact-finding mission. There's some oil deal the British are about to close with Libya. The planes will be available until Friday evening."

"Can one of them take my wife and my sister in-law to Saudi Arabia after we fly to Paris? We planned to fly there together after the symposium, but if there's a security threat, I'd rather they were out of the way."

"Let me check with the pilots. Jim, if you can be ready in two hours, one of the NSA planes will be flying to the Air Force base in Dover. Four commanding officers from the Four Thirty-Sixth Airlift Wing will be flying home. You can hop a ride."

"Thanks. I'll be in the lobby in thirty minutes." Jim turned to everyone. "I'll be in touch from the plane as soon as we're airborne."

"One of our security cars will take you directly to the plane," Mike said.

"Mike, please continue," Isaac said.

"My suggestion, we take the two planes. Isaac, me, and some of our security personnel on one, and Brahim, his wife, his sister-in-law, and Dov with additional security on the other."

"What time do we leave?" Dov asked.

"After breakfast. Nine o'clock?" Everybody nodded in agreement.

Brahim turned to leave. "I'm going to fill Abra in on the plans. I'll meet you in the morning, Isaac. Call me if you need anything." Dov and Jim followed him out.

"Charlie, can you and Isaac stay a few minutes?" Mike asked.

Isaac looked at him quizzically. "What's the matter?"

"My informant in Hong Kong said we're walking into a trap and I believe him. I'm waiting on more data from my source."

"Everything's already in motion," Charlie said. "What do you suggest?"

"I think we go through with Isaac's plan, but under no circumstance do you leave the plane once you've landed. I'm having one of my special agents accompany you. Around fifteen minutes before landing, you and the crew will be told to put on bulletproof clothing."

"Getting interesting," Charlie said with smile.

"The president wears the same clothing in public, and no one knows the difference. On the plane you'll be outfitted with weapons to defend yourself if needed."

"Let's hope that won't be necessary," Isaac said.

"Mike, can your people take me out to the plane in about an hour?" Charlie asked. "I want to talk to the pilot and the crew."

"Sure, my security guy will take you. He's the one flying with you."

Isaac looked worried.

"Isaac, please don't worry," said Charlie. "I'll be fine."

"Okay, but no hero stuff. You do exactly what Mike says. Got it?"

Charlie responded like a good soldier. "Yes, sir."

"We'll be in touch when you're in the air so we can check all our satellite relays." Isaac grabbed Charlie's hand. "May God protect you."

Charlie nodded and left to pack.

Isaac looked at Mike. "Mike, maybe you want to turn in for the night?"

"Not yet. What about you?"

"I need a good scotch. You want one?"

"I'm still on duty."

"I just relieved you."

"Scotch it is."

Isaac took a bottle of Glenlivet off the bar and poured two drinks. "We're in a tough situation, but we're gonna win. Keep an eye on Brahim. He's concerned about Abra."

"I'll assign someone to her. She'll be okay."

Ben walked in. "Mike, they're looking for you again at HQ."

"Cheers, really good stuff, Isaac, but I'd better go. I'll see you tomorrow."

Isaac sat down with his glass and took a large swallow. The phone rang.

"Hello. Yes, Brahim, I'm fine. Everything alright with Abra? Good. See you in the morning. Have a good night."

Isaac hung up the phone and took another drink. His phone rang again.

"Hello, Chava, yes, I'll take my cholesterol pill. Thanks for reminding me. I know it's because you love me. I love you too. Looking forward to seeing you in Paris tomorrow."

CHAPTER
23

Tuesday, June 3, 2014
Bekaa Valley, Lebanon

AT MIDNIGHT IN Bekaa Valley, Lebanon, the man in the moon was all you could see. Hard to believe that the moonlit path stretching all the way from Syria led straight to the strategic headquarters of the Hezbollah.

Deep in a cave dug out from the side of a mountain, agents from Iran, Syria, and Hezbollah sat on a dirt floor eating pita and hummus and discussing how to protect themselves from Israeli spy drones. Iran had summoned them for a meeting about the information they'd just received from California.

They each had the same goal: to gain control of what had once been called "the jewel of the Middle East." The Iranians and Syrians were like nomads, their sheep eating everything on the ground and moving on. For all of them, Beirut would be the final meal.

Tonight, with the information on the chip sent from California, Iran and Syria could take control of the Lebanese government, and the country would be in their hands.

"A suite in the Phoenicia InterContinental Hotel in Beirut has been set up with computers and satellite phone systems to start the liquidation of certain accounts in different banks around the world," said Halleem Amari, the Iranian agent in charge of the mission. "All of our men have been selected and trained in electronic espionage by the Revolutionary Guards in Tehran."

Otherwise known as the Army of the Guardians of the Islamic Revolution, the Revolutionary Guards were charged with protecting the Islamic system in Iran.

"Our mission is a joint effort headed by myself and my colleagues, Mohammad Saedi of the Hezbollah and Abul Elham from Syria. They all have experience working with international banks in London and Switzerland. Each held high-level positions in international finance after they left university. They're ready to execute the plan as soon as they receive the go-ahead from the Ayatollah Khamenei."

CHAPTER
24

Wednesday, June 4, 2014
Churchill Hotel, London

A HALF DOZEN security personnel stood around the lobby of the Churchill holding cups of coffee. It was eight o'clock in the morning. Mike and Ben walked through the entrance of the hotel and gathered everyone together to inform them about their meeting.

"I just finished being briefed by HQ, MI6, and the NSA. They all agree an attempt on Brahim's life is almost certain. They've deducted that Brahim has been selected so they can make an example of him before the Arab world. Between going into business with a Jew and now attempting to start a campaign for world peace, he's the poster boy for what Muslim fanatics don't want to encourage. They have reliable information it will take place in Paris, most probably at the symposium."

Ben stepped forward. "Here are your assignments." He handed packets out to each of them. "Any questions, I'm the address."

"The French were notified that we're bringing extra personnel from London," Mike added. "They agreed to cooperate fully."

Ben said, "If any of you want breakfast, now's the time."

"I'm taking breakfast on the eighth floor," Mike told Ben. He walked over to the elevator and pressed the button to go up. The doors opened, and in front of him stood Isaac still in the elevator.

"Good morning," Mike said. "It's too early to leave yet."

"I was looking for you. Care to join me for breakfast?"

Mike stepped into the elevator. "Perfect timing. I'd be glad to."

As they walked into the lounge on the eighth floor, they spotted Dov and Brahim having breakfast.

"Good morning," said Isaac. "Did you guys get any sleep?"

"Not enough," Dov answered.

"Maybe a couple hours," said Brahim. "By the time I finished dinner with Abra and her sister, it was past midnight, and then I was up talking with Abra until two thirty in the morning. Doesn't matter, I feel fine."

"Mike, what time should we be in the lobby?" Dov inquired.

"We should be in the SUVs at around a quarter to nine."

Dov stood up. "Excuse me, I think I'm going to grab a fast shower. I'll see you all soon." He turned to leave.

Brahim also stood up. "I better get going too and make sure the ladies are getting ready."

"It's no problem if we leave a little later," said Mike. "Don't rush them."

"Thanks, but I don't want to hold everybody up."

At that moment, Brahim's phone rang. "Hello, Abra. Yes, thank you." He hung up. "Abra said they're ready. She asked me to come to the suite before we meet in the lobby."

"Go ahead," said Isaac. "Mike and I were going to go over the schedule. We can update it and fill you in later."

"Isaac, you're looking tired. Please try to rest today."

"Thanks, I will."

Brahim left to check on the ladies.

Isaac looked at Mike. "Did you ever meet a guy like him? He's the one they're trying to kill, and he's worried about me looking tired."

They spent the next half hour discussing the itinerary and finalizing the details of Isaac's plan. As they were wrapping things up, Isaac's phone buzzed. "It's a text from Jim. He made it to New York okay. Thanks for arranging it."

Mike nodded. "I guess we'd better get a move on." He took a croissant and filled a paper cup with coffee. "I'll meet you in the lobby in ten minutes."

AT THIS TIME of the morning only security personnel and a few hotel staff were on duty. The concierge was eyeing the security detail; it was obvious they made him nervous. At each of the elevators stood a guard, two were positioned at the exit, and nine more surrounded the three SUVs waiting outside.

The sidewalk around the hotel entrance had been taped off. London police mounted on horses had the street blocked off. It was like a silent movie with the Keystone cops was in production. Some of the characters moved, while others observed.

The general manager, Mr. Blake, came out of his office holding a package. Ben walked up to him.

"Would you mind if I examine what's inside?"

"Please, by all means."

Ben opened the wrapping and saw a book.

"For Mr. Surin, a gift from the hotel. It's a signed book by Mr. Winston Churchill from when he stayed here."

Ben handed back the package. "I'm sorry I had to bother you. It could have been a bomb disguised as a gift."

MIKE WATCHED THE digital indicator of the elevator, waiting for the numbers to count down. As soon as he stepped out of the elevator, two of the security guards moved to flank him.

Fatima, Abra, and Brahim stepped out of the other elevator.

"Mike," said Brahim, "any news on our plane to Saudi Arabia?"

"We received clearance from HQ. The pilot's working on the flight plan."

"Is there a problem?" Abra inquired.

"No, they just need to confirm the times of takeoff and landing. I'm sure we'll receive the itinerary before we arrive in Paris."

"Thank you," said Brahim.

Mike gestured to the security guards at his sides. "Everybody, please go with these two men to the cars," he instructed.

Mr. Blake walked over to Brahim. "Please take this gift as a token of our appreciation for your friendship over the many years that you have stayed at the Churchill. I wanted to take this opportunity to thank you personally. Please visit us again soon."

Brahim smiled. "Thank you."

He took Abra by the hand and went out to the waiting car. Dov had stepped out of the elevator.

"We all set?" Mike asked.

"I'm as ready as I can be."

"Can I give you a hand with your luggage?" Mike offered nonchalantly.

"Thanks, be careful with that. It's a laptop.

They walked to the car. Ben waited in the front seat. In the back seat sat a security guard. Dov slid into the back next to him.

Mike leaned in and stuck his head in the front window. "Ben, you all set?"

"Yes. I'll be point. We'll move ahead of Brahim's car."

"Okay, I'll be with Isaac bringing up the rear."

Mike went back into the lobby to wait for Isaac, and his cell phone rang. It was Isaac.

"I'm on the phone with Hong Kong. I'll be down in five minutes."

"Okay, Isaac, take your time."

IN THE MIDDLE car, Abra was busy reading the Koran when Brahim's phone started buzzing.

"Hello, Nasim, how's the family? Okay, I'll inform Isaac. Jim will be in the office in the morning. If you need anything, touch base with Susan. Fine, I will tell your mother."

Brahim hung up his phone. Abra was praying, so he said nothing.

IN THE LOBBY Mike was pacing back and forth when Isaac walked off the elevator with a security guard.

"Sorry I held you up."

"No problem."

"Is everyone in the cars?"

"Yes, we're ready to go."

Mike and the security guard walked in front as Isaac exited. Brahim motioned for him to come over to his car.

"My son Nasim called me a few minutes ago. He said there's talk about a possible Iranian missile strike against Israel. Sounds like they're headed for war. If that happens, oil prices will go through the roof."

"I'll be on the phone to Israel in a few minutes," Isaac said. "I can check if the information is true."

"I told Nasim to be in touch with Jim in the morning and to stay in contact with Susan."

"Fine." Isaac walked away.

Mike was waiting by the open door of the car behind Brahim's. Isaac sat down in the middle seat, and Mike jumped in next to him. "Let's get going."

CHAPTER
25

THE SUVS PULLED away slowly from the driveway. The motor-cycle escorts pulled out in front as the caravan crossed Oxford Street and Marble Arch, lots of flashing lights but no sirens. They didn't need them; there were no traffic jams. They drove through Hyde Park on to the M25, which took them to Heathrow Airport.

Isaac tried to reach his contact, General Yaacov Solomon. General Solomon was head of an intelligence branch that ran clandestine operations even the director of the Mossad didn't know about. He was a valuable contact and a good friend.

After leaving a message for the general, Isaac turned to Mike. "I think we're heading for a full-scale war in the Middle East."

"What's going on in Hong Kong?"

"So far we're on schedule. Allan said everything's in place. He's standing by waiting for further instructions."

Mike turned on his two-way Motorola and started talking to Ben when his cell phone buzzed. "Ben, hold on. I need to answer my cell."

"Hello, when did this happen? Who are they blaming? Right, of course. Israel." Mike closed his phone. "Ben, you still on?"

"Yes."

"The Amir al-Momenin Mosque in Zahedan, Iran, has been blown up."

"Any idea who's at fault?"

"No, but this was the second time, and the Iranian news agency is demanding revenge against the Zionist regime in Israel."

"What do you think? Anything we should change in Paris, Mike?"

"No, let's keep to the same program."

"Okay, I think we should be at the airport in thirty minutes."

"What about security by the planes?"

"All set. Both pilots have been briefed on the procedures in case of any incidents. We received special clearance. We'll drive through the VIP gate right up to the planes."

"Make sure nobody gets out of the cars until we're all in position."

"Okay, I'll call you when we're on the runway."

Mike looked at Isaac. "Did you hear all that?"

Isaac nodded. "This is just the excuse they're looking for to start a war. More likely the Sunni minority was responsible. Their presidential elections are close. This is the sort of thing that helps people forget how bad their economic situation is."

SITTING IN THE other vehicle, Brahim looked at Abra. *How can I get her to sit down and talk with Isaac?*

"Brahim," said Fatima, "why all this security? I've traveled around the world with you two enough to know something is going on. We've never had this kind of security before."

Abra was listening. She closed her book. "Isaac has caused all of this, hasn't he?"

Brahim's face fell. He felt as if someone had stuck a knife deep into his heart. He looked at Fatima, glanced at the security guards, and with a steely look in his eyes leaned over and whispered, "Don't ever say anything like that about Isaac again."

"Brahim, please, calm down." Fatima handed him some bottled water. "Here, take a drink."

Abra showed no emotion. She picked up her Koran and started to read out loud. "'*And fulfill the Covenant of Allah when you have covenanted*' (al-Nahl 16:91)."

"Please, Abra, not now," Fatima begged.

Abra stared at her in silence, then closed the book and turned her face toward the window. The quiet was like a tranquilizer, the sound in the car was that of the tires hitting the cracks in the road. Fatima looked from Brahim to Abra, at a loss.

Brahim, looking for a distraction, opened his PDA and started dialing. Instantly an image appeared.

"Sammi, did you make the flight?"

The night before Brahim had contacted Sammi and told him to hop on the next flight to Paris.

"Yes, I'm on the same flight as Mrs. Green. We're landing in about an hour."

"Good."

"Boss, everything alright? You look tense."

"I'm fine. See you soon."

Brahim turned off his PDA and closed his eyes. He hadn't spoken to Abra like that since he was a hotheaded young man.

IN THE FIRST car, Ben checked with HQ on the latest situation in Iran. The traffic started to build as they approached the exit ramp to the airport.

Dov, sitting behind him, had been busy talking to his staff, making sure the press and television were going to give the symposium the coverage it needed. Working the phones nonstop, Dov booked Brahim and Isaac to appear on *Good Morning America* and *Fox News* to promote their philosophy of unity between Jews, Muslims, and Christians.

Traffic had come to a crawl. Mike was now on the two-way with Ben. "Can you figure out what's happening?" asked Mike.

"Two cars collided, and everybody's squeezing into the left-hand lane."

"It's getting late. Notify the escorts to start the sirens and get us moving."

Ben started calling. One motorcycle policeman stopped and dismounted his bike and started diverting the traffic. The others turned on their sirens. As soon as they started to move, Mike was back on the phone with the pilot. "We can leave for Saudi Arabia from Paris at one p.m.," the pilot announced.

"I'll ask Brahim if it's alright." He hung up the phone and called Brahim.

"ABRA, MIKE GOT word that you can leave Paris by one p.m. today. We're scheduled to arrive in Paris at eleven a.m. Unless you prefer to leave tomorrow as originally planned."

Fatima looked at Abra. Abra shook her head. "There's nothing for me in Paris. I would prefer to go on to Saudi Arabia as soon as possible."

"Fine, if that's what you want."

Brahim informed Mike of their plans and hung up just as Ben's car reached the VIP gate. Two minutes later, Brahim's car pulled up behind, followed by Isaac and Mike.

All the cars were now in position to enter the airport. Both planes stood at attention, side by side, their stairs lowered to receive passengers. The first to leave and board would be Dov. Brahim, Abra, Fatima, and their security guards would follow. Isaac and Mike, along with four security personnel would board the other aircraft.

Mike was on his mobile again. After a minute, he gave the order to proceed.

As one, everyone got out of the cars to board. Brahim allowed the others to go ahead and waited at the bottom of the staircase.

Isaac and Mike walked over to him. "Brahim everything alright?" Isaac asked.

"Mike, please give us a moment. I need to talk to Isaac privately."

"Okay, but we should get going."

"Just a moment, I promise."

Mike nodded and walked off. He didn't go far. He didn't want to leave Isaac unattended.

Brahim looked at Isaac. "Isaac, I'm losing my wife. She's going off the deep end."

"What happened?"

"She's blaming all the world's problems on the Jews, and she's somehow appointed you the representative of world Jewry. Her newest insanity is that you're the reason for all this security. She's not making sense. I thought you might have a chance to talk to her in Paris, but she's continuing on to Saudi Arabia soon after we land. What should I do?"

"Let me go on your plane and I'll talk to her."

"No, I'm afraid something might happen."

"Alright, but when we land in Paris I'll ask Mike to tell her she has to clear passport control before she and Fatima can board the plane again. I'll speak to her then."

"Are you sure?"

"Yes, I'll ask Mike to find us a private room so we can talk. You'll see, everything will be fine. Just stay calm while you're on the flight."

Mike returned. "We really have to go."

"I'm ready, Mike."

Mike walked Brahim up the stairs and watched as the plane's doors closed behind him, then escorted Isaac to their plane.

Snapping on his safety belt, Mike turned to Isaac. "Trouble?"

"I'll tell you about it once we're in the air."

What will I say to Abra when we meet?

"Mike," said Isaac, "I need you to call ahead and get me a private room when we land at the airport."

"Anything else?"

"Tell Abra she has to clear passport control before going on to Saudi Arabia. Take her passport first and then escort her to the room, then come and get me. Make sure she sees you collecting everyone's passport so she doesn't get suspicious. Keep everybody busy, I have to talk to her alone. "

"You got it."

"Thanks, I'm going to see if I can get a little sleep."

Mike headed up to the pilot's cabin and asked the pilot to call the control tower.

CHAPTER
26

Wednesday, June 4, 2014
Charles de Gaulle Airport

AS SOON AS the plane landed, it was directed to a runway far from the main terminal. Mike stared out the window with a look of surprise on his face.

"What's wrong?" Isaac asked.

"I don't know. But I want to find out."

Mike jumped up from his seat and went to the pilot's cabin. The door was partially open. He peeked his head in. "What's happening?"

The pilot looked at him with a worried expression. "Terrorists are in the main terminal holding hostages in the El-Al business lounge."

"Put me in touch with the control tower. Use the emergency frequency."

The pilot handed Mike a headset and pressed a button. The tower answered.

"I'm Special Agent Mike O'Shea with the United States National Security Agency. Patch me into whoever is in charge of security."

A pause and then, "Hello, this is Paul-Henri."

"Paul, this is Mike O'Shea, NSA. What's going on? I'm on a high-priority security assignment with two planes now sitting on a runway away from the main terminal."

"Mike, we had to close down the whole airport. We are diverting all air traffic to other airports in Europe or back to England. You're lucky you got in."

"I need more details. What's the situation?"

"We still aren't totally sure. What we do know is that at this moment, the terrorists are holding about twenty passengers inside the lounge. We heard a few shots early on, but it's been quiet since then. We aren't sure if anyone has been hurt."

"What's your plan?"

"We've secured every possible way out of the lounge, and we've almost finished emptying the terminal. The evacuation should be completed in the next few minutes. We've diverted all moving vehicles away from the airport, and all planes on the ground have shut down their engines."

"What's the next step?"

"Our French counterterrorist unit is already here with fifteen men. They just finished setting up a communication center."

"Okay, Paul, I need to talk to our people. Please keep your line open and keep me posted as updates come in."

"Fine, I'm leaving this line open."

Mike took off the headset and returned to the passenger compartment. He sat down next to Isaac. "We have a major problem. Terrorists have taken over the El-Al lounge, and the airport has been shut down. They have hostages. The French are about to try and negotiate a deal. We have to make some decisions now."

"Chava was supposed to be landing this morning on an Air France flight from New York. Can you check the status of flight AF2035? Tell me it's still in the air."

Mike went back to the cockpit to contact Paul.

Isaac looked out the window. He had a bad feeling. Impatient, he stood up and joined Mike in the cockpit. Paul-Henri was talking on the secure comm.

"Mike, that plane arrived ahead of schedule and unloaded its passengers. We believe some are in the lounge waiting for a transfer flight to Israel."

Mike related the information to Isaac. He grabbed Mike's arm. "Mike, my wife is in that lounge, I can feel it. If her plane arrived early, she'd wait for me in the El-Al lounge. Mike, get me off this plane."

Mike nodded. He talked into the headset. "Paul-Henri, look for the name Chava Green on the list of hostages. Find out if she's in the lounge."

"We're compiling a list of missing people right now. We should have it in fifteen minutes."

"Let me know when you do. In the meantime, can you get two of your security vans to pull up to our planes so we can get off? We need to get to your command center."

"Hold on a minute, Mike, the Minister of Defense wants to talk to you."

Another voice was heard on the comm. "Hello, Mike, this is Jacques. Sorry you have to fly into this mess. I was looking forward to seeing you guys later at the hotel. Tell us whatever you need. I'll get it done."

"Thanks. You already have a memo on who's on our two aircraft."

"Yes."

"I need one of our planes cleared to fly out as soon as you can refuel it so it can proceed to Saudi Arabia. We also have some security personnel on that plane with the passengers, Brahim, Abra, Fatima, and Dov. You already have copies of their passports. I'll inform you shortly who's continuing on and who's staying in Paris."

"As soon as we're finished talking, I'll have it done."

"From my plane, we'll all be disembarking." Mike's cell phone buzzed. It was Ben. "Jacques, hold on. This could be important." He picked up the call.

"Ben, what is it?"

"Brahim would like to talk to you."

"Put him on."

"Mike, what's happening?"

"Brahim, listen, we have a group of terrorists holding hostages in the El-Al business lounge."

"I heard about it on the radio. How's Isaac?"

"I'll put him on in a minute, but we have to make some decisions now. If your wife and sister-in-law still plan to fly on to Saudi Arabia, I can have your plane refueled and flying out to Saudi Arabia right away. Dov and some of the security guards will leave the plane. You decide what you're going to do. I have no idea how long it's going to take to resolve this situation."

"I'll stay with Isaac and Dov and send my wife on to Saudi Arabia. Give me a few moments to tell her what's going on and then have them pick me up and take me to Isaac."

"Okay, Brahim. Five minutes and we'll be at your door." Mike clicked off and talked into the comm.

"Jacques, are you still on?"

"I'm here."

"It's all set. Brahim and Dov are disembarking with security personnel. Abra and her sister are leaving as soon as you can fuel up and clear them for takeoff."

"Okay, Mike. I was just handed the list of hostages. We have no idea if it's complete."

Isaac stood nearby listening to Mike's side of the conversation.

"Is Chava Green on the list?" Mike asked. He waited for the answer.

Mike's face turned white. Isaac had his answer. "God almighty, she's in the lounge."

"Isaac, I promise you we'll get her out safely," Mike said as convincingly as he could.

Isaac sat down as a Vietnam flashback took him over. Visions of rescuing Jim, the heat, the bullets flying, it was all too much. He shook himself out of it. *This is Paris, and it's Chava's life that's on the line.*

"Does he know if any of the hostages have been hurt?"

Mike related Isaac's question to Jacques.

"No, we're trying to evaluate the next step. I just texted you with the confirmed names of the hostages we know are in the lounge."

Mike checked his PDA. "I got it. Wait a minute. Sammi Boaz? You sure?"

"Yes, he was in the seat next to Mrs. Green. Why?"

"He works for World. He's Brahim's private driver."

Mike looked at Isaac. "Sammi is with your wife."

"What?"

"Yes, it's confirmed."

Isaac glanced at his watch. It was 6 a.m. in New York. He opened his PDA and pressed a few buttons. Susan appeared on the screen.

Before he could say anything, she said, "I just heard. I'm really sorry, Isaac. It's gonna be okay."

"Thanks, Susan."

"I booked Sammi on that flight. Is he with Chava?"

"We believe so. Call Sammi's wife and tell her we're on top of the situation. And contact my children and tell them their mother's okay. I'll call them when we have more news." He clicked off and turned back to Mike.

"Mike, where are we holding?"

"The vans are all here. We should go."

A security guard handed them body armor. "Please put these on."

Isaac looked at Mike for confirmation.

"It's only a precaution until we're in the terminal."

Mike's phone buzzed.

"Mike, it's Ben."

"Go ahead."

"Dov is in one of the vans with a security guard. They're waiting for Brahim. He's still talking to Abra."

"Give him three more minutes and then go get him."

"Okay."

BRAHIM SAT FACING Abra and Fatima. "Terrorists have taken twenty hostages in the El-Al lounge. Chava and Sammi are among them. They were coming to meet us in Paris."

Abra put her hands together. "May Allah protect Sammi."

Fatima looked at her in horror. She tried to cover for her sister. "She didn't mean that, Brahim."

Abra looked straight into Brahim's eyes. Her expression was unapologetic. She said nothing.

Brahim sighed. He said, "The plane will be loading with fuel and you should be airborne shortly." He got up from his seat and walked to the exit without saying another word.

"Is something wrong?" Ben asked while handing him the body armor.

"Not at all." *I just found out who my wife really is.* Brahim's lips were drawn tight and his face was ashen as he put on the vest. "Let's get going. I want to see Isaac."

FATIMA STARED AT Abra. "How could you be so insensitive?" she said. "You're driving your husband away from you. He's going to leave you if you don't change something fast. I can feel it."

Abra shrugged. "I have Allah. Who needs a husband?" She opened the Koran that had been sitting in her lap and began to read, ending the discussion.

The plane door closed. *What does she think lies ahead for her in Saudi Arabia?* Fatima wondered.

THE VANS PARKED at Gate 40 opposite the El-Al lounge. Mike was the first one into the terminal, followed by Isaac and then the security team. Twenty meters away from the lounge, a command center was being set up. Isaac noticed that the terminal was too empty.

"What's happening?"

"The terrorists have given their first demand. They want the area cleared or they're gonna start killing people."

Jacques and Ben walked in with Brahim and Dov. Brahim squeezed Isaac's arm. "We'll get them out of there."

CHAPTER
27

Wednesday, June 4, 2014
Holland Tunnel, New York

THE NEW JERSEY Turnpike was always clogged with early morning commuters. Bumper-to-bumper traffic made the commute almost impossible. Jim sat in the back of his limousine, on his way from Dover Air Force Base to Manhattan. It was midweek, but the traffic made it feel like a holiday weekend.

His PDA buzzed.

"Jim, how are you?" It was Susan.

"I'm concerned I'm not going to make it to the office before the markets open. This traffic is horrendous."

"Where're you exactly?"

"We're approaching the Holland Tunnel, and the traffic is still bumper to bumper. Do you have any updates on the hostage situation in Paris?"

"Nothing yet. The terrorists haven't made any new demands. They're just waiting."

"Isaac must be going crazy. The hostages have been in there almost three hours. As soon as you hear anything, Susan, call me."

"I will. Listen, Jim, two agents from the FBI are here waiting to talk to you."

"About what?"

"Your brothers. It seems serious."

"Tell them I'll be there as soon as I can."

"Hold on, Frank's here too. He wants to talk to you."

"Put him on."

After a pause, he heard Frank's voice. "Jim, they arrested John and William."

"Where are they holding them?"

"In Chicago, Metropolitan Correction Center. It's a facility for Federal prisoners."

"Why there?"

"When the charges are related to national security issues, the accused appear before the federal courts. The FBI decided on the judicial district of northern Illinois."

Jim felt anger rising up. "I told you to take care of them, Frank."

"I tried. They won't listen to anyone."

"I'm out of the tunnel. I'll be there soon. Put Susan back on."

Frank handed the phone off to Susan. "Yes, Jim, what can I do?"

"Get me Guy Warren." Guy was the best criminal attorney in the country who also happened to be an old friend of Jim's. He worked out of Manhattan, on Park Avenue, not far from World headquarters.

"I'm on it. I'll get back to you as soon as I reach him."

Jim hung up his cell phone and gazed out of the car's window. *What's this gonna do to our mother? It's not enough that she lost my father too soon. It's only been two years and the wound is still fresh. Thank God, he wasn't alive to witness this. It would have killed him.*

Jim could see Battery Park, so he knew World headquarters was only a few minutes away.

The driver pulled into the underground garage. When Jim

stepped out of the elevator on the forty-eighth floor, Frank was wait-ing for him.

Jim stepped out of the elevator to greet his brother. "Frank, tell me everything."

"The FBI has had John and William under surveillance for the last year. On top of their involvement with neo-Nazis, it turns out they're part of cell of militant extremists from the far right. The group's agenda is to overthrow the government by any means neces-sary. Even if it means killing the president."

"What do the agents in the office want from me?"

"I have no idea."

"Okay, let's go talk to them."

SUSAN WAS WAITING outside Jim's office. "How are you, Jim?"

"I'm okay. Where are the agents?"

"I have them in the conference room on the forty-ninth floor."

"You and Frank, come with me."

In front of them was a small circular glass elevator that allowed access to the top four floors. As soon as the elevator doors closed, Susan began to speak. "I've been trying to reach Guy. I've called and left messages for him all over."

She paused to give a voice command. "Take us to the forty-ninth floor."

The elevator started moving. When its doors opened on the for-ty-ninth floor, Jim saw the agents through the glass-enclosed confer-ence room.

He entered the room first, followed by Frank and Susan. "Good morning. I'm Jim Murphy. What can I do to help you?"

"Nice to meet you. I'm Agent Dan Berk from the FBI." He shook Jim's hand. "This is Agent Ray Hardy."

"Susan, any of the staff around?"

"Sure, what do you need?"

"Do you guys want some coffee or cold drinks, perhaps something to eat?"

"Some coffee please," Dan answered.

"Ray?"

"Just some water for me, thank you."

"I'm fine," said Frank.

"Susan, I'll have a ham and Swiss cheese on a bagel and a milkshake." Susan typed the order into a computer on the desk, adding two black coffees.

"Mr. Murphy, we'll get straight to the point," said Agent Berk. "You are aware that both of your brothers have been arrested?"

"Unfortunately I am."

"The director of the FBI is personally handling this investigation, and due to the sensitivity of the allegations against you brothers, your company's security clearance is being questioned. He's asking you to refrain from direct contact with your brothers at this time."

Jim's face turned red. Before he could respond, there was a knock on the door. Susan jumped up from her chair and opened it. Their food had arrived.

"Please put everything over on the credenza," Susan said. "Thank you, that will be all."

Susan turned and saw the look on Jim's face. She'd seen this look before.

"Excuse me, gentlemen, I just received an urgent text message. I must speak to Jim privately for a minute."

She walked out the door and Jim followed, closing the door behind him. "What's going on?" Jim asked.

"I just had to get you out of the room before you blew your top. Listen to me. You have to be smart. If you get angry, it will make everything worse for your brothers."

"I can't just sit and do nothing. They're my brothers."

"You're right, but we're not without resources. Don't do anything until you've first talked to Guy. We have connections in every area of the government. Let's see if we can find out what they really have on them. "

"What then?"

"We'll get them out on bail, and then you can meet with them."

"Alright, let's go back in."

"Sorry for the holdup. The trading is already heavy and I really have to go. Do you need anything else?"

"Not at this time," Agent Berk said. "We'll file our report about this meeting with the director. Thank you for your cooperation, we'll be in touch."

Jim extended his hand to shake. Susan walked them to the elevator.

"What should we do, Jim?" Frank asked.

"Until we hear from our attorney, absolutely nothing."

Susan walked in. "Jim, the Stock Exchange is opening in a few minutes. You should probably get to it. Frank, you go see your mother before she hears about it on the radio or sees it on TV. I'll interface with everyone and give you a briefing as soon as developments warrant it. Jim, is that okay with you?"

"Do it."

"What should I tell Mom?" Frank asked.

"Just tell her the truth, that I'll take care of it and she shouldn't worry. If I know Mom, she'll go straight to the church to ask the priest to pray for our family."

"Okay, I'm on my way."

Susan's phone rang. It was Guy. Finally. Susan pressed the speaker button to allow everyone to hear the conversation.

"Hello, Guy, this is Susan. I'm in the room with Jim and Frank. How are you?"

"Great."

"Where are you?"

"I'm in Hong Kong."

"What you are doing there?" Jim asked.

"I adopted another Chinese baby, a girl. I had to take care of the paperwork. I just flew in from Beijing, and I'm on my way back home."

"That's great, Guy," said Jim. "Listen, I have a serious problem. John and William have been arrested. They're in a federal prison in Chicago."

"What's the charge?"

"Conspiring to overthrow the government and kill the president."

Guy whistled. "That is serious."

"I really need your help."

"You got it. Susan, I'll try to get a plane out as soon as possible. In the meantime, I'll contact my office to get in touch with the authorities and see if we can get to visit them. Then I'll give you an update."

"Wait a minute," said Jim. "I just had an idea. We have a couple of our private planes landing in the Hong Kong airport today. You can fly back on one of them."

"Great, that's perfect. Nobody does anything until you receive word from me, understood?"

"Yes. I'm texting Isaac and Brahim right now to be in contact with you via their PDA," Susan told him. "It's coded and they'll respond immediately." She didn't tell Guy that Brahim and Isaac were in Paris dealing with a hostage situation involving people they cared about. He'd refuse their offer of a ride, and they needed Guy back in New York.

"Fine, I got to go and take care of some personal things for my wife. I'll be in touch." He hung up.

Susan looked at Jim and Frank. "It will be fine."

Frank nodded, but his face was grim. He looked at Jim. "I'd better get going. I'll call you from Mom's house."

Jim's mobile buzzed. He glanced at the screen. "I'm needed on the trading floor." He turned to Frank, his face red like the hot summer sun. "If anything happens to our mother because of the situation they've gotten themselves into, they can rot in jail for the rest of their lives." He took a deep breath. "I have to go, Frank. Get to Mom's."

Jim turned and left the room. Frank looked at Susan and said, "Susan, you are the only one who can control my brother. Watch him, he's about to explode." Then he left too.

As Susan headed for her office on the forty-eighth floor, she reviewed the next steps she needed to take. Jim was her primary concern, but thoughts of Guy begged her to pay them attention. For a moment she let herself.

She'd first met him at a legal seminar and liked him right away. He was tall and good-looking. When he wasn't talking about legal issues, he was a joker. He loved to joke about being a double minority. "With a Jewish father and a Puerto Rican mother, I'm eligible for twice the government aid." Over the years, Guy had become a close friend. At some point, Susan thought he might ask her out on a date, but then suddenly he was announcing his engagement and now he was married with two kids.

Susan entered her office and her mind traveled back to the present. She had too much to coordinate to think of anything else right now. She sat down and took a sip of her coffee, forgetting that she had made it an hour ago. It was ice cold. She put the cup down. Time to get to work.

Susan tapped out a memo to all company personnel.

> Any inquiries about John or William Murphy are to be referred to me. No information about Jim, his relatives, or the company business is to be discussed privately. Your cooperation in this matter is mandatory. Susan Kais.

She pressed the Send button. She leaned back in the swivel chair and closed her eyes. Just last week she was in Canada planning a week off and dreaming about her upcoming trip to Hawaii. She knew full well her vacation plans would now be put on hold with the situation at hand. She couldn't leave New York at a time like this, and even if her bosses insisted she wouldn't want to.

Her PDA started to beep and she opened her eyes.

"Hello, Susan, it's Isaac. You alright?"

"Yes, I'm fine. How are you?"

"I'm holding up. We're waiting for word from the hostages. I was just on the phone with Jim. He told me about his brothers and the FBI visit. What do you think?"

"He told you about our call with Guy?"

"Yes."

"My advice, Isaac? We do nothing till Guy gets back. You're aware he's in Hong Kong?"

"Jim told me. I've already been in touch with Charlie. Even with what's happening here, we still have to be ready for the planes landing in Hong Kong. We're monitoring both Charlie's and Brahim's planes. The pilots decided to land at 11 p.m. Allan arranged for his people to pick up Guy and drop him off at HKI. He'll be there when the plane comes in to pick up the remains."

"Sounds like everything's covered," Susan said. "Let me know if there's anything you need from me."

"I will. I'll speak to you later."

CHAPTER
28

Wednesday, June 2014
Phoenicia Intercontinental Hotel, Beirut

IN THE LOBBY of the Phoenicia Intercontinental the same movie played itself over and over. Men and women sitting around tables in lounge chairs, drinking and smoking, dreamers and schemers all, everyone out to convince someone of something. Most of their business cards were for fictitious positions, like Monopoly money that was of no use in the real world of commerce. The dream of Beirut, once known as the Switzerland of the Middle East, had turned into a recurring nightmare.

The Lebanese were known for killing each other, only pausing long enough to pursue their continuing wars with Israel. All of the participants understood the game. They knew there was no real hope of peace as long as Hezbollah existed, but if they could make money off it, why not?

In a corner, out of sight, two men sat talking in a whisper.

"Terry, would you like a drink?" Pierre asked.

"Order me a Coke."

A few minutes later the waiter returned with their drinks. Pierre signed the bill. Terry had already started drinking his Coke.

Terry had recently received a call from his handler in Israel introducing him to Pierre. At first he was taken aback at his discovery that he would have to work with a Lebanese. After he read up on Pierre's background, his mind was put at ease.

Pierre Jamal was an explosives expert living in Beirut since the summer of 2006. He was thirty years old, a Christian Lebanese educated in Paris at the Sorbonne. He'd worked for the Mossad for three years. In the last twenty years, the Hezbollah had killed many members of his family, and now was the time for retribution.

Terry Shaun was an Israeli intelligence officer. Originally from Dublin, he had gone to Israel as an exchange student and decided to stay. He made aliyah and joined the IDF. Eventually he was recruited by the Mossad. He worked for the Associated Press as a cover and flew in and out of Beirut Airport every week. Now he and Pierre would be working together.

Terry put down his drink. "We have a lot to discuss, so let's get to it."

CHAPTER
29

Wednesday, June 4, 2014
Tehran, Iran

NINE HUNDRED AND thirty-eight air miles away, the Iranian government hosted the seventeenth summit of the Non-Aligned Movement. The agenda consisted of the UN's sanctions on Iran's nuclear program, human rights, and peace in the Middle East.

After the overthrow of half of the regimes in the Middle East in recent years, the Iranians were well on their way to dominating the Muslim world. Of their top concerns was protecting the wealthy Chinese and Russian delegations who had been invited to observe.

The Russians had come to show their support for Iran and keep their promise to help rebuild nuclear reactors previously damaged by Israel. China had also come to show its support for Iran, but they had another motive. China and Iran were about to finalize the largest oil deal in the history of the country. China needed Iranian oil to ensure the growth of their economy.

After the summit, Iran planned to hold a large signing ceremony with all the mullahs attending, followed by a state dinner. China would be in attendance.

CHAPTER
30

Wednesday, June 4, 2014
State Department, Washington, D.C.

AT THE STATE Department in D.C., a top-level meeting was taking place between Secretary of State Marge McCormick and two of her aides, Henry Gold, expert on Iran, and Joe Luck, the State Department liaison from the NSA.

Marge opened the conversation. "With Iran breaking the UN sanctions imposed on them, and China breaking the embargo on Iranian oil, our allies want to know how we'll be responding."

"What *will* our response be?" Henry asked curiously.

"The United States called its ambassador back from Beijing. That's all the president has authorized."

"Israel will blow a gut if all we do is call back the ambassador," said Joe. "That's never going to satisfy the Israelis. They have a nervous government over there. I spoke to some of our intel people in Tel Aviv. Something's in the works between Iran and China, and it's not the oil agreements."

Henry nodded in agreement.

"We've received intel from Iran that Wing Dang was at the

summit. He's the head of counterintelligence for China."

"He's the final word on planning operations and on gathering sensitive information on financial transactions in the world," Joe added.

Henry's voice was grim. "We think he's the one who authorized Lo Chi Xi to sell the chip to the Iranians."

CHAPTER
31

Wednesday, June 4, 2014
Charles de Gaulle Airport

INSIDE THE COMMAND center, a table sat in the middle of the room covered with the floor plan of the El-Al lounge. Officers from the French counterterrorism unit (GIGN) stood around it analyzing every angle, every strategy, searching for the one that might make the difference. They'd been at it for over four hours. The terrorists hadn't made any new demands. Mike and his people were using the time to find a way to rescue the hostages without getting anyone killed.

Used coffee cups littered the floor, and the wastebasket over-flowed with an assortment of half-eaten sandwiches. The informa-tion board for flight schedules flashed in red: "All flights have all been canceled." Terminal 4 felt like a morgue, and Isaac knew if they didn't come up with a plan soon, the feeling would become a real-ity. Next door, in the VIP lounge, Isaac and Mike had set up their own command center. Isaac had requested a construction plan of the lounge and was examining it. Mike had arranged to bring in com-puters and monitors so they could set up a communications system.

Isaac's PDA rang. It was Susan. "Susan? I'm putting you on speaker. Brahim and Dov are here with me."

"Isaac, Jim's been calling me every fifteen minutes for updates. He wanted me to tell you that the market strategy is working. He'll call with an update after the market closes in New York."

"Tell Jim I'm on top of things here. I hope to have good news soon."

"I'll let him know."

"Did you speak to my family?" Isaac asked.

"Yes, they're all worried, but they're holding up okay. Jim and I talked. We've decided to cancel the symposium. I hope you approve."

Isaac looked at Dov and Brahim. They both nodded. "Okay. Dov and Brahim agree with you too. The symposium is important, but we can't risk any more lives."

"Okay, Isaac, I'm on it." She clicked off.

A security agent walked toward them. "We have a message from the terrorists."

"What is it?" Isaac asked.

"An ultimatum: we have twelve hours to free Abu al-Mousavi in London and fly him to this airport."

"The terrorist who bombed the London Eye? You have to be kidding me."

"That's not all. They want a private jet fully loaded with fuel standing by and twenty million euros, one million for the life of each hostage. The money is to be delivered to the lounge by the time the banks close today. If we don't comply, they're threatening to blow up the entire area."

"It's already three thirty. That doesn't give us much time." Isaac looked at Brahim. "Call Jim and have him contact Bilas Baudins, the managing director of Société Générale in Paris. He's to take the money out of our special account. Give him the code EMGC. Have their airport security division bring it to Gate 40. If he encounters any difficulty, tell him to call me." Isaac motioned to Mike. "Mike can you call HQ in London and get me the prime minister? We'll need his help to arrange al-Mousavi's release."

"I'm on it."

"Thanks, the clock is ticking."

Brahim had hung up with Jim. He stood looking out the window at the airfield. Isaac walked up to him and put his hand on his shoulder. "Abra will be alright."

"She's gone. It's all over."

"Then we'll get her back. You know we've dealt with bigger things than this."

Brahim nodded. "You're right. Let's worry about Chava and Sammi right now. We'll worry about Abra tomorrow."

Mike rushed toward them. "We'll have the communications up and running within twenty minutes. The secure hotlines are ready whenever you need them."

"Where can we set up for TV and media announcements?" Dov looked around the room.

"Let's do it at the restaurant just down the hall."

"Sounds good. I'll contact my people to have a mobile satellite hookup. "

Isaac nodded. "Good. Now, Mike, let's get Susan on the line."

CHAPTER
32

MIKE LED ISAAC and Brahim to a table set up with a large screen. He grabbed a chair and sat down in front of it. Other screens had been installed around the room, broadcasting the news from different channels.

"Isaac, Brahim, all you have to do is talk to the screen and request who you want to speak to. The machine will be able to patch into the other person's PDA. Your voices are preregistered. It's connected to NSA headquarters."

Isaac spoke to the screen. "Call Susan Kais."

The machine responded, "One moment please. I'm processing your call."

Moments later Susan appeared on the screen. "What can I do for you?"

"Canceling the symposium under control?"

"Almost done. I'll be finished in less than half an hour."

"You were able to contact everyone on your list?"

"Our office has reached everyone but Prince Abdul al-Issa from Saudi Arabia. We're calling everyone we know to locate him. His office last heard from him yesterday. They said he could be anywhere."

"Keep working on it. Have you heard from Charlie?"

"They're all aware of the situation, and I'm sure they're very anxious and worried about Chava and Sammi. Charlie said he's praying for everyone."

"Thanks. I'll check on Charlie myself and then call you back."

Brahim had been pacing back and forth.

"Wait a minute. Isaac, I have a private number for Prince Abdul." He pulled out his wallet took out a small piece of paper and read out the number for Susan. "When you finish dialing a message will come on, just say my name, and then hang up."

"Okay." She hung up.

"What's next?" Mike asked Isaac.

"Can this screen system do multiple pictures and voices at one time?"

"Absolutely. What do you want to do?"

"In a half hour our planes will be approaching the coast of Hong Kong. Get my pilot, William, and Brahim's pilot, Thomas, on the line with me and Susan. I want to be on the system with them as they're landing."

"I'll take care of it."

"Isaac," Dov interrupted, "the media are waiting for information. I promised them we'd hold a press conference in two hours."

At that moment, Brahim's phone buzzed. It was Jim in New York.

"Brahim, put Isaac on the speaker so he can hear me."

Brahim called Isaac over and pressed the speaker button. Jim's voice was heard on the line.

"Isaac, we closed out eighty percent of our positions, and in the overnight trading we'll close out the rest. We've already taken positions in gold futures. It's been a great day in the market." He paused. "I wanted to give you some good news."

"Thank you. You did."

"Susan is keeping me up-to-date. I reached the bank in Paris, and everything is being arranged to get you the ransom money. Brahim has all the follow-up information. I had a chance to speak with Guy. I want to go to Chicago tonight and see if I can get in to visit my brothers. Guy can meet us there. What do you think?"

"Good idea. But don't see your brothers until Guy gets there."

"Is there anything else I can help you with?" Jim asked.

"Just pray."

"I am. Mary has gone to church to light a candle for Chava. That's all we can do right now. I'll be in touch with you later. Good luck." Mike was busy punching in the codes to contact the planes. He looked up at Isaac. "We should be live in a minute."

When the picture came on, the clarity of the image was astounding. It was as if they were sitting right there in the cabin with the pilots. Brahim, Dov, and Mike pulled their chairs close. No one spoke. Everyone sat watching.

Isaac looked into the monitor. "Can you all hear me?"

"Yes, I can hear you," William answered in a loud voice.

"Charlie, I see you're the copilot."

"We wanted to keep the crew minimal. How're you holding up?"

"I'm okay."

"Are there any new developments with Chava and the other hostages?"

"We're working on it."

"Hold a minute. William wants to talk to you."

"Mr. Green, we have to start to prepare for the landing. I want to close off the transmission part of this call until we're on the ground. I don't want the tower to get confused. You'll still be able to listen to our conversations. You just won't be able to talk to us."

"Fine, turn it off." Isaac turned his attention to Thomas on the other plane. "Thomas, how are you doing?"

"We're on schedule. I don't expect any delays at this time of night. I heard what William said. I'm gonna follow his lead and close the transmission too."

"Susan, did you hear all that?"

"Yes, it was very clear."

"God bless you all, and good luck."

Mike turned from the screen in front of him. "Amen. Let's do this."

Brahim's mobile began to vibrate. He walked away from where everyone was seated.

CHAPTER
33

AL SALAAM, BRAHIM. This is Prince Abdul. *Kayf haluk?* How are you?"

"*Ana bi-khayr.* I'm fine. Where are you, Your Highness?"

"I'm in Paris in my home. I had some business to attend to, so I arrived early for the symposium."

"We've been trying to reach you. Have you seen the news about the hostage situation at de Gaulle?"

"Yes, of course, terrible."

"Unfortunately we had to cancel the symposium. They are not allowing any flights into Paris. All the airports are closed until this is resolved. We have no idea when and how this is going to end."

"Of course. I understand. Please keep me informed, and if you need my assistance don't hesitate."

"Thank you, Your Highness." Brahim hung up the phone and sat down next to Isaac.

Isaac stared at the monitor, watching William. William was talking to the tower.

"Emergency request clearance to land on an open runway. I can't divert to HKI. I won't make it. My instruments are not working properly. I need to land now."

He cut out contact with the tower and said, "Isaac, I flipped the switch to put the tower radio on silent. The crosswinds are bouncing us around, but the runway is clear. I'm lowering the landing gear."

Isaac got on the phone with Allan as he watched William approach the runway. By now Allan should have been at Kai Tak, waiting with Lee, Kim Li, and Hui Ying.

"Are the packages ready to go, Allan?"

"They're in the FedEx truck, but I'm not with them. I'm on my way to HKI. I'm going with the other plane. It was a last-minute decision. I'll explain later."

Mike looked at Isaac. "Something's wrong."

"We can't do anything about it now. Time is running out."

William landed and turned the communication system back on. He taxied his plane into position for the FedEx truck to pull alongside.

"Pull off the runway, pull off the runway," the tower controller insisted.

William didn't respond. He could see the truck approaching. It pulled alongside the plane and the door opened. As soon as the truck was blocked from the tower's sight, Kim Li and Hui Ying jumped out and ran up the stairs onto the plane. The door to the plane closed and the truck pulled away. Once William saw the truck driving away, he called the tower.

"I apologize. We fixed the malfunction. A small transistor burnt out. It's been replaced and we are ready to go."

"Wait a minute. We have to clear you for takeoff."

Everyone held his breath.

William monitored the tower and the air traffic control. He got nothing but silence. Ten minutes passed. How long was this going to take? After a few more minutes, the controller's voice came over the radio.

"You're cleared. The runway is open for you to take off."

William turned the plane around and started down the runway.

He pulled the throttle back and the plane lifted off. Everyone exhaled. They'd done it.

"Congratulations, William," Isaac said, "you did an outstanding job."

Mike agreed with Isaac. "You did great."

William said to Isaac, "I'm on my way to Taiwan to refuel, as we agreed. I should be there in a few hours."

"William, I spoke to Thomas. He's on his final approach and he has been cleared to land. HKI is telling him to land on the northern Chek Lap Kok runway and follow the airport vehicle to a hangar at the end of the airport."

"Right on schedule. So all's good. I'm signing off for now."

CHAPTER
34

As THOMAS LOWERED his wheels, he saw the landing lights ahead of him on the runway. Thomas spoke in code, prearranged with Mike. "Tell my wife we just landed. The trip was bumpy. We had four heavy bouts of turbulence, but we are on the runway."

Mike translated the message for Isaac. "The plane landed, but there's trouble. The pickup truck was joined by four armed vehicles on both sides of the plane. We don't know if the Chinese will let them leave with the cargo."

"Allan said he's meeting Thomas's plane instead of William's. He'll know what's going on."

Mike nodded and dialed Allan. The phone rang and rang. When it finally picked up, there was a message: *This line has been disconnected.*

Mike started to dial the State Department. At that moment, Isaac's phone buzzed. Isaac answered it. "Please hold the line for the Prime Minister of Great Britain. He'll be with you shortly."

The prime minister's voice came on the line. "Isaac, you're on a speaker. I've asked several of my people to be available for this call. They're sitting around the table. I've been fully briefed on the situation. What can we do for you?"

"Sir, the terrorists are demanding that Abu al-Mousavi be freed and brought to Paris. They also asked for twenty million euros in exchange for the twenty hostages. World has arranged to obtain the money, but we need your help on the al-Mousavi matter. Mr. Prime Minister, the clock is ticking. The life of my wife and the other hostages are on the line. I know your government's policy regarding freeing terrorists." Isaac paused. "Mr. Prime Minister, can I ask you to take me off the speaker? I need to speak to you privately."

There was a pause and then, "Isaac, you're off the speaker. What is it?"

"Anthony, as long as we've been friends, I've never asked for a favor, business or personal. But I don't have another option now. I give you my word: give me Abu al-Mousavi, and I will give him back to you dead or alive."

"I'm putting you on hold."

A few minutes later, the prime minister came back on the line.

"Isaac, I'm putting you back on the speaker. One of my aides, Frederick, is going to handle everything. He's the only one in the office who knows about this, and I told him exactly what needs to be done. Here he is now."

"Isaac, this is Frederick. It will take me about an hour to arrange for al-Mousavi's release. We'll get him to Paris in three to four hours. That's the best I can do."

"Understood. When you're on your way to Heathrow, put him on the phone. We'll connect him to the lounge so they'll know he's on the way. Mr. Prime Minister, I want to thank you. You have my word this is going to work out."

"Isaac, my prayers are with you."

"I'll be in touch from Heathrow," said Frederick.

"HELLO, THIS IS Tony de Marco, State Department."

"This is Mike O'Shea. Have you had any contact with Allan Peters?"

"No, I couldn't reach him. They've already notified the local authorities in Hong Kong and told the embassy staff to put out an alert to all of our agents in the Far East."

"Okay, let me know what happens."

Mike turned his attention back to Thomas. Isaac's eyes were fixed on the monitor. The tower had directed Thomas to follow the armed vehicles to the hangar and shut down his engines.

Isaac turned to Brahim. "Do you have an update on the money?"

"It will be ready within the hour."

The monitor showed Thomas's stairs being lowered. Cameras placed inside the overhead compartment of the passengers' cabin recorded everything. Thomas walked slowly so the camera could relay the pictures to Paris. They could see Wen Tian with police guards standing beside him. They were holding machine guns. The plane was surrounded.

CHAPTER
35

Wednesday, June 4, 2014
Hong Kong International Airport

THOMAS STEPPED OFF the last step. Wen Tian walked up to him. "Welcome to Hong Kong," he said, and extended his hand.

"Thank you. We're pleased to be here."

"We were waiting for you."

"Why?"

"Some of your people say they have two coffins to deliver to you. They are waiting in the warehouse. Let's proceed there now."

Thomas walked with Tian. The security detail followed behind them surrounded by police. The warehouse was dark with just a single floodlight hanging overhead. Two wooden coffins draped with American flags sat in the middle of the room. No one spoke.

Tian opened the door to the office. He escorted Thomas in. Two police officers joined them. Guy Warren was waiting inside, along with someone Thomas didn't know.

The other man stood up and introduced himself. "Joe Whelan from the U.S. Consulate. How was your flight?"

"Great. Is everything in order so we can leave?"

"After you refuel and we load the coffins, you can leave."

"There has to be an inspection of the coffins before they're loaded onto the plane," Wen Tian asserted.

"Mr. Tian, the remains are to be flown home for a military burial in Washington, D.C.," said Joe. "Under orders from the United States State Department, the coffins aren't to be opened. They are diplomatic cargo."

Tian stood up, staring directly into Joe's eyes. "This isn't America. I'm in charge here. The coffins won't be leaving until I examine them."

"You're creating a diplomatic incident without any reason. I'm calling my embassy. They'll clear this up with your government."

Tian raised his voice. "No calls. You will open the coffins."

The police raised their guns and pointed them.

"Why are their guns pointed at us?" asked Guy.

"This is China. We're aware of your actions."

Joe looked confused. "What actions?"

"Spying and other crimes against the state. You have broken our laws."

Guy stepped forward. "Mr. Tian, you have put us in a difficult position. Mr. Whelan can't go against his orders. There has been a grave mistake here."

Wen Tian looked at Guy. "Who are you? I don't know you."

"I'm not from the embassy. I'm a lawyer from the States. I have clearance to fly back home with Thomas."

"What are you doing in Hong Kong?" Wen Tian asked.

"I'm here to finalize an adoption." Guy handed him a document to verify his story.

Wen Tian scanned it. "A criminal lawyer from New York. I'll need to verify this with my office."

"Mr. Tian, you can see from my file that I have already adopted one girl from China."

"That is of no importance to me."

"I have a lot of pull with the press. I'll make sure they hear about the innocent man who tried to adopt one of China's abandoned daughters only to be held at gunpoint for his decision. I'm under the impression that adoption has become an important revenue stream for your country."

Wen Tian handed the document back to Guy. "Enough talk. Sit down over there."

"Mr. Tian, with your permission, I would like a word with Mr. Whelan in private. I'm pretty sure there is a satisfactory way we can settle this."

Tian shook his head. "Sit down. No more talking."

"You don't want to create an international incident."

Tian waved his hand, motioning to his officers to point their weapons at Guy. "I'll open the coffins myself." Tian motioned to the guards. "Bring them outside."

Tian opened the door, and the guards pointed their weapons, directing Guy, Thomas, and Joe to move outside and into the warehouse. Tian slowly approached the coffins.

"Take off your flags."

Nobody moved. Joe looked at Guy. Guy nodded. Joe said to the two security guards who had accompanied Thomas, "Gentlemen, I'll need your help to remove the flags."

They nodded and stepped forward. Both of them had served. They knew what to do.

The guards held one flag waist high, then they folded it in half, from the bottom up to the top, the lower striped section of the flag over the blue field as the military manual instructed.

Tian studied every move, impatiently pacing up and down in front of the coffins. The two men continued folding, while Guy, Thomas, and Joe stood at attention with their right hands held up in a salute. As they folded the outer point of the triangle inward toward the stars, forming another triangle, Tian received a call on his cell phone and turned away with his back to the coffins. The security guards finished folding the flag. They picked up the second flag and repeated the whole folding ritual. They handed both flags to Joe and then stepped back.

Guy felt his phone vibrate. "Mr. Tian, I have to go to the bathroom."

Tian motioned to one of the guards to take Guy. The guard stood outside the door while Guy quickly pulled out his iPhone from his jacket pocket. A message from Susan read urgent. She had forwarded a text from Mike:

Get Tian to open the coffins.

The message had come a little late, thought Guy. Good thing everything was going to plan.

He slipped his iPhone back into his pocket and knocked on the door. The guard opened it and escorted Guy back to the others.

Wen Tian was standing in front of the coffins. "I was just on the phone to Beijing," he told Guy. "My government has approved my actions. All of you are going to be sent to jail while you await trial."

Guy looked at Joe.

"I have diplomatic status," Joe said. "You can't do this."

"Guards, open the coffins."

Tian stood at the foot of the caskets. They opened the top half of the coffins. Then the guards stepped back. Tian walked slowly to the side of the coffins, looked in, and saw two dead bodies. His eyes widened with surprise. He touched the faces of both bodies to confirm their authenticity. On top of the bodies lay a card: *"High Priority United States Military for burial at Arlington Cemetery by order of the President of the United States."*

Tian turned to the guards and motioned to them to close the coffins. His body language said it all. As they sealed the coffins, he stood frozen, as if he were on exhibit in London at Madam Tussauds wax museum and they were the tourists.

When the guards were done, Tian turned away to take a phone call. Joe and Guy walked over with the flags and draped them over the caskets. Thomas noticed a figure passing Tian at the entrance of the hangar. Someone was walking toward them. Joe spotted him too. When they recognized Allan, they ran to meet him.

"Allan, what happened to you?" Joe asked. "Are you alright?"

"A little shaken up, but otherwise I'm okay."

"We've been trying to reach you."

Allan glanced at the police officers and then silently motioned the others over to a corner away from the guards.

"Tian had men watching me. I couldn't risk going to Kai Tak. At the last minute, I changed plans and decided to meet Thomas's plane here. My driver was supposed to meet me at a prearranged pickup spot. The car was there, but my driver wasn't. An unmarked car pulled up and three guys jumped out, grabbed me, and threw me into their car. They said they were from the police and were taking me to HKI. They confiscated my phone so I had no way of contacting anyone about my change of plans. I showed them my consulate ID, but they refused to let me go. Since then I've been sitting in their car, unable to leave. A few minutes ago they pulled up outside this hangar and pushed me out. Then drove away as if nothing ever happened."

Tian walked back toward the guards. He whispered something to them, turned unceremoniously, and walked out of the hangar.

One of the police officers walked over and handed Allan an envelope. "Mr. Tian told us to tell you that you're free to leave with the bodies."

The police turned around to leave. Allan opened the envelope, took out his phone, studied it for a moment, and then pressed a button. Nothing happened. He opened the back and saw that his SIM card was missing. "Allan, you look troubled," Joe said.

"I'm going back to New York with Guy. It's too dangerous for me to be here after what just happened."

"I agree. I'll make the report at the embassy tomorrow."

Joe and Allan shook hands, and Joe left.

The security guards had gone ahead to load the caskets onto the plane. Thomas entered the cockpit to start up the jet's engines. A few minutes later, Guy and Allan entered the plane and sat down.

As the door closed Thomas looked at them. "Buckle up," he said.

Slowly he started to make a U-turn in the hangar with barely enough room to complete it. Heading toward the runway, he received a call from the air traffic controller telling him he had to wait for clearance.

"What's happening?" Guy asked.

"We're waiting to get the go-ahead from the tower to proceed," Lionel, the copilot, answered.

"One plane before us and we should be cleared for takeoff," Thomas added.

Thomas slowly moved the throttle into the takeoff position. Allan saw police cars with flashing lights in the distance heading toward them. "Thomas, I think we've got trouble."

"Tighten your seat beats and put on your body armor. The tower is telling me we can't take off, that we should move immediately to the side ramp."

Through a microphone, they heard Tian's voice. "Close down your engines or we'll shoot. You are to close down your engines now."

The airport police stood in a line on the runway in front of them. The sirens screeched, and the policemen pointed their weapons at the plane. Thomas looked at Lionel, then over his right shoulder at Guy and Allan, and gave the thumbs up.

Thomas put his hand firmly on the throttle as he pushed it forward. The plane moved faster and faster down the runway. The police cars held on as long as they could, but finally had to move out of the way before the plane ran them over. Police kept shooting as he cleared the runway, barely missing the tower and the high-voltage lines that surrounded it.

"Is everyone alright?" Thomas asked on the intercom.

"We're okay," Guy answered.

"Thomas," said Lionel, "look at the fuel gauge." Thomas looked. It was running low.

"Damn it, we never had a chance to refuel. Lionel, do the math. How much flying time do we have?"

"We don't have enough fuel for the return trip and may not have enough to make it to Taiwan. What are we going to do?"

CHAPTER
36

Wednesday, June 4, 2014
Charles de Gaulle Airport

IN PARIS, ALL eyes were fixed on the monitors. Every news channel was covering the events at the airport. Jacques and Paul-Henri walked in. Jacques handed Brahim a note. *"The money is in the Brink's armored truck at Gate 40."*

Brahim handed the note to Isaac. Isaac gave it a quick glance.

"Isaac, a call's coming in," said Mike. "It's Thomas."

"Answer it."

Thomas's image filled the screen in front of them. He briefed Mike and Isaac on the situation.

"Anything we can do from Paris?" Mike asked.

"Yes, as soon as Lionel tells me the amount of fuel left, I'll tell you. Hold on, Lionel just handed me his calculations. It shows we'll be flying on empty as we approach Taoyuan International Airport. We'll have to lighten the load to save fuel."

"How much time do you have?" Isaac asked.

"Not much. I know it's a tough call, but we should release the coffins over the ocean."

"We're not dumping American soldiers out of a plane," Mike said. "Have Danny and Eddie empty everything else out of the plane." Danny and Eddie were the security detail. "Start with the galley. Strip it. Just save the life preservers in case you have to make an emergency landing in the water."

"Yes, sir. Lionel will be at the controls. I'll help them in the back. We have about forty minutes until we're out of fuel."

Isaac's phone rang. It was Jim.

"What's happening over there?" Jim asked.

"The Brink's truck is here with the money. GIGN is in contact with the terrorists, keeping the lines open." GIGN was the counter-terrorism unit of the French Armed Forces. They had sent fifteen men to set up the command center at the airport. "They've been told the money is here at Gate 40. A plane is on its way from London with Frederick and Abu al-Mousavi."

"What about Chava and Sammi?"

"The GIGN informed us that one passenger has a minor wound. They said one of the hostages is a doctor. He's taking care of it."

Brahim signaled to Isaac.

"Jim, I have to go. Brahim needs me."

"I'll call you later."

"*Shalom.*"

Isaac walked over to Brahim. "What's doing?"

"I just got a call from the prince. He says he thinks he can help. He wants to come here and meet with us. I asked Ben to have his people pick him up. I should go with them."

"Good idea."

"I'll call you when we're on the way back. It shouldn't take more than ninety minutes."

"Okay. Take care."

"Excuse me, Mr. Green?"

Isaac turned.

"I'm Zvi Polack, head of El-Al security at the airport."

Mike walked up to them. "Hello, Zvi. Good to have you with us." He looked at Isaac. "Isaac, this man has been responsible for stopping several terrorist attempts to plant bombs on El-Al flights leaving Paris."

Isaac put out his hand to shake Zvi's hand. "How did this happen? You guys have the best security system in the world."

"All we know is that two of the terrorists, Ahmed Habibi and Salim Bahar, are Israeli Arabs from Acre."

"Israel?" Mike raised his voice in shock.

"They were screened and passed personal security at JFK. The Shin Bet in Israel is interrogating everyone connected to them. At the present time we have no additional information, but I'll keep you all posted."

Isaac walked over to the table to examine the blueprint of the lounge. At the bottom it read SWITCHGEAR. Isaac, with his background in engineering, knew that switchgear was designed to protect the high voltage for the whole city, including the airport. He motioned to Paul-Henri. "Get me the chief electrical engineer for the airport. I need to know more about how the system works."

Paul-Henri made a call. A few minutes later, Isaac was speaking to a man named Jean.

"Mr. Green, the power transmission networks are protected and controlled by high-voltage breakers, which are usually solenoid with current-sensing protective relays. They're operated through current transformers. In substations, the protection relay can be complex."

"Hold it. Can you close down this terminal without affecting everything else?"

"Everything except the El-Al lounge."

"Why?"

"The Israeli engineers wanted their own design in the lounge. A fifteen-kilovolt medium-voltage vacuum circuit breaker. They installed it themselves."

"Where's it located?"

"It's in the kitchen next to the storage room."

"Thanks, Jean, you've been a great help."

"Do you need me to stay?"

"No." Isaac turned to Mike. "Have the police take him home."

"Sure. Jean, follow me."

A few minutes later Mike was back. Isaac was still examining the blueprints.

"I've studied all of the blueprints," Isaac said. "The Israelis secured the lounge like it was the Dimona Nuclear Research Center. Can you believe they even put steel plates on the roof and covered it with cement, so no one could drill a hole through the roof and drop something into the lounge?"

"What, like a grenade?"

"The emergency exit door is made out of steel, like you'd use on a bank vault. It's dead-bolted from the inside. The door can only be opened with a coded electronic pad that reads hand prints by someone with the right clearance. With all that security, the terrorists were still able to practically walk right through the front door. "

Isaac shook his head back and forth, eyes closed. Suddenly he opened his eyes. "What time is it?"

At that moment his phone rang.

Hello, Isaac, it's Frederick."

"I hear you. Go ahead."

"I have Abu al-Mousavi in the security van. We'll be in the airport in fifteen minutes. The plane is at Heathrow ready to go. We have spoken to Paris, and they cleared our landing with GIGN. When do you want him to speak?"

"Stay on."

Isaac turned to Mike. "Mike, call GIGN and inform them to tell the terrorists that al-Mousavi is in a van and will be in the air in thirty minutes. Frederick will put him on the phone to prove he's been released. And we want the wounded hostage or there's no deal."

"Got it."

Isaac turned to Frederick. "What kind of plane is it?"

"A Falcon 7X nineteen-passenger business jet. Our government got it when the Royal Bank of Scotland canceled it during the financial crash a few years ago."

"Do you have any idea what the range is?"

"Almost six thousand nautical miles. Why?"

"Just thinking. Ask your pilot to see me as soon as he lands."

"Okay."

Jacques interrupted. "I just spoke to Ahmed Habibi. He's agreed to release the wounded hostage once he has heard from al-Mousavi, but said that if we try anything, he will start killing the passengers." Jacques paused. "He also said he wants to speak with Isaac directly."

"Connect me now." He talked into his phone. "Frederick, stay on the line."

Jacques pulled out a phone and dialed a number. He handed the phone to Isaac.

"This is Ahmed. I have agreed to the terms. Understand that if you deviate in any way, the first one to be killed will be Mrs. Green."

Isaac's face turned grim. "I'm getting you what you want, but let me make this very clear. You will not hurt my wife or anyone else in that lounge. This whole thing will be over in less than an hour. There will be no casualties, or the last time you and all of your associates saw your families will be the last time you'll ever see them."

Without waiting for a response, Isaac hung up the phone.

Mike looked at Isaac's face. It had turned deathly white. "Isaac, let me get you a drink. Did you take your pills?"

"I took them."

"I'll be right back."

"My people are ready to patch the call in when you give the go ahead," Jacques said.

Isaac picked up his phone. "Frederick, are you still there?"

"Yes."

"You have to call GIGN now. We gotta get al-Mousavi on the line with Ahmed."

"I'll do it now."

Isaac listened as Frederick contacted GIGN from another phone.

"Okay, they'll call me back in a minute with Ahmed on the line."

Isaac heard Frederick say to al-Mousavi, "You have thirty seconds. Tell your colleague that you are at Heathrow, and we will be taking off shortly. You tell him we are doing everything he asked. One word more or less and you'll be dead."

The other phone rang twice. Al-Mousavi put it to his ear. Frederick grabbed the phone and pressed the speaker button, then handed it back to Abu.

The voice on the other end asked, "*Salam*, Abu. Are you alright?"

"Yes, I'm at the airport. We're about to board. They're doing what you asked."

"With Allah's help, I'll see you soon."

Frederick clicked the phone and it disconnected. He picked up the other phone. "Did you get all that, Isaac?"

"Yes, thanks. See you soon."

At the Paris airport, Jacques was busy on his phone, talking to Paul-Henri. Isaac thought of Chava. *How is she holding up?* The frustration was overwhelming.

"They're sending him out in five minutes," Jacques told Isaac. He was talking about the wounded hostage. "They warned us nobody's to come near the lounge."

Isaac nervously walked back and forth looking at his PDA. Brahim had sent him a text. He was on his way back with the prince.

Mike walked up to him with bottled water. "Any news from William or Charlie?" he asked Mike.

"Not yet."

"What about Thomas?"

"They're tearing out everything they can." He handed Isaac the drink. "Isaac, how are you doing?"

Before Isaac could answer, his phone rang.

"Isaac, this is Yaacov Solomon."

"General, thanks for returning the call."

"Isaac, all of our prayers are with you."

"Thank you, General."

"We are following the events closely. Our government is using every available resource to help you. We are interrogating anyone remotely connected to the terrorists."

"I know that you have your hands full with other things, General, and I appreciate it. Is there anything you can tell me about the situation with Iran?"

CHAPTER
37

E'RE MONITORING IT by the hour. They appear to be getting ready for war. They've done this before in order to drive the oil prices up, but this time it looks more serious. We can't be sure but we have to be prepared. We're on high alert, we've already called up our reservists."

"I heard Iran's working with Beirut."

"You heard right. For the last several months Iran has been arming Hezbollah with the latest surface-to-air missiles. Our intelligence personnel is reporting from Lebanon. Yesterday they told us China is also working with them."

"I've heard rumors about that too." Isaac didn't want to let on how much he really knew.

"It's not a rumor. I had a conversation with the prime minister before I called you. He's on his way to meet with the president in the States. He said to tell you his prayers are with you and your wife."

"General, please thank him and everyone else for me. I have to go. If there are any new developments, please inform me as soon as you can."

"Of course."

Isaac turned off the phone, and Mike handed him a coffee.

"Black, no sugar?"

"You got it. Wait a minute. Susan is trying to reach me."

"Susan, what's the latest?"

"William has arrived in Taiwan to refuel, and everyone on the plane is safe. There's a new flight plan."

"Tell Charlie to call me as soon as he can."

"Isaac, is everything alright?"

"Yes, I just have to tell him something."

"I can patch Charlie in right now."

"Do it."

Charlie came on the line. "I'm here, Isaac."

"Okay, listen, I want you to tell William to wait for Thomas to land and have Allan and Guy fly here with you."

"Do you need anything else?"

"Not at the moment. Wait a minute, I just thought of something. Tell William to call me. Charlie, I see on the monitor that they just set free the wounded passenger. I'll call you back."

The hostage walked out of the lounge toward the police, his left arm in a sling, but appearing to be fine. Two plainclothes officers and a doctor greeted him.

"How are you doing?" the doctor asked.

"I'm just tired."

"Here, sit down." The doctor offered him a wheelchair.

"No, I'm fine. I need to see Mr. Green right away."

"Follow us to the VIP lounge."

When they opened the door, Isaac stood waiting for the man at the entrance with Mike and Dov. Everyone stopped to look at him as he entered the room.

Isaac stretched out his hand to shake his good hand. "You look familiar to me. What's your name?"

"Leka Galimoni. I was the general contractor on your house in Livingston, New Jersey. Must have been twenty years ago by now, Mr. Green."

Isaac studied the man's face. "Sure, I remember you now. Please come and sit down."

"First I must tell you, your wife is fine. She is worried about you." Galimoni reached into his pocket and took out a small box and a scrap of paper. He handed them to Isaac. "Your wife gave me this note and told me to tell you to make sure you take one of these pills."

Isaac looked at the box of blood pressure pills and unfolded the note. It read, "*I love you. Don't worry, we're fine. Just get us out of here, okay?*"

Isaac smiled. "My wife is being held hostage by terrorists, and she's worried that I make sure I take my medicine." *Amazing woman, that wife of mine.*

Leka interrupted Isaac's reverie. "Mr. Green, you gave me my first building contract. I'd just arrived in America from Macedonia. You recommended me to all your friends in the Jewish community, even though I was a Muslim. I've never forgotten that. Those recommendations made all the difference for me."

"Mr. Galimoni," Dov interrupted, "while the doctor's checking your arm, can you give us an update on the other passengers in the lounge?"

"I'm fine. The doctor in the lounge took care of me."

"What's the status of the other passengers?" Isaac repeated.

"They're scared. They're worried that if the demands of the terrorists aren't met, they'll be killed. I was sitting with your wife and Sammi in a corner of the lounge. Sammi was so mad he couldn't hold back any longer. One of them was taunting a young woman, and Sammi lashed out in Farsi, 'It's animals like you who give Muslims a bad name.' The terrorist was enraged and started toward Sammi. I thought the terrorist was going to shoot him, so I jumped up from my chair and he shot me in the arm."

"What happened next?"

"One of the other terrorists ran over and stopped him. He told

him that he could kill them all later, but that for now they still needed them."

"How did you end up in the lounge?"

"I'm a member of the King David Club. I fly Air France to Paris
all the time. I usually make a connection to Macedonia to see my
mother. This time my plane arrived early so I decided to wait in the
lounge. I was on my way to Mecca."

"Did you see or hear anything that could be helpful to us?"
Mike asked.

"What do you mean?"

"Did they have anything with them? Bags, explosives?"

"Packages, several. Why?"

"Could you see what was in them?"

"No, they kept them in the kitchen. It was hard to hear them
most of the time. They spoke in there. Two of them were always
near the desk by the front door. The others were guarding us. I did
hear one of them say that the plane had taken off. The other one
answered, 'We can fly anything.' I don't know exactly what that
means."

"Please think. It's important. Did they say anything else?" Mike
asked.

"Not really, but one thing seemed strange to me. I heard them
mention that they were going to have another passenger besides al-
Mousavi."

Mike looked at Isaac. "I'm done with my questions."

"Leka, is there anything we can do for you?"

"Yes, I want to call my wife and tell her I'm safe. Then, if you
can help me, I want to continue on to Mecca."

"Paul-Henri can help with that," said Mike. "You can stay here
until we find out about flights to Mecca. For now, all flights have
been grounded."

Dov looked at Isaac. "The press wants to interview Mr. Galimoni."

"What do you think, Mike?"

Mike shook his head. "The terrorists would love more press. Sorry, Dov, I say we don't give it to them."

"You got your answer," Isaac said to Dov. "Tell them we'll give a full press conference when all of the hostages are free."

Isaac turned to watch the plasma screen on the wall. The news flashed across the bottom of the screen: "*A bomb has gone off in front of the United States Embassy in Beijing. Ten people dead and many others wounded. No one has claimed responsibility.*"

Isaac's phone rang. It was Susan. "Thomas is on the other line. He's almost out of fuel and may not make it to the landing field. He has already notified everyone to prepare for a crash landing. It's going to be close."

CHAPTER
38

ISAAC GRIPPED HIS phone tight. "They're going to make it, damn it. They have to make it."

Suddenly there was silence on the PDA.

"Susan, Susan, can you hear me?" Isaac yelled into the PDA.

"I lost contact. My God, they've crashed!"

"I need the tower," Isaac demanded. "Somebody get me the tower."

Mike was already dialing the tower. Dov called his contacts in Taiwan.

A French TV show that was playing on one of the monitors was interrupted with breaking news: *"A private jet plane has crashed about one hundred meters short of the runway in Taiwan. We will update you as matters progress."*

Dov was already on with his media representative in Asia. He was told that CNN had dispatched a helicopter to cover the crash. They were relaying the pictures via satellite to their network.

"Switch all TV channels to CNN," he told Mike.

Mike stood with Isaac in front of a monitor. Ambulances were arriving to the site while fire engines covered most of the plane with foam. CNN reported: *"The plane's right wing was severed in half as the plane skidded across the ground in the crash. The pilot is being commended for having done an outstanding job. This is Clarence White for CNN."*

A helicopter now hovered near the plane. A moment later it cut its engine. A reporter and a cameraman jumped out of the helicopter and headed toward the staircase of the plane. In the VIP lounge, all eyes were glued to the TV.

Just then, Brahim arrived with the prince, along with Ben and his security people. With all of the commotion over the crash, they entered the room unnoticed. Brahim walked over to where Isaac was standing and touched him on the shoulder. "The prince is here."

Isaac turned. Prince Abdul al-Assi stood a few feet away watching the news. "Your Highness, I appreciate your being here."

"I'm here to assist in any way possible."

"Thank you."

Brahim interrupted. "Isaac, we've been following everything on the TV in the car."

The news broadcast blared. *"The door to the plane is being opened, and we'll find out the condition of the passengers in a moment."*

Everyone in the command center stopped talking. All eyes focused on the TV monitor. The cameraman zoomed in on the door as it opened. The first shot was on Allan. Though he appeared fine, airport personnel helped him down the stairs. Guy followed behind him with a grateful smile on his face. Lionel and Thomas appeared together, walking down the stairs, waving their hands, and giving the thumbs up sign.

Mike looked concerned. "Where are Danny and Eddie?"

CHAPTER
39

Wednesday, June 4, 2014
Taoyuan International Airport

THOMAS WAS BEING interviewed by the TV reporter. Allan and Guy moved out of sight of the reporter and cameraman. They spotted Charlie walking toward them waving.

"Are you guys alright?" Charlie asked when he caught up with them.

"We're fine," Guy answered.

"Same old, same old. Anything new with you?" Allan smirked.

"Very funny. After you're checked out by a doctor, Isaac would like you two to come on our plane to France. We're already cleared to go."

"What about Jim and Chicago?"

"Isaac, will get you a jet from Paris."

"Fine."

"Danny and Eddie, our security detail, are waiting with the caskets until they arrange a flight to D.C. They want to be in Arlington at the official burial. I want to thank them," Guy said.

"I'll wait with the car."

As soon as they walked away, Charlie called Isaac.

"Isaac, it's all set. Guy and Allan will be with me on the plane to Paris. We should be airborne within the hour."

"What about Thomas?"

"He and Lionel have to stay and fill out a report."

"What about Danny and Eddie? We didn't see them come out of the plane."

"They're fine. They want to be at the burial. They're arranging to have a military plane bring them to Arlington."

"Okay, call me later from the plane. Try to get some rest."

"What about you? You have to be exhausted."

"I'm fine. Thank God, everyone's safe, that's all that matters. Call Jim and tell him to sit tight. I needed Guy to come here for a meeting. I'll get him out of Paris as soon as possible."

CHAPTER
40

Wednesday, June 4, 2014
Charles de Gaulle Airport

BRAHIM AND THE prince were sitting in a corner of the room. Isaac pulled up a chair. "Your Highness, I apologize for keeping you waiting."

"Mr. Green, I have been speaking with Brahim. I'm prepared to talk with the men responsible and see if we can bring this to a peaceful conclusion."

"Fine, let's set it up. Let me get Mike and Jacques to coordinate it with the GIGN."

Isaac looked around for Mike. He didn't see him. He walked over to Ben on the other side of the room. "Ben, where's Mike?"

"He received a call from the States. He stepped outside to take it. He should be back in a minute. By the way, I just heard from GIGN that the flight from London is about to land."

"I need to talk to the pilot as soon as he lands. I told Frederick to bring him here."

"I'll go and get them."

Isaac walked back to Brahim and the prince. "Mike will be

with us in a few minutes."

"Isaac," said Brahim, "the prince and I have been discussing the best way to handle this."

The prince looked into Isaac's eyes. "They must believe that I'm on their side. I suggest that I go into the lounge and assure them that there will be no tricks. They will not want to harm me, as they're aware that the whole Arab world will be watching."

Brahim interrupted. "Isaac, what do you think?"

"Sounds okay so far. Then what?"

"I'll offer them myself as a hostage. I'll board the plane with them so as to give them confidence that their plan is working."

Isaac sank deeply into thought, then he said, "What if they decide to extort more money for your safe return?"

"That's a chance I'm willing to take."

"Let me run this by Mike and Jacques. If they agree, we'll set it in motion."

Isaac saw Jacques talking to Mike. He excused himself and walked over to them.

"Isaac," said Mike, "Frederick has landed, and I instructed my people to have them taxi up to Gate 40 next to the Brink's truck."

"The prince has offered to talk to the terrorists. He'll board the plane as a guarantee that nothing is going to happen once they set the hostages free."

Jacques looked surprised. "If that's what he wants to do, it's fine by me. Let me go brief him on how we'll be handling our end of things."

"Fine."

Jacques walked away. Isaac looked over at Mike, who hadn't said a word.

"What's the problem? You look like death warmed over."

"Let's go outside for a moment."

They left the room. Isaac had a bad feeling in his gut. "Mike, what was that call about?"

"It was from our NSA special communications division. It's not located in Washington so you wouldn't have heard about it. We set it up in 2002 in the South Pole as an experiment after September 11. The budget and the programs they're working on are so secret it's hidden in an offshore company that the NSA funds. They were able to develop a new spy satellite designed to listen in on multiple conversations in the world without using standard wire-taping devices. Impressive, but the most important feature is its ability to duplicate and alter conversations through voice recognition.

"Since 9/11 it has been focused on the Arab leaders. They have provided disinformation using the voices of radical leaders, which has led to the overthrow of certain governments."

Isaac listened attentively, trying to digest the information and figure out where the conversation was headed.

"Isaac, this is completely confidential. It would endanger many people around the world if this information got out."

"Before you tell me, I want to know who the other people are who know about this, Mike."

"The deputy director of the NSA and the chairman of the Joint Chiefs of Staff are two of the people."

"Who else?"

"Senator Richard Long, head of the appropriations committee, and Bill Waters, the CEO of AT&T."

"Is that it?"

"Yes."

"Okay, go ahead."

"Isaac, the call I just had was a conference call with the deputy director and the chief of staff. They played me a tape of several conversations that our people have been monitoring. One of the conversations was with the prince and the terrorists in the lounge a week before the hostages were taken."

CHAPTER
41

IT WAS JUST after the capture of Abu al-Mousavi. Abu is the prince's nephew. His sister's son, and the king's favorite grandson."

Isaac's silence concerned Mike. "Isaac, are you alright?"

"I'm following every word."

"He planned the whole operation. That's why he was conveniently in Paris when this all went down. We're being set up."

"What do you mean?"

"This isn't easy to say. But one of the other calls was the king of Saudi Arabia to the president. As is customary, the president was being monitored since he'd been receiving death threats from some white supremacy group on his personal iPhone. Somehow he forgot to turn on the special code that allows him privacy on personal calls. The actual conversation recorded went like this."

Mike played a recording on his phone. The king spoke first.

"Mr. President, are you alright?"

"Fine, Your Majesty. You are aware of the situation in Paris."

"Yes, I received a coded message via your ambassador in my office yesterday."

"After my staff decoded it, I talked with Prince Abdul in great detail about it. He has my full cooperation. I can assure you that whatever it takes me to free your nephew, I'll do it."

"Thank you, and may Allah bless you."

Isaac listened in disbelief. "The president was in on this whole operation?"

"There's more and it gets dirtier. They've been in constant contact. We learned of a secret deal made to disarm Israel's nuclear weapons as part of a Middle East nuclear-free zone. When that happens, the Arab countries will attack Israel. The president will conveniently be too busy to help Israel until it's too late.

"On his last trip to Egypt, he held private meetings with several Arab leaders and gave them his word on this matter. He will tell the world he did everything to bring peace, but Israel did not heed his advice. Furthermore, he'll announce that the United States no longer recognizes the State of Israel and now is opening diplomatic relations with the State of Palestine."

Isaac looked at Mike and raised a fist. "Like hell he will."

Isaac found it all a little hard to digest. Innocent people, including Isaac's wife and Brahim's friend, were in danger and the president intended to do nothing. More, he was colluding with the people who were responsible. With terrorists. Isaac realized they were in this alone. It was time to take things into his own hands. No one messed with his family and got away with it.

As they started to walk back into the VIP lounge, Isaac turned to Mike. "I have my own plan, just follow my lead."

"You got it."

When they entered the room, they saw Frederick and Ben standing next to the pilot. Isaac walked up to them. "Frederick, can I talk to you for a minute alone?"

"Sure."

Isaac led Frederick to the far corner of the room, where it was quiet.

"Frederick I can't tell you everything at this time, but I need you to trust that I know what I'm doing."

Frederick stared straight ahead. "What is it, Isaac?"

"I have information that the terrorists are going to use your plane to leave for North Africa. Their destination is Libya. I need you to have the pilot fix the fuel gauge on the plane."

"What? Why?"

"He has to make it look like the plane is fully loaded with fuel when they take off. But it should have have only enough fuel to fly until it reaches the middle of the Mediterranean. "

Frederick shook his head. "Everyone on board will be killed. We can't risk the prince's life."

"That's why I need you to trust me."

"I can't do this. You're asking me to crash a plane and kill all of its passengers. This is murder."

"I understand your position. I'll have someone else do it."

"Wait. Hold on a minute. Just tell me why."

"This whole thing's been set up to free al-Mousavi. The prince and the terrorists are working together." Isaac paused. Frederick waited. "Listen, I've told you more than I should have."

Mike walked over to greet Frederick. "Is everything alright?"

"Mike, are you aware of this plan of Isaac's?"

"He mentioned it in passing. He told me he has a plan but no details. Why? What's the plan?"

Isaac looked at Mike. "The plan is to crash the plane in the Mediterranean with everyone on board. Everyone on the plane will be killed."

Mike turned to look at Isaac. "How do you know they won't survive? Surely they'll have life preservers and a lifeboat on the plane."

"We'll take precautions to make sure of it. Faulty life vests, a punctured raft, there are ways."

"Then what are we waiting for. It's a go."

Frederick looked confused. He'd been sure that Mike would veto the idea. "I can't believe it. Mike, what are you saying?"

"Frederick, if we don't do something now, we're going to have to let them get away scot-free."

"I'll take full responsibility," Isaac said.

Mike looked at him for clarification. "Isaac, what is it we have to do?"

Before Isaac could answer, Frederick interrupted. "God help us, I'm in. Only one thing: my pilot and crew who flew here can't be part of this."

Isaac and Mike nodded in agreement.

"I'll fix the fuel gauge myself."

"Frederick, are you sure?"

"I'm sure. Before my current position I flew for the Royal Air Force." Frederick looked at his watch. "I'd better get a move on. Mike, how much time do I have?"

"I figure about two hours, maybe less."

"I'll tell the crew and my security personnel to leave the plane. Have your security people take charge of al-Mousavi. Also, have the airport send the fuel truck to the plane so it will seem like it's being refueled. The terrorists have to see the refueling, but make sure that the fuel truck is half empty. I'll be on the plane unloading the extra fuel with the emergency dumping switch. It will take some time to fix the instrument fuel indicator. I'd better get on it."

Isaac extended his hand. "If you need anything, talk to Mike. I have a few other things to take care of."

Mike looked at Frederick. "Take this. It's a two-way Motorola. Just press *M* if you need me. It's a secure line."

"Thanks."

Over in the other corner, the prince was speaking to Jacques. Isaac walked over to them.

"Prince, everything is set with the plane. The fuel truck is going to be pulling up shortly. When they finish refueling, we can start moving the hostages."

Isaac stared into the eyes of the prince. A part of him felt like getting a gun and killing him right then and there, but he'd been trained to control his emotions. Instead, in a concerned tone of voice, he said, "Prince, are you sure that this is the right thing?"

"Yes, Jacques has arranged with GIGN to clear the plane for takeoff. I just spoke to them inside the lounge. They've agreed to the switch and I'm prepared to go in now."

Isaac looked at Jacques. "How is this going to work?"

"The prince is going in by himself. As soon as we call the terrorists, he will enter the lounge and then they will release ten of the passengers, as agreed. As soon as that is done, two of the terrorists will exit the lounge through the back door and check the plane. After they finish inspecting it, they will tell us to bring over the money. When they finish with the counting, they will release five more hostages. The rest will be released once they have all boarded the plane."

"Who's going to fly the plane?" Mike asked. "Don't we have to file a flight plan with the tower?"

"They told me that they can fly it. They're all capable."

"And the flight plan?"

"They refused to disclose it to me."

Isaac seemed upset. "That's not good enough. Your Highness, they could fly anywhere. They could hold you for ransom or, worse, kill you. Once they realize you can identify them, they may think you'll put out a reward for them." Isaac paused. "I can't have this on my conscience. I can't agree to you risking your life, and they will not assure us your safety. The deal is off."

CHAPTER
42

MIKE WONDERED WHAT Isaac had planned now.

"Stop loading the fuel," Isaac ordered.

Jacques stopped him. "Wait a minute, Isaac. You're putting all those hostages at risk. Your wife could be killed."

"My wife would never forgive me if I traded her life for the life of someone else."

The prince looked shocked. He recovered quickly and said to Isaac, "I'll be fine. This is my decision to make. Jacques, I need to go in and convince them to tell me what country they plan to take me to."

"Fine, we'll trace them from our satellite from the moment they take off until they land. If they change course, we will notify our forces. They will be waiting for them in any country they land in."

Isaac looked at the prince. "Your Highness, you ready to go in?"

The prince squared his shoulders and nodded. "Ready."

Jacques said, "Come with me."

On their way out, Brahim grabbed the prince and kissed him on both cheeks. "May Allah be kind to you."

Mike shook the prince's hand. "Be careful."

"Your Highness, I won't forget this," Isaac said. "Thank you."

The prince walked toward the door with Jacques. Ben came over with Dov on his heels.

"Is everything all set?" Ben asked.

Mike answered, "We believe so."

"Have I covered everything?" Isaac asked Mike softly.

"You did what you could."

"You better have your people get al-Mousavi off the plane so he doesn't figure out what Frederick is doing."

"Right, I'm on it." Mike walked away to make the call.

"Isaac," said Dov, "the media is ready to start broadcasting as soon as the first hostage is released. We want them to show the plane as the terrorists are boarding. I'll release a statement that the prince has volunteered to be held as security to guarantee that the terrorists leave safely. When the last hostages are safely in the terminal, we'll hold a press conference."

"Good."

Mike returned. "Al-Mousavi is in a security car, and Frederick will be joining us in a moment."

"Excuse me," said Brahim, "I want to try and reach Abra. I'll be back in a few minutes."

Paul-Henri walked over to them. "Isaac, everything is in order. Just give the word. Ben checked to make sure all the security is in position. The sniper is in place if anything goes wrong. All of the closed-circuit cameras are focused on the front of the lounge and the loading ramp. Outside, airport security cars are waiting to escort the plane to the main runway for takeoff."

"Thanks, Paul." Isaac fidgeted with his mobile. He still hadn't heard from Frederick. "Mike, walk with me." He took Mike by the arm and walked him over to the door.

When they were standing right outside the room, Isaac said to Mike, "Give me your gun."

"What for?"

"If they pull any stunts and this plan goes wrong, I want the pleasure of killing the prince myself."

"Take it easy, Isaac, nothing's going to go wrong." Mike saw the strain on Isaac's face and said, "When was the last time you fired a weapon?"

"A month ago on the firing range," Isaac snapped. "My vet buddies and I have a night out once a month. We have dinner and then go shooting."

"Very nice, but I still can't give you my gun. Trust me, nothing would give me more pleasure than to kill this guy. If a problem arises, I'll take care of it."

At that moment, Frederick appeared. "Mission completed."

Isaac looked at both of them. "Mike, give Paul-Henri the go-ahead."

The three of them walked into the lounge, and Mike signaled to Paul-Henri. "It's a go."

Jacques and Paul-Henri left and proceeded to the GIGN command center. They would monitor the terrorists as they boarded the plane, ready to take action if anything went wrong. Mike and Isaac focused on the monitor that showed the door to the El-Al lounge.

Brahim returned. "I can't reach either Abra or her sister."

Isaac looked at him but said nothing. He was watching the monitor, waiting for the moment when the door to the El-Al lounge would open. His heart was thumping, and he began to sweat. He felt like he couldn't catch his breath. Everyone was so focused on the monitor that they didn't notice Isaac.

Dov walked in, took one look at Isaac, and yelled, "Somebody get me some water for Isaac."

Isaac shook his head. "I don't want water. Get me a single malt scotch."

Frederick walked to the bar. "I'm on it." He grabbed a bottle with several glasses and started pouring. He handed a glass to Isaac and said, "I can't watch a good friend drink alone. Can I join you?"

Isaac nodded his head in consent, looking better already. As

Isaac sipped his drink, he spotted the door to the El-Al lounge opening on the screen. One by one, the passengers started to emerge. The
color returned to Isaac's face, and a sense of relief filled the room. He
raised his glass. "Cheers!"

The scotch was passed around as they all turned their attention back to the monitors, observing the passengers as they walked
toward the security people. Medical personnel waited to take them
to an emergency area for checkups. The tenth person left the lounge
and the door closed. Isaac's face dropped.

"I'm sure Chava and Sammi will be in the next group," Mike
assured Isaac.

Isaac nodded and took another swallow of his drink.

"If you're feeling alright, I should go and brief the press," said
Dov. "I also have to meet with the passengers and prepare them for
the questions they're going to be asked."

Ben added, "I also have to go. GIGN will want to talk to each
one of them and I should be there."

Isaac nodded again. "Both of you go ahead. Mike and I will call
you as soon as the other passengers are released."

Jacques returned with Paul-Henri. "Two of the terrorists have
boarded the plane, and they've finished checking it out. They said
we should have the Brink's truck bring them the money now. The
security guards are to set it down inside the door of the plane. We
just gave Brink's the order."

The security cameras focused on the door of the plane. All the
monitors except one showed them the entrance to the plane. The
other monitor was still focused on the door to the El-Al lounge,
where two more terrorists and the prince were inside with the rest of
the hostages. Al-Mousavi wouldn't be allowed to join them until all
the hostages were released.

Everyone in the room watched the security guards walking up
the stairs with the delivery. Each one put the black bag he was carrying inside the door of the plane and turned around to head down

the stairs. Once the last bag was inside, the terrorists closed the door halfway. Everyone sat in silence and waited.

"It's always the money," Isaac murmured.

"What about the money?" Mike asked.

"Nothing, just a thought I had." *Thank God it's counterfeit.* The partners of World had planned for this in case one of their family members might be taken hostage for ransom. The code EMGC that Isaac had activated told the bank to release counterfeit bills that could be tracked.

The silence was broken when Jacques heard his phone ring. The GIGN told him that the terrorists had given their permission to release five more hostages. As he hung up, everyone watched the hostages coming through the door.

Mike watched the monitor intently. "I don't see Chava or Sammi."

"They're showing that they're in control of the situation, not us." Isaac slammed his fist down on the table, harder than he meant to, sending pain shooting through his wrist. "They know Chava is my wife and Sammi is valuable to Brahim. There's nothing random about this. I've had enough of their garbage." He turned to the defense minister. "Jacques, let's get the prince on the phone."

"What's going on?" Mike asked.

"In one minute you'll see what's going on. They want terror, I can do terror." He looked at Paul. "Paul-Henri, call your security guards. Tell them to take al-Mousavi out of the security car and have him kneel down on the ground as if he's praying. Make sure they can see him from inside the lounge. I want you to tell the security guards to put a gun to the back of his head and wait for you to give the order to shoot him."

Brahim looked at Isaac in horror. "Isaac, wait a minute. Don't do anything rash."

"Brahim, please let me handle this."

Jacques held his phone up. "Isaac, I have the prince on the phone."

Isaac put the call on speaker so everyone could hear.

"Prince, I want to speak to my wife immediately."

"What if they refuse?"

"If they refuse, just have them look out the window. Al-Mousavi will be killed immediately. As we are talking, the GIGN are being given orders to storm the lounge and board the plane and eliminate the terrorists."

"What about your wife and the other hostages?"

"The terrorists have proven they can't be trusted. I'll take my chances. With God's help, Sammi and Chava will be safe."

Brahim grabbed Isaac's shoulder. "Please, Isaac, let me talk to the prince."

At first it looked like Isaac was going to refuse, but then he handed Brahim the phone.

Brahim spoke into the phone. "Your Highness, please get them to do this."

"Alright, I'll call you back in a minute."

Jacques stared at Isaac intensely. Isaac began to pace back and forth. Dov walked one step behind him in silence, like Isaac's shadow. Brahim held on to the phone waiting for a miracle. The phone rang once. Isaac and Dov stopped pacing as Brahim answered it.

"Brahim, Mrs. Green is standing next to me. Put Isaac on the phone."

Brahim handed the phone to Isaac. Isaac's hand shook. He took the phone off of speaker and walked away so no one could hear the conversation.

"Chava, are you alright?"

"Yes, I'm fine."

"What about Sammi?"

"He's right here next to me. He's been a great help."

"Don't worry, honey, I'm gonna get you out of there very soon. I love you. Now please put the prince back on the phone."

A pause while Isaac waited for Chava to hand over the phone, then, "Isaac, she's fine."

"Thank you for your help, Your Highness. Are you on the phone by yourself. Can anyone hear me?"

"No one else can hear you. Go ahead."

"An agent from the Mossad in Israel called me fifteen minutes ago. They rounded up several of the terrorists' relatives in the West Bank. One of them was Abu al-Mousavi's mother, who was visiting relatives in Ramallah. She is being interrogated in Tel Aviv. They asked me what to do with her. Tell them to send out the rest of the passengers right now. No stalling and I'll see that she's set free. You have my word. Everything else will proceed as arranged. They can board the plane with you immediately."

"I'll talk to them."

Mike leaned over and whispered in Isaac's ear, "What call from the Mossad?"

Before Isaac could answer, the prince was back on the phone.

"They have agreed. I gave them my word that the rest of the passengers will be set free. The remaining hostages are being sent out of the lounge as we speak. Check your monitor. I'll be boarding the plane shortly. Is everything all set?"

"Yes, Your Highness."

Isaac watched as Chava and Sammi came out first, followed by the other passengers. Isaac turned to Mike with a big smile and hugged him.

"You're right. There was no call from the Mossad."

"I've never met anyone like you, Isaac. Not in my entire career. May the good Lord bless you."

"Let's go get Chava and Sammi."

"Just one second." Mike talked into his two-way. "Ben, can you see that all the terrorists get on the plane? Make sure the tower clears them for takeoff."

CHAPTER
43

AS ISAAC WALKED toward Chava, he was flooded with a rush of emotions. He remembered the night he married Chava. Her parents walked her to the canopy while he waited underneath it. Now, as he looked at her, she was more beautiful to him than the day she'd stood with him under the *chuppah*. In a moment she would be in his arms again. Nothing else in the world mattered. They were together, and the blessing the rabbi had given them on their wedding day had come true: their love for each other had grown every day.

Isaac started to cry. "Chava, thank God you're alright."

"I'm fine, dear. Don't worry. Did you take your heart medicine?"

Isaac's tear-strewn eyes met Chava's and he smiled. "Some things never change."

Brahim kissed Sammi on both cheeks.

Sammi looked exhausted. "Boss, I think I need a vacation."

Brahim burst out laughing. "You deserve one. All expenses paid."

Dov had waited the appropriate amount of time before interrupting. "So sorry to do this, but the media's waiting."

Isaac held Chava by the hand. "Can you handle a press conference?"

"I managed to handle you all these years. The press should be easy."

Everyone started to laugh as they felt the tension start to diminish. Isaac gave his wife a warm smile and sat down still holding on to her.

"I never in my life understood how precious freedom is until today," said Chava. "In only those few hours of captivity I realized it's something I can never take for granted again. When you described coming home from the war years ago, it was hard for me to understand what all the killing and suffering was for. I understand you now, Isaac. You're right. Freedom is worth defending at any cost."

"Chava, I'm so proud of you. I love you so much."

Chava was still wiping the tears from her eyes when Dov came over and asked, "Isaac, are you two ready?"

Isaac looked at Chava. She nodded.

"Let's do it."

Walking down the hall to the press conference, Isaac held Chava's hand tightly. Every few steps he looked at her. *I can't believe I almost lost you.*

Ben came over and handed Mike a note: *"The plane is about to take off."* Mike leaned over to Isaac and showed him the note.

"Chava," said Isaac, "go on ahead. I have to look at something with Mike." He put his arm on Mike's shoulder. "Come with me."

They walked to a large window to see the plane that had the terrorists on board slowly heading down the runway. Finally it lifted off and soon it was out of sight. A new kind of war for freedom had just begun.

BRAHIM STOOD WITH Sammi next to Chava and Mike in the press room that Dov had taken over. A makeshift platform had been set up. Dov was double-checking the speaker system. Isaac went over to Sammi and gave him a big hug. "Thanks for keeping Chava safe."

Sammi smiled. "Mrs. Green is one amazing woman. She never got depressed or cried like some of the other passengers. She kept everybody in good spirits even after the shooting. She kept telling everyone that you would get us out safely. She was amazing. At one point she stood up in the middle of the lounge and said to the terrorists, 'If you want to die here in the El-Al lounge, fine. If they hear guns going off from inside, they'll storm the lounge, and you'll all be killed along with us. What you set out to do will not get done. Is that what you really want? If you don't hurt anyone, I'm sure that your demands will be met.'"

"Sammi, please, that's enough." Chava blushed.

Isaac looked at Brahim and asked, "Do you want to say anything to the media?"

"No, Isaac, I really can't talk now. Please, you and Mike speak."

"Mike, how about you leading, then maybe Jacques or Paul-Henri would like to say something."

"That's fine with me."

Paul-Henri interrupted. "Isaac, I really think it should just be you and Mike. You led the operation."

"Isaac," said Chava, "everybody is drained. Please just say a few words. I'm sure the press is going to have lots of questions. Besides, I'm anxious to go and call the children."

"Fine, you're right."

Mike walked up to the podium. "Ladies and gentlemen, I want to introduce you to Mr. Isaac Green, chairman of World Corporation. Some of you may have heard about him or read about his company. What you may not know is that he's a decorated hero from the Vietnam War. He's also the man responsible for the safe return of all of these passengers."

Everyone stood up and applauded. Isaac walked up and grabbed Mike's hand to shake. With a big smile he leaned over and whispered into Mike's ear, "I'll get you for that."

Isaac turned to face the audience. "Please, if you could all be seated." Isaac glanced at Chava standing beside him. She smiled.

"My wife asked me to keep this short. It's been a long day for all of us, so I won't keep you for too long. First, let me thank God for bringing everyone to safety. All of our prayers were answered. Many individuals participated in this successful operation. The French GIGN, the minister of security, the airport personnel, they all did an outstanding job. But the real heroes are the passengers. You held yourself together in the face of life-threatening danger. You're our heroes."

Everyone applauded. When the clapping faded, Isaac continued.

"At this moment there are plans to change the democratic structure of the world. This is a war of religious fanatics who are determined to bring down our way of life. My partner Mr. Brahim Surin always quotes Churchill, so I will too.

"'It's not enough that we do our best. Sometimes we have to do what is required.' From today forward we must all do what is required of each of us to end terrorism. Today we have shown the world what that looks like. Thank you. May God bless you and all freedom-loving people."

Isaac took Chava by the hand and walked off the platform.

Chava whispered to Isaac, "Are you feeling alright?" She looked worried.

"I'm fine, just a little tired."

"No," Chava persisted, "there's something else you're not telling me. Is our family safe?"

"Yes, I promise you, Chava. Please, everything is fine. Let's call the kids."

Isaac's PDA rang. It was Susan. "I just wanted to know how Chava is."

"She's fine."

"Can she talk? I have some of your children on hold and they all want to say hello."

Isaac smiled, feeling relieved. "Chava, Susan has the children on the line."

"Put them on."

As he handed Chava the PDA, Brahim and Mike walked toward them. "Chava, tell the kids that I love them and we'll see them all soon."

Chava nodded. Isaac walked over to Brahim and Mike.

"Are we done here?" Isaac asked.

"Yes. Dov, Ben, and our security people are sitting with the GIGN personnel. Frederick is on the phone with London. But Brahim can't reach Abra or Fatima."

"They should have been in touch by now," Brahim confirmed.

"We've notified our people in Saudi Arabia. They said the plane arrived ahead of time, and some friends of Abra picked them up."

"I don't know why she's not answering my calls," Brahim said.

"You're right," Isaac agreed, "something doesn't add up."

Brahim looked at Mike. "Can you get me a plane to take me to Saudi Arabia within the hour?"

"You're right, Brahim," Isaac said, "you should go."

"I'm thinking of taking Sammi with me."

"That's a good idea. He'll look after you."

"What about that guy, Leka Galimoni? He wanted very much to go to Mecca. He can come with me."

Isaac nodded. "I'm sure he would appreciate it."

"I'll arrange everything," said Mike. "Now if you'll excuse me, I have to talk to the security personnel and see who else will be going with you." He walked away.

"I have a bad feeling about this trip," Brahim said, looking at Isaac.

Isaac had the same bad feeling. In moments like these, they became like identical twins, sharing the same feelings and the same thoughts.

"Listen to me very carefully, Brahim. Trust no one but Sammi over there. Make sure your security people are with you twenty-four/seven, and I want you to text me every couple of hours after you land, alright?"

"Yes, of course."

"If I don't hear from you or Sammi, I will send people to find you."

"Isaac, we're going to Saudi Arabia, not Israel. What will you be able to do?"

"Listen to me, I don't care where you end up. If you need me to, I'll get you out."

"These are my people, Isaac. What could happen?"

"We know your life is being threatened, and Abra isn't answering your calls. It won't hurt to take precautionary measures."

Brahim nodded in agreement. "You're right. When are you planning to go on to Israel?"

"The day after tomorrow. I want to be with the children for the Sabbath."

"Have you heard from Charlie?"

"He and the others should be arriving here in a few hours. I'll meet with them in the morning. I need to talk to Guy about Chicago. I also want to debrief Kim Li and Hui Ying. We need to know what the Chinese are planning to do about the dollar."

Mike walked in with Ben. "All set. The pilot is getting the current weather report, and the crew is making the final inspection before takeoff. Two of my people boarded the plane to scan it for bombs. They'll fly with you and stay on as part of your security detail during your stay in Saudi Arabia. Our embassy has been alerted. They will provide the additional security for you and your family."

Brahim shook Mike's hand. "I can't thank you enough."

"I guess we should inform Mr. Galimoni that he will be traveling to Mecca on a private jet."

CHAPTER
44

MIKE, HOW LONG has it been since the terrorists' plane departed?"

Mike and Isaac were the only ones left in the pressroom. Mike looked at his watch. It was already 10 p.m. "Two hours and fifteen minutes."

"How much longer before the plane with the prince is over the water?"

"Forty-five minutes, give or take fifteen minutes. What happened to your watch?"

Isaac looked at his watch. The glass face had shattered and the watch had stopped telling time. *If people would only realize how precious each minute of their life really is.*

"Patek Philippe took a break when I hit the table waiting to get Chava out of the lounge. For now he's just an expensive bracelet. Listen, Chava will be here in a minute. Don't speak about this in front of her."

"I understand."

"What are your plans?"

"I'm coming with you to Israel, and then we'll see."

"And Ben?"

"He's staying in Paris. He's been reassigned."

Chava came over and sat down next to Isaac. "Am I interrupting something?"

"No, just arranging our plans for tonight. I thought we might have time to go visit the rabbi, but it's late."

"And you have a busy day tomorrow. Let's just go straight to our place. We can have a fast bite and go to bed early. I didn't really sleep on the flight from New York." Chava smiled mischievously.

Isaac laughed. "Mike, we're going to our apartment."

Dov returned. "Isaac, my staff and I are finished with the last of the newspaper reporters. Anything more for me to do?"

"No, Chava and I decided we're going to our apartment. Can you be at my place at around eleven a.m.? I'm going to arrange for Charlie and the others who flew in from Hong Kong to come by for a debriefing."

"Sure. Good night, everyone. See you all in the morning."

Ben came in and said to Mike, "Brahim and Sammi are ready to board."

"Good. Let's escort them on board and then I'll take Isaac and Chava home." Mike looked at his watch. "Isaac, you ready to go?"

"We're ready."

At that moment Frederick walked into the room. "Isaac, I've been looking for you. Can I have a word?"

Isaac nodded. "Please excuse us."

Frederick and Isaac walked a short distance away. "What are we going to say after the plane crashes with the prince?" asked Frederick.

Isaac thought about it for a minute, then said, "I'll have Dov put out a press release."

"What's it going to say?"

"I've been thinking about it. I thought maybe something like, 'We are deeply saddened by the death of the prince. He understood terror, and he sacrificed his life so that we may defeat it. By doing so, he helped save the lives of the hostages. This was an unfortunate and unforeseeable accident and one that we will all mourn for a very long time.'"

Frederick smiled. "Isaac, you have a way with words."

"It's the truth. At least, most of it."

When they returned to the others, they saw Ben standing with Brahim, Sammi, and Leka Galimoni. Brahim gave Isaac a big hug and kisses on both cheeks.

"Take care of yourself. I'll meet you in the Holy Land with Allah's help."

"Good-bye, Brahim," Isaac said. "May our next meeting be less eventful."

Sammi turned to Isaac to shake his hand. "I'll take care of him. May God bless you."

Mike laughed. "Enough already with the hugging and kissing. You guys have to go."

They all left the room together. As Brahim and Sammi headed down the ramp to the plane, Isaac said to Mike and Ben, "If he were my own brother, I couldn't love him more."

"We can tell," Mike responded.

Brahim and Sammi disappeared into the plane. "Mike, what time is it?" Isaac asked.

"It's almost time."

Isaac walked over to where Chava was standing and escorted her to the car waiting outside the terminal. Mike opened the door for them. "I'll ride along in the front seat."

The driver pulled away from the terminal.

"Mike," said Isaac, "can you check if there's anything new happening in the world?"

Mike turned on Radio France International. "The Chinese finance minister has been asked to resign."

"It's starting," Isaac said. "They're going to crash the U.S. dollar, you can bet on it." *Why isn't there any news about the crash? How is the president going to react to the news?*

Looking over at Chava, Isaac saw that her eyes had closed and she had already fallen asleep. Unmarked police cars with horns blasting drove through red lights, forcing other cars to move aside as they turned onto Avenue des Champs-Élysées. Isaac looked out his window. The trees were lit up from one end of the avenue all the way to the Arc de Triomphe. Isaac leaned forward and tapped Mike on the shoulder. "Now you know why Paris is called the city of lights."

Isaac had been in almost every capital city around the world, and never had he seen such a beautiful sight as the Champs-Elysees at night. Every tree had hundreds of bulbs bringing light to the dark.

The world is heading into a dark place. We need to be part of bringing light back to the world.

Isaac suddenly noticed that their progress had slowed. "Can you find out what's going on, Mike? Why is the traffic so heavy?"

"One moment." Mike stepped out of the vehicle and returned a few minutes later. "Looks like we're in the middle of a demonstration. We should be clear of it in a few minutes."

"Were you able to find out what it's about?"

"Public employees are striking for better pay and less hours."

"So what else is new?"

Mike chuckled. "It looks like the government is trying to break the unions. I remember in November 2007, I was attached to a special mission on nuclear weapons storage in Europe. We had to travel to Belgium on a top-secret assignment. We made arrangements to go by SNFC rail that day to a secret military location. That morning they went on strike. The Paris Metro too. We figured it was only going to be for a few hours. It went on all that day. The next day the electric company started to reduce the electric supply by a few thousand megawatts. It was a disaster. This city is famous for strikes and demonstrations."

Mike's mobile beeped. "Yes, I hear you," he said into the phone. "I'll tell Isaac the news."

Mike turned around and looked at Isaac.

"Isaac, that was Frederick. The plane carrying the prince and all the terrorists crashed off the coast of Libya. They believe that there are no survivors. The British navy has some ships in the area and is trying to retrieve anything that might give them information on what happened."

Chava was now awake and heard Mike's report and looked at Isaac. She took his hand and asked in a low voice, "Are you responsible for this?"

"Chava, let's not discuss it now."

"Isaac, I trust you know what you're doing."

"The Torah Sages tell us, 'Where there are no men, be a man.' Today I had to be that man. Please understand. I did what I felt the situation *required*."

"I understand, Isaac. That's what I love about you. You're never afraid to do what needs to be done. But I couldn't live if anything happened to you."

"I love you too, and nothing is going to happen to either one of us."

Isaac and Chava sat holding hands and looking out their window until the car arrived at their building. Mike jumped out and opened the door. He extended his hand to help Chava. "I see you already have security at the front door," he said.

The doorman approached. "Welcome home, Mrs. Green."

"Thank you, it's good to be here. How is your family?"

"Fine, thank you for asking."

Mike smiled at Isaac. "It's been an interesting day."

"I'll give you that. I hope you get some rest tonight, Mike."

"I intend to. I've arranged with the GIGN to assign you a security detail until you leave Paris. They'll be right outside your door twenty-four/seven."

"God bless you, Mike. I'll see you in the morning."

"Right. Eleven a.m."

"No, be here by eight. And tell Frederick to come too. We have to discuss the other thing." Mike nodded. "Fine, have a good night."

Isaac walked into the house.

Mike walked toward his car. He turned on the radio. More updates about the plane that had crashed off the coast of Libya. After a minute he turned it off. *I bet by tomorrow there will already be a new top story.*

CHAPTER
45

Wednesday, June 4, 2014
Green home, Paris

CHAVA WAS UNPACKING in the bedroom.

Isaac walked in. "Are you alright?"

"I really don't know how I am right now."

"What is it?"

"Physically I'm fine, but emotionally I'm drained."

"Chava, forget the unpacking for a moment. Come sit down with me and let me make you a cup of tea."

"What about you? Did you eat anything today?"

"I was sort of busy."

Chava feigned a smile. "Sit down and I'll make you something."

"No, I just want a cup of tea."

Isaac followed Chava into the kitchen. She took out the tea pot and filled it with water. As she turned on the gas burner for the water to boil, Isaac stood up and put his arms around Chava. She leaned back, resting her head on his shoulders, and started to cry. Isaac held her close to his body, feeling every sob. His eyes filled with tears as he tried to hold back his own emotions. He knew he'd caused her pain.

"Chava, everything is fine now. Everyone's okay."

Chava composed herself and sat down as Isaac handed her some tissues. He sat next to her, waiting for her to say something.

"Forgive me for what I'm about to say, Isaac, but we've always been honest with each other and I'm not going to stop now. Today changed me. My eyes are open now. I know how you feel about Brahim and the trust you have in him, what the three of you have gone through together. Everyone admires you. I'm not talking about your business, but about your commitment to work together, who all of you are and where you come from. And I know what you're thinking—that a Catholic, a Muslim, and a Jew can help bring peace and brotherhood to the world.

"But I'm telling you now, Isaac, it has to stop." Isaac opened his mouth to say something, but Chava held up a hand to stop him. "Before you answer me, look around you. The fanatical Muslims are looking to kill all of our people. In Israel, years of bloodshed, buses, cafes, and hotels being attacked. Innocent people killed because they're Jews. It's not only Israel, it's everywhere. People are afraid to get on planes. You can't move freely anywhere."

"Chava—"

"Please let me finish. We are both still young enough to enjoy our children and grandchildren. I want us to spend more time with them. Brahim is a good person, but if Abra has her way, he'll also be caught up in the fever of Islam. His wife and children will bend his will and make him follow the mullahs' doctrine. I know you love him. I do too. But things need to change."

"Chava, what are you saying?"

Chava reached over and put a hand on Isaac's. "You can be friends with Brahim and Jim for the rest of your life, but I want you to sell your interest in World."

Isaac was overcome with surprise. Chava had never breathed a word about wanting him to slow down, let alone sell his part in the business. Isaac took both of her hands into his and exhaled slowly.

"Isaac, say something."

"I'm surprised, Chava. I had no idea this is how you felt. Or maybe you didn't feel like this until today. We both know a day can make all of the difference in a life. Right now I can only tell you that I love you and I'll give it serious thought. I want you to be happy, and what you say has a lot of truth to it. "

"That's not a good enough answer."

"About Brahim, I don't agree."

"Why do you say that?"

"Brahim is a strong man. I don't believe he'll be caught in the fever of fanatical Islam. We'll get Abra back. She's just let her mind run a little too wild. She'll tire of this quickly. And if not, we'll find a way to make her see the error in her newfound ways."

The teakettle started to whistle, signaling the end of the conversation.

"Chava, why don't you get some sleep?"

Chava sighed. "Sounds like a good idea."

Isaac asked, "Would you like to visit some museums tomorrow?"

Chava was surprised. Isaac had never offered to go to museums with her before. *Maybe he's seriously considering what I just asked him about.*

Chava smiled. "Maybe. Right now I'm going to take a bath and then read in bed for a while. I need to try and relax."

"Fine, you go ahead. I'm going to check my e-mails at my desk in the living room. And I want to check the news."

"Please finish your e-mails soon and come to bed."

"I'll make myself a drink, check the news, and then be right in."

At midnight, the news on the international news channel France 24 was in English. A panel of reporters were discussing the plane crash as reactions from around the world poured in. One reporter noted that Al-Qaeda was claiming that the British and French, in collaboration with Israel, were responsible for the plane crash and that they would pay for this.

Isaac finished his drink and turned off the TV. When he entered the bedroom, Chava was already sleeping. He sat on the edge of the bed for a moment and then lay down. Eyes wide open, he thought about Brahim.

Is he heading into a bad situation?

He looked at his watch, forgetting for a moment that it was broken, then looked at the clock on his night table. It was one a.m. With his head on the pillow, he looked over at Chava. He watched her sleeping, marveling, as always, at how she could lay in one place the whole night. Isaac hadn't had a quiet night's sleep since 'Nam. Exhausted, he closed his eyes and in a minute was fast asleep.

HE AWOKE WHAT felt like a short time later to a soft buzzing. He reached for the clock. It read six a.m. But the noise wasn't coming from the alarm. After a moment he realized someone was at the door.

Isaac jumped out of bed and closed the door to the bedroom before he went to the front door. The surveillance camera showed Mike standing with two security guards. He quickly opened the door.

"What's wrong?"

"Two hours ago Muslims started rioting in cities across France, mainly in the outskirts. Several people have been killed. The president of France is calling for a state of emergency."

"Please come in."

Mike turned to the men who were with him and told them to wait outside.

"Did you get any sleep?" Isaac asked as Mike entered the apartment.

"About three hours. I've been on and off the phone with Frederick. He's been in touch with 10 Downing Street. The prime minister has been getting calls from the White House. They want to know if the British had a hand in the plane crash."

"What did he tell them?"

"Nothing."

"Was there anything else?"

"Yes, the prime minister wanted to talk to you as soon as you were awake. Frederick said he would get the message to you."

"Okay, let me get dressed. Help yourself to some coffee."

Isaac walked back into his bedroom. Chava was still asleep in the same position. He looked at the clock on the night table. Six thirty a.m. Quietly he finished getting dressed and came back into the living room. Mike sat on the couch, one hand on the phone and the other holding a coffee mug.

Isaac walked into the kitchen and turned on the espresso machine. He stood waiting until the coffee dripped down into the special cup he had purchased at Harrods department store in London. He remembered Chava insisting he buy a pair of them. *Look, Isaac. They're made out of bone china. There are only six of this kind in the world.*

Mike walked in. "The call was from Washington. The director of the National Security Council wants a full report on his desk in twenty-four hours. He said the president plans to hold a meeting with all the security agencies. Afterward the president is going to make an announcement on TV."

"Have Frederick come over right away. When I talk to the prime minister, I want him to hear exactly what I have to say."

"Good idea, I'll call him."

By now the clock read seven a.m. Isaac walked into the living room and picked up the remote for the TV. He turned to the Al Jazeera channel. He wanted to see the Arab world's reaction to the plane crash.

During President Bush's term in office, one of Isaac's friends in the Defense Department told him that the president wanted to bomb the Arab-owned TV station. Bush claimed that they were flaming the fires during the Iraqi war. The problem was that Qatar was one of its key allies in the Gulf States, so the idea was shelved. As he sat down on the sofa with his cup of espresso, the TV showed pictures of the prince and the terrorists.

Mike joined him and Isaac turned off the TV. "They'll be running the same pictures all day."

"Frederick will be here in thirty minutes."

"Are we the only ones who knew about unloading the fuel off the plane?"

Mike looked curiously at Isaac. "Of course. Why?"

"It's going to get rough around here. What about the fuel truck driver?"

"He was told that due to the weight of the cargo and all the passengers, we had to lighten the load. I don't think he's a problem."

"Did Paul-Henri or Jacques get wind of what was going down?"

"No, I'm sure they would have said something if they had."

Isaac's phone rang. It was Charlie.

"Charlie, how're you doing? You make it to the hotel okay?"

"Fine, what about you?"

"Great, I'm sitting here with Mike. Where's Guy?"

"He's still in his room. We planned to meet for breakfast in the dining room at around eight. What do you need?"

"See if you can round up Allan, Kim Li, Hui Ying, and Guy. Have them all here by eleven if possible. Dov will be here too."

"You got it. "

"Did you speak to your wife and kids?"

"Yes, a couple of times from the plane."

"Is everything alright?"

"Fine, the kids just want to know when I'm coming home with their presents."

Isaac laughed. "See you soon."

Mike served himself another cup of coffee. "Isaac, can I fix you a refill?

"No thanks. I'm just going to check on Chava."

Isaac walked into the bedroom and saw Chava still fast asleep. *I've caused her so much trouble over the years. Always away on business trips while she took care of everything at home. Shuttling the kids here and there all the nights when the children were ill or needed something and I wasn't home. She never asked for anything. Never complained, not a word. How can I deny her the first thing she's asked of me in thirty-eight years, even if it means leaving World?*

Quietly he left the room, questions unanswered.

Mike sat drinking his coffee in front of the TV. "Come see this."

The French news channel showed a live demonstration in Vénissieux. Thousands of women marching in burkas filled the streets, their faces covered, only their eyes visible in defiance of the French law they were breaking. They carried signs: "We want Justice!" "Who killed the Prince?" Many yelled, "Down with the U.S.!" and burning Israeli and American flags.

Mike looked at Isaac intermittently as they watched the police fire tear gas at the rioters. "This is only the beginning," he said to Isaac.

Live from Paris, a reporter was standing on the steps of the Hall of Justice with Jacques, surrounded by gendarmes and the military police. The TV camera focused on his face in a close-up. Radio and news reporters waited for him to speak. He stepped forward.

"The French government will not allow people to flagrantly break the law. Only a few minutes before I was to speak, I received a report that three policemen were killed and several wounded in shootings in Lyon. The report said the policemen were dispersing men and women who were throwing rocks and burning automobiles. A curfew has been put on the city. The president will be making a speech later today to the Parliament at the Palace of Versailles. We're asking the public to remain calm and continue being law-abiding citizens."

As Jacques ended his comments, a large explosion went off. It seemed to come from around the corner. Everyone ran for cover.

CHAPTER
46

Thursday, June 5, 2014
Green home, Paris

ISAAC AND MIKE watched with disbelief as a gendarme grabbed Jacques and rushed into the Palais de Justice. Pandemonium filled the streets. In a matter of minutes, the live TV coverage shut off, and the TV commentator announced, "We have lost contact temporarily. Please stand by." The French national anthem took over the sound coming from the screen.

Isaac heard a knock on the door. He saw Frederick through the monitor and let him in.

"I just heard the news in my car," said Frederick when he entered the room.

The commentator on the TV announced that a second bomb had just gone off at the Palais de Justice. The gates had been blown up, and there were bodies lying in the street.

Mike looked at Isaac and Frederick. "We'd better get our answers ready about what went on in the airport and the subsequent plane crash."

"I've got my answer," said Frederick. "I have no idea what caused the plane to go down, and until they recover the black box I can't possibly speculate. As for the hostage situation, I think it's better if you and Isaac handle that. This way we minimize the information and any possibility of conflicting statements."

"I agree," Isaac said.

"I bet the president is going to demand a special investigative team due to his relationship with the Saudi king," Mike offered. "As soon as we're done, I'll check with Washington and see what's in the works."

"Frederick, can you try to contact the prime minister?" Isaac asked. "I want to talk to him before Charlie and the others arrive."

"Give me a few minutes. I'll try to reach him on his secure line."

Isaac flipped channels. On CNN, the news anchor informed his listeners that the prime minister of Israel had arrived in New York City before going on to Washington for a visit with the president.

"The British prime minister is coming to the telephone in a minute," said Frederick. "Here, take it." He handed his phone to Isaac. Another news alert ran across the screen: *"The British Navy has recovered the black box from the plane crash and will be sending it to London."*

Wonder what that will reveal, thought Isaac. At that moment, a voice came on the line.

"Hello, Isaac, this is the prime minister. How are you?"

"Fine, thank you, Mr. Prime Minister. Frederick told me that you wanted to speak to me."

"Isaac, I'm getting calls from all over the Arab world and from the president of the U.S. They want to know what happened on that plane. The Arab world is boiling. They're worried that their people are going to start attacking our embassies. I need to give them some information, something to satisfy them."

"Mr. Prime Minister, do you mind if I put the phone on speaker? I'm here with Frederick and Mike from the NSA."

"Yes, go ahead."

Isaac pressed the speaker button.

"Mr. Prime Minister, I have reliable information that the prince was the one who planned the hostage crisis so he could free his nephew. He arrived in Paris a few days early to control the operation. They planned to go to Libya and fund other terrorist operations with the ransom money."

"If that's the case, the king of Saudi Arabia is going to want proof. Isaac, I need to know how that plane crashed."

Isaac looked at Mike and Frederick. "The truth is, it ran out of fuel. That's it."

"I see." The prime minister paused, then said, "Listen, Isaac, even if you say you have proof that the prince was colluding with the terrorists, they'll say we fabricated it."

"Sir, when they examine the black box in London, you should insist that the ambassador from Saudi Arabia be in the laboratory."

"How can you be so sure that this is what happened?"

"Sir, trust me. The last time we spoke I promised you I would return al-Mousavi to you dead or alive."

"Yes, you did."

"I always will keep my word, sir."

Another pause. "I see," the prime minister said again. "Well, I'd better go. I have to figure out what I'm going to say to the Saudi king. Please give my best regards to your wife." The prime minister hung up.

Frederick looked at Mike, then Isaac. "That's telling it the way it is."

"Well, I'm sure that the prime minister is going to have a lot to think about," Mike added.

Isaac nodded in agreement. "We all have a lot to think about."

Chava walked through the bedroom door. "Good morning, everyone."

Isaac stood up to give his wife a peck on the cheek. "Did you sleep well?"

"I slept fine. I was reading and then I just closed my eyes for a moment and fell asleep."

"I hope we didn't disturb you," Mike said.

"You didn't disturb me at all, Mike."

"Chava, did Isaac ask you to join us today for a visit to some museums and perhaps dinner?" Frederick asked.

She looked at Isaac before she responded, "Yes, he did. I knew he didn't come up with that one on his own."

Isaac smiled. "Chava, this is Frederick from the British prime minister's office. I don't believe you've officially met."

"A pleasure to meet you, Frederick." She looked at Isaac. "So what do you have in mind for today?"

"We should be done by two p.m. with our meetings. That will give us plenty of time for the museum. We'll decide on dinner later."

"Can I make anyone breakfast?"

"I'm hungry," Isaac answered. "What about you guys?"

Mike nodded. "Thanks, that would be great."

"Give me a few minutes and I'll call you when it's ready." Chava went into the kitchen.

Mike's phone buzzed. "Isaac, I just received an SMS from the director."

"What did he say?"

"After he meets with the Israeli prime minister, the president is going to Saudi Arabia to pay his respects to the king for the loss of the prince and his nephew."

"Excuse me," Isaac said, "I just remembered I have to make a call." He disappeared into his office.

He dialed a number that would connect him directly to General Solomon. Isaac was one of a dozen people who had this number, and the phone he used had been operational for less than a year. It was a burner phone programmed to filter out anyone listening in on the conversation.

The phone rang and a recorded voice asked Isaac, "Please identify yourself."

Isaac pressed a six-digit number, and the voice said, "Please confirm your voice password."

Isaac said, "Green."

"Thank you, please wait."

A moment later, General Solomon was on the line with Isaac. "Hello, Isaac, how are you?"

"I'm fine. General, let me get to the point. I'm concerned about a situation that I think the prime minister should be aware of before he meets with the president."

"What is it?"

"The president is planning to meet with the king of Saudi Arabia."

"Yes, we're aware of that meeting."

"I'm sure you are, but I have information you're not aware of. There's a good chance he's going to make final plans to break off the security arrangements with Israel. He's going to declare that Jerusalem is the capital of Palestine, and the Israelis must return to the 1967 borders or the United States will break off diplomatic relations with them."

"When are you coming to Israel?"

"I was planning to be there for the Sabbath."

"We may be at war by then."

"It's that close?"

"Our people in Iran informed us that they're moving very fast on preparations for war since the prince's plane went down. We have also intercepted a coded message from Syria to the Ayatollah saying that Hezbollah is ready to start the war on his orders."

"It makes sense. The president's trip to pay his condolences is a smoke screen. He wants to be there when the war starts so he can force Israel to capitulate. He'll say that he's trying to make peace between the Arabs and Israel. When Israel refuses to give up Jerusalem, I believe he'll break off diplomatic relations and declare the Palestinian State.

"General, can you reach the prime minister? I want you to tell him what I just told you before he meets with the president."

"I'll get in touch with him right away and call you back. Do you have a secure line?"

"My PDA is secure. You have the number. I have to go. I think my wife has started serving breakfast, and she gets upset if I don't eat the eggs when they're hot."

"I'll be in touch."

Isaac walked out of the office. Chava stood by the door waiting for him. "Isaac, let me know when you're ready."

"Everyone else will be here shortly. Let's wait till they get here. We'll all eat together."

"What's going on?" Mike asked.

"I was just on the phone with my contact in Israel."

"Isaac," Chava said knowingly, "if you want to discuss something confidential, I'll leave."

"No, please stay."

CHAPTER
47

I'VE JUST SPOKEN to General Solomon," Isaac added. "He believes that war is imminent. It's quiet, but not for long."

"What are you going to do?" Frederick asked.

Isaac looked at Chava. The answer was already on her face.

"Chava and I are going to be with our family in Jerusalem."

"And my staff and I will be going with you," said Mike.

"I think it's best I head back to London," Frederick said. "There's a meeting scheduled with the prime minister regarding security on the Internet and I have to be there."

"We're having our own problems with hackers," Mike added. At that moment his phone rang. He picked it up. "Hello. Okay, let them through."

Mike turned to Isaac. "Everyone has arrived."

Chava got up and excused herself to set the table. The door opened. Charlie, Kim Li, and Hui Ying walked in first, followed by Allan and Guy. Charlie walked up to Isaac, grabbed his hand, and shook it with a big smile.

"You're looking great, Isaac. I see you must have gotten some sleep."

"A few hours." Isaac turned to Frederick and Mike. "Let me

introduce you. This is Kim Li and Hui Ying."

"Nice to meet you," Frederick said with a smile. "We're all glad you made it out of China and Hong Kong safely. You are both very brave."

"And this is Allan Peters and Guy Warren."

Allan went over to shake hands with Isaac. Guy was busy staring at the art hanging on the walls.

"You like Chagall?" Frederick asked him.

"His work is amazing."

Hui Ying extended his hand to Isaac. "Thank you for all of your help, Mr. Green."

"My pleasure. Everyone, please take a seat."

"Isaac, excuse me I have to go," Frederick said. "I'll keep in touch." He stood up and shook everyone's hands.

Mike said, "I'll go see if Chava needs any help."

"I'll come with you," said Allan.

Allan and Mike walked into the kitchen. "Chava, what can we do?" Mike asked.

"Why don't you pour some coffee and make up a tray for everyone? I'm going to go set us up in the dining room. The kitchen is too small for all of us." She gathered up some cutlery and plates and left the kitchen.

Mike placed mugs on a tray and started pouring coffee from the espresso machine. "So what is it you wanted to tell me, Allan?"

"Bad news. Kim Li's sister has been killed. One of my people contacted me and informed me about it after we flew out of Hong Kong. They say she was taken from her office at the airport. According to our information, the order was given by Wen Tian."

"Who's going to tell Kim Li?"

"I don't know. Maybe it's best if she hears it from Isaac. He has a way with people."

"Good idea." Mike placed sugar and milk on the tray. He picked it up and they exited the kitchen. When they entered the room, Dov had arrived and Isaac was on the phone with Brahim. Everyone sat watching Isaac as he paced back and forth.

Allan whispered in Mike's ear, "I have a feeling this is not the right time to bring up Kim Li's sister."

Mike set the tray down on the coffee table. "I agree."

Isaac hung up. "Brahim's wife is missing. The Saudi intelligence agency has put out a special alert throughout the Middle East. They've contacted Interpol and, believe it or not, are asking Israel for help."

"What happened to her?" Dov asked.

"Nobody knows. When Brahim got to Saudi Arabia, she'd already disappeared."

Charlie spooned some sugar into one of the coffee mugs. "What about Fatima? They were together, weren't they? She must have some information."

"Only that they were both at the Ka'bah shrine in Mecca, and they got separated. Fatima searched for her sister for hours and then called the police and reported her missing."

"How long ago was that?" Allan asked, looking at his watch.

"I don't know. I'll check back with Brahim in a few minutes."

"I'm gonna make some calls," said Allan. "We have people on the ground there."

Kim Li and Hui Ying sat listening silently.

"Sorry about all this," Charlie said to them. "We're dealing with a situation in Saudi Arabia."

"That's all right," Kim Li said. "We are just glad to be here."

Isaac turned his attention to his guests. "So tell me, from what you've deciphered, what do you think the Chinese are planning to do with the dollar?"

Kim Li looked at Hui Ying before answering, "According to the information Hui Ying has gathered, when the Chinese conclude a secret arrangement with the Russians on a proposed new currency basket, they will create a major incident with Taiwan."

"Any idea what that incident's going to be?" Isaac asked.

"We believe they'll send in their navy, set up a blockade, and threaten anyone who tries to break through it. They anticipate that the United States will intervene, and that is when they will crash the dollar."

Allan had returned from making his calls just as Kim Li was speaking. "That could trigger a war," he remarked.

Kim Li nodded. "They are ready. But they don't believe the U.S. will go to war over Taiwan."

"That's an awfully big bet," said Mike.

Charlie nodded in agreement. "You're right. But they have other ways to bring down the dollar. We all know the Chinese are big gamblers, and right now they're holding a very strong hand: a trillion dollars or more in U.S. Treasury bonds that they could decide to cash in at any time. They could bankrupt America in a snap. Today they are the second largest economy in the world. Now they want to become number one."

CHAPTER
48

ISAAC'S PDA RANG.

"Yes, Susan, what is it?" It was about 6 a.m. in New York.

"I just received a call from Jim. His brother was in a prison fight. He killed another prisoner."

"Which brother?"

"John Jr."

"Listen, Susan, I have Guy here with me. Give me ten minutes. I'll call you back. Set up a conference call with Jim. In the meantime, I'll talk to Guy."

"I'm waiting for your call."

Isaac hung up and turned to Guy. "Guy, would you please come into my office?"

"What happened?" Guy asked when they were alone.

"Jim's brother John Jr. killed a prisoner in a jail fight."

"Guess I'm on my way to Chicago."

"I was hoping we'd have more time to discuss Jim's situation face-to-face, but you need to get over there immediately. I'll ask Charlie to arrange a flight right away."

Guy gave Isaac a nod. "Thanks, Isaac."

Isaac was silent.

Guy stood up to leave. "Well, if that's all—"

"Wait a minute, Guy. There's something else."

"What is it?"

"Look, Jim is like a brother to me and I know him that well. I'm afraid he's going to do something rash. You have to convince him that he'll do more harm than good if he gets involved in his brothers' case."

"I hear your concern, but it's not going to be easy. You know how Jim is about his family."

"I know. If Jim's mother dies from all this aggravation, he'll go crazy."

"Don't worry, I'll handle Jim."

A knock at the door signaled the conversation's end.

"What is it?" Isaac called out.

Charlie opened the door and ducked his head in. "You left your PDA in the other room. General Solomon called. He said it's urgent."

"Charlie, Guy has to fly to Chicago right away. Please get him a private plane, arrange everything he needs. Call Susan and tell her that Guy will be in touch." He turned back to Guy. "Excuse me, Guy, I have to deal with this. Charlie will take care of you."

"What about Kim Li and Hui Ying?" Charlie asked.

"Tell them I'll be with them in a minute."

Guy turned toward the door. "I'd better get going. I'll keep you posted."

"If you need anything, just call me or Susan."

Once Guy and Charlie had left, Isaac locked the door and started to dial General Solomon. Isaac heard a knock on the door, and put the call on hold. When he opened the door, Chava stood in the threshold. She looked shaken.

"Someone attempted to blow up the Knesset," she said. "I just saw it on TV." She was trembling and her face was pale. "They don't have an exact number yet, but they're saying a lot of people lost their lives."

Isaac put a hand on her back and gently guided her to a chair.

"Chava, sit down. Let me get you some water."

"I'll be alright. I'll just sit here for a moment."

"Is everyone in the family okay?"

"Yes, thank God, but it's so terrible. All those innocent people killed."

"Look, Chava, I'm sorry. I really have to make a call. Please, wait just a minute."

Isaac released the hold button, and after a minute the general came on the line.

"Hello, Isaac."

"Chava just told me that a bomb went off in the Knesset. What's the situation?"

"So far about twenty-five Japanese tourists killed and dozens wounded."

"How many Israelis?"

"We're not sure, but we have an early count of six."

"How did they get in with a bomb?"

"We think it was planted with a timing device in one of the backpacks of a Japanese tourist. They were standing in line at the gate about to go through security when it went off."

There was a short pause, then the general said, "Isaac, you alone?"

"No, Chava is with me."

"The prime minister asked to speak to you privately."

Isaac walked over to Chava and took hold of her hands. They felt cold. "Chava, I need to finish this phone call in private. Will you be alright?"

"I'm just tired of the senseless killings. When will it end?"

Isaac put his arms around her and held her close. Chava clung to him. He had never seen her like this. For the first time in their marriage, he felt she was on the edge of breaking down. They had been through a lot together, but the events of the last few days had shaken her to the core. He kissed her, trying to calm her.

"Chava, things are going to change, I promise you."

"I love you, Isaac."

"I love you, Chava, with all of my heart."

Chava gave Isaac a kiss and left.

Isaac picked up the phone. "General, are you still there?"

"Yes, I'm going to patch the call into the prime minister's private number. Hold for a minute until I secure the line." A minute of silence passed before the general's voice came back on the line. "Mr. Prime Minister, this is General Solomon. I have Isaac Green on the line. All is secured. Please go ahead."

"Isaac, how have you been?" the Israeli prime minister greeted him. The prime minister was still in New York. Isaac glanced at his desk clock. It was about 6 a.m. over there.

"Could be better. I just heard the news about the bombing."

"Yes, I just got off the phone with our people. Hamas was behind it. The Japanese were duped by a travel agent who was acting as their tour guide. When they got in line, he detonated the bomb with the SIM card in his phone. Two off-duty policemen noticed him running away. He's being held by the Shin Bet in the Russian Compound in Jerusalem and being interrogated as we speak."

"That's good. Mr. Prime Minister, you wanted to speak to me?"

"Yes Isaac. We have information that your partner Brahim's wife, Abra, is in Iran."

"Is she alright? What happened?"

"As far as we can tell, she's fine."

"Do you have any idea how she got to Iran?"

"Our people on the ground have information that she left Mecca with four men and then was flown to Beirut. She spent several hours in the Hezbollah headquarters before they flew her to Tehran."

"What do you mean, she left with four men? Was she their prisoner or was it by free choice?"

"We're not sure. We have all our people in Iran working on figuring out where she's being held and what's going on."

"What about Brahim? What should I tell him?"

"For now just say that she's alive and uninjured and that we're working on getting him more details. I understood that you and he were going to be in Israel together. When are you planning to come?"

"My wife and I are planning to leave first thing tomorrow morning."

"Tell Brahim I said he should come too. We should have more information by the time you're all here."

"Mike O'Shea from NSA and his people are coming with me."

"Fine. General, get a list of everyone who will be with Isaac and have them cleared to land at Hatzerim Air Force Base."

"Yes, sir."

"Isaac, I have to go and prepare some notes for my meeting with the American president."

"Sir, all I can say is be careful with the information you share with him."

"What do you mean?"

"He's no friend of Israel."

"We're aware of that."

"Are you aware that he's going to break off diplomatic relations with Israel when he's in Saudi Arabia?"

"Are you sure?"

"Yes, at some time during the imminent war, he will turn on Israel."

"Where did you get this information?"

"Sir, please trust me. This information is from one of the highest sources inside the president's administration. I would never say something like this if I didn't know it to be true."

"Thank you, Isaac. Stay in touch with General Solomon. I have to go. *Shalom*."

"Isaac," said the general, "stay on the line. I want to talk to you about your flight information. It's very important to contact Brahim right away and tell him to be in constant contact with you. I need to know the soonest he can fly to meet us in Israel."

CHAPTER
49

ISAAC DIALED SUSAN the minute he finished the call with the general.

"Hi, Isaac, are you ready to talk to Jim?"

"Put him on."

"Hold for a moment. I'll connect you."

Jim came on the line a moment later. "Isaac, are you on the line?"

"Jim, what's going on?"

"They have John Jr. in solitary confinement. They say it's to protect him from the other inmates."

"Guy is leaving Paris in the next hour. He'll be in Chicago by the morning."

"That's good. I wanted to speak to John Jr., but they're saying he can only speak to his attorney."

"What about William?"

"The same. I feel useless."

"And your mother?"

"I just got off the phone. She still hasn't heard the news. She keeps asking about John Jr. and William. She's worried that they haven't been in touch."

"Jim, listen to me. Call your wife and have her go and stay with your mother. Distract her. Take her to a movie. You'll feel better."

"That's a good idea. I'll call her as soon as I hang up. Now tell me, what's really happening over there?"

"The news from Israel isn't good. Chava is nervous."

"I've been listening to the news. What do you think is going to happen?"

"All the indicators show we'll be at war before the month is up. By the way, I've just heard that Abra is in Iran."

"What happened? Was she kidnapped?"

"We're not sure. I'll keep you informed as soon as I know more. Take care of yourself."

Isaac hung up the phone and walked back into the living room. It was empty. Everyone had gone into the dining room to eat what had turned into an early lunch.

Charlie looked up from his plate of eggs when Isaac walked in. "Is everything okay, Isaac?"

"Yes, Charlie." Isaac sat down and filled a plate with food. He took a few bites before he spoke. "Let's get back to what Kim Li told us just before I left the room. How did Hui Ying come by this information?"

Hui Ying spoke up for the first time. "I had been in the office of the director of currency on other business," he said. "When the director stepped out to go to the washroom, I noticed a memo on his desk marked confidential. I read it as quickly as I could. It disclosed the plan to take down the U.S. dollar."

"What were you doing in the director's office in the first place?" Isaac asked.

"He had called me in. When the director came back, he said that I was going to be the head of a new department, and then proceeded to hand me the confidential memo. I acted surprised and read it very slowly. After a few minutes, he gave me a list of people who were cleared to see this information."

Hui Ying stopped talking.

"Is there anything else?" Isaac asked.

"No, nothing else. I just left."

Isaac raised an eyebrow. "That's all? No further conversations or instructions from the director?"

"That's all."

He's hiding something, Isaac thought.

He turned to Charlie. "Contact Jacques and Paul-Henri and ask them to arrange for us to be cleared for takeoff to Israel in the morning. Mike, can your people be ready?"

"No problem. We have two planes ready to go if we need them. Who's going?"

"Everyone present."

"I think it's better if we use both planes," Mike suggested. "What do you think?"

"I agree."

"You, your wife, Dov, and myself, plus a couple of my people will be on the first plane. Allan and Charlie will be on the second plane, with the rest of my staff, along with Kim Li and Hui Ying."

Everyone shook their heads in agreement.

Dov looked at Isaac. "I would like to bring my wife if it's okay with you?"

"I wouldn't mind spending some time with Sara," Chava said.

"Fine," said Isaac. "Are there any other items?"

"As soon as you're ready," Mike said, "I'll have my people take all of you back to your hotel."

Dov stood up. "I'll call my wife and tell her to start packing. I have to go. I need to pick up some stuff from my office for the Israeli press."

The others stood up to leave too. Allan touched Isaac's arm.

"We have to talk privately."

"Fine, let me just tell Chava I'll be a few more minutes. We have plans for the afternoon." He left the room.

Allan went over to the rolling bar and selected a bottle of Macallan. He poured himself a drink and sat down, thinking about Kim Li's sister. He wondered how Isaac might break the news to Kim Li.

As he sipped his drink, his cell phone rang. It was a call from Hong Kong. He didn't recognize the number.

"Hello, who is this?"

"Allan, it's Lee. Can you hear me?"

"Yes."

"I have some terrible news. Robert was murdered. He'd just left our law offices. He was sitting in his car."

"Where you are now?"

"I'm driving to the U.S. Consulate."

"Stop and listen to me," Allan said. "Don't go near there. If it was the secret police, that's the first place they'll expect you to go. Go to the Park Hotel in Kowloon. At the cashier's desk, ask them to ring suite 1818. The call will be forwarded to me by SMS. I'll tell them to let my guest in. It's a safe house. Stay there until we find out what's going on. Get rid of your mobile and don't make contact with anyone from the hotel. If you need to reach me, dial A1818 from the suite and I'll get back to you as soon as I can."

"Okay, I'll be in touch." Lee hung up.

Isaac walked in to see Allan with a glass in his hand. "I think I'll join you."

"Good, I could use someone to drink with right now. I do enjoy Macallan."

"Good choice." Isaac picked up the bottle and said, "I received this as gift from a hotel casino in Atlantic City. I'd been winning big that night, and I think they gave me this bottle just to get me to go up to my suite and drink it before I took all of their money. If I tell you how much it cost, you won't believe it."

"Tell me."

"Seriously, you won't believe it. Thirty-eight thousand dollars."

"Are you kidding?"

"Would I make that up? There aren't many bottles of Macallan

1926 around." Isaac sat down and lifted his glass. "To life."

Allan looked at his half-full glass, then looked down toward the table.

"Allan, what's wrong?"

Allan put down his glass. "I received some bad news earlier today, and more on a phone call I got just now when you were out of the room."

"What's going on?"

"I just got off the phone with Lee. I am sorry to tell you this, but Robert was murdered."

In shock, Isaac sat down and took a sip of his drink. "What happened?"

"We're not sure. He was sitting in his car in front of the law office."

"Where's Lee now?"

"I sent him to one of our safe houses."

Isaac sat looking at the glass of Macallan he was no longer interested in finishing.

"There's more. Kim Li's sister Daiyu was taken from the airport by Wen Tian's people for questioning. Twenty-four hours later she was found dead. The authorities just released a statement saying that she committed suicide. We both know it wasn't a suicide. We have to tell Kim Li."

Isaac nodded grimly. "Wait until we get to Israel. Once she feels safe and things calm down a little, I'll tell her."

"What about Lee?"

"I think we should get Lee out of there right away. Let's bring Mike in on that."

Chava walked into the room. "Isaac, I just spoke to our son Mordechai. The country is on high alert, and they're asking everyone to check their gas masks. He thought maybe we should delay our trip."

"What do you say?"

"What do you think I'm gonna say?"

Isaac smiled. "Do you need help packing?"

Mike walked in and handed Isaac a folded note. Allan poured another drink for himself. "Mike, you want one?"

"Thanks, I could use it."

Allan stared at Isaac as he read the note. More bad news, he was sure of it. Isaac read the note out loud. "It's from Frederick. The British prime minister was rushed to the hospital thirty minutes ago. It appears he's had a massive heart attack."

CHAPTER
50

Friday, June 6, 2014
Green home, Paris

MIKE WAS WAITING at the front door at 7 a.m. "Are we ready to go?"

Isaac nodded. "I'll get Chava."

Isaac walked into the bedroom where Chava was sitting on the bed talking on the phone. He sat down next to her as she hung up. He put his arms around her.

"I love you. Let's go home."

Isaac and Chava grabbed their luggage and walked out of the house.

Isaac looked around. There were more security guards than there had been the night before. Mike noticed the expression on Isaac's face. He leaned over and whispered, "Nothing to be concerned about. I just wanted to make sure you and Chava arrive in Israel safely."

One of the security personnel opened the door to the SUV. Chava entered and Isaac followed. Mike jumped in the front seat and signaled the driver to go. Isaac held Chava's hands while they sat in silence. Isaac's eyes started to close when his PDA rang. It was Frederick.

"Frederick, are you alright?"

"We're all concerned about the prime minister."

"As are we. How is he?" asked Isaac. "Hang on a minute, Isaac. I've got to take this call."

Isaac looked at Chava. Her eyes were closed. *This is a time in our lives when we should be enjoying ourselves. But the whole world seems to be knocking at our door looking for help. How can I not answer?*

Frederick came back on the line. "Isaac, you're not going to believe this. I just received word. The prime minister is dead."

"What! It can't be."

"Listen, I have to go," said Frederick. He disconnected.

Something's wrong. Too many horrible events one after another. There has got to be a connection. Isaac opened his PDA and dialed Frederick back. After several rings and no answer, he sent a text message:

Urgent. Please call me.

Isaac's PDA rang. Isaac answered it, hoping it was Frederick.

It was Susan.

"Brahim left a short while ago from Saudi Arabia. He's on his way to meet you in Israel. He's with Sammi and one of the special agents."

"Did he say anything about Abra?" Isaac asked.

"Nothing, but he sounded awful."

"Call my family and tell them we're on our way to Israel."

"Are we still on schedule for Canada?"

"Yes, why do you ask?"

"It's just that you're involved in so many situations right now that require your full attention. I assumed Canada would be put on hold."

"Don't worry, I can handle all that. Listen, we're driving up to the planes right now. I'll talk to you from Israel."

The SUV stopped at the side of the plane. Mike jumped out and opened the door.

Chava looked at Isaac. "We're finally going home."

She walked up the stairs onto the plane and sat down. Isaac decided to stand with Mike, watching everybody board the planes.

"How do you handle all this pressure?"

Isaac looked at him, and then with a big smile said, "What pressure?"

They both started to laugh, then walked up the stairs onto the plane.

CHAPTER
51

Friday, June 6, 2014
Phoenicia InterContinental Hotel, Beirut

MOHAMMED ZAEEM STOOD out on the balcony of his suite wearing only pajama bottoms. At six thirty a.m. it was already hot and humid. In one hand he held a cigarette and in the other a cell phone pressed against his ear. He looked out at the harbor. *How calm the sea is today.* Ships with flags from all over the world anchored, waiting to unload their cargo. They'd stand idle for months; the port couldn't handle all the goods the Arab world was buying. The ships came anyway, praying for a miracle that they would get unloaded.

Mohammed's cousin Hussein Zaeem walked out onto the balcony. "We have word it's on." He held up a text:

> A chameleon does not leave one tree until he is
> sure of another.

Mohammed smiled. "*Allahu Akbar.*"
They hugged one another and went inside.

"When will we do it?" Hussein asked.

"Let's check the time zones of the major banks. In honor of the holiday Laylatul Bara'ah (Night of Salvation), let us start the program after our morning prayers. Tonight we celebrate."

Hussein nodded. "Let's go now to the mosque and pray. Then let's get something to eat. I'm starved."

TERRY SHAUN AND Pierre Jamal entered the hotel lobby. They walked over to a table with a card that read, *Reserved.* Terry removed it and sat down to a view of the elevators.

Terry motioned to a waiter.

"Good morning. Can I serve you something?"

"Two espressos, please," Pierre answered. He placed a folded hundred-dollar bill on the waiter's tray, then turned his chair so he was also facing the elevators.

A few minutes later, the waiter came back and served the espressos. He handed Pierre the bill on a tray. Under the bill a note read, "Ready."

Pierre sipped his espresso. When the elevator doors opened, he spotted Mohammed and Hussein, followed by Abul Elham. He was amazed that all of them had left the suite and were now leaving the hotel. It was just the opportunity they needed.

The waiter was still standing there. He picked up the "Reserved" card and placed it back on the table. Pierre and Terry stood up and walked into the elevator. They pressed the button for the ninth floor. Terry and Pierre walked out of the elevator and headed for the door marked "EXIT ONLY FOR USE IN CASE OF FIRE."

They hurried down the steps to the seventh floor. When they opened the steel door and looked around, no one was there. They headed to suite 711. Terry took out a special master key from his pocket and opened the door. They walked in and closed the door behind them. Pierre started shooting pictures with a special camera supplied by the Mossad. It took 3D digital photos in color and automatically downloaded the pictures to Israel.

Terry took out a microtransmitter. He connected the wires to the back of the laptop sitting on the desk, then went into the bathroom and placed a small plastic bag of PE-4 explosives in the tank of the commode. He then proceeded to the bedroom and placed more explosives under the bed. Last, he attached a microphone the size of a pinhead under the couch.

They would never know what hit them.

Pierre looked at his watch and motioned to Terry that they had two minutes. Terry checked the transmitter again, and then motioned to the door that they should leave. Terry slowly opened the door and looked around, then gave the all-clear sign. They left the suite, retracing their route. When they arrived back in the lobby, Terry checked his watch again. The whole operation had taken them less than ten minutes.

They walked back to the table and removed the "Reserved" sign. The waiter came over.

"Is everything alright? Can I get you some more espresso?"

"Please," said Pierre, "and if you don't mind, bring me my change."

Terry stared at the entrance. "Let me have a cigarette and your lighter."

As Terry lit his cigarette, he saw Mohammed come in and head for the elevators. A few minutes later Hussein and Abul walked in, followed by a Chinese guy. They recognized him as a man named Chang Li.

Terry looked at Pierre, surprised, and said, "That's the guy that the NSA has a hit on. One of their agents, James Brown, has been tracking him in Beirut. Chang is a double agent working in the Chinese Embassy here. He's been coordinating activities between Iran and China."

Pierre watched them as they entered the elevator. "So that's why he's here with Hussein."

Terry nodded. "Let's finish our coffee. We need to go for a walk."

The waiter served them their espressos. They each took a sip. The waiter put the change in front of Pierre.

"Keep it."

The waiter looked at them. "Thank you, I hope you have a successful day."

They walked out of the lobby. The beach was a short distance from the hotel. They spotted a place to sit that was empty of people. Terry took a quick look around to make sure they were out of earshot. Then he opened his phone and put it on video so Pierre could both see and hear everything that was about to take place.

They heard Mohammed telling Abul to start up the program. Abul put the chip into the computer. The program started running. Hussein sat next to him, watching the screen. The screen filled with the names of banks and individual's and companies' accounts.

"Is it okay?" Abul asked.

"Yes," answered Mohammed.

"Are our banks set to receive the transfers?"

"One minute and I'll tell you."

Mohammed typed in a code of numbers and then the letters CBI for Central Bank of Iran. Next he typed CBOS for Central Bank of Syria, and finally Hezbollah's bank, Bangue du Liban.

"All is ready," Mohammed said.

Abul nodded. "Let's begin with the American list. Select twenty of the richest Jews first and then the billionaires."

Isaac Green's name was the first to pop up on the screen, followed by a list of other Jewish world leaders in industry, banking, and public service.

"You can start running the program," Abul said.

"What about Europe?" Hussein asked.

"Everyone on that list too. In Asia start in China, with Liu Yong Xing and Lee Shau Kee. Then pick twenty others at random."

"Make sure you get the wealthy Indians like Lakshmi Mittal, and Adi Godrej."

"What about our brothers?" Abul asked.

"Yes, all of the traitors to our faith, with pleasure. Start with Prince al-Walid ibn Talal and Crown Prince Abdullah. Go down the list, whoever has a history of siding with the American's or the Zionist, clean out their accounts."

Terry handed Pierre the phone. "Keep listening." He opened his shirt. Attached to his body was a money belt. He unzipped the pouch and took out a microtransmitter. He started typing:

Wolves are attacking the lambs.

CHAPTER
52

Friday, June 6, 2014
Over the Mediterranean Sea

OFF THE COAST of Lebanon, in international waters, a converted Israeli Airborne Early Warning and Control Center (AEW&C) plane flew, outfitted with special decoding equipment. Only the Israeli prime minister, six of his inner cabinet members, and General Solomon were aware of its assignment. Major Dan Levy, commander of the plane, read the coded message from Beirut. After he finished reading the message, he took out a note from a sealed brown envelope marked "Top Secret."

Following instructions, he reached for a small metal box. He removed the chip from the box and handed it to Sergeant Meir Miller.

"Insert the chip and type the words 'Temple Mount' at seven minutes past." He sent a coded message:

> The lambs have escaped and are going home to the shepherd.

CHAPTER
53

Friday, June 6, 2014
Phoenicia InterContinental Hotel, Beirut

TERRY RECEIVED THE message and closed the transmitter. He said to Pierre, "Have you heard anything important?"

"They're checking to see if any of the funds have arrived at their banks," Pierre answered.

"Pierre, we should go."

"Wait a minute, they're all laughing. Mohammed just saw the first money to arrive in the Beirut bank."

Terry turned up the volume. They heard Hussein say, "All of the wire transfers on the list have been sent."

"Call Fahd in LA," Abul said, "and tell him to call the Ayatollah. He should say, 'The chameleon is in the other tree.'"

Terry disconnected the phone. "Let's go."

They walked to their car in the hotel parking lot. Inside the car sat the waiter. Terry jumped into the back seat. Pierre sat down next to the driver.

"Andre, my brother, is everyone okay at home?"

"Our mother has a cold. Everyone else is fine. She sends her love."

"Has everyone got the word?" Terry asked.

"Yes, everybody," Andre replied. "The hall and elevator videos have all been destroyed."

"What time is it?"

Andre checked the time. "Eleven fifty-five."

"Okay," said Terry, "in five minutes we go."

At exactly noon, Andre turned on the ignition and started to pull away. The car moved slowly. As they were about to turn onto the main road, there was a huge explosion. Terry looked out the back window to see one whole side of the seventh floor of the hotel blown out.

"The NSA owes us one. Chang is taken care of. Andre, pull over. Pierre, take pictures."

Terry reached into the glove compartment and pulled out a pair of high-powered binoculars. Outside the car, he surveyed the damage. Sirens blasted in the distance, fire trucks honked, all trying to get to the victims while Terry stood there and watched. People ran from the hotel in all directions. The panic was palpable.

Terry looked at Pierre. "It's done. Let's go."

They jumped back into the car. Pierre and Andre looked out the window as police cars raced passed them. No one spoke until Terry interrupted the silence.

"Andre, to the boat now, as fast as you can."

CHAPTER
54

Friday, June 6, 2014
Over the Suez Canal

AT THIRTY THOUSAND feet there was no turbulence. Brahim slept soundly. Sammi debated waking his boss, but Brahim had requested to be awoken when they were close.

Sammi touched Brahim gently on the shoulder. "Boss, we're about to fly over the Suez Canal. You wanted me to wake you."

"Thanks, Sammi. Please ask Gail to bring me a black coffee."

As he walked to the back of the plane, Sammi saw James Brown III standing in the galley talking to the flight attendant. James had accompanied them to Saudi Arabia and was now escorting them to Israel. Mike always chose James for security when he had a special assignment. James was a West Point graduate. He served two tours of duty in Iraq and one in Afghanistan.

"Gail, Mr. Surin would like some coffee. Black with no sugar."

"Yes, sir, I'll bring it to him right away."

James looked at Sammi. "Have you ever been to Israel?"

"No, but I have some good friends there."

"I've been there a dozen times. It's an amazing place. Everybody is someone's relative. You're having a conversation and you mention a name and it doesn't matter who you just mentioned. Either whoever you're talking to 'served with him in the army' or he's his 'wife's first cousin.' Warm people. I love it when they send me on assignment there."

"Where are you from originally?" Sammi asked.

"Brooklyn. You can't tell?"

While they talked, Sammi kept his eyes focused on the front of the plane, making sure Brahim didn't need him.

"James, can you tell me what our schedule is?"

"After we land at the air base, our orders are to take you and Mr. Surin to Herzliya."

Sammi saw Brahim motioning to him. "Excuse me, my boss needs me."

Sammi walked over to Brahim. "Yes, boss?"

"Do you have any idea when we're going to land?"

"In about a half hour. Something you need?"

"Just have a seat."

Sammi knew Brahim well enough to know that "have a seat" meant something was really bothering him. Sammi sat down.

"Boss, everything is going to be alright."

"For the love of Allah, I can't understand how this could happen."

Brahim held up the e-mail he'd received an hour before from the U.S. Embassy in Iran:

> We regret to inform you that Mrs. Surin is no longer classified as a missing person. Her kidnappers have made contact, and her case is being handed over to higher authorities. We wish you luck on her safe return.

"How could she have been kidnapped? Something is wrong here.

What about her personal security detail? Where the hell were they?"

"We'll get her back, boss."

"But why in Mecca? Why now?" He rubbed his eyes, weary. "Sammi, why are they doing this?"

Over the intercom the pilot made an announcement. "We're approaching the borders of Israel. Please put on your seat belts. If you look out your windows in a minute, you'll see two Israeli jets flying alongside us."

James came over and looked out the window. He said, "Did you ever see a more beautiful plane than the F-35 fighter jet?"

"You're right," said Sammi. "It's the most beautiful plane ever built."

Sammi remembered how back in 2010 Isaac, Jim, and Brahim were going to make a big investment in Lockheed Martin Corp. The top management of LMC met with them at World's offices in New York. The main conference room on the forty-ninth floor was set up to do a live hookup via satellite to the cockpit of a new prototype, the F-35. A test pilot was going to put it through its maneuvers, creating an outstanding show of all its capabilities. The plane was the ultimate stealth fighter, and the U.S. and its allies would be ordering hundreds.

"Can someone get me a list of which of our allies are going to purchase the planes?" Brahim asked.

LMC presented a list of the countries to the partners. Brahim looked across the table at the chairman. "How come Israel isn't on the list?"

"The president told us not to include Israel at this time, as it could affect the peace in the Middle East."

Brahim glanced at Isaac, who was unusually quiet. "Gentlemen, if my partners agree, we'll make a twenty-billion-dollar investment into your company."

Isaac and Jim stared at Brahim. After a long pause he continued, "But only if Israel gets the first planes off the assembly line." He closed the file in front of him. "Let me know once you have an answer for us. We're late for another meeting."

That same day the chairman left for Washington. A week later he called Brahim and informed him of his meeting with the president. He'd told the president that if they couldn't get the financing from World, ten thousand people in the States would lose their jobs over the next twelve months. The president was very upset. His top political advisors told him the mid-term elections were just around the corner, so reluctantly he gave in.

James's voice interrupted his reverie. "Mr. Surin, we'll be landing in a matter of minutes at Hatzerim Air Force Base."

CHAPTER
55

Friday, June 6, 2014
Hatzerim Air Force Base, Negev

HATZERIM AIR FORCE Base was located in the Negev Desert close to the Dimona Research Center. Only a few government officials were aware of its real function. Israel had built twenty-four top-secret deep underground silos, ready to launch nuclear missiles at its enemies if attacked. Inside, twelve hangars located throughout the base were specially designed with remote early-warning launching systems. All foreign spy satellites would see were an array of old planes in different locations, including some captured Russian MiG's. But with the press of a button, the missiles rolled away from the silos on titanium rollers, allowing the missiles to be launched in less than five minutes.

When the plane's door opened and the staircase was lowered, James and another security guard walked off the plane. Brahim and Sammi followed behind them with the rest of the security detail, Sammi carrying Brahim's attaché case. At the bottom of the stairs, General Solomon waited to greet them. As soon as Brahim was on the ground, the general saluted him, much to everyone's surprise.

"I have to thank you again for getting us those F-35s," said the general.

Brahim smiled. "They've proven to be a good investment."

"Only because of you. They not only gave us the planes, but allowed us to improve them with our own avionics and radar systems."

"It's a beautiful plane," Brahim responded.

James smiled and shook his head.

"Please, Brahim," said the general, "accompany me to my office in the hangar."

The two men walked off. Sammi, James, and the other security guards waited by the plane.

James said to Sammi, "Your boss is a really special guy."

"Very few people know all the good he does. The partners in World are all unbelievable. They've contributed millions to fight terrorism. World has a trust fund set up to educate people in poor countries. Al-Qaeda is known for recruiting the poor and destitute, so the fund ensures that they have less people to choose from."

James's phone buzzed. "Excuse me, I have to take this call."

James paced back and forth as he spoke into the phone. Sammi sensed something important was being discussed. After a short conversation, James hung up and walked over to Sammi.

"Sorry about that."

"Is everything alright?"

"Not exactly. You'll hear the news shortly, so I might as well tell you now. Someone just tried to assassinate the president."

Sammi was stunned. "Do you know what happened?"

"It was the head of the Executive Clerk's Office. He was in the Oval Office to pick up a document signed by the president. Apparently his gun jammed. He panicked and ran. A Marine guard was there as an escort. He grabbed him when he heard the president yell."

"Does anyone have any idea why he did it?"

"That's all I was told." At that moment James's phone buzzed. "Hold on a minute."

It was a text from Mike:

> The planes from Paris are going to start landing in ten minutes.

James put away his phone. "Your friends from Paris are here. I have to tell Brahim."

"Let's go."

Inside the office, General Solomon was on the phone with the prime minister. Brahim was listening in on the speakerphone. James knocked on the door and walked in, followed by Sammi.

The general signaled to them not to speak by covering his mouth. "Mr. Prime Minister," he said, "Brahim and myself have been joined by James Brown and Sammi Boaz, is that alright?"

"Surely. Welcome to Israel."

Sammi responded first. "I'm looking forward to visiting the holy sites, sir. It's my first time here."

"We'll do our best to see your request is filled. James, how are you? I haven't seen you in a while."

"Yes, sir, it's been almost two years."

"Gentlemen, please keep me posted. When you have decided a course of action, I'll inform the agencies involved."

The prime minister hung up. Brahim looked at James. "Did you need something?"

"I just got news that someone made an attempt on the president's life. I thought you'd want to know."

"Yes, the prime minister informed us what happened. He's cutting his visit in Washington short. The White House canceled all meetings with foreign dignitaries for the time being. Anything else?"

"I was just informed that the planes from Paris landed and are taxiing up to the hangar."

"Let's go meet them," Brahim said. "I need to talk to Isaac immediately."

While everyone walked toward the plane, Brahim pulled Sammi aside. "Sammi, would you come with me to Iran?"

"Of course. You know I'd follow you anywhere. I'd go to hell with you if you asked."

Brahim threw his arms around Sammi. "You truly are my brother. Thank you."

Ahead, General Solomon stood at the bottom of the staircase of Isaac's plane. Mike was the first one to exit. Isaac and Chava started down behind him, followed by Dov and his wife. Allan, Charlie, Kim Li, and Hui Ying exited the other plane and started walking toward them. After exchanging hellos with everyone, Isaac and Brahim excused themselves.

"Brahim, how are you holding up?" Isaac asked.

"To be honest, I'm worried about Abra. Listen, can you and I go together in a separate car? I need to talk to you alone."

"Of course." Isaac walked over to Chava. "Would you mind taking Dov and Sara home ? Brahim and I have something to discuss."

"Not at all. I need to call the children and prepare for the Sabbath. When do you think you'll be done?"

"We have to make a stop in Herzliya Pituach and then I'll go on to Jerusalem. I should be home by around five o'clock."

"Candle lighting is at seven."

"I won't be late." Isaac walked over to where Brahim was standing. "Okay, let's go."

Mike was arranging who went in which limo. General Solomon took him aside. "Mike, I'm sorry, but Hui Ying and Kim Li can't go with us to our headquarters."

"What should we do with them?"

"There's a great hotel on the waterfront with a private beach. They can relax and freshen up there. It's not far from our headquarters."

"Which one is it?"

"The Dan Arcadia. We have a few secured rooms available for special occasions. They can use them, no problem."

"Okay, I'll tell them about the change of plans."

"I'll have my staff arrange for whatever they need."

Mike walked toward Allan and Charlie, who were deep in conversation.

"Allan and I need your help, Mike. When are we going to tell Kim Li about her sister?"

"It's up to Isaac."

"What about Lee? We have to arrange for Lee to get out of Hong Kong immediately."

"I have some people I can call," said Allan, "but I could use your help, Mike."

"How about if we talk about it after the meeting with the general?"

Charlie looked at Allan. "Right after. We have to move on this."

"You two are in the third limo. See you later."

Mike made one last check of all the limos and then gave the go-ahead to the drivers.

CHAPTER
56

AFTER PASSING THROUGH the security gate of the air base, the limos sped toward the main highway that would take them north to Herzliya. It would take less than two hours to reach the headquarters of the Tree of Life Foundation, the clandestine operation that the general had founded and directed from its inception.

The headquarters was situated in Herzliya Pituach, a wealthy beachfront district in Israel. It was an unusual decision to locate the Tree of Life building in a residential neighborhood. To the ordinary eye, it looked like one of the homes that had been built for the upscale residents of Herzliya Pituach. Only a select few were aware that on this quiet street, lined with weeping willow trees, stood the most secret agency of Israeli intelligence, the Tree of Life Foundation.

The area was dotted with the homes of many foreign dignitaries and several embassies. This gave General Solomon's agents opportunities to come in close contact with foreign informants, mostly at social events, without raising suspicion. To qualify for the unit, the general's agents had to be able to speak at least six languages fluently. They'd all lived and worked in Arab countries and most of the European capitals. From time to time, they served at the Israeli Embassy in the United States. Some had also been sent to Washington, D.C., as part of their counterintelligence training.

The Tree of Life headquarters had eleven rooms, all on one level. Eight rooms were filled with the most advanced computers and decoding equipment in the world. Early on in the formation of the organization, it was decided to send a specially designed Amos satellite into outer space only to service the needs of the Tree of Life Foundation. The satellite picked up chatter in Arab villages throughout the country. The information was sent directly to Herzliya, where it was analyzed by some of the most sophisticated computers in the world. Tree of Life secret agents were constantly repositioned around the globe based on this information.

Two other rooms consisted of the general's office and a small dining room. The other room was off limits to all personnel except the general and three experts in esoteric knowledge, affectionately referred to as "the space cadets." The team focused all of their time researching mysteries of the universe. With special laser technology they were able to lift encryptions from ancient writings and artifacts without harming them and decipher them. After preparing a detailed report, they'd pass it on to the general, which he then passed on to the IDF. The secret codes they had discovered enhanced Israel's military capabilities to what they were today.

On the road, the limos drove on toward their destination. Mike was in the first car with the general. "There seems to be a lot of activity going on around here," Mike noted. "A few years ago all you could see for miles and miles was desert."

"The Negev has grown a lot over the last ten years."

"What inspired the growth?"

"The government made it a priority for development. We closed lots of small bases around the country and transferred their operations to this area. All together they account for over thirty thousand of our troops."

In the limo behind theirs, Charlie had just finished talking to his wife. "Allan, my wife is nervous. All the news channels are saying that a war is imminent between Israel and the Arab nations."

Allan was busy sending texts to his contacts in the State Department in D.C. looking for assistance with the Lee situation. Allan turned to Charlie. "Unfortunately, I agree with your wife. If Iran continues on the path it has taken until now, it will blow up the whole Middle East."

"They threatened the same thing a few years back and nothing happened."

"Things are different this time."

"How?"

"We believe they've made a deal with the Chinese and the Russians. We know the Russians want more influence in the Gulf states. That's why they keep backing Syria. We also know the Chinese need oil and they're looking to back the strongest force in the region. The crazy thing is that the war won't give either of them what they want—control of the Middle East and its oil."

Allan looked out the window at the Bedouin tents that dotted the landscape. "Maybe the Bedouins have the right idea."

"Yeah, I can see my wife washing clothes by hand and my kids without TV or computer games."

"What makes you think they don't have video games? I've heard of Bedouin caves with wireless Internet."

"Very funny."

"I'm completely serious."

"How do they make a living?"

"They raise sheep and camels and sell them."

"How do you know so much about Bedouins?" Charlie asked.

"I lived with them for a summer when I was in college. My thesis was on Bedouin women and their traditional healing methods."

Charlie looked out of his window. "Why have the cars stopped?"

"I'll find out." Allan opened his door and stepped out. A moment later he came back. "Just some Bedouin crossing the road with a herd of his sheep."

"Great," Charlie remarked. "Where's the sheep crossing sign when you need it?"

In the third limo, James, Hui Ying, and Kim Li opened their windows. The hot air rushed over Kim Li's face.

"This reminds me of the Gobi Desert and the village where I was born. It's in the northwestern part of China, near the Mongolian border. The Bedouin tents are very similar to the tents I lived in as a young child. At night it would get so cold, snow would appear on the dunes." She got chills, reliving the cold winter nights in her mind.

The beeping of a car horn brought her back to the present. Hui Ying sat reading a map of Israel. "Do you think we can visit the Golan Heights?" he asked James.

James was surprised by the request. "We'll see."

Mike had briefed him about the Hong Kong situation. He assumed they weren't going anywhere for a while. James started checking e-mail on his iPhone. His other mobile rang. It was Mike.

"How is everyone?"

"Everyone is fine. But I believe Kim Li and Hui Ying want to speak to you."

"After we drop everyone off at the hotel, I'm going on with Isaac and Brahim to meet the general. I'll meet with them as soon as I get back to the hotel. James, the traffic is starting to move. I'll talk to you later."

CHAPTER
57

Friday, June 6, 2014
On the road to Herzliya

ISAAC AND BRAHIM'S limo was sandwiched between two other limos carrying more security personnel.

"So, Brahim, what is it you wanted to tell me?" Isaac asked.

"Before you landed, I spoke to the Israeli prime minister. He offered to do everything he can to help locate Abra. I've asked Sammi to go with me to Iran and try to find her. Do you think I should contact the Iranian government through our private channels? Fatima's been calling all over, looking for people with connections to the Iranian Revolutionary Guards. So far we have very little to go on. I can't just sit around and do nothing. I'm going crazy."

"For the moment, God willing, let's assume she's safe," Isaac responded. "If she's been kidnapped, as the police believe, the kidnappers will be contacting you. For you to go to Iran with Sammi would be extremely dangerous. What if the only reason they took Abra was to lure you to Iran? What if that's the goal? To get you to Iran searching for Abra so they can kidnap you too and hold you both for ransom. It wouldn't take a rocket scientist to realize that

World would have no problem paying a lot of money to get the two of you home safely."

Brahim's lips tightened. "You have a point."

"And what if they want more than money? Like our PCM-26 chip. Iran would do anything to get their hands on it. If that's what they're after, we both know our hands are tied. The United States wouldn't allow us to hand it over, kidnapping or not."

"What do you suggest? She's my wife. What if she's hurt?"

"They're not going to hurt her. They wouldn't have taken her if they didn't need her. Listen, it's Friday. Let's finish our business with the general, then we'll go to Jerusalem and talk solutions. You're at the King David Hotel, right?"

"Yes, Mike's security people have cleared a floor with several suites. Mike and some of the U.S. Embassy staff in Tel Aviv are planning to stay at the hotel too. They'll be updating me as needed."

"Did they make arrangements for you to go to the Al Aqsa Mosque?"

"Yes, I planned to pray there on Saturday with Sammi."

"I suggest Mike get some of his key personnel with knowledge on Iran to join us at my home after the Sabbath."

Brahim's PDA buzzed. It was Fatima. "Hello, Fatima. Do you have any news?"

"A friend of mine in the Iranian police force sent me a message. Abra is alive. She's being held in a security house in Lavizan Park about twenty minutes from Tehran."

"Did they say anything else?"

"Only that they've closed the park to all visitors. The Revolutionary Guards are in charge of the security. They've taken over."

Brahim was silent, trying to digest the information.

"Why aren't you saying anything, Brahim? What are you going to do? Whoever is holding her could kill her."

Fatima's voice was loud enough for Isaac to overhear the conversation. He scribbled a note and handed it to Brahim. It read: "*Tell her you'll get back to her shortly, then hang up."*

"Fatima, I'll get back to you shortly."

"I want to go to Tehran right away," Fatima insisted. "You should come with me, Brahim."

"Fatima, please, I'll call you back in a moment."

"I'm waiting for your call."

Brahim hung up the phone and turned his attention to Isaac. "What do you think?"

"There's no way to know what's really going on. Fatima could be part of a setup and not even know it. The kidnappers knew she would contact you immediately. The good news is Abra is safe. Let's see what the intelligence agencies come up with. Let's give them a little time to work their magic. Mike and all the NSA resources are on it. Nobody is going to rest until we get Abra back."

"And what should I do in the meantime?"

"For now, call Fatima back and tell her you're working on a plan, and she is to sit tight until further notice. Tell her that the last thing we need is one more kidnapping of a family member in Iran."

"I'll make the call."

Isaac checked the time on his PDA. It was already two p.m. It would be six a.m. in Chicago. "I'm going to try to reach Jim and see how he's doing."

"Good idea. He has got to be going crazy over this thing with his brothers."

Isaac hit the direct dial button on his PDA. Before Isaac could speak, Jim came on. "Are you with Brahim?"

"Yes, we're together, and he's listening. We're on the way to Herzliya to General Solomon's office."

"Is there any news about Abra?"

"Brahim just received some information. We believe she's safe. Hopefully we'll have more to tell you soon. Jim, how is your mother?"

"Not so good. A reporter from the *New York Post* showed up

on her doorstep last night asking about John Jr. and William. She slammed the door in his face. Thank God I had called my wife earlier and told her to go stay with my mom. When she arrived, my mother was crying hysterically. My wife called our doctor. He came right over and gave her a sedative to calm her down."

"When are you meeting your brothers?"

"Guy has to speak to them first. He'll be meeting with them this morning. Then he'll come by the hotel. I hope he'll tell me he's arranged for me to talk to them."

"Make sure to stay calm, Jim," Brahim interrupted. "Don't let them get you angry."

"Me, get angry? I don't get angry."

"Jim, please control that Irish temper, we can't afford to have you in jail with them."

"Isaac, my mobile is ringing it must be Mary. I'll be in touch with you after your Sabbath. Brahim, everything will be alright. Abra's a fighter. Guys, you take care."

"It looks like the whole world is going crazy." Brahim thought about Abra. *How is she? Will she be okay? He regretted now the harsh words he had with her when he saw her last.*

Isaac looked out the window and saw a large green sign. It read, "HERZLIYA NEXT EXIT." He turned to Brahim. "We should be there in a few minutes."

Exiting the highway, they turned onto Ramat Yam Street. They passed the Okeanos apartment hotel. Isaac remembered some of the holidays he and Chava had spent there years ago. Their eighth-floor apartment was just for the two of them, one bedroom, a small kitchen, and a living room. The view of the Mediterranean from the balcony at sunset was incredible. Chava loved eating sushi at the Daniel Hotel next door. After dinner they would take a slow walk on the promenade.

The world was a very different place back then. Now things moved too fast. The world felt like it was in a freefall. His business had grown beyond his wildest dreams. In spite of all of his success, Isaac knew that the only permanent thing in his world was his devotion to God and his family.

The limos stopped in front of the Dan Arcadia Hotel. A group of security personnel waited to greet them. Mike stepped out of the limo first, followed by the general. Both huddled with their security. Kim Li and Hui Ying exited their limo and stood together at the entrance waiting for their luggage to be unloaded.

Charlie and Allan approached Isaac when he exited his vehicle. "Isaac," Charlie said, "when are we going to break the news to Kim Li?"

Isaac looked at the hotel entrance to see that Kim Li had just received her luggage.

"Let's all meet on Sunday morning. We'll tell her then."

Brahim nodded. "She's been under tremendous pressure. Let her rest up on Saturday."

"How about if we have breakfast at my home?" Isaac suggested. "Chava will be there and she could help us with Kim Li."

"What time should we meet?" Allan asked.

"Sunday morning, around ten a.m. Allan, can you please ask Mike if he can arrange for the security? The traffic should be light at that time in the morning."

"I'll take care of it right away."

"Brahim, before we go, I just want to take a minute and wish Kim Li and Hui Ying a pleasant stay."

"Okay, but I want to get going. I need to know what the general plans to do about Abra."

"I'll only be a few minutes." Isaac walked away.

Allan looked at Brahim. "Brahim, Abra is going to be alright. Everyone is working on it. They'll come up with a plan."

"I'm not worried about that. It's the unknown that's getting to me. Why haven't they made demands?"

"We're all asking the same question."

"There's not much we can do now," said Charlie. "I'm sure we'll have an update on Abra shortly."

Isaac came up to them. "Charlie, what are your plans for the Sabbath? Why don't you come and spend it with me and Chava?"

"Thanks, I would love to, but I already called a cousin of mine in Raanana."

"I understand. Have a good time. I'll see you on Sunday."

"Thanks, I'd better go check in and make sure Kim Li and Hui Ying are settled. James is going to be staying with them. Mike's security detail will be here too."

"Sounds good." Isaac looked at Brahim. "Let's go. I have to be home by five o'clock."

Mike joined Isaac and Brahim in one of the limos and it pulled away. In less than five minutes they arrived at the Tree of Life headquarters. There were no cars parked outside on the street. The limo entered the driveway on the side of the house and proceeded to the parking area in the back.

Looking out of a bulletproof window, a guard attended the walled gate. The general stepped out of the car and motioned to him to open the metal security door. Mike left his car and joined Isaac and Brahim. The rest of the security personnel stayed with the cars. The three of them walked into the yard as the security door closed behind them.

General Solomon walked up to the entrance to the house and put his hand on an electronic pad next to the glass door. "I'm sorry, we all have to go through a full body scanner," he said.

"I hope it takes good pictures." Isaac laughed.

"It does." The general was serious. "We have your medical records from your military service showing where you were wounded for comparison. The scanner will also measure your pulse to see if you are nervous, and it can check if you're carrying any chemicals or explosives. The team who designed it called it 'Rambam,' after one of the greatest Jewish doctors and thinkers."

After they had proceeded through the scanner, one of the general's aides stood by to take them to the conference room, where the staff had set out an assortment of drinks and sandwiches. Before he left the room, the aide handed the general a note.

"Please sit. Help yourself," the general said. After everyone was seated, the general spoke. "A short while ago we intercepted a communication from Iran." He proceeded to read from the note he'd just been handed.

"'The Iranian Supreme Council has set the amount of money for the release of Abra Surin at one billion U.S. dollars.'" The general looked up. "It further states that the Revolutionary Guards will handle all arrangements concerning this matter. It's signed by the Ayatollah. This was sent to the commander of the Revolutionary Guards thirty minutes ago."

All eyes focused on Brahim. "What now?" he asked.

"You can expect to hear from them through the Swiss or German embassies within twenty-four hours. It's crucial that they not be aware that we're intercepting any of their communications."

"So we can't move until we hear from them," Isaac said.

"What's the plan then?" Brahim asked.

"If all they're after is money, we can arrange that through the Swiss or German embassies," the general said matter-of-factly.

Mike chimed in. "Our people will be on top of it, as soon as we get the go-ahead."

A knock on the door interrupted Brahim's next question. All conversation stopped as the general pressed a button to open the door. An aide walked in, handed him a note, then left. The general's face turned red. He slammed his fist on the table and said, "They can go to hell."

He passed the note to Isaac. Isaac picked up the note and read it aloud.

"This is the latest intercept: 'We have to force the Israelis to free Aswad along with one thousand Lebanese and Palestinian prisoners. Brahim will get them to agree, he has done a lot for the Israelis. Threaten to kill her if our demands are not met.'"

"This is a whole new ball game," said the general. "Aswad was taken prisoner by the Israelis in 2006 in the beginning of the second Lebanese war. He's been in isolation since then." General Solomon looked at Brahim. "He's our ace card. If they capture one of our soldiers in the next war, the plan is to offer him in exchange."

"What makes him so valuable?"

"He's the brother-in-law of the Hezbollah leader, Nasrallah. I'm sorry, Brahim, but we can't let him go."

Isaac studied Brahim's face. "I'm sure we'll find another way to free her."

Brahim said only, "General, is there anything else at this time?"

"No, finding a way to get your wife back to you safely is the only thing I'm interested in."

Isaac stood up. "General, thank you for all your help. I don't want to be late getting home before the Sabbath."

Everyone shook the general's hand, and he walked them to the exit.

Sammi walked next to Brahim. "Boss, what are you going to do?" Sammi said in a whisper.

"Not now. We'll talk about it later."

Isaac walked with the general. He stopped suddenly. "I must have dropped my phone in the conference room."

"I'll go with you."

They walked back into the conference room.

"General, I apologize. I just needed a minute with you alone. I have to tell you, Brahim was devastated when he saw your reaction about the swap for Aswad. I want you to reconsider. I believe that the prime minister will agree with me."

"If we cave in to their demands, it will never end. What happens when they take another hostage? No, we have to find another way. We have some time. We're gathering more information from our agents in Iran as we speak. Due to the sensitivity of this matter, I'm not at liberty to disclose certain operations that are ongoing. They could change the whole situation overnight."

"Brahim is going to need a plan after the Sabbath," Isaac warned.

"Tell Brahim he'll have it." The general walked Isaac to the exit. "*Shabbat Shalom.*"

Isaac climbed into the limo and sat down next to Brahim.

"What was that all about?" Brahim asked.

"I had a few words with the general. We're going to get your wife back, trust me."

"There's no one in the world I trust more than you." Brahim grabbed Isaac's hand. "Her life is in your hands."

CHAPTER
58

Friday, June 6, 2014
Metropolitan Correction Center, Chicago

T HE METROPOLITAN CORRECTION Center (MCC) was located on Clark and Van Buren Street in downtown Chicago. The limousine stopped in front of the building. Guy looked at his watch. It was nine a.m.. He was reviewing the notes on the charges against the Murphy brothers when his mobile rang.

"Good morning, Jim."

"I'm at the hotel," Jim said. "Call me as soon as you've see my brothers."

"It could be a while. I'll be in touch."

Guy hung up and gathered his papers. He stepped out of the limo, then bent down to speak to the driver through his open window. "I'll be at least an hour. If you want to grab some breakfast, go ahead. But please make sure your phone is on."

Guy proceeded to the visitor's door.

"Proof of your identity," the guard asked in a matter-of-fact tone. "I also need the name of the prisoner you are visiting."

The guard typed the names into his computer. "Have a seat. It will take a few minutes."

"I've been here before, I know the routine."

Guy sat down, looking at the guard. He knew the penal system too well. It was a system designed to punish anyone who had a connection to the perpetrator. Victims, families, witnesses, and lawyers would all pay a price in one way or another.

Guy spotted a no cell phone sign on the wall across from him. He took out his mobile and shut it off. When he finished putting his phone away, the guard motioned for Guy to get up. "This way."

Waiting for him was a female guard. "Your credentials, please."

"This is a letter from the United States attorney general," Guy told her. He handed her the document.

"Empty your pockets."

Guy put all his belongings on the conveyer belt with his iPad and walked through the scanner. A red light started blinking.

The guard walked up to him. "Please step out and stretch out your arms."

She ran a hand scanner over his body. At his left wrist. the scanner started to buzz. He turned his head and saw his Rolex. "Excuse me, I forgot to send my watch through." He slipped off his watch and added it to the rest of his things.

"Take your items and follow me."

Guy hurriedly grabbed his stuff. The guard walked down the hall briskly without looking back to see if he was following. He struggled to catch up with her. Finally she stopped at an elevator and with a key opened the door. She motioned to Guy to go in first.

As he entered, she pressed the third floor. *What a lousy job for a woman.* He was about to ask her how she liked her job when the elevator doors opened. In a stern voice, she said, "Follow me."

Every few feet there was another closed door with a sign hanging on it that read "Lawyers Only." Two men in prison uniforms rolled a wagon of uniforms stacked neatly.

"Hey," one of the prisoners taunted, "what are you in for?"

Guy ignored him and kept walking, following closely behind the guard. Finally they reached another gate, with another guard. The guard Guy had been following opened the gate. She said, "Follow me."

After a few meters, both guards moved away from Guy. They stood to the side talking to each other, and then the female guard turned and left abruptly. The other guard walked to a door that read, "High Security Only." He unlocked it. "Wait in this room. If you need me, press the red button on the table." The guard closed the door and left.

The room had a plastic chair and a desk counter with a glass divider in the center. In the middle of the glass was a speaker, and on each side was a small microphone.

Guy opened his attaché case and was looking at his notes when he saw the door open. Through the glass the guard looked at him and then stepped aside as John Jr. walked in. The guard closed the door. John Jr. sat down.

Guy talked into the microphone on his side of the glass. "How are you holding up?" Guy asked.

"I could be better."

"Your brother Jim is waiting at the airport hotel. He's not allowed to see you or William until you've seen your lawyer."

"I understand. What am I up against?"

"I won't kid you. These are very serious charges, attempting to murder the president of the United States and then compounding it by killing a prisoner."

"Can you get me out on bail?"

"I can try, but it probably won't happen."

John Jr. nodded, as if he already knew the answer. "What about William?"

"Maybe, but it all depends on you both cooperating with the government."

"No way in hell." John Jr. raised his voice.

Guy leaned forward. "Let me explain this another way. My associates have obtained some damaging information that the FBI in D.C. has on you and your friends. The FBI started following your group over four years ago. When you had a meeting in Madison. Wisconsin, you were recorded on tape with the head of the organization for several hours. Since then you and William have been photographed attending meetings with six neo-Nazi groups."

John Jr. shrugged. "So what? So we went to a few meetings. That doesn't prove anything."

"I'll tell you what that proves," said Guy. "It proves they're smarter than you are. They were able to infiltrate your groups, and they have you and William both on tape planning to kill the president. That's hard evidence."

John Jr. looked down at his hands. He was silent.

Guy said, "If you want to spend the rest of your lives in a maximum security federal prison, fine. At the rate you're going, that won't be difficult. You'll end up spending the better part of your life in isolation. Let me tell you something. I know a murderer that's in for life. He's serving his time there. He told me, 'It's like being buried alive.'"

Guy paused to gauge John Jr.'s reaction to his words. Nothing.

"You're putting your family through hell, you realize that, right? This will kill your mother, John. Frank and Jim are ready to do anything to get you out of this mess. For her sake, please try. If I'm going to help you, I need you to tell me what you're going to do right now. John, this is your call. William will follow you. You know that."

John picked up his head and looked at Guy through the glass. "These people are destroying our country. Muslims, Jews, and blacks. If we don't stop them, in twenty or thirty years *they'll* be the majority, and us whites, we'll be finished. The Muslim nations have taken control of our economy. They're building more mosques then we're building churches. Look at what they did in New York. The politicians are afraid to say anything for fear of their voting power.

Soon the Muslims will have control of the Congress. The blacks and the Jews are running the Supreme Court already."

Guy looked at John Jr. in disbelief. "Are you finished?"

John Jr. shrugged. "Yeah."

"Not that it will matter to you, but you should know it was Isaac, a Jew, who insisted I get on the first plane to come here to help you. Time is running out. Our visiting time is almost over. What should I tell Jim?"

"Tell him I'm not making a deal, and I'm not giving away any information."

John Jr. got up from his seat and turned his back on Guy. He pressed the button to summon the guard, and the guard opened the door.

Guy sat there for a few minutes, then pressed the red button, closed his attaché case, and stood up as the door behind him opened.

What could I have said to change John's mind?

The guard walked in front of Guy with a phone to his ear. He hung up the phone and turned to Guy with a stunned expression. "Someone tried to assassinate the president."

Guy walked faster. He retrieved his things and turned on his iPhone. He pulled up Fox News. The headline read, **PRESIDENT IS SAFE AFTER ESCAPING A NEAR ATTEMPT ON HIS LIFE HE IS ON HIS WAY TO AN UNDISCLOSED LOCATION.**

Guy wondered if John Jr. was connected to the assassination attempt. The guard escorted Guy through the last gate. Guy stood outside on the sidewalk, about to call his driver when his phone rang. It was Jim.

"Hello, Jim, have you heard the news?"

"It's all over the TV. What about my brother. What did he say?"

"Let's talk about it when I get to the hotel."

"I'll be in the lobby."

Guy saw his driver across the street. "I'll be right there, sir," the driver yelled out the window.

The driver made a fast U-turn and pulled up to the curb where Guy stood. Guy opened the door and sat down in the back seat.

"Did you hear the news about the president?" the driver asked.

"Yes, get me to the Hilton at the airport as soon as you can."

"Yes, sir." The driver made a left at the next corner. "I've been listening to the radio. It's strange. They aren't saying much. It seems like the White House isn't telling the whole story."

"Turn on your radio. Let's see."

The driver searched for an all-news station and finally got WBBM.

"The time is ten thirty a.m. In the latest news, the Associated Press has announced that the White House will hold a press conference at one p.m. to discuss the attempted assassination of the president. They have released a statement that president and his wife are safe. We'll now go to our affiliate WFED for the latest news from Washington."

"It'll be the same," said Guy. "We won't hear anything until one o'clock. You can turn it off."

"How about some music, sir?""

"Thank you."

Guy opened his mobile and dialed Susan. The phone rang and rang. After ten rings, there was still no answer. He left her a message. "Susan, it's me. Give me a call."

Guy looked out the window. The traffic was terrible. Everywhere he looked, he saw people talking on their cell phones. "I bet there's a cop up at the corner," the driver said.

Sure enough, as they approached the intersection, a police officer stood in the middle of the street with his hand waving at the traffic. After a short stop at the intersection, the traffic started to move faster.

"We should be at the hotel in a matter of minutes, sir."

"Thank you." Guy's phone rang. "Susan, are you alright?"

"I'm fine. Sorry I missed your call."

"I just wanted to fill you in on the meeting with John Jr."

"Go ahead. What did he say?"

"Basically nothing. He refuses to cooperate. He just rants."

"Did you have a chance to speak to William?"

"No, I'll have to go back tomorrow to see him, but without John Jr. cooperating I'm afraid it will be useless. Susan, inform Isaac of this conversation. Tell him to contact me as soon as possible."

"Sure."

"Thanks, I'm on my way into meet Jim. "

Ten minutes later, Guy entered the lobby of the Hilton. Jim stood there waiting. He extended his hand to Guy. "Let's go have a cup of coffee."

"Maybe we should go somewhere we can be alone."

Jim nodded. "We can talk in my suite."

On the way up in the elevator, Guy could smell that Jim had already been drinking. It wasn't even noon.

"Jim, you have to be strong for your mother. Alcohol isn't going to help. I'm going to need you to keep a clear head if we have any chance to help your brothers."

"I'm Irish, Guy, this is what we do."

"Well, this time, don't."

"I hear you. I'll stop. You have my word."

They exited the elevator, and Jim opened the door to his suite. Guy sat down on the sofa. "Hey, Jim, I'll take that coffee now, black no sugar."

"You got it."

A few minutes later, Jim joined Guy and sat down in a chair opposite the lawyer. He leaned forward. "Don't pull any punches. How bad is it?"

"If John Jr. isn't going to cooperate with the FBI, his chances are slim to nothing of getting off without a long prison sentence. That's without the charge of killing the other prisoner. We may have some leeway with William. My staff is working on obtaining documentation on how the FBI obtained their information and if it was legal."

"What can you do right now?"

"Tomorrow I'll go with you to see both of them. I'll talk to William and you'll visit John Jr."

"What time?"

"Visiting hours start at eight thirty. Be ready to go at eight a.m. I'll be waiting outside with my driver. I'll brief you on the way to the prison. Jim, I need you to stay calm when you talk to John Jr., understood?"

"I understand. Listen, I just heard about the attempt on the president. Do you think my brother had something to do with that?"

"I have no idea. Whether or not he's involved, it's not good news for his case."

CHAPTER
59

Friday, June 6, 2014
On the road to Jerusalem

THE LIMO TURNED onto Highway 1 toward Jerusalem. Isaac thought about his last words to Brahim.

How will I keep my word? Did I speak too fast when I promised we would get Abra back?

The mullahs were not rational, driven by their fanaticism. The Sunnis had hated the Shiites for centuries. The Shiites want control of Mecca and all of the oil in the Middle East. No one had ever been able to reason with either of them. What did he think he could do?

He also knew they would have no compunctions about killing Abra if their demands weren't met. *If it was only money it would be simple, but they want more. More than anyone is willing to give.*

Isaac knew that Aswad's release was just the beginning. Isaac glanced at Brahim, who was dozing in the seat next to him. Brahim was aging under the pressure. It was amazing what worry could do.

Isaac's PDA vibrated.

"Yes, Charlie, what is it?"

"I just received a message from Xu Ming. He's attending a United Nations World Health Symposium. He says it's very important that I meet with him while he's in New York."

"You still have plenty of time before sundown. Call Susan to check on the availability of one of our planes. If it's not being used, see if it can be ready to fly you home on Sunday from Ben Gurion."

"Are you sure you want me to go?"

"No, I'm not sure, but I'm sure your wife and children will be glad to see you. Besides, if he's planning to defect, he'll need your help. Oh, and while you're at it, tell Susan to have her friend Mindy Zinger call me. I'd like to set up a meeting with her on Sunday."

"Okay, I'll be in touch."

"What did Charlie have to say?" Brahim asked, opening his eyes.

"He received a call from Xu Ming, the Chinese scientist who developed the antidote for the virus."

Mike overheard their conversation from the front seat. "The one who wants to defect?"

"That's right. Xu Ming told Charlie that he's in the States and wants to meet him in New York right away. I told him to make arrangements to leave on Sunday."

Brahim nodded. "Let me know how that goes."

"I will."

Forty-five minutes later the limo arrived in Jerusalem. The driver glanced at Brahim and Isaac in the mirror. "Gentlemen, where you would like to go first?"

Brahim looked at his watch. It was past five o'clock. "Please go straight to Isaac's home. It's getting late."

Isaac looked at his new watch. Chava had picked it up for him as a thank you gift at the duty-free shop in Paris. It wasn't a Patek Philippe, but with the Abra situation still unresolved Chava knew he might be slamming a few more desks before they got her back.

"You're right. I told Chava I'd be home by five."

Isaac's Israel home was in Talbiya, not far from the Israeli president's residence. The four-story house was built to accommodate their children and their families when they visited for holidays. One floor was set aside for visiting guests with a private entrance and an elevator.

Chava had commissioned the famous Israeli architect Bezalel Yaakov to design the house. It took five years to build. When it was completed, the mayor of Jerusalem awarded the Frank Lloyd Wright Award for original house design to Bezalel at a party Isaac and Chava threw to celebrate the completion of their new home.

When the limo arrived in front of Isaac's house, they saw several security guards standing outside the gate. Several unmarked cars were sitting nearby. The scene was not much different from that in front of the president's residence.

The car came to a stop. Mike stepped out of the car and opened the door for Isaac. Before getting out, Isaac asked Brahim, "Would you like to come in and have something to eat?"

'Thank you, but I'm really tired. I think I'll just go to the hotel."

"Whatever you want, but call me right after the Sabbath."

"I will. Have a restful one. All the best to Chava and the family."

"Thanks, will do."

Isaac stepped out of the car, gave Brahim a hug, then closed the car door.

"Don't worry, I'll take care of him," Mike said.

Isaac shook Mike's hand and entered the house. Mike sat in the back seat of the limo with Brahim and they were off.

THE RIDE TO the King David Hotel took only five minutes. They didn't speak; Mike understood that until Abra was free, everything was superfluous. As they pulled into the circular driveway of the King David Hotel, Mike recalled the time he'd stayed there with the previous president of the United States. The president had ordered everyone in the Secret Service to learn the hotel's extraordinary history.

On July 22, 1946, the hotel had been bombed by Israeli freedom fighters. It was the beginning of Israel's struggle to become a Jewish state, and the hotel was the British administrative headquarters for Palestine. The attack on the hotel was a response to British raids on the Jewish Agency. Menachem Begin, the sixth prime minister of Israel, was the leader at the underground organization who had implemented the attack, the Irgun.

Mike remembered the meetings that the U.S. State Department had set up between NSA agents and some of the old members of the Irgun. One evening the president asked Mike and another agent on duty to take him to Begin's grave on the Mount of Olives. Since it wasn't an official state visit, only a handful of people went. In the Israeli government only three people had any knowledge that the visit ever took place.

It was winter and it was cold. The wind went right through him. It had been raining all day, and the ground was wet on the mountain that night. An Israeli from the foreign office accompanied them. He provided flashlights, and they followed him to the grave site. The president had Mike bring a flower arrangement, which he placed at the foot of the tombstone. He then bent down and picked up a small rock and placed it on the grave, as was the Jewish custom.

On the drive back to the hotel, the president said, "He was the greatest world leader I ever met. He was a fighter, an honest politician, with a vision for his nation. Most of all, he was humble."

"We're here, sir."

Mike didn't hear the driver. He was still stuck in his memory. Brahim looked at Mike. "Are you all right?"

"Yes, I was just thinking of what someone had told me a while back and how right he was."

Mike joined Brahim in front of the hotel and gave last-minute instructions to his people. The doorman took their luggage from the limo and brought it inside.

They met Charlie in the lobby talking on his cell phone. Mike walked over. "Let's get you to Raanana."

"Give me a minute. I'm talking to my kids."

After Charlie finished the call, Mike said, "You really miss them."

"You bet. I can't wait to see them. You know I'm flying back on Sunday."

Mike nodded.

"What about you, Mike? Are you married?"

"I'm in love with the job. Keeping a wife takes work, and I don't have time for that."

"I hear you. But as much as I love my work, I love my family more. So where are you off to after you take me to Raanana?"

"Back to the Dan Arcadia Hotel to meet with Allan. We have to talk to Washington. The Lee situation needs our attention right away."

"If you need me to do anything while I'm in the States, let me know."

The ride to Raanana took only forty-five minutes. They made good time. They turned into Ahuza Street, Raanana's main thoroughfare.

"My cousin's home is a few blocks from a park," Charlie said.

The driver checked the GPS. "It's showing up now. It's on Hanesiim Street, right?"

"That's it."

Charlie looked at Mike. "There's a great boutique wine store on this street." He spotted the store. "Can you pull over and stop?" he asked the driver. "I want to bring a gift for my cousin."

"I'll go with you," Mike said.

The store was lined with shelves that held wine imported from all over the world. "Mike, would you believe all this wine is kosher?" said Charlie.

Mike picked up a bottle of Baron Rothschild Haut-Medoc 2005. "Have you had any of this one?" He turned the bottle to show Charlie.

"Excellent choice. It's sixty percent cabernet, forty percent merlot. It's imported from France."

Impressed, Mike took the bottle and walked over to the cash register. Charlie motioned to the owner. "Do you have any Dalton Single Vineyard Cabernet Sauvignon?"

"Let me check." After a few minutes, the shop owner returned. "We just received a shipment today. How many do you want?"

"Three bottles, please."

After paying their bill, they left the store and went to the car. Charlie handed one of the Dalton bottles to Mike. "Try this. It's made here in Israel."

"Thanks, Charlie." He put the bottle in the bag with the bottle he'd bought. A few minutes later, the driver stopped the car in front of the address Charlie had given him.

"Call me when you're finished with the Sabbath," said Mike. "I'll send my people to pick you up."

"Thanks, Mike, have a great day."

Mike waited until the door of the house opened and Charlie waved him off.

"Take me to the Dan Arcadia Hotel in Herzliya, please," Mike said.

Mike noticed the red light on his security mobile blinking. Frederick had left him a message asking him to call immediately. *It's urgent*, he said.

"How close are we to the hotel?" Mike asked the driver.

"Ten minutes, if we don't get stuck in traffic."

Mikes punched in a security code that automatically dialed Frederick's number. It would ensure that the line was secure.

"I was just about to call you," Frederick said when he answered. "Mike, I just had a conversation with the head of MI5."

"About what?"

"The prime minister's death."

CHAPTER
60

Friday, June 6, 2014
Dan Arcadia Hotel, Herzliya

W E BELIEVE HE was poisoned."

"What makes you think so?" Mike asked Frederick.

"The family insisted on an autopsy. His wife said he was in top physical condition and had just undergone a series of stress tests. The forensic pathologist informed the family that the prime minister died of ischemic cardiomyopathy. It's a weakening of the heart muscle, which reduces the flow of blood supply."

"Okay, so why do you think poison?"

"I'm getting there. When he checked further, he found a virus planted in his food."

"Are you positive?"

"Without a doubt. The autopsy was conclusive. MI5 had its laboratory confirm the results. It's a strain of an unknown virus they've never seen before."

"What's your government going to do?"

"So far we're keeping it as quiet as possible. It's a matter of national security. Anyone who had a meal with the prime minister in the last two days has been brought to a private hospital near the London Bridge. They've all been quarantined for monitoring. My colleagues and I believe that he was the sole target."

"If you're right and they can put a virus in the food, terrorists can select their targets on an individual basis. It's a whole new level of strategic terrorism."

"We're dealing with a whole new ball game."

"As soon as the Sabbath is over for Isaac, I'll inform him and Charlie."

"Please keep this on a need-to-know basis," Frederick said. "I'll be in touch with you when I have more information." He hung up the phone.

Mike tried to digest the information he'd just heard. Looking at the bottles of wine he'd just bought, he realized that thousands of innocent people could by killed simply by putting a virus into the casks at the wineries. He remembered when the United States was almost brought to a standstill over envelopes coated with white powder sent to people in Congress. The last thing they needed was another anthrax scare.

Allan was waiting for him outside when Mike's car pulled up. Mike stepped out. "I guess you heard about London."

"Yes. I still can't believe it."

"Where are Kim Li and Hui Ying?"

"They're sitting by the pool. She's really nervous. She wants to speak to Isaac. I told her he wouldn't be available until after sundown on Saturday."

"What's with her and the nerves?"

"She won't say."

"What about Hui Ying?"

"He seems to be alright."

"Let's call Washington. Lee's situation is more dire right now."

"Your team has already scanned your room for bugs. Let's go there."

James found them on their way to Mike's room. "Kim Li wants to talk to you and Allan right now."

"We have to make a call to Washington. Tell her we can meet in thirty minutes."

"She wants to meet you without Hui Ying."

"Why?" Mike asked.

"Something must have happened between them. They've hardly talked to each other since we left Paris."

"Are we going to tell her?" asked Allan. He was talking about her sister's murder in Hong Kong.

"No, Isaac wants to do it himself. I just want to see what's on her mind."

"Okay," said James, "I'll tell her you'll meet with her in a half hour." He walked off, leaving Mike and Allan to take care of their phone call.

As they entered Mike's room, his phone rang. Mike picked it up. "Hello."

"Hello, Mike."

On the other end of the call was Paul Britt, the deputy director of the NSA and Mike's boss.

"The president has decided he's flying Sunday to meet the Saudi king."

"Yes, sir."

"He's considering making a short stop in London, so he can pay his respects to the family of the prime minister. What's your situation?"

"Sir, I'm with Allan Peters. We were about to call the office."

"What about?"

"We have to get a U.S. citizen named Lee Henry out of Hong Kong right away."

"Send me all the data on my TS1 and I'll put some of our people on it immediately. Mike, I want you in London with the president."

"How long?"

"Around four hours, from the time his plane touches down at Heathrow until he takes off for Saudi Arabia. As soon as the president's plane is airborne, you can fly back to Israel."

"I'll make arrangements. Send me the details on the security detail for the president. I'll be in touch, I have to go."

"I'm going to try and reach Lee and tell him we're working on getting him out of there," Allan said and left.

Mike called James on his mobile. "Bring Kim Li to the room in five minutes."

While he waited, he turned on the TV. The president's trip was the top story. "*The president of the United States will be leaving shortly on his trip to Saudi Arabia to meet with the king to discuss the situation in the Middle East.*"

The news anchor was interrupted by someone handing him a note. His expression turned somber. "*We've just been notified on the funeral arrangements of the prime minister, more to follow in a moment. In the meantime, Israel's prime minister is boarding a special EL-Al flight to London so he can attend the funeral.*"

There was a knock at the door. James stood there with Kim Li. Mike waved them inside. "Please come in. Would you like a drink?"

Kim shook her head. "No, thanks, I'm fine." She sat down on one of the beds. "Actually, could I please have a Diet Coke?"

"Sure."

Mike took a bottle of soda out of the minibar and poured her a drink. She took a sip. "Agent O'Shea, I really have to meet with Isaac."

"Call me Mike. Isaac's planning to meet with you on Sunday."

"It can't wait until Sunday. It's very important that I see him today."

Mike looked at her as she lifted her drink with a shaking hand. "Kim Li, I'm sorry, this is Isaac's Sabbath. He doesn't take meetings."

Kim Li stared at her Coke.

"Tell us what's so urgent, Kim Li. Then we can decide what to do."

Before Kim Li could answer, there was a knock at the door. James answered it.

Allan walked in and sat down in a chair next to Mike. "Hello, Kim Li." He smiled almost shyly.

"Allan," said Mike, "Kim Li wants to see Isaac today. I told her he wasn't available."

Allan took his chair and moved it next to where Kim Li was sitting. He saw that her face was full of fear. He took her hand. "Kim Li, something's bothering you. Tell us what's so important, and then we can try and help you."

Kim Li was hesitant. Finally she whispered, "I'm afraid."

CHAPTER
61

KIM LI REACHED up to the locket she was wearing and lifted the chain over her head. Her hands trembled as she handed the locket to Allan.

"Please open it carefully."

Allan opened the clasp. On one side was a picture of Kim Li, and on the other side that of another young woman.

"That is my sister, Daiyu. Please lift up the picture of my sister very carefully."

James stood looking over Allan's shoulder. Mike's eyes focused on Kim Li. Allan gently removed the picture and held it in the palm of his hand.

"Turn it over," Kim Li said softly.

Allan turned the picture over, hardly able to believe what he saw. Embedded on the back of the photo was a dot as small as a pinhead. He carefully handed the picture to Mike. Mike looked at it for a moment. "Kim Li, where did you get this?"

"Until yesterday, I knew nothing about it. I was sitting in my room feeling lonely. Then I remembered what my sister told me when she put me on the plane. She fastened this locket around my neck and told me that I should never take it off. That it would be good luck for me. I've been missing her so much. I guess that's what made me open the locket and look at her picture. When I opened it, I saw the picture had become loose. I was going to get some glue and put it on the back of picture to fix it. When I turned it over, I spotted the dot. At first I thought it was just something stuck to the back of the picture by mistake, but then when I tried to dust it off I realized it was something more, so I brought it to you. She never said a word."

"It's a microchip," Mike said. He reached out and took the photo with the chip attached to it.

"I'm worried about my sister. She wouldn't have given it to me unless it wasn't safe in China. Something's wrong. I think she's in danger."

"Don't mention this to anyone else yet." Mike's voice was clipped. "I'll get back to you as soon as I can."

Kim Li looked at Allan. "I'm tired. I'm going to my room to lie down."

Allan nodded. "James, would you mind showing Kim Li to her room? I have to finish up some other business with Mike."

"Fine, I'll be outside her room if you need me."

Allan smiled at Kim Li. "I'll see you later for dinner. Let's meet in the lounge at eight o'clock."

Kim Li smiled weakly. "Yes, alright."

"See you then."

James and Kim Li left. Mike stood, staring at the dot on the back of the picture.

"You have any ideas, Mike?" Allan asked.

"A few, but first I'll call the general and see if we can have some of his people tell us what this thing really is."

"There's something else, Mike, we have a problem," Allan said urgently. "I didn't want to say anything when Kim Li was here. She'd only worry more."

"What is it?"

"When I was in my room, I received a call from one of my security people in Hong Kong. I had given instructions that they check on Lee daily. This morning, when they tried to reach him, they said he wasn't in the hotel. I called the desk and spoke to my guy there. He said he never saw him leave. I called the room with the code and there was no answer. I asked my guy to go and check the room. It was empty."

"That's great. Now how can we help him?"

"My people are asking around discreetly. They'll make contact with our informers and see if they've heard anything from the authorities."

Mike listened while Allan spoke, but he'd already dialed the general's private number. The phone rang a dozen times. There was no answer.

Mike started to pace back and forth. "It's Friday. Maybe he went home early." He sat down and held up the picture of Kim Li's sister. "Daiyu gave her life for this chip. It has to be extremely important. Allan, let's take a chance. Let's drive over to the house in Herzliya Pituach. Someone there will know how to contact the general for sure."

"Let's go."

Mike was heading to the lobby with Allan when his mobile rang.

"Hello, General, I was trying to reach you."

"I was on with the prime minister. Everything alright?"

"Can I see you right away? It's very important."

"Where do you want to meet?"

"I need you to look at something that will require the use of the facilities at your office."

"Come right over. I'll have my people clear you straight through. I'll be there shortly."

"Thanks, we're on our way."

Mike and Allan walked toward the exit of the hotel. On their way out, Mike spotted Hui Ying standing off in a corner talking to a man. Mike took out his Motorola and contacted James.

"James, Hui Ying is talking to some guy in a corner of the lobby. Who is he?"

"I have no idea."

"Where's the rest of the unit?"

"I'm standing here with Joe outside Kim Li's room. I have another four outside with the limos."

Mike's face turned red. "Well, one of you had better check out who he's talking to. He's not to be left alone, no matter what."

Mike hung up and looked at Allan. "What are they thinking? This is some kind of holiday?"

They walked to where the limos were parked and got into one of them. "Where to?" the driver asked.

Mike gave him the address of the Tree of Life headquarters. A few minutes later, the car was pulling up to the house in Herzliya Pituach. Remembering his previous visit, Mike directed the driver to go around to the back.

At that moment, Mike's phone rang. It was James calling.

"What is it?"

"Mike, Hui Ying told me the guy he's talking to is a cousin from China. He's been an exchange student at Hebrew University for the last year."

"How did Hui Ying contact him?"

"He said he called him when he went to his room after we checked them in."

"Make sure they're not out of your sight until Allan and I get back."

"Of course."

"If the cousin tries to leave, tell him that Hui Ying's life could be in danger and that you have to take them upstairs."

"I got it."

They came to a stop. Mike was surprised to see that the general was waiting at the gate. "*Shalom*," the general greeted them, "it's nice to see you again."

Once they were inside, the general took them to his office.

"So what's so urgent?"

Mike reached into his pocket and removed the envelope where he'd placed the picture. "General, please look at the other side of this picture."

It took a minute for the general to notice the dot. He reached for a magnifying glass on the desk and adjusted it.

"My son-in-law works in the diamond exchange," said the general. "He gave this to me when he married my daughter. It was a joke. He wanted me to see how perfect her ring was. But funnily enough, it sometimes comes in handy around here."

He held the magnifying glass over the picture and examined the microchip. "How did you come by this?"

"Kim Li gave it to us. She had no idea she had it until today. She was wearing it around her neck in a locket since she left China."

"Come with me." The general motioned for them to get up.

They followed him out of the office to the end of the hallway. The general placed his thumb on a pad next to a door that had an OFF LIMITS sign on it. When they entered, Mike and Allan looked around expecting to see a room full of people. Instead they saw a single figure working at a computer.

"Except for Tzvika," said the general, "everyone is already gone for the Sabbath."

Tzvika stood up from his desk, smiled, and nodded hello. "*Shalom*. General, how can I help you?"

The general handed him the picture of Kim Li's sister. He pointed to what was attached to the back of it. "I want you to remove this chip from the picture. I need to know what's on that chip."

Tzvika took the picture and placed it between two small pieces of blue glass. The glass had a very thin wire running through it. He put the glass into what looked like an infrared oven and pressed a button. A digital clock on the machine counted down from two minutes.

"What's that, General?" Mike asked.

"Tzvika, please explain what you are doing for Mike."

"Before we insert any chips into our system, we kill any viruses, Trojans, or worms they may contain. Chip designers sometimes embed viruses to keep the chips from getting into the wrong hands. This extractor computer was designed and built especially for analyzing and removing them. But often if you kill the virus, you also destroy the information on the chip. So we designed a special chemically coated beryllium copper wire embedded in the glass to prevent that from happening."

The clock on the virus extractor showed five seconds. When the light went off, Tzvika removed the slide from the oven. He put on a pair of surgical gloves and proceeded to separate the two pieces of glass. He then picked up a four-prong tool with a rubber suction cup attached to it and lifted the chip off the back of the picture. He placed the chip into a special integrated circuit board.

Mike and Allan looked at each other. Tzvika saw they were getting anxious.

"It will only be a few more minutes."

He proceeded to place the board between two sheets of diamond glass film. He opened up a door on a heavy metal box on the floor and put in the circuit board with the chip.

"What's that?" Mike asked.

"It's a process called encapsulation. This is a hydrogen heat-sealing box. It seals the chip with the board, and the hydrogen removes any air with contaminants that could degrade the chip or the board."

After a minute, Tzvika opened the door and took the chip to his computer. "I'm ready, General."

The general started punching numbers into the computer. "I'm the only one who knows all of the passwords," he explained.

Seconds later symbols, some letters, and a bunch of numbers popped up on the screen.

"The computer is reading it," Tzvika said excitedly. Mike waited a minute to see if the screen was going to reveal anything that was readable.

"This is a multilevel coded communication system employing frequency-expanding code conversions," Tzvika said. "I'm going to override it and substitute my own encryption system."

He started typing numbers and letters. In a matter of seconds, more numbers, letters, and a strange configuration of symbols appeared. Tzvika leaned back in his chair and looked at the ceiling, waiting. The general, Mike, and Allan stood like mannequins behind him, focused only on the screen.

Soon words appeared on the monitor. It was a letter from Daiyu.
Dear Kim Li,

If you're looking at this message, you are safe and hopefully with people you trust. The information on this chip is from one of the highest government officials in the politburo in China. I can't disclose his name for fear that if this chip fell into the wrong hands he would be killed. At some time in the future he will identify himself to you. He will tell you some of our childhood secrets and you will know it is him. He has put together the following list of countries in which highly placed citizens of that country are spying for the Chinese government. Most important are their double agents. They're feeding misinformation on all levels of military, industry, and finance around the world. They intend to bring down the United States and other democracies with whatever means they can. This list can help prevent that. You must make sure that only those you trust with your life will see it.

Remember when we moved to the city with our beloved parents? Our first night in Beijing we were excited but scared. Our mother came into our room and told us an old Chinese proverb. "A child's life is like a piece of paper on which every person leaves a mark." It has taken me a lifetime to understand that. Now I do.

Love, Daiyu.

They all stood silently for a moment.

"Tzvika, scroll down slowly," the general commanded.

They studied the list of double agents. First to appear was the United States. Allan looked at some of the names in disbelief. Some were people he had worked with over the years, who worked for him at the consulate in Hong Kong. He'd been to their homes for dinner and Fourth of July picnics. *How could they have turned against America?*

At the end of the U.S. list, three names with asterisks next to them came up. Hui Ying was the first name. The second was the commercial attaché for trade at the U.S. Embassy in Beijing, Kenneth Anderson. The last was the special assistant to the president, Wilbur Jackson, the man in charge of the negotiations on the nuclear arms treaty that was to be signed by the end of the year with Iran.

"General," said Mike, "I have to make a call right away."

The general nodded. "Come into my office."

"Can Tzvika make a copy of the data for me on a disk?" Allan asked.

"Yes, of course."

Mike and Allan walked down the hall into the general's office. As soon as they closed the door, Mike turned to Allan. "Hui Ying is sitting in the lobby with a man who claims to be his cousin. I'm pretty sure he's there to update him on our every move. What do you think we should do?"

"I say we do nothing for now," said the general. "Let's track him. See who else he contacts here in Israel."

"In the meantime," said Mike, "I'll have some of my people put a surveillance team on this 'cousin.'"

"I think you should monitor all of Hui Ying's calls from his room starting immediately," the general suggested. "He'll be more useful to us if he's free to move around for now. We can feed him information we want the Chinese to buy."

"Agreed. I have to call James." Mike dialed James's number. "What's happening? Where are Hui Ying and his cousin?"

"They're still sitting where they were when you left. They just ordered lunch."

"Tell Hui Ying I would like to meet his cousin. We'll be there in thirty minutes. He should wait for us."

Mike hung up. There was a knock on the door. The general hit a button on his desk, and Tzvika walked in. He handed a disk and a printout to the general. "This has everything that was on the disk."

"Thank you, Tzvika," said the general. "Lock up the chip in the vault."

"Is there anything else you need?"

"No, you can go home. I'll see you on Sunday."

Tzvika shook Mike and Allan's hands. "Nice meeting both of you. *Shabbat Shalom.*"

"Mike," said Allan, "we should get going."

Mike turned to the general and shook his hand. "Thank you for all of your help."

"This is valuable information for us as well. I need not tell you what that list means to both of our countries."

A few minutes later, Allan and Mike were driving away.

"Allan, let me see the list."

Allan handed it to Mike.

"Take a look at the countries on this list. Who's missing?"

Allan scoured the list. Over forty countries appeared on it.

"The list contains not only names of agents and double agents but also their handlers and secret bank accounts," Allan noted. "There are also forged passport numbers."

"But what's missing?"

Allan skimmed over it again. "Now I see it. Tzvika cleaned the list of Israeli agents. We're really stupid. We were standing right there and we didn't catch it."

"And they have the chip in the vault with the full list, including the names of the Israeli double agents."

"I can't believe this. He's not gonna get away with this."

"Allan, take it easy. Let's take care of Hui Ying and his cousin for now, and then we'll figure out how to handle this."

The limo pulled into the hotel driveway. As soon as the car stopped, Allan jumped out. "Mike, I'll be right back. I want to check on Kim Li, make sure she's okay."

"Sure thing. Meet me back here in five minutes."

James was waiting for Mike in the lobby. Mike walked up to him. "Where are they?"

"They're both sitting outside by the pool waiting for you. I have one of our guys keeping an eye on them."

"What about Kim Li?"

"She's still in her room."

"Okay, tell them I'll be there in few minutes."

Mike's phone rang. It was General Solomon. "Hello, Mike."

"Yes, General?"

"I assume you took a closer look at the list?"

"Yes, sir, we did." Mike's tone wasn't friendly.

"I know you're upset with me, and I understand that, but it was my duty to inform the prime minister about this information before you or anyone else could have access to it. I've cleared it with him. I can give you the missing part of your list."

"Thanks, General, but we're also going to need back that chip."

"I have to get clearance for that."

"If it wasn't for us, you would never had gotten it. You have all the data. Let us have the chip."

"True, but without our facilities you wouldn't have found out what was on it so quickly."

"Look, why don't you come by the hotel later. Drinks are on me. In the meantime, I'll call Washington, and you bring me the list."

"Alright. See you then."

The general hung up. Allan walked up to him. His face was pale.

"Lee's dead. I just spoke to Hong Kong."

Mike swore. "I knew we should've gotten him out of there sooner. How did it happen?"

"They found his body in his office. He was shot in the head. One of my staff members, Pat Muller, called his office to see if he might have gone there. He kept getting a busy signal. After an hour he decided to go check it out. The security guard let him in. The office had been ripped apart. Apparently whoever did this was looking for something."

"It's highly unlikely he had secret documents in his office."

"I don't know about that. He and Robert had major industrial clients. Their office had just completed an agreement between World and the Chinese government. That's what Isaac was doing in Hong Kong before he came to London."

"I don't buy it. This has something to do with Hui Ying. We have to get him alone and question him. By the way, just before you knocked, I got off the phone with the general. He's bringing over the missing part of the list tonight."

"That's good news. Hui Ying and his cousin are waiting at the pool. I want to see this piece of dirt's face now that we really know who he is."

"Let's go."

They headed outside to the pool. James was sitting at a table near Hui Ying and his cousin, reading a newspaper. Another one of Mike's guys was stretched out on a deck chair ostensibly checking e-mail on his iPhone.

Mike and Allan walked over to Hui Ying.

"I hope you're enjoying yourselves," said Mike.

"Great weather here in Israel," Allan added.

Hui Ying stood up. "Fantastic. Thank you for your hospitality. The accommodations are great. Let me introduce you to my cousin Feng."

Feng was already standing. He extended his hand to Mike and then to Allan.

"Feng. That's a great name," Allan said.

"It means 'Wants to change the world,'" Feng said in soft voice. "I guess my parents knew me even when I was small."

"Doesn't it also mean 'Changes like the wind'?" asked Allan, catching him off guard.

"Impressive. Hui told me that you're with the U.S. consul in Hong Kong. But I see your knowledge of Chinese is more expansive than that of your peers there. My name also means 'Upright and honest.' In China many things have more than one meaning."

"I understand that you're an exchange student at the Hebrew University in Jerusalem," Mike chimed in. "It's a great school. What's your interest?"

"This is my first year. I'm at the Truman Institute for the Advancement of Peace." Feng looked at his watch. "I'm really sorry. I have a date for dinner tonight, and I have to catch a bus to Jerusalem."

He stood up. "Hui, great to see you. We'll speak soon."

"I'll walk him to the entrance if it's okay with you, Mike?" said Hui Ying.

"Sure. We'll be here when you come back."

Mike motioned to James. He folded his newspaper and came over.

"James, follow Hui Ying. When he's heading back, grab him by the arm and tell him you just got a text saying that there may be a bomb in the hotel. Take him to the underground bomb shelter in the basement. There are signs directing you there. I'll fill you in later."

A few minutes later James intercepted Hui Ying just as he reached the entrance to the pool area. He slipped his hand under the Chinese man's elbow.

"There's been a bomb threat, and I need to get you to safety. Come with me."

CHAPTER
62

HUI YING FOLLOWED James stoically.

When James disappeared with Hui Ying, Mike turned to Allan.

"Allan, go to the front desk and inform them that someone left a suspicious package in the locker room near the pool. They should call the bomb squad and evacuate the area. After the call, tell our people to man their assignments. No one is to leave under any circumstances unless they hear from you or me. I'm heading down to the bomb shelter. Wait until I call."

"I got it."

Mike headed down to the basement. At the bottom of the stairs were two arrows pointing to the laundry room and the bomb shelter. The long narrow hallway was lined with carts full of sheets and pillowcases waiting to be laundered.

He walked by the open door to the laundry room, peeking his head in for a second. Industrial washing machines and dryers worked, spinning and making noise. The sound reminded him of jets warming up to take off. Tables lined one of the walls where several women worked, ironing and folding freshly washed items. Mike proceeded next door to the bomb shelter. He knew that every building in Israel had to have one, but the thickness and size of this steel door surprised him. Inside he found James and Hui Ying sitting alone on a bench.

The door had been half open when Mike entered, and he turned to close it, but the large handle would not turn.

James saw he was struggling. "Let me help you."

After pushing with all of their strength, they were finally able to close it. Mike scanned the room. There were signs everywhere. One read, "One hundred and fifty occupants maximum." Another read, "No smoking." There were only a few metal benches to sit on, and the white paint on the walls was peeling. There were no windows, but there was a six-inch pipe sticking out of the wall with a metal screen over the front of it to let in air from the outside.

Mike sat down and said to Hui Ying, "You okay?"

"I'm fine, but I don't understand what's going on. Where are the rest of the guests?"

"They'll be coming," Mike lied. "We were able to evacuate most of them, so many are waiting outside until the Israeli bomb squad assesses the threat. Allan will come and notify me when it's all clear. I'm sure it's nothing."

Hui Ying sat with his back against the wall, legs crossed. One of his feet jiggled, like he was trying to take off a piece of gum stuck to the bottom of his shoe.

Mike pulled another metal bench over and sat down. "Hui Ying, I lied."

Hui Ying stiffened. "About what?"

"When I heard about the bomb threat, I asked James to get you down here alone where we could talk without anyone disturbing us."

Hui Ying sat up. "What do want to talk about?"

"Your cousin Feng, can we trust him?"

"Of course, why would you ask that?"

"I would like him to help us when he returns to China."

"As a spy?"

"I have nothing specific at this time, but I think he could be an asset for us. His English is excellent. I assume he's learning Hebrew while he's studying here. You could be his handler. We would pay you, of course."

Hui Ying sat still, poker-faced. Mike looked straight into his eyes, and then glanced at his watch, quietly waiting.

Hui Ying broke the silence. "I need to think about it."

Mike decided to take the conversation up a notch. "I also thought you should know, Lee Henry's office was just found completely torn apart. He's been murdered. Whoever did it wanted us to believe that they were searching for something."

"What makes you say that?"

"I've been in this job a long time." Mike stood up and started pacing back and forth. He stopped in front of Hui Ying. "Kim Li's boss, Robert Lewis, was also killed the other day. Shot in his car."

Hui Ying leaned forward, looking at his hands. "That is terrible."

James watched in silence. Mike continued to pace back and forth, then suddenly stopped and sat down. "I need your help, Hui."

Hui Ying kept his face carefully blank. "What do you need from me?"

"You have to tell Kim Li that her sister has been murdered by Wen Tian."

Hui Ying made a good show of looking shocked. "Daiyu? When did this happen?"

Mike stood up and, turning his back on Hui Ying, looked at James. "We're all trying to figure that out right now."

Inside Mike was boiling. He thought about all of the people Hui Ying had set up to be killed by the Chinese secret police. Daiyu, Robert, and now Lee, they were all dead because of him.

It took all of Mike's self-control not to pull out his Sig Sauer and shoot Hui Ying then and there. Suddenly Mike said to James, "Go find Allan. Ask him what the situation is and how much longer we have to be here. If it's all clear, send me a text and we'll come up."

Mike walked James to the door. "Let me help you."

Together they pulled it open. Mike took a few steps outside with James and shouted back to Hui, "Wait here! You'll be safe. I'll be back in a few minutes."

"James, quickly help me push the door enough so that I'll be able to close it."

James looked at him.

"Do it," Mike demanded.

They both pushed the door until it left an opening small enough for just one person to squeeze in or out. Mike examined the wheel on the front of the door. He saw that it locked so that the door couldn't be opened from the inside. He'd been on a few submarines that had the hatches designed the same way.

"James, you can go up," Mike said.

"Mike, what the hell is going on here?"

"I'll tell you later. Go upstairs and see Allan. Wait for me in the lobby."

James left.

Mike walked back into the shelter and sat on the bench right next to Hui Ying.

"Hui, I have a big problem."

"What is it?"

Mike turned his face to look into Hui Ying's eyes. "It's you."

Hui Ying jumped up as if someone had placed a firecracker underneath him. "What do you mean by that?"

Mike stood up in front of Hui Ying and stepped forward until they were nose-to-nose. "Sit down. I'm trying very hard not to kill you right now. Don't give me a good reason to."

Hui Ying sat down, looking at the floor. Mike's face turned red as a beet. "Listen, you bastard, you're going to tell me everything you know about the murders of Robert, Lee, and Daiyu. If you want to leave this room alive, you're going to start talking."

Hui Ying raised his head and looked straight into Mike's eyes, defiant. "I don't have any idea what you're talking about."

"You're the one who's been leaking information about our every move. How are you getting it? Everyone who's been killed, I know it's because you passed on the information to Wen Tian. I want to know how and when."

Hui Ying said nothing.

Mike pulled his gun out of his holster. "Your choice, live or die." Adrenaline rushed through Mike's bloodstream.

Hui Ying didn't say a word.

"Why don't I leave you here for a bit to think about your decision? I'll be back soon and then it's time to make your choice."

Walking backward, Mike slipped through the door, then leaned against it to push it closed with his shoulder. He turned the wheel and locked Hui Ying in.

Upstairs, Allan stood at the reception desk with James. Mike walked over to them. "Let's all go to my room."

"Where's Hui Ying?" Allan asked.

"He's safe for now."

Mike walked fast. James and Allan followed closely behind. As soon as the door closed behind them, James demanded, "Now tell us what the hell is going on?"

Mike said, "Hui Ying is locked up in the bomb shelter down in the basement until we decide what to do with him."

"What do you mean 'we'?" said James. "You've already decided what to do, right?" He looked from Mike to Allan and back to Mike. "What haven't you told me?"

"That chip that Kim Li's been carrying around with her? It contains a list of Chinese double agents around the globe. Hui Ying's on it. He's a top-level intelligence officer for the Chinese Ministry of State Security. His code name is Steepen."

"According to the data on the chip," said Allan, "Hui Ying and other double agents like him received special orders from the chairman of the politburo to create a clandestine unit to gather top-secret information from other nations. Their main focus is to infiltrate the intelligence service of the United States."

James whistled. "So Hui Ying's a double agent? I didn't see that one coming."

"When Isaac first came to me about rescuing Kim Li and Hui Ying, we did a background check on him. We know he's thirty-eight years old, born in northern China not far from where Kim Li was born. He must have started out as a minor intelligence officer and moved up the ladder uncovering spies in the politburo."

James glanced at the door as if Hui Ying might burst through at any moment seeking retribution. "Is this going to escalate into a major political situation? I mean, what's already begun could have a bad ending."

Mike checked his watch. "It's been about a half hour since I locked him in the shelter. Let's go check on him."

"The general feels he's more valuable to us free," said Allan. "He might lead us to other agents."

"James, what are your thoughts?" Mike asked.

"It's a high-risk game. But I'm ready to play."

"We'd better play it fast," said Allan. "We're having dinner at eight with Kim Li."

"James and I will go down together and see if he's ready to co-operate. I'll call you if I need you, Allan."

Mike and James left the room. James didn't speak until they entered the elevator.

"Mike, we've been working together a long time."

Mike opened his mouth, but James held up a hand to stop him. "Stop right there. I know what you're thinking. You're gonna kill him."

Mike's lips tightened into a flat line. "He has one chance to live."

"What's that?"

"I believe he has names of American double agents who are not on the coded chip. Our servicemen are dying every day fighting for our freedom, and these traitors are betraying our country. If he has that type of information, he can trade it for his life."

James nodded. "You don't have to say anything else. I'm with you."

Mike patted James on the back. "Just like old times. I remember when you first joined the Secret Service after your tour in the army. Do you remember, we had information that a drug cartel out of Mexico had ordered a hit on our last president? He was touring the proposed site for the security fence in El Paso. An informant passed on information to the FBI, and they gave us a briefing. The cartel had hired a local drug dealer to do the job. One of his junkies was the informant. You and I staked out the dealer's house. We had his phone tapped when he ordered the hit on the president, and we moved in on him. We got him, but the sniper made a run for it and you killed him."

"That's not the end," said James. "You dragged the dealer into the basement. I was upstairs, and I could hear everything. How you 'encouraged' him to give you the name of the cartel leader who ordered the president's assassination. He wouldn't budge. Thirty minutes later I heard a shot. You came up smoking a cigarette. Said he tried to attack you. Two weeks later we received a special commendation from the President."

The elevator doors opened to the sublevel. "You have a good memory, but let's get going."

As they approached the door to the shelter, James said, "Let's give him a chance."

CHAPTER
63

THEY TURNED THE wheel to the shelter. When the door finally opened, it was pitch black inside. Mike reached in and hit the light switch. The light bulb hanging from the ceiling flickered and then illuminated Hui Ying's body hanging from a steam pipe that ran to the laundry room next door. Mike looked down at the bench that was now lying on the floor.

"It looks like that bench was more useful than we expected it to be."

James looked at Hui Ying hanging there. "I'd better get Allan."

"Okay, I'm going to try and reach the general. Keep this between us for now."

James turned to go back upstairs. Mike pushed a bench over to Hui Ying's body and stood on it so he could search Hui's pockets. He reached into Hui's back pocket and pulled out his wallet. Then he stepped down and started to go through it.

Everything looked normal: some Hong Kong dollars, a driver's license, a few credit cards, and a picture of Kim Li. Mike was about to put it back, but when he ran his hand on the inside of the wallet he felt a little rise in the leather, He pushed his finger between the two soft pieces of leather and pulled out a small piece of microfilm. He looked at it for a moment and then slipped it into his own wallet before returned Hui's wallet to his pocket.

What's on that piece of film and why didn't Hui destroy it before he hanged himself?

At that moment James walked in with Allan and two of the security guards. Allan looked up to see Hui hanging from the pipe. "Did you reach the general?"

"Not yet."

"We should take him down."

"He stays right there. The general may want to call the local police, and they won't like it if we move the body."

James agreed. "Close and lock the door."

Mike followed James and Allan up to the lobby where they found a quiet corner.

"This has been one hell of a day," said James.

Allan nodded. "Sure has."

Mike got down to business. "Before I call the general to tell him about Hui Ying, I want to go over the schedule for the next forty-eight hours. We might not have time later. First off, Paul called me earlier. I have to fly out of here early Sunday morning. He wants me to be in London when the president arrives."

"How long is he planning to stay?" James asked.

"Till he takes off for Saudi Arabia, around four hours. It's not an official state visit. He's only stopping to pay his respects to the family of the late prime minister and stay a short time for the burial. My plane is leaving Ben Gurion at five a.m. I'll be at Heathrow with time to spare before he lands. I plan to fly back here as soon as he's in the air. James will be in charge while I'm gone."

James nodded.

"Next item. I'm due to meet Isaac tomorrow night to discuss the Iran situation. On Sunday Isaac is meeting with Kim Li to tell her about Daiyu and the other recent deaths."

"What are we going to tell Kim Li about Hui Ying?" Allan asked. "I'm supposed to be having dinner with her soon."

"To tell you the truth, I don't know. It's a lot for her to take in." Mike looked at his watch. "It's getting late, and I want to shower before the general gets here. He was supposed to meet me for drinks, but I'd better call him and tell him what to expect."

"Anyone want to join me and Kim Li for dinner?" Allan asked.

Everyone looked at him and they all started to laugh.

Allan looked at them, taken aback. "What?"

"Sure you want company?" James teased.

"What are you talking about?"

James laughed. "Sure, I'll be there. I wouldn't miss it."

Allan gave him a look.

"I'll join you after my meeting with the general."

"Alright." Allan stood up to leave. "I'll see you all later."

"One last thing, James," Mike said to the other agent before he too stood up to leave. "Do we have anyone from our security detail who understands Hebrew?"

"A couple of the guys. What do you need?"

"I need someone who can understand the general when he's talking to his people."

"I'll work on it." James walked off.

Mike decided to check the front desk for any messages before he went up to his room. When he approached the desk, he was surprised to see General Solomon talking to the attendant at the reception desk. He walked over.

"Good evening, General. I wasn't expecting you yet."

The general turned around. "Mike, I was just telling them to ring your room. Do you have a minute?" He extended his hand.

"For you, General, all the time you need."

"Maybe we can find a spot that's quiet."

"Follow me. I just left one." He pointed to the table where he had just been sitting with Allan and James.

"Mike, I saw you tried to phone me. I figured I should come sooner than later."

"That's right."

"It's about Hui Ying, is that right? What are we going to do about him?"

"That's why I was calling you, General."

"Mike, I love you Americans."

Mike was confused, unsure where Solomon was going with this. "What do you mean, General?"

"You Americans with all your manpower and money sometimes overlook the small things."

Mike was puzzled. He looked around the room for a waiter. "General, I think I need a drink."

"Hold off for a minute, I want to give you something."

Mike took the envelope without opening it and put it in his pocket. He figured it must be the list the general had promised to bring.

"Don't you want to look at it?"

"I'll look at it later."

The general stood up to leave. "Wait, General, please sit down, I need to tell you about something else."

"If you are talking about Hui Ying hanging himself in the bomb shelter, there's no need. I already know."

Mike's jaw dropped. "How?"

"We have it all on tape. All up until you turned off the lights and left."

Mike was stunned.

"We have microcameras hidden in the bomb shelters of every major building in Israel. The Tree of Life Foundation developed a special system that alerts us when there is an entry. One of my guys is always on standby. When he received an alert on his mobile, he immediately went back to the office. He called me the moment you walked in with Hui Ying. Next time you're scanning a room check the screws in the light switches for a camera and a microphone."

Mike picked up the envelope that the general had given him. In it was a bug. He assumed that was the one that had recorded what had transpired between him and Hui Ying.

He shook his head. Never underestimate the Israelis. "So what do we do with Hui Ying?"

"My people are handling it as we speak."

"Can you fill me in?"

"They're going to take him to his room."

"How are they going to do that?"

"In a laundry cart, of course. They'll put him in his bed and inject him with a drug that will make his death show up on a coroner's report as a massive heart attack."

"What about his neck? Won't it be obvious that he hanged himself?"

"Our coroner will take care of all the details." Once again the general stood up to leave. Then he turned around and said, "Oh, one more thing. The microfiche in your wallet, when can we look at it?"

"Whenever you want, sir."

"Saturday night okay with you?"

"I'm flying out in the morning. I'll call you when I get back."

"Alright. And I almost forgot." The general pulled out a disk and handed it to Mike. "Your list." The general turned to leave, got into his car, and was gone within seconds.

Mike's phone rang. He slipped the disk into his pocket and said into his phone, "What is it, Allan?"

"I'm picking Kim Li up at her room in a few minutes. She just called me and asked if we could speak alone before we all have dinner together."

"It turns out that I won't be having drinks with the general tonight, so I'll see you as soon as I shower and change."

"Did you tell him about Hui Ying?"

"I'll give you the lowdown later. But for now, don't tell Kim Li about Hui Ying. As far as we're concerned, he decided to turn in early."

"Okay, got it."

"I'm on my way to her room. I'll meet you in the dining room in ten minutes."

CHAPTER
64

ALLAN APPROACHED KIM LI's room. A huge man with dark glasses and arms folded across his chest stood next to her door.

"How's it going?" Allan asked.

"Quiet."

"That's a good thing."

Allan knocked on the door lightly.

"Who is it?"

"It's Allan."

"One minute, please."

"Take your time."

Since the security guard didn't seem to be up for conversation, Allan stood in silence, rocking on his heels, until the door opened.

"I'm so sorry to keep you waiting," said Kim Li. She looked calmer and a little more rested.

"Not a problem. Are you ready to go?"

The security guard accompanied them as they walked to the dining room.

"Were you able to get some rest?" Allan asked.

"A little. I have so much on my mind, it's hard for me to sleep."

When they entered the dining room, the maître d' was waiting to show them to their table. The security guard looked around and pointed. "I'll be standing over there if you need me."

Kim Li and Allan sat down. "Can I order you a drink until the others join us?"

"That would be nice, thank you."

Allan handed the wine list to the maître d' without even looking at it. "Please bring us the best bottle of Israeli wine you have."

The maître d' motioned to a waiter. The waiter picked up a bottle and brought it over.

"I highly recommend this 2005 Zauberman Cabernet Sauvignon limited edition," said the maître d'. He took it from the waiter and held it up so that Allan could read the label. "This is the last bottle we have. I'm sure you will enjoy it."

"Thank you."

The maître d' opened the wine and poured a small amount into Allan's glass. Allan lifted up the glass to look at the color, then gently swirled it, finally inhaling the aroma.

Kim Li watched as Allan took a small sip and said to the maître d', "Very nice. You can pour the lady some. We'll order when our other guests arrive."

The wine-pouring ritual over, Allan looked at Kim Li. "What do you think?"

"About what?"

"The wine. Do you like it?"

"Oh." Kim Li tasted it. "It's very nice."

They were quiet as they sipped their wine. Kim Li broke the silence. "Allan, I apologize. I know I seem distracted. My thoughts are with my sister. Ever since I found out about the locket, I've been so afraid for her safety."

"No need to apologize."

"The truth is, I'm glad James and Mike aren't here yet. I wanted some time to speak to you alone."

"Before you start, I want to tell you how beautiful you look."

Kim Li blushed. "Thank you." She paused and took a deep breath. "Allan, I am worried that my sister is dead."

She looked like she was about to cry. Allan took her hand. He wanted to tell her that she was right but held back. He didn't want to be the man she'd always remember as having told her the worst news of her life.

"Kim Li, please, drink a little wine. It will help you relax."

Kim Li dried her eyes with a tissue. "I'm sorry. I didn't mean to get so emotional." She lifted the glass and took a sip.

"Now," said Allan, "what makes you think your sister is dead?" Even as he said it, he felt guilty.

"It's Hui Ying," she said. "His behavior is strange lately. I sense he knows something about Daiyu that he's not telling me." She ran a finger around the rim of her glass. "It's difficult for me to explain. It's just something I've been feeling over the last week. Please don't think badly of me."

"Never. Why do you say that?"

"I don't like to speak ill of people, but Hui Ying has changed."

Allan held back telling her exactly how much had changed about Hui Ying lately.

"Give me your dominant hand, the one you write with." Kim Li stretched out her hand palm side up for Allan to rest his hand in. She had clearly decided a change of subject was in order.

Allan put his right hand into hers.

Kim Li took his hand and flipped it over to see the lines in his palm.

"My parents moved us to Beijing when we were children. Not long afterward, both of my parents were killed in a train accident." She studied Allan's palm. "We were brought up by our aunt and uncle. They both read palms. You'd be surprised how much you can learn about a person from his palm."

Allan gave into the moment. Looking at Kim Li as she focused on his palm, he said, "So what can you tell me?"

She pressed his fingers back a little so the lines in his palm were more pronounced. "I see the sun. That represents your deep desire to share. It's part of your soul."

She stopped for a moment and then pressed his fingers back further so she could see the lines even clearer. "You can transcend limitations. Your success, charisma, and integrity, they are intrinsically a part of you."

Kim Li released Allan's hand and looked into his eyes. "Many times I asked Hui Ying to let me study his hands. He always refused. He said he didn't believe in any of that foolishness. Then the other day we were alone for a while, and he was acting strange, very nervous, smoking one cigarette after another. I was on the couch watching him when suddenly he said, 'Go ahead and read my palm.' I studied Hui Ying's hand intensely. I could not believe what it revealed to me."

Allan listened in silence.

"What I read was very disturbing. The islands in his hand indicated an inauspicious symbol. It was very pronounced in his career line. He had many small lines crossing it. I told him he was facing many political difficulties. When he heard that, his demeanor changed. The thing that upset him the most was when I told him that something serious could cut his career short."

"What did he say?"

"He called me a fool and said he never wanted to hear about this silly fortune-telling again, that since the Cultural Revolution and Maoism there is no place in our society for any of this. Then he just got up and walked away."

Allan had no idea what to say. He checked his watch It was 7:48. Mike and James would be joining them soon. He decided to say nothing.

Kim Li looked out the window. "It's really a beautiful sight to see the sun set into the sea. It's dark outside and the clouds have hidden the stars." She turned back to Allan. Her expression was bleak.

"My life feels like the sky, dark. I can never go back to China. I don't know what I will do."

Allan said gently, "When we see Isaac tomorrow, I'm sure he'll be able to help you. Everything will be fine."

James had entered the restaurant and observed Allan and Kim Li from a few feet away before he walked over.

"Is it okay if I join you?"

"Only if you're buying drinks," Allan quipped.

"What are you drinking?"

"Try it. It's a great Israeli wine."

Allan poured James a glass, and Mike came over and sat down, accepting a glass of wine for himself. Mike looked at Kim Li. He could tell she'd been crying. In an attempt to change the atmosphere, he lifted up his glass and said, "Cheers, everyone."

Allan and James did the same. Kim Li placed her hand on her glass but said nothing.

"Let's eat," Mike said. "I don't know about all of you, but I'm starved."

Allan motioned to the waiter to come over. The waiter handed everyone a menu. Kim Li studied it, then lifted her face to Allan. "I will just have soup. I am not really hungry."

James looked over the menu. It was all in Hebrew. He handed it back to the waiter. "Can I have a steak, rare, with fries and a salad?"

The waiter nodded his head and looked at Allan.

"What do you recommend?" Allan asked.

"The entrecote is excellent."

"Sounds good. Medium rare with a baked potato and an Israeli salad, thank you."

Mike's phone rang. He stood up. "I'll have the same as you, Allan." He left to find a quiet place to take the call.

"Allan," Kim Li asked once the waiter had left, "do you have any plans for tomorrow? I understand it's the Sabbath, so it will be pretty quiet."

"How would you like to go see the Dead Sea? Unless you have something else you would prefer to do."

"Hui said he wanted to visit the Golan Heights. Perhaps we can all go together."

Allan's face darkened. Kim Li noticed immediately.

"Did I say something wrong?"

"Kim Li, no, it's not what you said," James said hurriedly. "It's where you want to go."

"I don't understand. What's the problem?"

"The Golan Heights is under tight security. Israel is expecting a war, possibly with Iran or their surrogate Hezbollah. We'll be subject to all kinds of checkpoints."

Allan nodded in agreement. "It's not the place to go at this time."

The three of them fell silent. Kim Li looked into her glass like it was a crystal ball. Allan looked at James, hoping he would say something smart to break the silence. *What's taking Mike so long?*

The waiter brought over their food. "What should I do with the other meal?" he asked Allan, looking at Mike's empty chair.

"Leave it. I see him coming now."

Mike sat down. "I apologize for holding everyone up."

"They just started to serve. Is everything alright?"

"It was just Paul to give me some information about London." Mike checked his watch.

"Is everything on schedule?" Allan asked.

"It appears that way. Anything else I'll get when I'm on the plane in the morning."

James signaled to the waiter. "I feel like another drink. Would anyone care to join me? Kim Li, what about you?"

"Can they make me a mojito?" she asked the waiter.

"Of course."

"I'll have a double Macallan on the rocks," Mike said.

"The same for me," said James.

Mike checked his watch again.

"You're nervous about something?" James asked.

"How do you know that?"

"I can see it in your face, Mike. And you keep checking your watch."

"I wouldn't say I'm nervous, but I am concerned about the trip to England and what's going to take place in Saudi Arabia."

Allan leaned forward. "Mike, Kim Li can read your palm. She's good."

Mike looked at Kim Li. She smiled shyly.

"Why not?"

"Good, let's switch seats."

Mike got up to change his seat with Allan. "I can't believe I'm doing this." He gave Kim Li his right hand. She pushed it aside.

"I need your left hand as it is your dominant one." The tone of her voice was confident. "Some readers say that the right hand is for men and the left is for women. I believe both hands are important."

Kim Li studied Mike's hand. "Your left hand is the doorway to your persona. Your hands are not flexible, which indicates a strong character. Whatever you do, you must believe in it strongly. You will never compromise your beliefs. This is the foundation of how you live your life. The shape and color of your nails tell me you are in good health." She looked up at Mike. "There are many more details on the fingers, but it would take too much time for me to elaborate now. I'll just mention one other thing: the middle part of your palm shows aggression, courage, and bravery."

She released his hand.

Mike looked into her eyes. "What about my life line? Is it long?"

Kim Li took her glass of wine and raised it. "I suggest we make a toast."

Mike was silent for a few moments, then nodded. "When in Rome..." He poured some wine into his glass. "The Jewish custom is to say 'Lechaim'—to life—when you toast." He raised his glass. Everyone else did the same. "To long and meaningful lives. To all of us."

Everybody said "*lechaim*" and took a swig of their wine. They ate and talked, avoiding any more mention of Hui Ying or Daiyu.

An half hour later, Kim Li pushed away her half-full bowl of soup and stood up. "Excuse me, if you don't mind, I'm going to ring Hui's room and say good night to him, and then I think I'll see if I can get some sleep."

Allan looked to James for an intervention.

James said, "Sorry, I completely forgot to tell you that Hui told me he was going for a walk on the beach and then to sleep early. He didn't want to be bothered."

Allan stood up too. "Let me walk you to your room."

She nodded and turned to Mike and James. "Good night, gentlemen. Thank you for a lovely evening."

Allan motioned to the security guard that they were leaving.

Mike leaned over and spoke to James in a low voice. "Go to reception and tell them that Hui Ying requested a wake-up call at eight a.m. But under no circumstances is he to receive any further calls this evening. Say that he wanted to go to sleep early."

James stood up. "Got it."

"I'll wait for you here. I need to go over some information with you. Could you ask the waiter to give me a refill on your way back?"

"No problem."

Mike looked out the window. It was pitch black outside. In the distance, out on the sea, he could see an array of small lights. The fishing boats were out in full force. He thought about all of the places his job had taken him. Africa, Lebanon, South America, and most of the islands in the South Pacific.

He envied the fishermen. He'd always loved fishing. He dreamed about owning his own boat and traveling in different waters to fish. Fishermen everywhere were alike. Late at night or early in the morning they banded together like fraternity brothers at their college reunion. But even with all of the small talk on their radios about the weather and yesterday's catch, in the end it all came down to making a living. This thought reminded him he didn't have the time to fish. He was in the same boat; he had to make a living.

He looked up to see the waiter placing a glass on the table. "Your friend told me to bring you another drink. Macallan. Right, sir?"

"Yes, thank you."

"Is there anything else I can do for you, sir?"

"Come to think of it, there is. Leave the bottle of Macallan on the table and bring some pistachio nuts and pretzels, if you have it. And do you have those big green olives?"

The waiter smiled. "Are you sure that's it, sir?"

Mike smiled back, then reached into his pocket, pulled out a twenty-dollar bill, and handed it to him. "That's it. Thank you."

The waiter took the twenty dollars and put it in his pocket. "I'll be back in a few minutes."

Mike sipped his drink and stared at the lights of the fishing boats some more. He went over everything in his mind, what Kim Li had told him and the whole situation with the general. But it was Hui Ying who disturbed him the most.

I should have been more careful. If he were still alive, with the right interrogation tactics he could have revealed more of China's intentions toward the U.S.

CHAPTER
65

THE TELEPHONE CONVERSATION with the deputy director had created a major problem for Mike. That's what he'd been so nervous about, but he hadn't wanted to say anything.

The director put me in the middle of a house on fire and left it up to me to extinguish it or be consumed by it.

James returned and sat down. The waiter placed the bottle of Macallan right in front of Mike.

James looked from the bottle to Mike. "How many have you had?"

"You drinking or lecturing?"

"Okay, no lectures." He took the bottle and poured a drink for Mike and one for himself. "You had something you wanted to talk to me about."

"Where did Allan disappear to?"

"When I went to the reception desk, he was sitting and talking to Kim Li in the lobby."

Mike took another swallow of his drink. "It's better we talk alone anyway."

"Go ahead."

"What I'm about to tell you may put your life in danger, but I have no other option."

James downed the rest of his drink and stared at Mike. "Spill it."

"That call I had earlier was a conference with our boss and the chairman of the Joint Chiefs of Staff. They were together in the war room at the Pentagon and informed me that they are planning to remove the president from office and declare a national emergency. The plan is to install the vice president."

James was about to pour himself another drink. He put down his glass. "Mike, don't tell me anymore."

"They asked me to tell you everything that's going on."

"I don't give a damn about what they said. This is crazy, it's treason. I don't understand what the hell is behind this."

"Lower your voice. Calm down. That was my reaction too. Then they played me the tape." Mike pulled out his mobile and turned on his voice mail. "Listen to this."

James looked at Mike for a long time, trying to decide whether to press the on button or not.

"If you listen and don't want any part of this, I'll report back that I felt I couldn't trust you so I decided not to tell you about the plan."

James nodded. "Okay." He pressed the button, then put the mobile to his ear and turned his face toward the window.

"Yes, Your Majesty, of course. Yes, I'm here in the Oval Office. This is a secure line. We can speak freely... I'm aware. I want to extend my deepest sympathy and condolences on the loss of your nephew. We'll find out who is responsible for that plane going down, and I assure you he will pay... The plan went horribly wrong. I am prepared to do anything you need. You have my full support... We will succeed. And we will be praying together in Mecca soon."

James turned off Mike's phone and slowly put it down. "You sure that was the president?"

"I wish I wasn't."

James sat motionless, then said, "Mike, pour me another drink.

I want to hear it again."

Mike poured the drink and handed it to him. James took a swallow and put the phone back to his ear. He closed his eyes as if he was replaying the president's words in his mind. Mike waited for a reaction. They had survived stakeouts, drug busts, and whatever else their bosses told them to do.

They could survive this too.

James finished listening to the recording again and handed the phone back to Mike.

"What do you think?" Mike asked.

"Assuming the tape is real and the plan you already described is in motion, we have a major problem. This isn't something we can be a part of and not take responsibility. Who's involved in the conspiracy other than our president and the king of Saudi Arabia?"

"I don't know. What I do know is secret meetings with concerned individuals are ongoing, and the list is growing by the day. As I said before, they'll be contacting me on the plane. When I hear from them, I'll fill you in immediately. One thing I can promise you for sure. I'm not gonna let anyone hang us out to dry for this one."

"What about Allan?" James asked.

"Let's wait to tell him. I'll need to clear it with the director."

"So what's next?"

The waiter was back with a pot of coffee. Allan walked in behind him.

Mike looked at James. "We can finish this conversation later."

Allan sat down. "I see Mr. Macallan is treating you well."

"I've had enough." Mike poured coffee into his cup.

"Allan, if you have one, I'll join you," James said. "I haven't had nearly enough."

Allan poured himself and James a drink, finishing the rest of the bottle.

James lifted his glass. "Cheers to the three of us and to long life."

"*Lechaim*," they said in unison. Mike put his cup of coffee down and took the empty whiskey bottle and laid it down on the table in front of him.

"What's that about?" Allan asked.

Mike shrugged. "I've seen Isaac do it when there was an empty bottle on the table. That's what he does. I asked him about it once, and he told me it's a Jewish thing. Something about bad luck. Something about empty bottles means empty pockets." Mike took another sip of the coffee, put the cup down, and grinned. "Isaac's done pretty well, so I figure it can't hurt."

Allan smiled. "I had a long talk with Kim Li. I told her that Isaac would make sure she wouldn't have to worry about money or a position in the U.S. But right now all she cares about is her sister. I told her we'd do what we can to get information about her."

James nodded. He felt lightheaded. All the Macallan he'd consumed had started to take its toll. "Mike, I have to get to bed. It's after midnight. What time do we meet in the morning?"

"Eight o'clock for breakfast. Okay with you?"

"That's good, see you in the morning."

James got up, leaving Mike and Allan alone at the table.

"What's the latest news from D.C.?" Allan asked casually.

"Just the same old stuff. Why?"

"Just curious."

"Well, there's nothing to be curious about."

Allan wasn't buying it. "Something's up, right? If you don't want to tell me, fine, but don't give me a story. There's no such thing as the 'same old stuff' in our line of work."

Mike scowled. "Stop pressing me, Allan. You're better off not being involved."

Allan exhaled. "It's that serious. When will you tell me?"

"Damn it, Allan, when you need to know." Mike turned to leave before Allan could ask anything else. "I'll see you at breakfast."

Left alone, Allan checked his watch to see what time it was in the States. It was around five o'clock over there, the end of the workday. He decided to call some of his contacts in Washington. Maybe he could figure this out without Mike.

He scanned the private numbers in his phone, then dialed one of them. Ted Wallace was an old college buddy and a friend of the president's top-secret advisory board for covert operations involving military actions in foreign countries. If something big was going on, he was the guy who would know what it was.

The phone rang several times before Ted picked up.

"Hello."

"Ted, it's Allan."

"Where are you?"

"Israel."

"I thought you're based in Hong Kong. What are you doing in Israel?"

"I just left Hong Kong. I'll explain it to you later."

"Actually, I was going to call you. I heard that there were some major problems over there in Hong Kong."

Allan grimaced. "You could say I've had my hands full. But that's not why I'm calling."

"What's on your mind?"

"I can't put my finger on it, but I have a feeling something big is going down. Maybe something connected to national security. Do you have any update on what's going on in the White House?"

"To tell you the truth, I haven't heard anything out of the ordinary, just the same old stuff."

"Thanks, Ted. I appreciate your help. Please give my regards to your wife."

Allan hung up, thinking. There it was again. That phrase. *The same old stuff.*

He scanned his phone again. He'd have to ask his questions more carefully, be less direct. He pressed the number of the White House assistant press secretary. One ring and a female voice came on the line. "Press office. Jasmine Yona speaking. Can I help you?"

"How are you, sweetie?"

"Allan, where are you? Are you in D.C.?" Nobody called her "sweetie" but Allan.

"No, I'm in Israel."

"I can't remember the last time I saw you."

"It's been at least two years. We had a great dinner in Georgetown, and then I took off for Hong Kong."

"You're right, it's been too long. What can I do for you, darlin'?"

"You must have heard what happened in Hong Kong with the Chinese."

"Yes, but not all the details."

"Well, I can't return at this time due to difficult circumstances that have recently arisen as a result. Anyway I want to be back in Washington. I need to bypass the State Department, or they'll send me someplace like Kosovo. I need a minute with the chief of staff. Can you arrange it?"

"Allan, I can try, but everyone is in over their heads with the imminent trip to Saudi Arabia, and now with the stopover in London it's going to be tough."

"Maybe I can meet him in London. I assume he's going to be there?"

"After paying his respects to the prime minister's wife, the president is having a brief meeting with the foreign minister of China. The chief of staff and a few other key people will have to be there. They won't have time to see you."

"Where will the meeting take place?"

"That's the strange thing. No one knows. I checked with the Secret Service so I could put together a press release about the visit. They were only told that there would be a meeting and they wouldn't be informed when the meeting would take place until they were in London. They're mad as hell about it too. Hard to arrange security when you don't know what you need to secure."

"Well, do what you can, sweetie. I'll be in touch."

Allan hung up. *What the hell is going on?*

He looked at his watch again. It was already after one a.m. He started walking toward his room, trying to decide who else to call. When he reached his room, he heard the phone ringing inside. He quickly slipped his electronic key in the lock and ran in to get the phone.

"Hello."

"Allan, it's Frederick. How are you?"

"Fine. Something wrong?"

"I'm sorry to call you so late. I left a message for Mike, but the operator said his phone was off until six thirty in the morning. I took a chance on calling you."

"Wait, Frederick. I'll call you back on my cell phone. It's more secure."

Allan hung up and called Frederick back on his mobile.

"So what's up?"

"I had a meeting with MI5 earlier. I thought that your government should be apprised of the latest information due to the president's trip to London."

"What is it?"

"They traced the virus that was in the prime minister's food to the chef. They took him in for questioning. While they were running his file, he was put in a cell alone for about half an hour. When they came to get him for interrogation, he was dead."

"How did it happen?"

"They found a small plastic envelope with a pill casing in it sewn in the lining of his jacket lapel. The laboratory analyzed the remains. The report showed it was a new advanced form of cyanide. From what we can ascertain, he was gone within a few minutes. He knew that if they found out about his activities, they would torture him. Maybe even kill him."

"What was his motive for poisoning the prime minister?"

"Honestly we haven't figured it out yet. He was born in Shanghai. He'd been in the UK for five years and applied to be the chef in the prime minister's house. He had solid references and they all checked out, including a reference from the Chinese ambassador in Great Britain."

"That's really bizarre. What's the next step?"

"MI5 has assigned their best people. Their agents are all over his house, and they're talking to anyone he's had contact with."

"Do you want me to tell Mike about this?"

"No, I have to talk to him anyway about his trip to London."

"Okay, thanks for the call. I've got to get some sleep, talk to you tomorrow."

Allan lay down on the bed fully clothed, his mind still racing. He kicked off his shoes, grabbed the second pillow on the bed, and placed it on top of the other pillow. If he could just rest for a minute, maybe it would clear his mind.

He closed his eyes and within a few minutes fell fast asleep.

CHAPTER
66

THE SHIN BET arrived in the lobby under the general's orders. Local police stood talking to each other. Most of the guests had retired for the night.

Someone from the hotel had reported Hui Ying's death. The report had come from one of the general's men, after he had transported Hui Ying's body up to his room in a laundry cart, but the police didn't know that. The Shin Bet agents showed up soon after, claiming jurisdiction since Hui Ying was a visiting national.

Shin Bet agents removed Hui Ying's body from his room as discreetly as possible. A few minutes later, the hearse arrived. They loaded the body into it and they all left.

CHAPTER
67

MIKE COULDN'T SLEEP. He'd been through this scene before. It was part of the job description.

He decided to head down to the lobby. He spotted a coffee urn near the front desk. He took a cup of black coffee and sat down on the sofa. The lounge was empty. The guy who had been pounding out old melodies on the Steinway had left for the night. Mike sat admiring the piano.

He tried not to think about his assignment in London. He finished his coffee and stared out at the sea. The lights on the fishing boats were gone. It was as if everyone was sleeping. The fish and the fisherman had both called it a night.

"Can I join you?"

Mike jumped up and turned around to see General Solomon standing there.

"What are you doing here at this hour, General?"

The general smiled. "I was in the neighborhood. We have some unfinished business, Mike."

Mike nodded and offered the general a chair.

The general shook his head. "We'll go to my office. I can offer you better coffee there. Also, I want to see what's on that microfiche."

"Let's go. I have it here in my wallet."

"My driver is waiting outside."

Fifteen minutes later the security guard opened the gate to the Tree of Life headquarters and waved them in. *How different the night makes things appear*, Mike thought.

The house was completely dark. It appeared as if the people inside it were sleeping, just like every other house on the block. So few people knew about the activities in the house or how much they could affect their lives.

They went directly to the general's office. The general reached for two cups on the table. "You drink your coffee black without sugar, isn't that right?" He started pouring coffee into a cup.

"You got it." Mike took a sip. "This is great coffee."

"It's Turkish. A friend of mine always brings me a case when he visits Israel. Let me give you some to take home. I have plenty."

"Thank you."

The general took Mike back into the room they were in earlier that day. The room was empty.

"Who's going to decrypt it?" Mike asked.

"I am."

Mike reached into his pocket and pulled out his wallet. He took out the microfiche and handed it to the general.

"The U.S. government uses Advanced Encryption Standard for its decryptions," Mike commented.

"We have something better." The general placed the microfiche into a projection machine, then pressed a switch. Up on the screen came a bunch of what looked like gibberish.

Mike understood what he was seeing. He'd been in the Pentagon decoding room plenty of times.

"Solomon, can you decrypt it?"

"Just give me a few minutes and I'll tell you." He punched in a symmetric key decryption using the template his team designed.

Mike pulled up a chair and sat next to the general, trying to keep track of the general's programming commands. But his fingers moved so fast they were impossible to follow.

"We're almost there." The general continued tapping the keys. "When the USSR broke up in the nineties, we were fortunate to welcome Russian computer engineers into our country. They had been working on advanced research to break some of the most advanced codes that existed." The general stopped typing and glanced at Mike. "Some of them even broke some of your country's top-secret codes for us."

"That's encouraging," Mike said wryly.

"Mike, keep your eyes on the screen so you can read the information as soon as it starts to appear."

A moment later words showed up on the screen.

Top Secret:

- Top priority: get all the working plans of the space-based defense systems Israel is working on.
- The name of the person on the team working on it.
- His code name, plus the information on the drop-off points.
- Chinese students in the universities in Israel will use a coded microfiche.
- We need a detailed list of leading-edge technology companies that are working with the U.S.
- Last, we have a mole inside the Dimona nuclear facility. He has made a chip of new developments on their enhanced neutron and hydrogen bombs. We need that chip.

Almost as soon as Mike had finished reading, the screen went blank.

The general said, "If they have access to the Dimona facility, they already have information on our next-generation warheads." The general looked at his watch. Four thirty a.m. "Mike, I have to get going. Why don't you try to get a little sleep?"

"Good idea. I'll be seeing Isaac after the Sabbath to inform him of the new developments."

"I'll join you. I have a few things I need to speak to him about as well. Mike, do you want a copy of the microfiche?"

"You keep it for now. I'll have to figure out a way to get it to Washington." He didn't tell the general that right now he wasn't sure who in Washington he could trust. "I'll call you when I need it."

"Fine, let's go."

In the driveway, the general's beeper went off. He scrolled down and read what appeared to be a long message. Mike could see that it must be something important. The general closed the beeper and said to the driver, "Take us to GOC."

Mike knew what the GOC was. Unofficially known as Mazi, it was the headquarters of the Israel Defense Forces located near Herzliya.

The general looked at Mike. "Mike, I'm sorry, but I have to get there right away. All the commanders of the IDF are assembling. As soon as my driver drops me off, he will take you back to the hotel."

"What's happening?"

"The message I just received is our satellite has sent pictures of a massive movement of troops and equipment from Syria into Lebanon."

"I see."

"There's more. Our people inside the Syrian military have sent us a coded message. They're planning to attack us midday tomorrow, during the Sabbath."

Mike pulled out his phone. "I have to alert my people right away."

"You can, right after we confirm that the information we received is correct."

How am I going to get to London in the middle of a war? Mike thought.

"Listen, General, let me come with you to the meeting."

The general thought about it for a few moments, then nodded. "Alright. You have the clearance for it. I already did a background check before I cleared you to enter the Tree of Life headquarters. This will be a good opportunity. I need you to convey to your superiors in the National Security Agency the threat from all sides of the Arab world that we face."

It seemed like it took no time to arrive at GOC headquarters. Cars pulled up one after another. It was still dark as they waited in line, the headlights of each car silhouetting the car in front of them. At the gate they paused for a few seconds to identify themselves. When he saw the general, the soldier at the gate said, "Sir, they're waiting for you in Building Three."

The driver proceeded to the building. Inside, the general led Mike down a long corridor where they found a frenzy of people at work. The general stopped at a door. Two guards stood with their Mini-Uzis slung over their shoulders. The general touched an electronic pad, and the door opened into an elevator. They both stepped inside. There were no buttons to press.

The general said, "Code ten." Immediately the elevator started to move. He looked at Mike. "Your ears may pop."

As the elevator descended, Mike asked, "How far down are we going?"

"It's the equivalent of ten stories below the ground."

Before Mike could ask anything else, the door opened and they walked out into the middle of the war room. It was completely silent. Everyone was wearing earphones, their eyes focused on something he couldn't see. Mike scanned the room, impressed at the size of the facility. It was as long as a football field.

The general took Mike by the arm, urging him forward. In the center of the room, there was a circular table with at least thirty people standing around it. The general positioned Mike next to him at the table and handed him earphones. Mike slipped them over his head.

What he experienced next was more advanced than anything he'd ever seen. It was a voice recognition multi-touch system. It allowed people to use finger-touch commands and voice commands simultaneously. Its touch-sensitive screen included a layer of capacitive material, not unlike a normal touch screen, except everything was three-dimensional. With a voice command, any person around the table could change the battle plan based on the data he was receiving through the integrated circuit.

Mike focused on the large screens on the walls. One of them continually showed pictures of each city in Israel, zooming in and out on government buildings and military bases. Another relayed pictures from the latest Ofck-9 military spy satellite. Mike watched as the screen focused on downtown Beirut.

It transmitted conversations too. Every word being relayed by voice transmission was simultaneously translated into Hebrew and English.

Something caught Mike's eye. He turned to the general. "What can you tell me about that breastplate hanging on the wall with the four lights going on and off?"

"That's a replica of the breastplate the high priest wore in the Holy Temple."

"What are the lights for?"

"The four lights are symbolic of some of the stones embedded in the breastplate. Mike, hold on. I'll be right back with you."

Mike observed the general giving orders into his headset. Mike heard the words the general was saying, but he didn't understand the Hebrew, and he wasn't programmed for simultaneous submission, which left him more than a step behind. It was times like this he wished he knew the language.

From the images on the screen in front of him and snatches of the conversation, he could glean that the general had positioned four submarines stationed in the Persian Gulf loaded with nuclear missiles, ready to launch at Iran and Lebanon.

In a matter of minutes, the atmosphere had changed. Mike could feel the nervous tension in the room. Something big was about to happen. Everyone around the table was moving the screens in front of them. He watched live pictures of Israel Air Force planes taking off from different bases. One screen showed personnel of an armored tank division on the Golan Heights moving into formation. On the Lebanese border thousands of young men with blackened faces and night-vision glasses were adjusting their camouflage outfits. Some smoked cigarettes, others prayed. The personnel carriers sat waiting for the orders to move them across the border.

Down south in Gaza, Hamas was still in power even after the last two wars. From what Mike saw, it was going to end with this war. No more cease-fires imposed on them by the United States and European countries. No political interference, international or domestic, would stop Israel from destroying the enemy.

Mike's eyes moved back and forth from the table to the blinking lights on the breastplate. He thought he was beginning to understand the code. The next light would indicate that the war was about to start. He waited, holding his breath, for the light to flash.

All the lights suddenly went off and then immediately turned back on. The general took off his headset and turned to Mike. "The exercise is over."

Exercise? What the hell?

An aide walked up to the general and handed him a phone. "It's the prime minister, sir."

The general took the phone and talked into it. "Good evening, sir. Yes, sir, it went the way we planned it. Agent O'Shea is right here with me, I'll put him on."

The general handed Mike the phone.

"How are you, Mr. Prime Minister?"

"Fine. I understand you're headed to London. I hope to see you there if you have time."

"I'll contact you as soon as I can."

"Mike, what did you think of the exercise?"

"Let's pray it stays an exercise."

"With the help of God, it will." The prime minister hung up the phone.

The general led Mike out of the compound. "Needless to say, Mike, what you witnessed here shouldn't be discussed with anyone besides your superiors at the National Security Agency."

As they walked out to the car, Mike ran the drill over in his head again. *Good thing Israel's a friend to the U.S. I wouldn't want to see that warfare in action.*

A half hour later, the car pulled up to the entrance of the hotel. The general's mobile rang. "Yes, what is it?" His expression sharpened. Something was wrong. "Fine, I'll be back in the office in ten minutes." He hung up and said to Mike, "I have to go now."

"What is it? What happened?"

"A delivery truck just blew up near the prime minister's residence."

CHAPTER
68

MIKE WAVED GOOD-BYE as the driver pulled away and walked through the revolving door into the hotel. He stopped in the lobby, where he saw Allan and James sitting at a table having coffee.

"Good morning."

Allan looked up. "We've been trying to reach you. Where have you been?"

"None of your phones are on," said James.

Mike took out his phones and turned them on. "I'm sorry about that. I was with the general. He just dropped me off after receiving a call about the bomb."

"Yeah, we just heard the announcement on TV," said James. "A terrorist tried to blow up the prime minister's house."

Mike nodded. God, he was tired. "I'm going up to my room to get some sleep. James, can you knock on my door at noon?"

"Yes, I will."

"Thanks. I'll see you later." Mike turned and left.

Allan looked at James. "Something major's going down, and

Mike is keeping me in the dark. You know what it is?"

"I don't have a clue," James lied. "But I'm sure Mike will tell us when he's ready." He changed the subject. "What are we going to do about Kim Li? How do we break the news to her about Hui Ying?"

Allan said, "I'll handle it. I'll tell her that Hui Ying called my room in the middle of the night. Said he wasn't feeling well, that he was having chest pains, that at first he thought it could have been something he'd eaten, but I told him not to risk it, so I immediately had security call for a doctor. By the time the doctor arrived, he was already gone."

"She's smart, so you better be ready for some tough questioning. She might be soft-spoken, but she *is* a lawyer."

"I'm aware. I'll call her and invite her to have breakfast with me. I'll tell her then."

"I'd better go over the security assignments with the guys. If you need me for anything, just beep me."

"Okay, catch up with you later, James."

As they got up to leave, they saw Kim Li walking to the reception desk.

"Over here, Kim Li," Allan called and rushed forward to intercept her. He was relieved when she turned and started walking toward him. It would have been a disaster if she had asked for Hui Ying at the desk.

"We just finished our meeting," he said. "I was going to call you and invite you to have breakfast with me at the pool."

She smiled. "I was about to call Hui's room and see how he's feeling."

Allan took her by the hand and led her to a chair. "Kim Li, please sit down. We have to talk."

CHAPTER
69

I S IT ABOUT my sister?" Kim Lee's brow knitted.

"No, something else. It's Hui. He had a heart attack last night. I'm so sorry, but he didn't make it."

Kim Li folded her arms around herself. Her voice was shaky when she spoke. "I saw it in the palm of his hand, but I never should have told him."

"We'll do everything we can to see that his body is returned to the Chinese government as soon as possible."

Kim Li stared at the floor. "Allan, I would like to go to my room if you don't mind. I'm sorry, I'm not in the mood to eat right now and I will not be good company."

"Of course. Whatever you want."

Allan walked her up to her room. The security guard saw them approaching and unlocked the door.

"Kim Li, please call me if you need anything. I intend to stay in the hotel all day."

"Thank you."

She entered her room and closed the door behind her. Allan turned to the guard. "If she leaves the room you're to call me immediately."

ALLAN FOUND JAMES eating breakfast by the pool.

"How did it go?" James asked.

"Hard to tell. After I told her, she went back to her room, said she wasn't in the mood to eat."

James finished eating. "I'm going to take some downtime, take a walk on the marina. I have my best guys watching over Kim Li, so I'm not needed here right now. I suggest we all meet in the lobby tonight and go together to meet Isaac in Jerusalem."

Allan nodded. "See you later."

James left Allan brooding about Kim Li and the situation in Washington. He still hadn't managed to find out anything. *What isn't Mike telling me?*

He took out his mobile to make a call. He realized his phone had been off. He turned it on. There was a text message from Jasmine.

> The chief of staff has arranged for you to be in London with Mike and will try to get you a few minutes with the president. The president will be at the Dorchester Hotel until he leaves for Saudi Arabia.

Allan replied immediately.

> Sweetie, I owe you big time.

He finished his coffee and headed for his room. Upon entering, he noticed a small envelope on the floor. He bent down, picked it up, and opened it. The message was from Guy. *"Please call. Very important."*

A note attached to the message said it had been delivered to his room at nine a.m. by the front desk. Allan checked his watch and calculated the time difference from Chicago to Israel. It was the middle of the night for Guy. He sat down and pressed the automatic dial button to Guy's mobile. A voice came on. "Hold please. Your call is being forwarded."

In seconds Guy was on the phone. "Allan, thanks for getting back to me."

"I took a gamble that you might still be awake. You said it was important. What's going on?"

"I've been waiting for your call. A few hours ago I received a call from the FBI office here in Chicago. They told me that for security reasons John Jr. and William had been transferred to a safe house."

"Do you know where?"

"They said somewhere along the Jersey shore."

"That's strange. The government usually only does that in witness protection cases. Did John have a change of heart? Is he going to name other people?"

"I don't know. I called you to ask if you could get the message to Isaac. I know it's his Sabbath and he won't be answering the phone."

"Sure I'll tell him. We're meeting him tonight. Any idea when they'll let you see them?"

"They informed me the director himself would call me Monday morning. That's all they would say."

"Where's Jim?"

"He went back to New York to see his mother. I'm due to fly back today."

"This is a hell of a mess. I'll make sure to get the message to Isaac."

"Thanks, Allan."

Allan turned on the TV and picked up the Saturday edition of the *International New York Times*. He flipped from channel to channel while he browsed the headlines. *Casablanca* was playing. He stopped to watch it, but he felt restless.

He put down the paper and looked at his watch. It was almost eleven. In one hour he was due to meet with Mike. He sank into the couch and let himself become engrossed in *Casablanca*. The sound of gunshots brought him back to the present.

Allan jumped up. It sounded like several rounds going off one after the other. He ran to his door and opened it. He saw Mike standing over a body in the hallway with his revolver in his hand. A second body was lying against Kim Li's door. Allan ran toward Mike. He could hear Kim Li screaming inside her room.

"Mike, what the hell happened?"

When Allan got closer, he realized that the body slumped against the door was Feng. Mike leaned over the security guard's body to check his pulse. "He's dead."

Allan pounded on the door. "Kim Li, it's me, Allan. Open the door. You're safe. I'm here."

Mike called James. A maid walked by, saw the bodies, and began to scream. Mike looked at her, still holding the gun. "Get out of here. You didn't see anything."

The maid turned and ran down the hall, tears streaming from her eyes. Kim Li opened the door to find Feng's body lying in the hallway at her feet. She started to cry again. Allan put his arm around her.

"Allan, get a sheet and cover up this body," said Mike.

When James arrived, Mike was standing by the dead security guard.

"I'll explain everything later," Mike said. "Help me carry him into my room. No one can know this happened, not like this."

They quickly lifted him up. Mike opened his door. "Let's put him in my bed and cover him with a sheet. You make sure that one of our guys is standing outside. Don't let anyone in without our permission."

"What about the police?" James asked.

Mike shook his head. "I said no one." He hung a "Do Not Disturb" sign on his door and said to James, "Let's go to Kim Li's room."

As Mike raised a fist to knock on Kim Li's door, he saw General Solomon walking toward him with a police officer.

"Mike, this is Commander Ari Levin of the Yasam Anti-Crime Force. We were in a meeting when Ari got a call about a shooting at the hotel. We just intercepted some very interesting information regarding Feng."

Mike shook the commander's hand. "Let's go to my room so we can speak in private."

"Fine."

"James, tell Allan that I'm in my room with the general. You stay with him in case he needs help with Kim Li."

James looked at Mike. "You sure I shouldn't come with you?"

"No, I'll brief you later."

James shrugged. "Okay."

Mike turned to his guests. "Please, right this way."

They entered the suite. The general and Commander Levin sat on the sofa. The general got straight to the point.

"Mike, what happened?"

"I was just about to leave my room when I heard gunshots. I pulled out my revolver and opened the door slowly to check out the situation. For a moment, I couldn't see anything. One of the lights in the hallway was out. I started walking toward Kim Li's room when I saw our security guard on the floor and Feng with a gun in his hand. He saw me and fired. I fired back two rounds. One hit him in the chest and the other in the head. You saw the results.

"I immediately checked my security guy, but he was already dead. Allan heard the shots and came running. I called James. He showed up a few minutes later. We moved my guy into my room and covered him with a sheet. He's in the bed behind you."

"Thank God you were in your room," said the general. "Early this morning we intercepted a message to Feng's phone. Since we met last night, we've been listening in on all his telephone conversations. We placed a bug in his room at the university and have been monitoring his movements. This morning he received a coded message from China. My guy was still working on it when we got the call about the shooting and I headed straight here, stopping only to pick up the commander."

"Did you ever find out what the message says?"

"My guy called as we approached the hotel. He'd deciphered the code. It was from Wen Tian in Beijing. The message said, '*Hui Ying is dead. Today is Kim Li's last day. Make sure of it, and retrieve the chip at all costs. WT.*'"

"How did they find out about Hui Ying?"

The general ignored the question. "Ari, what are you going to do about the bodies? We have to remove them."

"If you can get him to a morgue, I can have one of my people make arrangements with our embassy to pick up my guy and fly him to the States," Mike said.

The commander nodded. "Alright, here's my card. Let me know when you have completed your arrangements." He stood up and walked toward the door.

"General, I want an answer to my question," Mike said.

"Let's go to Kim Li's room and see if we can get you those answers."

They finished their drinks and left the room together.

When they approached Kim Li's room, the door was already open. They walked in and saw Commander Levin standing and watching as two men put Feng's body in a bag and placed it on a rolling gurney.

"We're finished here for now," said the commander.

Allan walked over to Kim Li, who was standing on the patio with her back to the others, looking out at the sea. "Kim Li, Feng's body is gone."

She didn't respond.

Mike handed the commander's card to James. "See that our guy's body is properly taken care of. When you have time, start your report for Washington. I'll go over it with you before I leave for London."

Allan walked over to Mike. "Mike, she won't talk. All she'll say is that she wants to speak to you."

"Hui's death and Feng being killed at her door, it's a lot to handle."

"Of course. But what's disturbing her most is her sister. She's desperate to meet with Isaac and find out why Daiyu hasn't been in touch with her. Come on, let's talk to her."

Mike and Allan walked out to the patio and sat down. The general was out there, standing next to Kim Li.

"Kim Li, you wanted to speak to me?" Mike asked.

"Yes."

She turned around and sat down. "When Allan told me about Hui's death, we were in the lobby. I was shocked. I asked him to take me to my room. I sat on the couch, my head pounding. Then my telephone rang. It was Feng. He said he had news about my sister, and he was on his way to the hotel. He did not want to talk on the phone. He said the information was too sensitive. Then he asked about Hui. He told me that Hui wasn't answering his phone."

"What did you say?" Mike asked.

"I told him Hui was dead. He didn't react at all. Not a word. He just asked me if I was alone and if there were guards outside my room. At first I thought it was a strange question, but I was still in shock from the news about Hui and didn't pay it much attention. I told him there was one guard. He told me not tell anyone he was coming to see me. When I heard gunfire outside my door, I ran into my bathroom and locked the door. I stayed there until I heard Allan calling me and knew it was safe to come out."

Kim Li lifted her hands to her face. They were still shaking. "Mike, I'm so confused. I don't know what's going on. I know you're keeping something from me. I know Isaac is the only one who will tell me what you won't. I want to see Isaac, I need to see him. Please, I know you have the authority to make this happen. Please help me."

Mike stood up. "Let me see what I can do." He turned to the

general. "General, Allan, can I see you inside for a moment?"

Allan stood up. "Will you be alright here for a few minutes, Kim Li?"

She nodded.

The general and Allan followed Mike into the living room. "What's on your mind, Mike?"

Mike looked at Allan. "She's not buying that we have to wait until tonight to tell her what's going on with her sister."

Allan raked his fingers through his hair. "We should have told her right away. We shouldn't have dragged it out like this."

"I thought Isaac was the one to tell her, but now I'm not so sure."

Allan nodded grimly. "She's not going to take it well, that's for sure."

Mike looked at the general. "I want to know how Wen Tian heard about Hui Ying's death."

"Every morning Hui Ying sent a text to his sister, who works for Wen Tian. He'd ask about their mother, and in the evening he'd receive an answer. It was prearranged with Wen Tian that if he sent the message, it meant he was alive. No message meant he was dead. Tian knew almost instantaneously. "

"Well, nothing we can do about it now. But what about Kim Li?"

"Let me handle it," Allan said. "She'll take it best coming from me."

Mike nodded. "You're right, Allan. Good call."

Allan walked back out to the patio and sat down.

"Kim Li, can I speak to you alone for a moment?"

"Of course."

He took a deep breath and exhaled slowly. Kim Li looked at him, waiting.

"I know you want to speak to Isaac, but I'm pretty sure I can answer the question you've been wanting to ask him."

"Oh, God, I was right, wasn't I?"

"I'm sorry, she's gone."

Kim Li crumpled and her body doubled over. She put her head into her hands and gave in to her tears.

"Come here." Allan reached over and pulled her close to him. "I'm so sorry."

She let herself melt into him for a moment as the pain engulfed her. A few minutes later, she struggled to regain her composure.

"How did it happen?"

"She was taken away for questioning, and then she was gone. Wen Tian released a statement that it was a suicide, but we know that wasn't the case. I'm so sorry for your loss."

Kim Li nodded and reached up to wipe her eyes. "I could feel her presence wasn't in the world any longer. I felt something had changed. I wish this wasn't the truth, but I thank you for your kindness and honesty."

Mike slid open the door to the patio and came outside to join them. "Sorry to interrupt, but I just got word from the general that they want us on the road as soon as possible. He said he'll wait for us down in the lobby. When can you be ready to leave?"

"I can be packed in fifteen minutes," Kim Li said.

"Allan?"

"I packed this morning. I just have to go to my room and grab my flight bag and I'm good to go."

"Good. We'll meet you downstairs."

Kim Li went into her bedroom and started packing. Allan left to get his bag. Mike remained on the patio looking at the sea. Kim Li appeared a few minutes later. "I'm ready, Mike."

Mike didn't move, still staring at the sea. The waves were filled with surfers.

"Kim Li, have you ever been to Hawaii and seen them surf there? Oahu in the winter is the best. If the wind is right, it's incredible. You've never seen waves that big. I could sit on the beach and watch them for hours. I was there guarding our last president and his family for a week. It was amazing."

Mike paused and glanced at Kim Li. He could tell she wasn't listening.

"Come," he said gently. "It's time to go."

When they walked into the lobby, Allan was waiting for them near the reception desk. "Kim Li, are you okay?" he asked.

She nodded. "I'm okay. Thank you, Allan."

"I need to have a few words with James and the guys," said Mike. "Allan, can you stay with Kim Li?"

"Of course."

As soon as Mike left, Kim Li looked at Allan. "They're trying to kill me, aren't they? It's the locket, isn't it?"

"Nobody is going to kill you. I promise you. We are all here to keep you safe."

CHAPTER
70

THE GENERAL'S SUV sat behind a police car. Four other SUVs were lined up behind his.

James exited the hotel and walked over to Mike, who was waiting for the others to join him. "I just received this message on my mobile." He gave the phone to Mike so that he could read it.

> The Associated Press has reported that the prime minister of England was poisoned by a Chinese undercover agent working in the prime minister's house as a chef. Scotland Yard has confirmed the information is true.

"This information was supposed to be secret," Mike said. Allan had briefed Mike on the London situation after he went to get his bag.

"Read the rest."

> We have recalled our ambassador back from China. Parliament is being summoned to a special meeting, and some ministers are asking for military action against the Chinese. Please have Mike call me as soon as possible. Frederick.

At that moment the general stepped out of his SUV and motioned to Mike.

"I just received word that the Chinese are moving several navy vessels—aircraft carriers and submarines—from the South China Sea to the Taiwan Strait. We intercepted a coded message that they intend to blockade Taiwan. As the first step, they're sending their army to take over Quemoy, an island off the coast of mainland China that is administered by Taiwan. A text was sent to their ambassadors in the United States and Great Britain. They've both been instructed to deliver the message to the secretary of state in the U.S. and the foreign secretary in London warning them not to intervene in China's internal affairs."

Mike swore. "We're going to war, damn it. We've been playing into their hands since Nixon. They control our economy, our currency, and most of the strategic materials we need for our defense industry. The president needs to do something, and it better be fast." He pulled out his phone. "Please excuse me, I need to contact some people in Washington."

Mike went back inside to find a quiet corner. He dialed the chairman of the Joint Chiefs of Staff in Washington.

"Hello, Mike, what's up?"

"Sir, the Israelis have broken a Chinese coded message. They're in the process of sending their military to invade Quemoy and surround Taiwan with submarines and aircraft carriers. Where is the president?"

"He's on his way to London, Mike. We're aware of the situation. We've been tracking it for several days via our satellites. Before he left, we were all briefed."

"What was his reaction?"

"He said he'd be in touch with us from London, but not to do anything to provoke the Chinese. He made that very clear."

"You have to do something. Has anyone notified the Taiwanese government that they're about to be invaded by the Chinese and betrayed by the United States government?"

"No, but I can tell you that our previous conversation is more important now than ever. I will be in touch as things move along."

Mike hung up and walked back outside where General Solomon was waiting.

"Mike, it looks like we're going to be delayed."

"What happened?"

"I just received an SMS from my office. The whole city of Jerusalem is closed off. Someone has launched a laser-guided rocket from inside the Old City and blew apart the roof of the Dome of the Rock. The preliminary report is that there are many dead buried under the rubble inside."

"What about Brahim and Isaac? Are they okay?"

"I sent people over to Isaac's home to check if he and his family are all right. Brahim and Sammi should be safe at the King David Hotel, but I'm having my security people check on them too. While we wait for transport to Jerusalem, we can sit in the hotel's conference room. Please join me as soon as you can."

Mike walked back inside the hotel to find Allan and Kim Li.

They were standing at reception with their luggage. "There's been a delay. We're waiting for news about a rocket attack that has just taken place on the Dome of the Rock. Jerusalem's been sealed off while they look for the perpetrators. The general is arranging for alternative means of transport. I'm meeting him in the conference room in the meantime."

"What about Isaac?" Allan asked.

"The general has his people checking on everyone as we speak."

Kim Li put a hand on Mike's arm. "Mike, I'm really sorry for all the trouble I'm causing you. I have been so nervous. It's not like me."

"Forget it, you've been through a lot. Listen, I've got to go now." He walked off.

ALLAN LED KIM Li to the lounge. "Let's sit down over there for a minute." He pointed to two old green velvet chairs in a corner. "We can take a breather while they figure out what comes next."

Kim Li took Allan's hand, and they walking toward the seating area.

"Allan, do you remember when I read your palm? I told you your sign is the sun, which gives energy to the world. When I'm with you, I feel that energy. Your palm also told me that you're lonely and need someone to share your life with."

Allan looked up, surprised.

"Am I upsetting you?" Kim Li asked.

"I just didn't realize you could see all that in my hand."

Kim Li smiled.

MIKE ENTERED THE conference room. He took a cup and poured himself some coffee.

"We'll leave here in thirty minutes by helicopter," the general informed Mike when he had sat down. "We'll land at the Knesset heliport in Jerusalem. After I have met with some of the prime minister's inner security cabinet, we will go see Isaac."

"Did you get any word from your people about Isaac?"

"They're fine. Brahim and Sammi will meet us at Isaac's. My people are with them."

"Thank God they're all safe. I'd better inform my people about the plan."

Mike pulled out his phone and dialed James. "Round up everyone and have them ready to meet me on the roof. We're going to Jerusalem by helicopter. I'll fill you in on the details when we're together. Are Allan and Kim Li with you?"

"They're in the lounge."

"Tell them to meet us in a half hour." Mike clicked off.

The general's aide walked into the conference room. "Commander Levin is here. He wants to talk to you."

"Show him in."

The commander walked in and sat down. "Yaacov, I asked you to meet us here because I didn't want to give information this sensitive over a phone line. Even ours."

"What is it?"

"After the explosion, we sealed off the Old City so no one could enter or leave. Every house was being searched. Initially we thought it might be someone from a right-wing Jewish group, so we started in the Jewish Quarter. But we came up empty. Then we moved on to the Cardo, while our anti-terror squad proceeded to the streets closest to the Wall that had the best vantage point to launch a rocket. We still hadn't located the launcher, but then we got a break."

"What did you find?"

"One of my people got a lead about two young Chinese men who were spotted taking pictures of the Dome yesterday afternoon. Apparently they had some expensive-looking piece of luggage they took turns keeping their hands on. One would take a picture, while the other one held on to the luggage. Then one of them would make a phone call on his mobile. My informant said this happened at least six times. He found this all peculiar enough to follow them. They ended up at the Austrian Hospice on the Via Dolorosa.

"I sent two officers there to interview the rector. He told them that the two young men checked out early in the morning. When they had checked in on Wednesday, they told him they were from Beijing and were going to visit some relatives at the Chinese Embassy."

The general's eyebrows rose. "And?"

"Our people called the embassy. The story was bogus, as we suspected. Our people immediately called our CCTV surveillance system office. They monitor all foreign embassies. The video showed two young Chinese men going in and out of the Chinese Embassy several times. Sometimes the pictures showed them carrying pieces of luggage. On Friday they both left with their luggage at six p.m."

"I assume they no longer have their luggage with them?"

The commander nodded. "Today they came back without the luggage. The last video we have of them is thirty minutes ago entering the embassy. That's where they are now."

"What are your people doing to calm the Palestinians until we get to the bottom of this?"

"We're in touch with all their leaders, and they're in touch with the rest of the Arab world. Most important, they're calling on all their people not to take to the streets."

"That's not going to last, unless we capture the people who did this."

"Any idea how to do that?" the commander asked.

"Yes, but I have to speak to the prime minister first." The general checked his watch. "I have to go. I'm leaving for Jerusalem in a few minutes. Ari, thank you for the update." He turned to Mike. "Let's get everyone on the helicopters."

As they headed for the elevators to take them up to the roof, the general's aide handed him a coded message. He stopped and read it. It said, *"Red Ball of Fire, Joel 3:16."*

"It's from the prime minister," said the aide.

Mike glanced at the general, but the general didn't say anything. It wasn't the first message from the prime minister the general had gotten quoting Joel.

They went up to the roof and saw James standing with his mobile to his ear. They walked over to him.

"Is everyone on the choppers?" Mike asked.

"Yes, we're just waiting for you to give the go-ahead."

General Solomon took Mike by the arm and walked with him away from the helicopters.

"What's the problem?" Mike asked.

The general put his hand into his pocket and pulled out the message he had just received. He handed it to Mike. "Read this."

Mike scanned the note. "I read Joel when I was a kid in church." He handed back the note. "What does 'Red Balls of Fire' mean?"

"It means we've just been ordered by the prime minister to go on our highest top-secret alert. He's ready to launch nuclear missiles from our submarines."

Mike looked at General Solomon. "This is not like that exercise you put me through, is it?"

"I wish to God it was."

The helicopters motors roared and the blades churned. Mike boarded first and then the general got on. He signaled to the pilot. "Let's go before the world blows up."

As they lifted off, Mike let his eyes drift closed. He wondered how many more wars Israel would fight before it could live in peace.

The flight was short. After ten minutes in the air, the general said, "We'll be touching down in a minute."

Mike opened his eyes and looked out the window. "What's the schedule?"

"The defense minister just sent me a text. The meeting with the other ministers is going to be delayed. He wants to meet with us alone. Kim Li and Allan will be taken directly to Isaac's house."

"Alright," said Mike. "I'll call James and ask him to go pick up Brahim and Sammi. I'd feel better knowing he's with them."

The general's helicopter was the first to land. Within a few seconds, the second one followed. When the general stepped onto the pad, he was greeted by the defense minister, Mordechai Sharon, and a couple of his aides. The defense minister shook both of their hands and motioned the others to follow him without saying a word.

CHAPTER
71

Saturday, June 7, 2014
The Knesset, Jerusalem

THE MINISTER LED them to his office.

Once they were seated, he said, "General Solomon, the prime minister is waiting to hear from us. He has to have something to tell the press in London. He's going to force a meeting with the president of the U.S. to discuss the crises Israel is facing."

"We'll announce that we've found the rocket launcher and arrested a group of militant extremists. They're being held in a secret location pending arraignment. Our government will immediately start to restore the Dome and pay any other damages related to it. The families who lost loved ones in the attack will be compensated, and the government will do everything in its power to prevent this from ever happening again."

"We had better make it sound believable," Minister Sharon responded.

"I'll call Ari and have him pick up some of the usual suspects and leak the news to the press. When we do locate the rocket launchers, it needs to be kept confidential. Based on the information we have now, either the Chinese consul has outright lied to us, or his people are running their own espionage program and he doesn't have a clue."

"As long as the two suspects are harbored in the embassy, we have to play their game."

The general looked at his watch. "The Sabbath is over. I must go. Please keep me posted."

They all shook hands and Mike and the general left.

"What's the real plan?" Mike asked once they were outside.

The general smiled. "I see you have a *Yiddishe kup*. Are you sure you are not Jewish? Never mind, I'll fill you in on the drive over to Isaac's."

An SUV pulled up in front of them and they got inside.

"So," said Mike, "what's the plan?"

"We're going to kidnap them."

"How are you going to do that? They're holed up in the Chinese Embassy."

"Do you know the name Adolf Eichmann?"

"Of course I do. The Nazi responsible for the mass deportation of Jews to extermination camps. He was living in Argentina when the Mossad kidnapped him in 1960."

"Then you must be aware that we are experts in difficult situations. The Chinese terrorists are inside their embassy. We cannot go in and pull them out. They are protected under international law. When we were on the chopper to Jerusalem, I asked my agents to come up with a plan. They did, but I didn't want to involve the minister of defense. It could get ugly. The less people involved, the better."

"How are you going to do it?"

"We have a very small window to put this into operation. Within the next hour, my people will make sure that the entire international media has heard the news about the extremists and their arrest. The Argentine Embassy in Herzliya Pituach is hosting a cocktail party for the Chinese ambassador and his wife tonight. At the party, we're going to slip some arsenic into his drink. He has a strange habit. He only drinks apple juice outside his residence. It's perfect. The arsenic will never be detected."

"That could work. Arsenic tastes slightly sweet. The juice will mask it."

"When the ambassador lived in China, he was known for eating as many as five apples a day. The farmers use huge amounts of pesticide, which contain high levels of arsenic. Arsenic stays in a hair follicle for years. They will never be able to track it."

"How are you going to get in?"

"It's not out of the ordinary to have one of our security staff inside an embassy function as a waiter. The waiter who is going to help us tonight is from your country. He made aliyah five years ago. After doing his service in the IDF, we recruited him for my unit. He is a Yale graduate who majored in pharmacology. He will give the ambassador and his wife a new form of arsenic he developed himself. It's untraceable. We have the only antidote. We applied it twice in the last year in Iran. A few minutes after they ingest it, they will start getting symptoms—headaches and confusion. Then they will start to complain of stomach pains and start vomiting. Finally they will black out.

"Someone will call for an ambulance. My people will man the ambulance, of course. They will administer the new drug to neutralize the arsenic but keep them asleep. Along the way they will be transferred to an army ambulance that will then take them to the airbase where you landed. By the time they arrive, they'll have been blindfolded. When they get there, we'll put them in separate rooms."

"What happens after that?"

"Ari has his instructions. He'll notify the staff at the embassy that the ambassador and his wife were kidnapped on the way to the hospital. He'll tell them the Shin Bet has located the ambulance and that inside on the dashboard was a note demanding that the militant extremists give themselves up.

"In the note, the kidnappers will claim they were glad that the Dome was blown up, but their group had nothing to do with it. The note will say that if they don't turn themselves in by the morning, the ambassador and his wife will be killed.

"As soon as the ambassador comes to, we'll tell him that if he wants to save both of their lives he can record the following message:

"*'This is the ambassador. My wife and I are alive and have not been harmed. The two men who blew up the Dome must come out of the embassy by this Sunday at ten a.m. They'll be met by officers of the Shin Bet and taken to a courtroom with a judge. They will confess their crime before him and the international media. The Chinese minister of foreign affairs is to contact Wen Tian to make sure that they do this. This is his doing, and the two agents are his responsibility. If not, my wife and I will be killed.'*"

"Wen Tian?"

"The ambassador's wife is his sister. She informs him of everything that is going on in the embassy. Over the last year we have intercepted reports on the ambassador's activities that she sent by code. The ball will be in Tian's court. Either he gives over his two agents or sacrifices his sister. I'm pretty sure we know what he will decide.

"We've been trying to get the ambassador to work with us for the last few years, but until now there's been no success. It's a very slow process, as you know, to turn someone against his own country. Maybe this situation will help."

The SUV stopped in front of Isaac's house. As Mike left the car, he spotted Charlie getting out of a car a short distance away.

"Go ahead inside," Mike said to the general. "I'll wait for Charlie."

Charlie walked over. "How are you?"

"Who dropped you off? I told you to call me when the Sabbath was over, and I would have one of my people pick you up."

"My cousin drove. She wanted to go to the Old City and pray at the Wall."

"Have you heard the news about what happened at the Dome? I don't think your cousin is going to be able to pray at the Wall today."

"Yes, it was on every radio station in the country. The BBC is blasting Israel for not doing more to protect the Dome from extremists in Israel."

"We should go inside. This is going to be a long night."

CHAPTER
72

Saturday, June 7, 2014
Green home, Jerusalem

CHAVA GREETED THEM as they entered the house. "How was your Shabbos?"

"It was great, thank you," Charlie answered.

"Mike, did you get any rest?"

"To tell you the truth, I was kinda busy."

Isaac descended the stairs and came over to greet them. "Good evening. Chava, the general and I will be in the study with Charlie and Mike. Some of the general's staff will be arriving soon. Can you please show them into the conference room? We'll join them when our meeting is over."

The general had arranged for his staff to come by so they could discuss Abra's situation.

Chava smiled at Isaac. "Of course. I'll be with Kim Li and Allan in the living room if you need me."

Isaac looked around. "Where's Dov?"

"He's upstairs with Sara."

"Would you mind asking him to come down?"

Charlie and Mike followed Isaac into the study. The general was already inside. Isaac closed the door.

"Would anyone care to join me for a drink?"

"Count me in," said Charlie.

"I never refuse a good Scotch," Mike said.

The general smiled. "Every time I am around Mike, he makes me drink. The way his mind works, I asked him if he was Jewish. With all I have been drinking with this guy, pretty soon he is going to wonder if I am part Irish."

Everyone laughed. Isaac started to pour drinks.

"Let me help you," said Charlie. "By the way, where are Brahim and Sammi?"

"As soon as Shabbos finished, he called to tell me he'd be a bit late. He was in the middle of contacting his children in America. He wanted us to get started without him. I'll update him when he arrives."

"I sent James to go pick him up," Mike said. "I'm sure they'll be here soon."

Charlie handed everyone their drink. He raised his glass. "Le-chaim."

Everyone looked at the general as they raised their glasses. The general had a sober look on his face. "To peace in our lifetime."

They drank and put their glasses down.

"General, this is your meeting," said Isaac. "Please go ahead."

The general took another sip of his drink, then put the glass down.

"First, I want to thank Isaac for all he has done for our country. The hospitality that Isaac and Chava have always offered us is beyond any thank you I can offer. I know that we had set up this meeting to talk about Abra's situation. We'll get to that.

"Right now I have something to tell you that is more urgent, something that will affect all of you."

The room grew very still. Everyone's attention was focused

WORLDS TOGETHER, WORLDS APART 377

on the general.

"In the last week, there have been many critical events, events planned to bring the Western world to the brink of extinction. You may have only heard about a few of them."

The others nodded.

"Over the last forty-eight hours, Mike and I have been collaborating. What I am about to tell you stays inside this room."

"What about Brahim?" Isaac asked.

"Isaac, I'm sorry, but not even him. He is too vulnerable right now. It is best if as few people as possible know about this." General Solomon paused to look each of them in the eye. "If questioned, you would have to deny any knowledge of what you are about to hear. Even if you are asked to swear under oath. Understood?"

They all agreed, nodding their heads.

"This Monday morning, as international banks open to do business, they will be in trouble with their prime customers. As the clients attempt to withdraw or transfer money, the funds that were in their customers' accounts will have disappeared. Thousands of customers will be, for all intent and purposes, wiped out.

"All of the bank's electronic records will show that an authorized transfer of money was received and the money went to Beirut. The records will show the receiving banks were Bangue du Liban— Hezbollah's Bank—Syria's Central Bank, and the Central Bank of Iran. We are talking about at least twenty trillion dollars. Without those funds, the banks will have to close until they resolve the situation. And it may take weeks.

"Payments that China was to make to Iran through wealthy Chinese individuals will not be made. Russia will back out of its arms deal with Syria as the transfers from Syria's central bank will be frozen. Every country in the world will be affected by this gridlock. The national banks will have insufficient liquidity to settle securities and money market accounts."

Isaac had a sudden urge to check his accounts. "What are you doing to stop this?" he demanded.

"We became aware of this plan over a year ago and decided we had to take radical action. Israel has been able to secure all of these funds, and over the next month we'll return every last dollar to our friends."

Isaac exhaled in relief. "How did you do it?"

The general smiled. "They didn't know that the chip they used to access the account information of all those people was originally developed in Israel. We included a fail-safe code in case it ever got into the wrong hands. And that's exactly what the Chinese did with the chip: they sold it to the wrong people. The moment they attempted to access the information we knew about it. While it looked like they were transferring funds to their accounts in Iran and Beirut, the money was being secured by us."

"As someone who knows a thing or two about chips," said Isaac, "all I can say is thank God."

"This is just the beginning," said the general. "Our enemies are planning to destroy us and have convinced one-time friends of Israel that Israel has to be eliminated from the Middle East. They insist that if the world wants peace, they must agree on their terms. Now our strongest ally has joined them."

Mike looked worried. "Don't worry, Mike," Isaac said, "the United States Mint and the Federal Reserve are experts in printing more money. I'm sure your paycheck will be covered."

"Don't be so confident. What I'm sure about is that you would help me out with a no-interest loan to tide me over."

The general smiled. "Sorry, we have the bulk of Isaac's cash for now. He couldn't give you a shekel."

The mood turned serious again when the general continued, "This is going to be the week of choosing to be a free world of independent individuals living in a generous society, respectful of all religions, or a world of religious fanatics who want mankind to be like robots so they can program them. We know from the Bible that

God created this world for good, not evil. Our purpose on earth is for humanity to protect and nourish the good to grow. Israel is ready to defend itself against evil even if it has to stand by itself. If the action that we have taken proves ineffective in stopping our enemies, our government has given orders to arm our submarines and long-range bombers with nuclear weapons."

He paused to finish the rest of his drink. "Time has run out."

He turned to Mike. "You're scheduled to leave for London tomorrow morning to meet up with the president's security detail, if I understand correctly."

"Yes, the director said as soon as the president leaves for Saudi Arabia I can fly back here."

"Mike, I'm setting up a meeting between you and our prime minister. I need you to take an envelope with a coded message to him. Make sure you see him no matter what it takes, and you have to see that it happens while he and the president are both in London."

Isaac looked at his watch. "General, I have some questions for you, but they can wait until later. I should meet with Kim Li and Allan now. If you want to use my office, please do. Otherwise, you can ask Chava to show you into the conference room."

"Thanks, Isaac, I'll go meet with my people in the conference room now. Mike, why don't you join me? We can discuss London. Afterward we'll all meet again to discuss freeing Abra."

"Good idea." Mike stood up and followed the general out of the room.

Charlie stood too. "I'll go and get Kim Li and Allan."

"Thanks. Bring Dov in as well."

At that moment Charlie's phone rang. "Good evening, Mao Li. Or should I say good morning?" Then a pause and Charlie's face turned grim. "I'm so sorry to hear that your brother was killed in Lebanon. You have my deepest condolences." He hung up the phone.

Isaac had been listening. He looked at Charlie.

"You heard?" Charlie said.

Isaac nodded. There was nothing they could do for Moa Li now. He'd lost his bargaining chip, they'd lost a source of information, but they had other, more immediate concerns right now.

Charlie knew it. "I'd better get the others." He left the room.

While he waited, Isaac picked up a speech by Sir Winston Churchill that he kept on his desk. It was Churchill's famous "Blood, Toil, Tears, and Sweat" speech. He sat down in his armchair with his drink in one hand and the document in the other. As he read, he felt the strength of Churchill's words. The speech had been delivered to Parliament in 1940, inspiring them to go on to victory against Nazi Germany.

There was a knock on the door, and Charlie walked in with Kim Li, Allan, and Dov.

"Kim Li, I'm sorry that I wasn't able to see you on my Sabbath. I know how difficult all of this has been for you. Allan informed me that you heard about your sister's untimely death. I'm so sorry for your loss. I'm here to help you in every way I can."

"All I want now is the truth. So many terrible things have happened since I left Hong Kong. I feel like I'm in the middle of a tsunami. The wave has taken me out to sea, and I'm drowning."

Tears started to flow from her eyes. Charlie reached for some tissues and handed them to her. Allan handed her a glass of water, then took her hand. Isaac looked at Kim Li's face as if she were one of his children.

"You've been on my mind for some time now. You took a leap of faith that day in your office in Beijing with Lee and Robert. For that alone, you deserve the facts and the whole truth." Isaac lifted his glass and took a drink, giving himself a moment to gather his thoughts and stay in control of his emotions. "I'm sorry to tell you this, but Lee and Robert were both murdered. Information is limited at this time. We'll have to be patient until we find out more."

"Oh, my God." Kim Li put her face in her hands and started to sob.

"I'm sorry I couldn't tell you about your sister myself. I wanted to. But the timing just didn't work out for that."

Allan put his arm around her. "I'm so sorry."

Kim Li lifted her tear-streaked face to look at Isaac. "Is there any way there's been a mistake? I mean, about Daiyu?"

"I wish there was, but it's been confirmed."

Kim Li started crying again.

"Dov, can you please ask Chava to come in here?"

Dov left and returned with Chava. Allan got up so that Chava could sit down next to Kim Li.

Chava put her arm around her. "Kim Li, I'm so sorry. When I lost my brother, the pain was indescribable. I'm here for you if there's anything you need." She gave Kim Li a kiss on the forehead. "I know your parents are gone, and now your sister too. If you'll have us, we'll be your new family, Isaac and I. We always wanted more children."

"You're so kind, Chava." Kim Li smiled and everyone exhaled.

"Besides," said Isaac, "I need someone around who I can trust who understands Chinese. Not just the language, but how the business culture works and how the Chinese think about the world situation." He turned to Charlie. "You've been looking for the right associate for ages. Kim Li'll be a perfect fit."

Charlie nodded. "I would love it if you'd join me," he said to Kim Li. "In fact, I have to go to New York tomorrow on some business which involves a Chinese gentleman."

Kim Li looked to Allan for guidance.

"I told you Isaac would take care of you," he said. "This is a great opportunity for you. You should take it."

"Give her a chance to think about it," Chava insisted.

Isaac nodded in agreement. "Chava is right. Kim Li, please stay with us tonight. You can sleep on it, and tomorrow you can decide what you want to do."

There was a light knock on the door. Charlie walked over and opened it. Mike stood there with the general.

"Can you tell Isaac that we need to speak to him for a moment outside?"

Charlie walked over to Isaac, leaned over, and whispered the message in his ear.

Isaac stood up. "Please excuse me. Mike needs me. I'll return shortly."

When Isaac came to the door, General Solomon said, "The others can join us if they'd like."

Isaac turned to the others. "Chava, maybe you should show Kim Li to her room." He knew Kim Li needed his wife right now. "The rest of you can come with me."

CHAPTER
73

WHEN HE ENTERED the conference room, Isaac could sense that something was wrong. Something serious had happened, he could tell.

Since he often had business meetings when he traveled to Israel, Isaac had set up a conference room in the house. The walls were paneled with agarwood; at thirty thousand dollars a kilo it was the most expensive wood in the world. One wall was filled with pictures of Isaac shaking the hands of presidents, kings, and other dignitaries. On another wall hung plaques presented to Isaac as an honoree from universities that he endowed around the globe. Another wall held framed letters and awards from religious leaders, including the pope and the Dalai Lama.

Isaac sat down at the head of the conference table. "What's going on?" he asked.

"James called me," Mike said. He was sitting to Isaac's left. "He was waiting in the lobby of the King David to bring Brahim and Sammi here. Apparently Brahim had a heart attack. Sammi and the security detail went to the hospital with him."

"What hospital?"

"They've taken him to Hadassah on Mount Scopus."

Isaac stood up. "Let's go."

"I told my people to wait outside," said the general. "They're ready to take us."

"Dov, can you tell Chava what happened and ask if she would stay with Kim Li? I'll call her from the hospital as soon as I have an update on Brahim's condition."

Dov nodded. "Okay. And I'd better go tell Sara what happened too."

"I think I should stay here with Chava and Kim Li," said Allan.

"You're right, Allan, you stay."

"Isaac, I'm going to stick around here too," said Charlie. "I have some business to take care of."

"Alright, Charlie. Now let's get going."

Isaac needed to see Brahim for himself. He couldn't believe this was happening on top of everything else. You live for today and you pray for a good tomorrow. That was how Brahim lived. It was a philosophy that had stood him in good stead until now. *With the help of God, he'll be fine.*

They arrived at the hospital in less than fifteen minutes. When they approached the emergency room, it was obvious that half of the city had waited until Saturday night to get sick or have a baby. The general, followed by Mike and Isaac, approached the security scanner as fast as they could. The security guard ignored the red light as the scanner buzzed.

The crowd stood silent as they were ushered through. They walked down the hall to the elevators, where Mike saw James standing with Sammi.

"James, what floor is Brahim on?"

"Eighth. He's in the Coronary Care Unit."

"How's he doing?"

"The doctors said he's gonna be alright," said Sammi. "They're monitoring him. He's on a ventilator to help him breathe."

The elevator doors opened.

"Sammi," said Isaac as they stepped inside. "Did you call anyone in the States?"

"No, I was waiting for you to decide what we should do."

The elevator door opened onto the eighth floor. A plaque placed directly across from the elevator stared at them. It read, "The Chava and Isaac Green Intensive Care Wing." Standing by the sign was Dr. Jerry Brooks with two other doctors.

"Isaac, how are you?" the doctor greeted him.

"I'm fine, Jerry. How've you been?"

"I'm good, Isaac. I'd be better if I was meeting Brahim on the tennis court instead of in my wing. But he's gonna be alright."

"Have you seen him?"

"Of course. I'm taking the lead on his case. At first I thought it was congestive heart failure, but we're waiting for the results of his blood test before we decide on the next step. Right now he's resting comfortably."

"Can I see him?"

"Of course, but make it short."

Isaac turned to Sammi. "Come with me."

They both walked into the room. Brahim lay in a bed next to the window. The other bed was empty. Isaac walked over to the side of the bed and looked at Brahim. His arm had a needle in it with a tube running up to a bag of intravenous fluid hanging on a hook. Other than that he looked fine.

Sammi and Isaac stood silently for what seemed like forever. Finally, Brahim opened his eyes and smiled.

He squeezed Isaac's arm. "You're the guy with the heart problems, and here I'm in this damn bed with a heart attack."

Isaac looked at Sammi. "I told you he'd be fine."

"Boss, anything I can do for you?"

"Thank you, but they're taking good care of me here. You stick with Isaac for now. Whatever he asks you to do, do it, just like if it were me asking, okay?"

"I got it, boss."

Isaac took Brahim's hand. "You get some rest, and I'll take care of everything. The doctor is an old friend of mine. He's one of the best. Don't concern yourself with anything, just get better. I need you. We still have to finish what we've started."

"What about Abra?"

"I told you in Paris that I'll take care of it and I will. Get some rest. I am going to go speak to the doctor again."

Sammi shook Brahim's hand, and then Isaac leaned over and said, "I know God will bless you. You'll be just fine."

Brahim closed his eyes. Sammi and Isaac walked out of the room. Dr. Brooks was standing in the corridor with Mike and James.

"How's he doing?" Mike asked.

Isaac looked at Dr. Brooks. "What's the diagnosis?"

"He had a heart attack. The electrocardiogram shows he's had some muscle damage. But he's going to be fine. He's in the most advanced medical center in the Middle East, and he's receiving the best medical care you can get anywhere. I have to check on some other patients. Call me later and I'll give you an update on Brahim."

"James, set up a security detail here twenty four/seven," Mike said.

"You can work with Commander Levin's people," the general informed James.

"I'm on it," James said. "Where are you going now?"

"I have a few things to go over with Isaac. But the first thing I have to do is check in with Washington about the schedule in London."

"Sammi, I'd like you to stay at my home," Isaac said. "You shouldn't be alone."

"Thank you. I have to pick up our things from the hotel."

"One of my people will take you," James said.

"Thanks. Isaac, what about calling everyone in the States?"

"I'll have Dov prepare some kind of press release before the markets open for trading on Monday."

"I have some things I have to attend to," said the general. "Mike, I will see you in the morning." He left.

Isaac turned to the others. "Wait here. There's something I need to do. I'll be back in a moment."

Isaac entered Brahim's room. Brahim was sleeping restfully, his breathing even. Isaac opened a book of Psalms that he kept in his pocket and began to recite, "*He asked of You life, and You gave it to him—long life, forever and ever. His glory is great in Your deliverance; You have placed majesty and splendor upon him. For you make him a blessing forever; You gladden him with the joy of your continence...*"

A few minutes later Isaac came out. "I'm ready. Now let's get going."

"I'll catch up with you guys later," James said. Sammi had already left to go get his things from the hotel.

"Mike," said Isaac once they had entered the car, "if you don't mind, I'd like to make a short detour to the Western Wall. The general informed me that they lifted the closure of the Old City. I think Brahim could use a few extra prayers."

"It's fine with me."

Mike directed the driver to take them to the Western Wall. "Can you please ask the other cars to follow us?"

Isaac called Chava. "I'm going to the Kotel to pray for Brahim."

"Good idea, Isaac. We could all do with some extra prayers."

"By the way, I invited Sammi to stay with us. He's at the hotel picking up all of his and Brahim's stuff. He should be there within an hour."

"Fine."

"Tell him to make himself comfortable, and I'll see him when I get back."

"Alright."

"Did Dov leave yet? I need him to take care of something." Dov had booked a flight back to Paris. It was leaving tonight.

"Yes, he asked me to say good-bye for him. He left for the airport a half hour ago."

"Thanks, Chava. I'll call him tomorrow." Isaac hung up the phone.

"Mike, I gotta tell ya, best deal I ever made was when I convinced that woman to marry me. Never a complaint from her. Whenever things aren't going well, she'll say, 'You'll see, Isaac, it will be good with help of the One above.'"

"You're a lucky man, Isaac."

"I sure am. I've had the same motto my whole marriage: My wife is my life. Believe me, it's true."

CHAPTER
74

Saturday, June 7, 2014
Western Wall Plaza, Jerusalem

T HE STREETS WERE almost empty except for the police cars escorting them. Soon they were passing the outer walls of the Old City. Looking out the window, Mike was amazed by the lines of people rushing to board buses.

They drove up to the VIP entrance to the Western Wall. The large metal gates opened once the policeman in the lead car said the magic words: "U.S. delegation."

All of the vehicles drove in and the gates closed. The police had cornered off a section for them to park in. As Isaac was getting out of the SUV, he looked at Mike and saw him putting on a black skullcap.

"Where did you get that?"

"At the Churchill. The caterer provided them together with the kosher food. I figured it would come in handy in Israel, so I kept one."

Isaac started walking toward the Wall. He looked up at the sky. *Midnight at the Western Wall. It's beautiful. No matter what the*

season, cold and rainy winter nights or sweltering summer heat, we
all have something to pray for.

"*Tzedakah, tzedakah,* please, sir, anything you can spare?"

An elderly woman stood in front of them with her hand out. Other charity collectors also walked around, begging for a donation. Isaac knew that some of them were collecting for themselves, and some on behalf of others—a poor bride, a hungry family, a sick child.

Isaac turned to Mike. "I don't have any cash on me. Can you loan me something until we get to my home?"

Mike opened his wallet. "How much do you want?"

"Let me have a hundred and eighty dollars."

Mike gave Isaac a hundred-dollar bill and four twenties, and Isaac started handing them out. The elderly woman took two red strings from the bunch in her hand and put them on Mike and Isaac's hands. The red strings were said to ward off the evil eye.

Mike and Isaac left the plaza and entered the area designated for those who came to pray. A partition separated men and women, allowing their thoughts to focus on their Creator.

The idea of God as father was an easy one for most, but here, in front of the wall, you had no doubt that God was king. It made so much more sense here in his palace. In front of the Wall, body and soul could unite. You could feel your oneness with the Creator. Silent prayers and whispers shifted to emotions being let out of boxes they'd been held in for years. Pleas for help were uttered by people from all over the world.

As Isaac approached the Wall, he turned and saw Mike writing something on a tiny piece of paper and then placing it inside one of the crevices between the stones.

"Mike, can I borrow your pen and some paper?"

"You can have what I've got. That was a receipt. I think I have another one in here."

Mike dug in his pocket and pulled out another small piece of paper. Isaac wrote a short note and placed it in the Wall. He opened his book of Psalms and started to utter the words softly.

Mike stood back about a foot from the wall, his eyes closed. All of sudden he felt a strange rush of warmth in his body. His eyes started to tear, and he moved closer to the Wall, hiding his face so that no one could see that he was sobbing. After a few minutes, Isaac, who had finished praying, walked over and gently tapped him on his shoulder.

"Mike, we have to go."

Isaac walked away knowing exactly what Mike had just experienced. He thought of his first visit to the Wall when he came back from Vietnam. He stood there for over an hour crying.

As they walked back to the SUV, Mike looked at Isaac. "I don't know what the hell just happened to me back there."

Isaac looked up from the stone walkway in front of him, gave a brief smile, and kept walking. Mike continued looking for some kind of answer. "I got to get some sleep."

When they approached the door of the SUV, Isaac stopped and turned to Mike.

"Your tears just opened the gates to the kingdom of Heaven. This mountain where the Holy Temple stood is the holiest place on the face of this earth. And you just got to experience it firsthand.

"You know what it says in the Bible: 'I will bless those who bless you, and whoever curses you I will curse; and all peoples on earth will be blessed through you.' Mike, everything you've been doing lately is to help me and the nation of Israel, and tonight you were blessed. We need you, Mike. Israel and America have both come a long way, but mankind is still worlds apart."

Mike grabbed Isaac and hugged him.

On the way back to Isaac's house, Mike kept looking at his mobile, scanning his numerous messages, finely stopping at the one from the deputy director:

Joining you in London. Will brief you then.

He closed his mobile. *This can't be good.*

When they entered the house, they saw Chava coming down the staircase.

"Isaac," she said, "Kim Li is sleeping, but Sammi waited up for you. He's in your office. He's worried about Brahim. How is he?"

"The doctor said he's doing fine. I'll get a report later when they get the results from the latest blood work."

"Do you guys want something to eat?"

"Nothing for me, thank you," Mike answered.

"Chava, if we want something, we'll help ourselves. It's almost two a.m. Please go to sleep. You need to have your strength for the grandchildren tomorrow."

"Alright, but make sure you take your pills. I put them on your desk." She gave him a kiss on the cheek and went upstairs.

Isaac looked at Mike. "Now you know who the real boss is."

"No offense, Isaac, but I figured it out at the airport in France."

They both smiled and walked into Isaac's office. Sammi was inside, looking at the pictures on the walls. There were many of Brahim and Isaac.

"Sammi, are you alright?" Isaac asked.

"I'm okay, thanks." His tense expression betrayed his words.

"It's late so let's get to the point. We need to discuss what to do regarding Abra. Brahim will want to know our plan tomorrow."

Isaac led them to a seating area opposite his desk. After they had sat down on the armchairs and sofa, he asked, "Sammi, what do you think we should do?"

"Brahim and I were planning to go to Tehran. With Brahim is out of commission, it's even more important that I go. It's not just that I speak Farsi, I still have relatives and other contacts there. Most important, Abra knows me. She'll feel safer once she knows I am there. Brahim would want me to go."

"Mike, what do you think?"

"We have agents there, of course, but our intel is sketchy. Sammi has a point. If there's going to be a meeting with the kidnappers to make an exchange for Abra, no question Sammi would be the best one to go. I think we should discuss this with the general before we make any moves. He's due to pick me up in a couple of hours to take me to the airport. We can ask him about it then."

"You're right," Isaac agreed. "The general told us he has a plan. Let's see if Sammi fits into that plan."

"Thanks," Sammi said, looking a little better now that they had a plan of action. "I'm going to try to get some sleep." He left.

Mike stood up. "Isaac, I have to make a few calls and I might try to get some sleep myself. I'll set my phone alarm to wake me up in time."

"Wait a minute, Mike." Isaac walked over to the wall behind his desk and slid Chagall's *I and the Village* to the side to reveal a safe. He opened the safe, pulled out a small envelope, and handed Mike the envelope. Inside was a microchip.

"What's this for?" Mike asked.

"Keep it on you. If you're in a jam and you need help, put it into your mobile and press 613. It can only be activated once, so control yourself from trying a test run."

"Thanks, Isaac." Mike put the chip inside his wallet, then turned to leave.

At that moment, Isaac's phone rang. He held up a finger, telling Mike to wait.

"Hello, Frederick."

"Isaac, is Mike with you?"

"Yeah, he's right next to me."

"Put me on speaker."

Isaac pressed the speaker button. "Go ahead."

"Mike, can you hear me?"

"I'm all ears."

"You're flying to London in a couple of hours, right?"

"Yes, I'm leaving shortly."

"We've been informed that the president is going to meet with the foreign minister of China at the Dorchester. Everyone in the Parliament is anxious. They're trying to decide how to react to the situation with the Chinese. I need to meet with you before you see the president."

"That shouldn't be a problem. I'm due to arrive a couple of hours before the president."

"There's a private hangar I use when I don't want anyone to know I'm leaving the country. You can land there. I'll meet you." Frederick gave Mike instructions to give to the pilot.

"Fine, see you soon."

Isaac clicked off. Mike said, "Now I really need to go. I have a few things to take care of before I leave for the airport."

As Mike headed up the stairs to his room, his phone rang. It was his boss.

"Hello, sir. Give me a minute. I want to make sure I'm alone."

Mike entered his room and sat down on the bed. "Okay, sir. We can talk."

"Mike, a couple of hours ago a special unit of the FBI picked up Senator Long and Bill Waters from their homes in Virginia. They're being questioned regarding the conspiracy to remove the president. My contact in the FBI informed me that there are more arrests to come."

Mike was silent. They both understood what had just happened. Everyone who had knowledge of the plot to remove the president was now a candidate to be picked up by the FBI.

Mike wanted to call James and alert him. He thought about how Allan had pressed him for information about what was going on in Washington. Now he knew he'd done the right thing in freezing him out. He wondered how many more would be arrested by the time he arrived in London.

CHAPTER
75

Sunday, June 8, 2014
Green home, Jerusalem

ISAAC SAW GENERAL Solomon on the security camera, about to ring the front doorbell. Isaac opened the door to admit him.

"Isaac, I didn't expect you to be awake at this hour." It was four in the morning.

"I was waiting up for you."

"Then I might as well tell you the good news. We have the two Chinese militants who blew up the Dome of the Rock in custody. They confessed. By morning they will be facing a judge and the world media. We've convinced them to come completely clean. They'll be implicating Wen Tian."

Isaac smiled. "That's good news. A win for us. Listen, Sammi wants to talk to you about going to Iran to find Abra. I thought you might have a few minutes for him before you leave."

The general looked at his watch. "Please tell him I'm running late. I suggest we all meet this afternoon and discuss the plan my people worked on." He looked around. "Where's Mike?"

"He's in the kitchen having a coffee."

"When Mike is ready, I'll be in my car. I have to make a few calls."

Isaac walked into the kitchen.

"Isaac, is the general here?"

"Yes, he's waiting for you in his car. He said he'll meet with Sammi later. He's running late."

Mike downed the rest of his coffee. "Then I'd better go."

"Mike, I need you to do me a favor."

"What is it?"

"Keep in touch. Text me. I'm concerned about your trip to London."

"Don't worry, I have a four-leaf clover in my wallet, and the luck of the Irish is always with me. I got to go."

Isaac reached out to shake Mike's hand. "God bless you and keep you safe."

He accompanied Mike outside to the SUV and waved as they pulled away. Before going inside, he paused to look at the security guards sitting in their vehicles, guarding his house. He shook his head. *Will there ever be peace in this world?*

Isaac went to his office, where he knew Sammi would be waiting.

"Everything all right?" Sammi said. "Where's the general?"

"He told me to tell you that he's working on a plan, and he wants to meet with us later to discuss it. He was running late getting Mike to the airport."

"I understand. I'm planning to go visit Brahim today. He'll be happy to know we're moving forward to get Abra back."

Sammi left to try and get some more sleep. Isaac sat down in his favorite armchair. The clock on the desk read four thirty. He reached for his favorite book, *Faith and Trust*. He read it whenever he needed guidance, and this was as good a time as any.

He opened the book to where his marker guided him. "*Never fear,*" it said. "*One who trusts in God will not be afraid, as the*

prophet said, 'Behold, God is my salvation; I shall trust and not fear'
(Isaiah 12:2)."

The page blurred and Isaac's eyes drifted closed. Soon he was asleep.

CHAPTER
76

Sunday, June 8, 2014
On the way to Ben Gurion Airport

THE SUV SPED down the highway.

"What time is the president due to arrive in London?" the general asked.

"My latest info says twelve o'clock," Mike replied.

"And you're arriving at around nine this morning."

"Right, I'm meeting up with Frederick before the president arrives."

"Any idea when you are coming back? I'd like you to be here when I meet with Sammi and Isaac about getting Abra Surin back from Iran."

"I'm hoping later tonight. The president is scheduled to pay his respects to the prime minister's wife and proceed right on to Saudi Arabia to meet with the king." At least, that was the official line. The president would also be meeting with the Chinese foreign minister at the Dorchester Hotel before leaving for Saudi Arabia. "And, of course, there's my meeting with your prime minister," Mike acknowledged.

"Ah, yes," said the general. "Here is the package you must deliver to him."

He pulled an envelope from his jacket pocket and handed it to Mike.

Mike took it and put it away.

"Listen, Mike, call me if you need me."

"Yaacov," Mike said, "even this short time together with you tells me that you're the first call I would make. You can bet on that."

The SUV pulled up alongside the waiting jet. It had already started its engines. Mike shook the general's hand and got out of the vehicle. Mike started walking to the plane. The general yelled to him, "Mike, let me know when you're leaving London so I can pick you up."

Mike waved over the noise of the jet. "Will do."

Mike boarded the plane.

"Good morning, sir," the flight attendant greeted him.

Mike nodded and walked through the passenger's compartment to find a seat. He was taken aback to find Allan and one of his security guards inside, already seated.

Allan stood up with a smile. "Nice to see you, Mike."

"Nobody informed me you were accompanying me to London," Mike said.

"The chief of staff's office told me they sent you a message. He arranged for me to meet him in London. Is that a problem?"

"Not at all. Just surprised."

Over the loudspeaker, the pilot announced, "We're cleared for takeoff."

"Allan, if you don't mind, I'm not in the mood to talk. I was up all night. I'm going to try and get some shuteye."

"That's fine. I have to catch up on my e-mails anyway."

Mike covered himself with a blanket, kicked off his shoes, and put his seat into the reclining position. Allan started reading e-mails on his iPhone. Scrolling down, he stopped at an e-mail from Kim Li.

Sorry I didn't meet you before you left. I wanted to thank you for all you have done for me. It has been wonderful getting to know you, Allan. Take care of yourself. Yours, Kim Li.

As the screen went blank, Allan wondered when he would see her again.

CHAPTER
77

Sunday, June 8, 2014
Green home, Jerusalem

WHEN CHAVA AWOKE, she noticed that Isaac's bed had not been slept in. She checked Isaac's office.

A note on his desk read, *"Chava, I left early to pray at the Wall. Afterward I'm going to visit Brahim. Tell Sammi and Kim Li to go ahead and have breakfast without me, and tell Charlie to be ready to meet with me later to discuss his trip to New York. I expect to be home around nine o'clock. I'm on my cell if you need me. Love, Isaac."*

Outside Brahim's room James sat drinking a cup of coffee. He saw Isaac walk past the nurse's desk. He put down his cup and stood up as Isaac walked toward him.

"Good morning. Everything alright last night?"

James nodded. "Quiet. The doctor is inside with Mr. Surin."

"Thanks."

Isaac knocked on Brahim's door and entered. Dr. Brooks held a clipboard with papers. Brahim sat up in a chair.

"Good morning, Doctor," said Isaac.

"Good morning."

"Brahim, how do you feel? Did you get any sleep?"

"I'm fine, but how's Abra?"

"Our reports say she's fine. Plans are under way to get her back. Right now you just need to focus on getting better." Isaac turned to the doctor. "How's he doing?"

"All of his tests say he's doing well. A few days of rest here and some medication, and he should be good as new. He's gonna need a special diet and exercise plan, though." The doctor turned to his patient. "Brahim, I'll check back with you later after I make my rounds."

"Thanks for everything, Doc."

After the doctor left, Brahim stood up, a little shaky on his feet. "Isaac," he said, "I've got to get out of here now. No few days. Today."

"Brahim, sit down. Take it easy. I'll be right back."

Isaac walked out of the room and headed toward the nurse's station. The doctor was writing his report. He looked up. "Isaac, can I help you?"

"Yes, where can I speak to you alone?"

"Come to my office." Dr. Brooks led him to an office at the end of the corridor and closed the door. When they were seated, he said, "Isaac, what can I do for you?"

"Brahim wants to leave the hospital now. Jerry, listen, I'm telling you this as a friend, you can't tell anyone. Brahim's wife, Abra, is in Iran. She's been kidnapped. Do me a favor, discharge him. I'll bring him to my home. Just to be on the safe side, I'll arrange to have a nurse be with him around the clock. You can stop by and check on his condition whenever you want. What do you say?"

"Isaac, you know I can't say no to you. I'll arrange for a schedule of nurses to be at your home within a few hours. Let me get the paperwork finished and write out his prescriptions. It'll be about a half hour."

"Thanks."

Isaac walked out of the office and headed back to Brahim's room. On the way he took out his phone and dialed home. "Chava," he said when she picked up, "we're bringing Brahim home. Can you get the guest apartment ready?"

"Of course. It will be ready by the time you arrive. Send Brahim my love."

"Thank you, Chava, I will."

When Isaac walked back into Brahim's room, Brahim was standing at the foot of his bed, fully dressed and ready to leave.

"You look surprised," Brahim said. "I knew you would get it done." He winked at his friend. "Let's get outta here."

"Sit down, it's gonna be a few more minutes, brother. The doctor's filling out the discharge papers. He's only letting you go on the condition that I take you home with me. The fourth floor is unoccupied. It has its own elevator and a private entrance. I'm arranging for a full-time nurse until the doctor gives you a clean bill of health."

Brahim nodded and sat down.

"Now I know you're worried about Abra, but we're working on it. You've got to take it easy. Turns out I couldn't reschedule the world falling apart, so do your best."

"Okay, I got the message, Rabbi Green. Whatever you say."

"Now wait here. I'll tell James to get ready to transport you to my house."

Isaac went into the corridor to speak to James. "James, we're taking Brahim home now. He's staying with me."

"Okay, I'll inform my people of their new assignments. I'll follow your car and meet you at your home."

The doctor walked over to them. "Everything is arranged," he said. "You can leave now. A nurse is on her way to your home." He handed Isaac an envelope and a small package. "Here are his medicines and discharge papers. I'll call you a little later to see how he's doing. You're to make sure he gets plenty of rest and takes his pills.

He's not out of the woods yet."

"Thanks again, Doctor."

The doctor left. Isaac turned to James. "Okay, that's it. Let's go."

Isaac walked back into Brahim's room. "I've got everything. Are you ready?"

"Absolutely. Let's get out of here."

WHEN THEY ARRIVED at the house, Chava and Sammi were waiting at the door. Sammi rushed over to Brahim. "Are you alright?"

"I'm fine. Though I think I need to sit down."

Sammi led Brahim into the living room and the others followed. Isaac smiled at his wife. "Is everything all set, Chava?"

"All ready." She turned to Brahim. "Brahim, let me know if you need anything. I'm so happy you're staying with us."

"I can't think of a better place to get back on my feet."

"Does anyone want to eat or drink something?" Chava asked.

Before someone could respond, the doorbell rang. Isaac looked at the video by the door to see who it was. The general was standing on the porch. Isaac went to let him in. "Come in, General."

The general saw Brahim standing behind Isaac and gave him a big smile. "I'm glad to see you're out of the hospital so soon, Brahim."

"No more than me."

"Brahim, would like to go upstairs to rest up for a while?" Isaac asked.

"No, I want to discuss Abra and our plans to get her back."

"Let's go into my office."

Brahim walked slowly behind Isaac, with Sammi close by in case he needed a support. "Boss, maybe you should rest for a while," said Sammi.

"I'll have plenty of time to rest later. We need a plan to save my wife."

"Yes, boss, of course."

When they were all seated around Isaac's desk, Brahim turned to General Solomon. "General, what do you suggest?"

"On my way back from the airport, my office called me with new information. The Swiss Embassy has received a demand. It's the exact one we intercepted."

Brahim looked at the general. "What are you going to do?"

"I've already spoken to our prime minister and certain members of the cabinet. They have agreed to let me handle it. I intend to go ahead after we have positively verified that your wife is alive and safe. We'll then make the trade. Isaac agreed that World would take care of the transfer of the billion dollars."

"How do you plan to verify that Abra is safe before all of this happens?" Brahim asked.

The general looked at Sammi. "Sammi's the one to go and get her, isn't that right, Sammi?"

"That's right, General."

"How long before you can arrange everything?" Brahim asked impatiently.

"Twenty-four hours. My team is ready to meet with Sammi and brief him. A plane will fly him to Zurich with our people on board. From there he will fly on a private Swiss plane to Tehran. The Swiss have agreed to assist us in any way they can."

All eyes focused on Brahim. Brahim looked at Sammi. "This is very dangerous. Are you sure you want to do this?"

"Boss, I want to do this. I'll be fine."

Brahim suddenly looked very tired. "Brahim," said Isaac, "the nurse is upstairs. Sammi, do me a favor and go upstairs with Brahim. Make sure he has everything he needs."

"You got it."

Brahim stood up slowly and Sammi helped him out of the room.

"General, I need more details," Isaac said matter-of-factly when they had left. "There's something you're not saying."

The general gave a grim smile. "I didn't want to discuss this in front of Brahim. There has been a new development in the Abra case. We recently learned that Abra wasn't actually kidnapped."

"What are you saying? She went with those men of her own volition? But what about the message you intercepted?"

"This gets complicated."

Isaac leaned forward. "I'm all ears."

"She didn't leave Brahim, but he might want to leave her after he hears this. She is part of the plot to extort money from World. And there's more: they plan to kidnap Sammi during the exchange. Once they get the money, they plan to up the ante and force World to give over their newest chip, or she and Sammi will both be murdered."

"How reliable is this information?"

"We have two of our best people on intel. One's a top Mossad agent. He's been giving us the play-by-play on Abra's every move. We know that Abra has been staying in Lavizan Park in a private house since she arrived in Iran. She has been meeting with different officials daily. Abra has had meetings with mullahs who are in direct contact with the Ayatollah. It looks like she is collaborating with the regime and has no plans of ever returning to the U.S."

"You mentioned another agent. Who is he?"

"Dr. Kamiar Fard. In Iran he is a renowned heart specialist. He has been treating all the top people in the Revolutionary Guard for the past three years. But he wants to defect to the U.S. The NSA and my people have been collaborating on how to get him and his family out."

"How do you communicate?"

"Since the embargos on Iran, we have been using the Swiss government to deliver the medications he needs, with our own Teva pharmaceutical company as the provider. The labels on some of the bottles are coded. They contain messages for him. When he returns the empty bottles, inside is another prescription to refill, but it also contains his coded messages to us. Yesterday we received a communiqué that two days ago he was called to visit Abra. She was experiencing angina pectoris."

"What the hell's that?"

"It's a fancy way of saying chest pains. He examined her, but couldn't find a cause. He attributed it to the stress of the situation. He ordered some blood tests and an anti-anxiety medicine. As soon as we received that information, we started to develop a plan to get him out together with Abra."

"But I thought you said she doesn't want to leave?"

"I have a feeling Abra does not know what she wants right now. They got to her somehow. I can't put my finger on it yet, but this is not coming from Abra, even if she thinks it is."

Isaac nodded in agreement. "You have a point. I've known Abra for most of my adult life. This isn't the woman Brahim married, that's for sure."

"Before I came, I sent a text to my office that it's a go. The Iranian authorities are being notified that Sammi is going to be on the Swiss plane to Iran. Once he verifies that Abra is fine, the transfer of funds can be made and the rest of the agreement can be completed."

Isaac sat up. "Wait a minute, you still plan on going through with the exchange? Even with what you know? What about Sammi? Are you planning on telling him that you're setting him up?"

"No one is going to get hurt. We know about their plan, ours just has to be better."

Isaac exhaled. "I hope you're right. I couldn't forgive myself if Sammi or Abra were injured and I had anything to do with it."

"Everyone will be fine. Sammi will be monitored at every moment."

Isaac sat back and folded his arms. "Okay, so what's the plan?"

"We have prepared all the medications our agent has requested. They will be on the plane with Sammi. In that batch is a special vial with a drug we developed. The drug slows the heartbeat down. Dr. Fard will inject Abra, telling her that it is a flu shot. All of Abra's vital signs will make it appear that her heart is giving out. In actuality, she will be in no danger. She will just sleep for a few of days.

"The doctor will tell the authorities that she needs a complex operation that he only performs in Switzerland with a colleague who is a specialist in this procedure. It will be made clear that this is her only hope for survival and that the terms of the financial arrangements are that she is alive and well. They'll let him take her to Switzerland."

"It's a hell of a plan. When do you want to meet with Sammi to give him his instructions?"

"If it's all right with you and Brahim, I would like him to come with me now. We must set the plan in action as soon as possible."

"Fine, I'll call him."

Isaac reached for the phone just as Sammi walked in.

"How's he doing?" asked Isaac.

"He's sleeping."

"Sammi," said the general, "my team is waiting to brief you. Everything is set with the Swiss. I understand the money is in place."

Isaac interrupted. "Sammi, I'm sure the general will tell you that there is no guarantee that this will come off without a hitch and he's right. It's more complicated than we originally thought. I know how much Brahim means to you, I know you'd do anything for him, but I also know that he wouldn't think any less of you if you decided not to do this." Isaac placed a hand on Sammi's shoulder. "Sammi, they might try and take you to extort more money from Brahim."

The general looked pained. "Isaac, that is not exactly—"

"Isaac," said Sammi, "I've seen enough movies to know how many different ways this could play out. I've spoken to my wife, and she gave me her blessing. General, if you could just give me fifteen minutes to pack and say good-bye?"

"Of course. My people will be waiting outside."

Sammi extended his hand to the general. "Thanks for all of your help."

"Everything will be fine. We will be monitoring you the whole time. Just follow the instructions my team will give you."

Isaac grabbed Sammi's hand to shake it. "You take care. Don't worry about Brahim. I'll take care of him."

"I know you will. *JazakAllahu khair.* May Allah bless you."

Isaac showed the general to the door, then walked back into his study. Kim Li sat inside, talking to Charlie.

"Good morning, Isaac," Charlie said.

"Charlie, Kim Li, did you have breakfast?"

"We both ate while you were in your meeting with the general."

Kim Li smiled. "Chava took good care of us, thank you."

"Isaac," said Charlie, "Kim Li and I have been talking. She's agreed to go to New York with me."

"Yes, Charlie and I are off to a good start. We've already exchanged some ideas about how we should approach business with the Chinese government in the future."

"Great, when do you plan to go?"

"Susan booked us on an El Al flight. We're leaving in a couple of hours."

"Did you talk to Xu Ming?"

"Yes, but only for a minute. He's going to try to meet us Tuesday morning at World. He's being watched and he's very nervous."

"Kim Li, when you see him, tell him that World will fund his research center in the U.S. and he will be in charge of it. I believe that coming from you it will have more meaning."

Charlie nodded in agreement. "Have you thought about where he's going to stay until the government gives him asylum?"

"Yes, we'll put him up in our corporate apartment at World. That's probably the most secure building in the city."

Kim Li interrupted. "Isaac, do you have any idea if Allan is coming to New York?"

"Mike called me earlier to tell me that Allan is with him on the flight to London. I expect to hear from Mike shortly."

"Excuse me," said Charlie, standing up, "I've got to make some arrangements. Isaac, if I don't see you later, then take care."

Isaac stood and shook his hand. "I'll see you in New York." He turned to Kim Li. "I'll ask Susan to arrange a place for you to stay as well. If there's anything else I can do for you, please let me know."

Kim Li smiled and nodded. "Thank you again."

CHAPTER
78

Sunday, June 8, 2014
Heathrow Airport

GOOD MORNING, MR. O'Shea. It's nine a.m. Soon we'll be
on our final approach to Heathrow Airport. Would you like some
coffee?"

"Thanks. Black, no sugar."

Mike pulled off his blanket and reached over to lift the window
shade. They were flying inside a gray cloud. Rainy weather in London. No surprise there.

Soon I'll be back in Israel, breathing the Mediterranean air.

The flight attendant stood before him. "Sir, here's your coffee.
Would you like to eat something?"

"No, thanks, I'm fine."

Allan walked in from the pilot's cabin. "Good morning."

"Good morning. Any news?"

"I was checking on the weather. Light rain that will clear around
noon. The pilot said we'll be landing on time."

An announcement came over the intercom. "This is your captain. We'll be running into some turbulence as we approach Heath-

row. Please buckle your seat belts."

At that moment Mike's beeper went off. He had a message from Frederick:

> The president's plane landed early. He was sched-
> uled to be here at twelve. Our office was not in-
> formed until one hour ago that he has arrived.
> Something's up.

Mike texted back:

> We should be on the ground in ten minutes.

Mike didn't like this. *Why did the president change his schedule?*

As the plane started to descend through the clouds, Mike looked out his window and could see the magnificent 260-foot control tower. The plane had already lowered its wheels, and it taxied to the prearranged hangar. In the distance, Mike saw the president's plane, sitting apart from Terminal 5, the main terminal.

Mike looked at Allan. "Did you notice the president's plane? He wasn't due here till noon."

"Yeah, security must have heard something and they decided to leave D.C. early. It's good for me. He should have time to see me now."

The plane came to a stop inside the hangar, and the flight attendant opened the door and lowered the stairs. Allan and the security guard were the first to leave. Mike shook hands with the pilot and copilot.

As he descended the staircase, Mike saw Frederick standing alone. Allan and the security guard stood off to the side with three men he didn't recognize. Mike waved to Frederick and started walking toward him. Before he could reach Frederick, two of the men Allan had been talking to approached him.

"Mike O'Shea?" said the taller one.

Mike nodded.

"We're special agents with the FBI. We were sent here to detain you and Allan Peters in Heathrow until we can have you flown back to the States later today. There are some questions regarding a plot to remove the president from office that need to be answered."

Mike's face remained expressionless. "I don't know anything about that."

Allan walked over with the third agent. "What the hell is going on here?" he asked Mike.

Mike shrugged. "I don't know, but I'll find out soon." He turned to the agent who had addressed him. "I want to speak to the deputy director of the NSA right now."

The agent shook his head. "Don't make this more difficult than it has to be. The deputy director has already been detained in his home for questioning."

"Who else are you detaining?"

"I'm not at liberty to tell you."

"The hell with this. I'm going to find out what's going on." Mike took out his mobile and started to dial. There was no signal.

"It must be the hangar," he said. "I'm going outside."

"There's no use," said the FBI agent. "They blocked your SIM card."

Allan pulled out his phone.

"I'm sorry, but they did the same to yours."

"Mike," said Frederick, "some of my people are going along with the president's detail to the Dorchester as security. I was supposed to be with them. When he finished his meeting with the Chinese foreign minister, I was going to accompany him to pay his respects to the prime minister's widow. I will talk to the chief of staff and the president personally. I'm sure this is all just a big mistake and we'll get you out of this. Let me handle this, okay?"

"Thanks, Frederick."

"Where's the bathroom?" Mike asked one of the agents after Frederick had left.

"It's in the office over there," the agent replied and pointed.

Mike walked into the office and entered the bathroom, pulled off his belt, and removed a SIM card he kept hidden on the inside of his belt. He replaced the one in his mobile and dialed James.

"Mike, what's wrong? Why are you calling on this number?"

"As soon as we arrived at Heathrow, Allan and I were detained by the FBI. We're being held in a hangar. They're planning to fly us back to the U.S. today. They're questioning everyone regarding the alleged removal of the president. They're already interrogating Paul in his home."

"What can I do?"

"Frederick is on his way to meet with the chief of staff at the Dorchester. Please call him and give him this number. When I hear back from him, I'll update you. Unless you hear from me, stay put in Israel. Contact General Solomon and Isaac and let them know I've been detained and might not make it back. I've got to go."

As Mike walked back toward the hangar, he heard yelling. The FBI agents and Allan were running toward the agents' cars. Allan spotted Mike and shouted, "Mike, the president's been killed. We've got to go."

Mike stopped in his tracks, stunned. One of the agents rushed over to him and took him by the arm. "Mike, the director wants you and Allan to come with me. We're to take you to the U.S. Embassy."

Mike and Allan jumped into the back seat of the SUV. The agent who was driving turned on his siren and flashing lights. The sound was deafening as it bounced off the metal walls and ceiling of the hangar. As soon as the SUV was outside, Mike turned to Allan. "What happened?"

"All I know is one of the agents got a call saying that the president had been killed. Then we were all told to start moving to the cars."

A phone rang. It belonged to the agent sitting in the front passenger seat. He answered it. "Yes, sir." He listened and then turned around to look at Mike. "It's the chief of staff. He wants to talk to you."

Mike took the phone. "Hello."

"Agent O'Shea, you've heard the news?"

"I heard the president was killed. Is it true? How the hell did it happen?"

"It's true. We just received information that al-Qaeda is about to broadcast a message claiming they assassinated the president for killing Osama bin Laden. They're also claiming that the Israelis were responsible for the plane crash that killed Abu al-Mousavi and Prince Abdul. They are preparing for a jihad against Israel and the U.S."

"How did it happen? He was surrounded by security."

"The president was in the elevator on his way to meet with the Chinese foreign minister. When it reached his floor, a bomb went off. By the time we got there, the president and his entire security detail were dead. It was bad. There were body parts everywhere."

"No doubt the Chinese were in on it. Any clues on how they were able to do it?"

"PETN."

PETN was a powerful explosive.

"How did they plant it in the elevator?"

"It's not conclusive, but we think that the elevator control panel was rigged with the explosive so it couldn't be detected. Somehow they shorted the electrical system remotely, causing a fire which set off the pentaerythritol tetranitrate. Hold on a minute, I've got another call."

Mike turned to Allan. "It was PETN," he informed Allan. "How did our guys miss that?"

The chief of staff came back on the line. "Agent, you still there?"

"Yeah, go ahead."

"Look, it's insane here. I've got calls backed up, and I have to get the president's body on his plane by two p.m. We're flying to Dover Air Force Base. The president's wife is in California, and they're flying her there. Mike, hold it, I just got a text. They're about to swear in the vice president. I'll call you back."

Mike hung up the phone. "Somebody, turn on the radio."

The agent in the driver's seat turned on the radio to BBC.

"It's eleven a.m. and this is the BBC World Service. We interrupt our regular news program to inform you that the president of the United States of America has been assassinated. His death resulted from a bomb detonated in an elevator at the Dorchester Hotel in London. Two Secret Service agents who accompanied the president were also killed in the explosion. The total amount injured or dead is not known at this time. The president was scheduled to pay his respects to the widow of the late prime minister today and continue on to Saudi Arabia for a meeting with the king."

As they listened, the SUV sped on to the American Embassy.

"I still can't figure out why he came early," said Mike. "It doesn't make sense. Someone with inside knowledge of the president's early arrival had to be involved. The terrorist would not have placed the explosive earlier, taking the chance that the bomb would detonate prematurely. This had to be done at the last minute."

The agent in the passenger seat turned to Mike. "I just received a text saying that your cell phones have been turned on. Agent O'Shea, you're to call the NSA deputy director immediately."

"Great," Allan said, "now maybe I can find out what's really going on."

Mike surreptitiously switched back the SIM cards and dialed his direct superior's number. Paul's line was busy. Mike pressed the resend button, and after a minute the call connected.

"Mike," said Paul, "are you alright?"

"Tell me what's happening, Paul."

"I'm in my car on my way back to NSA headquarters. After the vice president was sworn in, a select few of us had a closed meeting with him. He told us that as soon as he was informed of the president's death, he ordered the director of the FBI to release all of us who were being detained and brought to the White House immediately. He's declaring a national emergency tonight on TV. '*Yesterday is gone. Tomorrow has yet to come. We have only today. Let's begin.* Mother Teresa.' That's how he closed the meeting. I was the last one to shake his hand and wish him well. Everyone had left. He took me by the arm and said, 'Tell Mike O'Shea to get over here.'"

"Listen, Paul, I have to return to Israel. I have some unfinished business there."

"You've got twenty-four hours. Then I want you on a plane to Washington."

"Paul, I have Allan Peters with the State Department here with me. He was stationed at the U.S. Embassy in Hong Kong. What should I tell him?"

"I'm aware of the situation in Hong Kong. He's being reassigned. He should fly to the States immediately. I'll arrange for him to be on the plane with the president's body."

"I'll tell him."

"Now let me speak to the agent."

Mike handed his phone to the FBI agent. After a minute of listening, the agent spoke into the phone. "Yes, sir, I understand, right away."

Allan looked at Mike. "What unfinished business?"

"The Abra situation for one. I've got to see this through with Isaac and Brahim. What are your plans?"

Allan smiled. "I've got my own unfinished business. First with the State Department, and then with Kim Li."

As soon as they had heard the news about the president, the SUV had turned around to return to the airport and now stopped outside the hangar. The agent in the passenger seat jumped out and opened the door for Mike.

"Agent O'Shea, I'm really sorry about this." He extended his hand. "No hard feelings, I hope."

"Forget it. You were just following orders." Mike took the other man's hand and shook it.

The pilot walked up to them. "Mr. O'Shea, we are refueled and cleared to return to Israel whenever you're ready."

"Thanks, I'll be with you in a few minutes." Mike went to say good-by to Allan, who had just hung up his phone, an odd smile on his face.

"Mike, if you need anything, you have my number." Allan extended his hand to shake Mike's.

"Were you just talking to Kim Li?"

"How do you know?"

Mike smiled. "It's all over your face. Have a safe flight."

Mike walked back into the hangar and boarded the plane. As the plane left the runway and ascended into the sky, Mike hit the reclining position in his chair, hoping to get some shuteye. Alone with his thoughts, the day's events rushed over him. He leaned back and closed his eyes. A moment later he was asleep.

CHAPTER
79

Sunday, June 8, 2014
Tree of Life headquarters, Herzliya

IT WAS TEN a.m. in Israel. The personnel at the Tree of Life headquarters were in high gear after hearing the news that the U.S. president had been assassinated. General Solomon was in his office. He had just finished a conference call with the Israeli prime minister and members of the cabinet. He was about to call Mike when there was a knock on his door. He pressed a button and the door opened.

"Yes, what is it?"

One of his agents entered. "Sir, we just received this message marked urgent." He handed it to the general.

The note read, "*Al-Qaeda is not responsible for killing the president. It was the chairman of the Joint Chiefs of Staff. Full report to follow.*"

The note was signed *Treasure Island.*

The general stared at the note as if it was a rare document from his ancient manuscript collection.

"Is there anything I can do?" the agent asked.

"No, thank you. Just inform everyone that I am not to be disturbed."

"Yes, sir." The aide turned and left.

The general unlocked a drawer in his desk. He pulled out a cell phone and pressed a button connecting him to the prime minister.

"Hello, General."

"Mr. Prime Minister, I've just received an urgent message saying that it wasn't Al-Qaeda who was responsible for the assassination."

"Then who?"

"The chairman of the Joint Chiefs of Staff. I'm waiting for a full report from our source."

"Who was the source?"

"Treasure Island."

"Alright, I'm canceling my plans to return to Israel. I'm going back to the States. I'll talk with you later." The prime minister hung up.

The general called his aide. "Cancel all my appointments and tell my driver I'm going to Jerusalem." On his way out, he texted Isaac to let him know he was coming.

As the general got into his car, the same agent ran toward it and handed him another message. "Sir, this is marked urgent. It's the follow-up report."

The general took the report. "Thank you. Please notify me of any updates." To the driver, he said, "Please take me to Isaac Green's house."

He started to read the report when his cell phone rang.

"Hello, General. Can you hear me? It's Mike."

"Go ahead."

"I'm on my way back. I'm due to land in about three hours."

"Alright, I'll meet you."

General Solomon resumed reading the report. He read it twice, then put it into his attaché case. As the driver pulled up to Isaac's house, the general saw Isaac kiss Chava and then Chava got into a car. Her car pulled away just as the general approached Isaac.

"Isaac, how's the family?"

"Fine. In fact, Chava just left to spend the day visiting with some of the grandchildren. With Brahim here and everything else, I decided to stay home.

"I got your message. Let's speak inside."

"Is everything alright? Is Sammi okay?" asked Isaac.

"Sammi is fine. My people are briefing him right now, and he is scheduled to fly to Iran soon. That's not why I am here. I have something to show you. You'd better sit down." He handed Isaac the report.

Every few seconds Isaac's eyes looked up at the general in disbelief. "It's like the gates of hell have opened, and all of the demons have been let out to destroy the United States."

Isaac continued reading until he came to the last paragraph of the report. "General, what are we doing with this information? You've got to inform Mike."

"I just heard from Mike. He's due to arrive in about three hours. I'm going to pick him up. I'll tell him then."

"I'd like to go along. There's something I want to discuss with Mike too."

"Fine. How is Brahim?"

"I was with him for a short time earlier. When he heard the news about the president, the nurse thought he was going to lose it."

A few minutes later they were on their way to the airport. Isaac sat looking out the window as they drove past the Shrine of the Book on the way to the Tel Aviv highway. Isaac had just read an article about when the Dead Sea Scrolls were discovered in 1947 and how, later, they had built this edifice to house them. The design of the structure was meant to symbolize an imaginary war between the Sons of Light and the Sons of Darkness. He knew that the report he'd just read was not imaginary, and as of today the Sons of Darkness were winning the war.

As they approached the entrance to the airport, Isaac said, "General, I've been wondering. Why'd you show me this report? This is obviously top-secret information from one of your undercover agents."

"That's right."

"So why'd you show it to me?"

"Isaac, you've used your position to influence the United States to cooperate with us in so many areas. With war imminent, I think this is definitely such a time. You need to know exactly who you are dealing with."

"General, you know I'll do everything I can."

They arrived at the airport. The driver paused at the security gate for a moment. The security guard waved them in. Mike's plane had just taxied off the runway and was about to park. As soon as they lowered the stairs, Mike quickly descended.

"Isaac, I didn't know you were coming."

Isaac shook Mike's hand. "What's your plan now that the president has been killed?"

"The deputy director has ordered me to fly back to Washington. I told him I had some unfinished business in Israel. He gave me twenty-four hours to tie things up here. By the way," he said, turning to the general, "here's the envelope. I'm sorry I wasn't able to deliver it to the prime minister."

The general took the package and nodded. "I will find another way."

Isaac looked at the general and raised an eyebrow. The general nodded and handed Mike the report. "I received this today from one of my undercover operatives."

Mike took his time as he studied each page. When he came to the last page, he handed it back to the general. His face had turned red with anger. "They won't get away with this. I won't let them."

The general's mobile rang. It was a text from his office. "I have to go," he said. "They need me to go over some last-minute items with Sammi. I'll have my driver drop me off and then take you both to Jerusalem. When I'm finished with Sammi, I will join you at Isaac's house."

Mike dialed James. "James, where are you?"

"Outside Isaac's home, sitting in a car. Where are you?"

"I'm with Isaac and the general. I'll be there within an hour."

Mike hung up.

The drive to the Tree of Life headquarters took less than thirty minutes. There were no interrupting phone calls and no conversation. The last line of the report played itself over and over in Mike's head.

"Once the president is dead, we'll set up Mike O'Shea and James Brown to take the fall, and we'll come up smelling like roses."

The days ahead would be filled with enormous difficulties. The world was in a free fall. The potential for war was imminent, Iran and its pawns versus the United States and its allies. The survival of the free world was at stake. A nuclear war, economic collapse, and now the planning and killing of the president of the United States. It was a lot to take in. Even harder to take was that they would repay all the sacrifices Mike had made for his country like this.

The SUV stopped at Tree of Life, and the general got out. A few minutes later, the driver was on the main highway to Jerusalem. From years of experience, Isaac understood that silence like this was a bad sign.

Mike was looking out the window as they drove past the sign for Ben Gurion airport. The report required a response, and Mike was plotting it.

"I can't let them get away with this."

"You're a liability they can't afford. They planned this from the beginning. But why did they have to kill the two Secret Service agents?"

Mike grimaced. "In their twisted minds, this is war and those agents were collateral damage."

"Who else is involved?"

"That's my problem. I've got to find out. This information had to be from someone close to the chairman of the Joint Chiefs of Staff. He's the address. We need to find out who this person is."

"Listen, Mike, the reason I came to meet you was that I wanted to give you a proposal. This situation tells me that it's a timely one."

"What is it?"

"What do you make? Two hundred fifty thousand a year?"

Mike laughed. "You're too generous. I make less than two hundred. And this is as good as it gets. I'm at the top of my pay scale, even though I'm one of the three highest-ranking agents in the NSA."

"Mike, I want to hire you to take over security for World. You can pick your own staff—James and whoever else you need to provide security for World. You have carte blanche, and you'll answer only to me and my partners. It'll mean a considerable raise in your salary plus I'll give you stock options in World."

"Isaac, I can't thank you enough. With these new developments, it looks like I'll be out of a job, so your timing couldn't be better."

"You're an asset, Mike. We'd be lucky to have you."

"Listen, Isaac, I want to give you back your chip. Obviously I didn't get a chance to use it so—"

"Just keep it. I'm sure you'll need it one day."

"Are you going to tell me what it does?"

Isaac was silent for a moment. "Okay, I'll tell you. When you were at the Western Wall, I saw something in you that's rare in your field."

"What's that?"

"Your sensitivity."

"Thanks, but what does this have to do with the chip?"

"That chip was a way of saying thank you for all you've done for me and Brahim. If you activate it, you will find the number of a bank account in Liechtensteinische Landesbank in Liechtenstein. There is one million dollars on deposit under a code name. All you have to do is type in the code and the money is yours. No strings attached."

"Isaac, I can't take this money for doing my job."

"You're now employed by World. Think of it as a signing bonus."

"Thanks, Isaac." Mike extended his hand.

Isaac smiled and shook it. "Welcome to World."

The car pulled up to Isaac's home, and they stepped out of the vehicle. James saw them arrive and walked up to them. "What's going on?" he asked Mike.

"Come inside."

"Mike, if you need some privacy, you can use my office. I'm going to visit with Brahim."

"Thanks." Mike led James to Isaac's study. He stared at the paintings on the wall, wondering where to start.

James studied Mike. "Mike, you look like you're in another world."

"Sorry, James, I'm with you. Have you received any updates from D.C.?"

"Not a word. Last news I heard was on the radio that Al-Qaeda claimed they killed the president and that the VP was being sworn in."

"James, the president was not killed by Al-Qaeda." Mike's voice had an urgency to it. "It was the chairman of the Joint Chiefs of Staff who gave the order."

"What? Where the hell did you get that information?"

"It's reliable. Do you remember the conversation we had in the lobby of the hotel? About that phone conversation the president had with the king?"

"Yeah, that's not the type of thing you forget."

"I told you that we would never take the rap if something went wrong."

"I remember."

"The plan they told us that day was a setup and we were the

patsies. If something went wrong, we'd take the blame. Now they're covering their backs, feeding the media misinformation about Al-Qaeda. But we present a problem. They know that we can bring down several people who were involved in the original plan. The chairman had decided to make us the fall guys from the beginning."

"How?"

"I don't know exactly. I do know that he killed two of our top security guys and that if he has his way, we're next."

"Who else is involved?"

"There could be several members of the cabinet, maybe heads of the other armed forces, NSA, Defense."

"How the hell are we going to find out? Can we trust anyone?"

"No one in Washington, that's for damn sure. After we dropped the general off, Isaac and I had a long talk. He offered me a job as head of security for World Corporation. He made me an offer I couldn't refuse. I want you to join me. You know how Isaac is, money is never an object. Doing what's right is the only thing he cares about. He's agreed that I can take whatever time I need and do whatever it takes to set the record straight regarding the killing of the president. He and World will back us all the way."

"What do you want me to do?"

"We need a couple of our guys that we can trust, but are still with the service. They'll be our eyes and ears, but they can't be told about the information I just gave you."

"What can I tell them?"

"Tell them we've been assigned to track down the killers of the president and the two agents."

"I'll get Ben on board, and we can trust Joe. What else?"

"I want to make sure this thing with Abra Surin is wrapped up, and then I plan to head to the States."

There was a knock at the door.

"May I come in?"

"Isaac, of course. I just filled James in on our conversation. He will be joining me at World."

"I'm happy to have you on the team, James." Isaac extended his hand and shook James's hand.

"Thanks, happy to be with you."

"How is Brahim doing?" Mike asked.

"He's doing well. While I was with him, Sammi called to tell him he had finished his meeting with the general and was on his way to the airport." The general had updated Mike on their plans for rescuing Abra on the way to his headquarters.

James stood up. "I'd better make those calls. See you later." He left.

"So," said Isaac, "what's your plan, Mike?"

"I need the general to get me more information on who else is in on this. This couldn't have been carried out without the assistance of top people in the government. I want James to stay behind to take care of the security for you and Brahim. I'm planning to go to the States as soon as I can."

"Brahim and I were just discussing the whole situation. As soon as we hear back from Sammi that Abra is okay, we'll have Susan notify everyone that the symposium that was to take place in Paris is being rescheduled to be held in New York. We just have to set the date. This will give you a reason to be in the States with Brahim and myself. We believe it's best that as far as everyone is concerned that you are still with the NSA on an assignment to protect us until this thing with president is cleared up."

"I'm with you on that. For now, James is the only one of my people who knows about my changed circumstances."

Isaac's phone rang. "Hello," he said. "Patch him in, Susan, and stay on the line."

CHAPTER
80

Sunday, June 8, 2014
Green home, Jerusalem

ISAAC, I'M WITH Jim and Guy in our office." It was around 10 a.m. in New York. "Guy wants to speak to you. I'm putting you on speaker." A moment later, Susan had them on speaker.

"Isaac, we have a problem."

"What is it, Guy?"

"I just found out that Jim's brothers are being sent back to Chicago."

"What do you think happened?"

"I don't like to speculate, but the president being killed has everyone in Washington nervous. I'd venture to guess that the attorney general felt since they were involved in a plot to kill the president, he would feel better if they were back in prison. They're being transferred as we speak."

"Anything at all we can do?"

"Not a chance."

"Jim, I'm really sorry."

"It's okay. Guy is doing everything he can to get them out of there."

"Guy, what are your plans?"

"The FBI delivered the discovery on their case against Jim's brothers to my offices. There's a lot to go through. I'll be working in World's headquarters so that Susan can assist."

"Keep me updated."

"Sure thing," said Guy, and the line disconnected.

There was a light tapping on the door. "Come in."

It was Mike. "Isaac, the general just called me. Sammi left and he's on his way back here. He should arrive in ten minutes."

"Have a seat. I just got off the phone with Guy and Jim. The attorney general ordered John Jr. and William to be escorted back to prison in Chicago. The whole business with the killing of the president has everyone on edge."

"You can't blame them."

The doorbell rang. Isaac focused on the monitor on his desk, and he saw the general at the door. "General, I'm buzzing you in," he said through the intercom.

Mike's cell phone rang. "Hello," he said into the phone. "All right, as soon as I can."

"Mike, everything all right?" Isaac asked.

"That was the deputy director. He said they are declaring a state of emergency. The military is on full alert. They're preparing to confront the Chinese. He wants me to come to D.C. right away."

There was a knock on the door and the general walked in.

"General, Mike was just saying that the United States is preparing for a showdown with China."

The general nodded. "Our people tell us that this has been in the planning stage for quite a while. We have confirmation that the chairman of the Joint Chiefs of Staff gave the order to kill the president when he obtained a coded message that the president wrote to the president of China. It said, 'The United States will not interfere with China's conflict with Taiwan. I'm on my way to pay my respects to the British prime minister's family. Please arrange a meeting with the Chinese foreign minister in England, and I will discuss my position further with him there.'

"It was signed by the president a few days before the Chinese started their military actions."

"Can you find out who else was involved?" Mike asked. "I need to know who else I can trust."

"I may have the answer in a few hours."

"I'll go update James on your intel. Please excuse me."

As soon as the door closed behind Mike, Isaac said, "General, how dangerous is it for Mike to go to Washington now?"

"As of now, nobody knows that he's aware of what actually took place at the Dorchester. They want him to return to D.C. so they can set him up. It will be easier if he's on home ground."

"Mike won't leave until he knows Abra is safe. How soon will we have information about Sammi?" Isaac asked.

"We've been monitoring him via our orbiting satellite from the moment he left my office. He agreed to let us put a small nitroglycerin patch on his chest. It's used for people with heart problems, but actually it contains a microtransmitter the size of a pinhead. Anyone checking for listening devices will never be able to discover it. If someone removes the patch and confiscates it, special chemical agents in the pad surrounding it will dissolve it, and we'll know he's in trouble."

"Anything else?"

"I thought you'd want to know that the prime minister has authorized us to release the funds we secured from the bank accounts that the Iranians tried to access. That's being handled as we speak."

Mike knocked and entered the room.

"Mike, is everything alright?" Isaac asked.

"I just briefed James. General, I need that information as soon as you can. I'm flying back to Washington tonight. I spoke to a few of my contacts in D.C. One of them won't speak on the phone, and he's the one I need to talk to the most. He works in the West Wing of the White House."

"Mike," said Isaac, "don't go to Washington. It's too dangerous."

"I know what you're concerned about, and you have nothing to worry about. I have no intention of showing up at NSA headquarters until I resolve this. My friend is meeting me at the airport in Washington and then I'm driving to New York. I have an alias I can use that they don't know about."

Isaac nodded. "Just be careful."

The general shook Mike's hand. "I must go. Sammi will be landing in Iran soon, and I want to monitor the situation from headquarters."

"Isaac," said Mike after the general left, "James is going to drive me to the airport. He'll be in charge while I'm gone. I'll be in touch with you as soon as I have any more information."

"Mike, be careful," Isaac said again. "Anything you need just call. I'm looking forward to greeting you in your new office at World headquarters."

Mike smiled, shook Isaac's hand, and left. Isaac stood for a moment, looking at the closed door. *Maybe I should have pushed him harder about not going to D.C.*

Chava walked into the room. She had just returned from visiting the grandchildren, and she looked happy.

"I wish you could have come with me today, Isaac. How are you, dear?"

"I'm fine, Chava."

Chava could tell there was more. She poured herself a glass of water and waited for the bomb to drop.

"Chava, I need to go back to New York right away, and I want you to come with me."

"Need to go, or want to go?"

"Jim has a lot to handle with his brothers and Brahim is ill. I've decided to reschedule the symposium. It's going to be held in New York, and there are numerous business matters I need to go over with Susan besides. I need to be there."

"When do you want to leave?"

"Tonight."

Chava nodded. "I'll call the children and let them know we're leaving and then I'll pack."

Isaac put his arm around Chava. "I think about our conversation in Paris every day. I'm working on what you asked of me. It's just going to take some time."

"Thank you, Isaac. I love you." She gave him a hug and then turned to leave.

Isaac picked up his PDA and dialed Susan's number.

"What can I do for you, Isaac?"

"Call William and tell him to prepare the plane. We're leaving Israel tonight. Make arrangements for another private jet to be ready just in case we need it."

"Anything wrong, Isaac?"

"No, I just think I should be there with everything going on with Jim and the symposium rescheduled. I want to hold the symposium as soon as it's feasible. Make the arrangements at the Waldorf."

"Everyone who was on the original list?"

"Yes, plus Mike and his security people."

"I'll confirm everything and get back to you."

"Thanks, Susan."

Isaac hung up and tried to think of what else had to be done. He dialed another number.

"Hello, Dov, we're leaving for New York tonight. We're rescheduling the symposium Susan will be in touch with the details. What are your plans?"

"Nothing in particular. I need to spend a couple of days in the office here in Paris, but afterward I can fly to New York and work with Susan on the media package for the symposium."

"Excellent."

Isaac sat at his desk and closed his eyes, exhausted. Thoughts of China, the president's assassination, the chairman of the Joint Chiefs of Staff, and Abra all fought for top position in his mind. After a few moments he gave into his fatigue and fell into a deep sleep.

CHAPTER
81

Sunday, June 8, 2014
World headquarters, New York

B
Y ELEVEN A.M. Guy was in the conference room on the forty-ninth floor at World's corporate office. He buzzed Susan.

"Susan, can you spare a moment?"

Susan walked in to see Guy surrounded by opened files from the FBI. They covered every inch of his desk and the floor.

"Susan, I need you to look at the three files in front of you and tell me what you think."

"What am I looking for?"

"You'll know it when you see it. I'm fixing myself a cup of coffee. Would you care for one?"

"No, thanks."

Guy took his drink and sat down watching Susan go through each file. He knew she would confirm what he'd already discovered. After fifteen minutes, she closed the last file.

"Miranda rights. The FBI questioned them in the beginning without telling them their rights."

"Yes, I've read the files countless times. There are at least half a dozen violations of John and William's rights. They have no case. At this point all they have is John killing the guy in prison. But we can prove it was self-defense."

All of a sudden, the door crashed open. Jim barged in, yelling, "Turn on the news!"

Susan pressed a button to turn on *Fox News*. Pictures of John and William were displayed on the screen as the news anchor reported.

"*In breaking news, two prisoners accused of plotting to assassinate the president, John Murphy and his brother William Murphy, were killed earlier today by FBI agents in an attempted escape while being transported back to the federal prison in Illinois. Local FBI agents are still searching for two white males who they believe to have been involved in the escape.*"

Guy and Susan looked at each other, then at Jim. "I'm so sorry, Jim," said Susan.

"We're going to find out how this happened," said Guy.

Jim sighed. "I know. For now, I need you to contact the authorities and find out when they will release the bodies. I need to make arrangements to bury them in our family plot. This is going to kill my mother."

"I'll take care of it right away."

"Thanks, Guy. I'm going home to be with Mary. If anyone calls, I'm unavailable. Unless it's Isaac or Brahim. I don't want to talk to anyone else right now."

Guy walked Jim to the elevator. "I'm so sorry. Do you want me to come with you?"

"I'll be okay. You know, my parents worked so hard to bring us up right. Thank the good Lord that at least my father didn't have to see this. Both of my parents were immigrants from Ireland. They fought to be treated like equals in a place that constantly reminded them they weren't. People hated the Irish when my parents got here. It wasn't any better for the Jews. But look at how the world has changed. Look at how far America's come. Still, neo-Nazis, fanatic Muslims, and other whackos are trying to tear us apart. We won't let it happen. It's too important."

The elevator doors opened and Jim entered. "We'll bet the world on it."

Susan was watching the news when Guy returned.

"Is there anything new?"

"Nothing more about John and William, but the president called for a UN Security Council meeting regarding China."

"It's lunchtime. I'm going to get something to eat. Want to join me?"

"Yes, I'm starved. I need about fifteen minutes to finish sending out the invitations to the symposium and then I'll be ready to go."

"Just buzz me when you're ready, and you can choose the restaurant.

CHAPTER
82

Sunday, June 8, 2014
Imam Khomeini International Airport, Tehran

ON THE APPROACH to Tehran, the pilot of the Swiss chartered flight announced that the weather was twenty-six degrees Celsius, partly cloudy and pleasantly warm. June in Tehran was balmy even at night.

The tower instructed the pilot to land and proceed to a hangar far away from the main terminal. As the pilot lowered the plane's wheels, Sammi's heart began to beat faster. He took a deep breath to relax. One of the agents noticed and handed him a glass of water. "Have a drink. You'll be okay."

As the plane taxied into the hanger, Sammi remembered a trip he took to Tehran with his parents when he was a young boy. The visit to the Grand Bazaar was still vivid in his mind. The merchants shouting, the crowds, the rushing and pushing. He was petrified to let go of his mother's hand.

Sammi was brought back to the present when he realized the plane had come to a stop and the stairs had been lowered. Walking down the stairs, he noticed there were half a dozen men in black suits standing next to three Samand LX cars manufactured in Iran.

"*As salamu aleiykum.* Welcome home." Akbar Hussein, secretary of the Guardian Council, extended his hand. Sammi and Hussein had spoken briefly to arrange the meetup.

"*Waleiykum assalum.*"

"Please follow me to my car."

"What about my associates?"

"They'll be in the cars behind us."

They drove along Valisar Street, the longest street in Tehran. Taxis, private cars, and buses weaved in and out. Crossing the street felt like walking through a minefield.

"Driver, take us to Shahr Park," the secretary said.

At his briefing in Israel, Sammi had been informed that Abra was being held in Lavizan Park. "Isn't Mrs. Surin in Lavizan Park?"

"Yes, we're taking you to the drop-off point so you can deliver the ransom money."

AT THE TREE of Life headquarters, the general was listening to every word being said. Two of his men sat next to him. Another agent tracked the delivery of the drug that was to be administered to Abra.

"General, we just received word that the vial has been delivered to the Razi Hospital a short walk from Shahr Park. I've received confirmation that Dr. Fard signed for it."

"Good. Check that the plane is ready to go, and test the listening device Sammi just placed in the car. And get me an update from the NSA on the doctor's family."

THE CARS STOPPED outside a tall wrought-iron gate. The park's guards rushed to open it so they could drive through. Only a few feet inside the park, the cars suddenly stopped.

The secretary got out of the car, motioning to Sammi to follow.

"We'll wait here. Come, we can sit on a bench near the pond."

Sammi sat down, looking around. The park appeared empty except for men in black suits stationed at different locations. A loud minaret called worshippers to pray. Akbar's mobile rang. Sammi could see from the look on Akbar's face that he'd just been told something terrible.

"We must go."

"Why? What happened?"

"Mrs. Surin is ill. They want us to come to her."

"What's wrong?"

"I only know that she is unconscious. Her physician, Dr. Fard, is with her."

"I must call Mr. Surin and inform him."

"You can call him after we meet with the doctor."

They went back into their vehicle and drove out of the park. A few minutes later, they pulled up to a building. Akbar led Sammi inside and they walked through a narrow hallway. A man whom Sammi assumed to be Dr. Fard stood in front of a steel door.

"What happened?" Akbar asked.

"Her heart. I need to get her into surgery. It's a complicated procedure. I called the Bern University heart clinic in Switzerland. One of the top surgeons in the world is there, and he is a good friend of mine. He has agreed to assist me with the operation. We need to fly Mrs. Surin there immediately."

Akbar picked up his mobile and walked around a corner out of sight. General Solomon and his staff listened to every word as an unsuspecting Akbar dialed the Ayatollah.

"Ayatollah, Mrs. Surin is in need of emergency heart surgery. She will die without it. Dr. Fard has made arrangements to have the operation performed in Switzerland. The exchange hasn't happened yet. How should I proceed?"

"You can release her once the ransom has been paid."

"And the chip?"

"There are other ways. For now, make sure that she doesn't die. We have controlled her this long. It would be a pity to lose our best pawn when she has set us up so well for a checkmate."

"I'll handle it. Thank you."

Akbar returned to where Sammi and the doctor were standing.

"I just spoke with the Ayatollah. He has agreed to release Mrs. Surin under certain conditions. The money transfer has to take place now."

"One moment." Sammi pulled out his phone to call Brahim. "My mobile isn't working. I need to talk to Mr. Surin."

"Hold on." Akbar dialed a number and spoke into his phone. When he hung up, he said, "Your phone should be in service now."

"Hello, boss," said Sammi when he reached Brahim. "I'm with Abra. She needs an operation. Dr. Fard arranged for the top heart surgeon in Switzerland to perform the operation. They won't release her until they have the money. We don't have much time."

"Tell them that by the time they land in Bern, they will have confirmation of the money. I'll meet you in Bern. And Sammi, tell them that if she dies, I'll hunt every one of them down and kill them myself."

CHAPTER
83

Sunday, June 8, 2014
Green home, Jerusalem

BRAHIM HUNG UP the phone and walked into Isaac's office. "Isaac, they're moving Abra to Switzerland. I'm going there right away."

"Hold it a minute, let me answer this call."

"General? Yes, I'll put him on the speaker." Isaac pressed a button. "Okay, go ahead."

"Brahim, I need to update you on what's really going on. Abra is fine. We are monitoring her vital signs in our office. The drug is performing the way it's supposed to. She is sleeping peacefully. Dr. Fard is right by her side. One minute, please hold on." A pause and then, "My aide just handed me a note. The plane is preparing to take off for Switzerland as we speak. Sammi is on the plane with some of our personnel. They should be landing in Bern-Belp Airport in a few hours."

"Thanks, I was telling Isaac I'm going there now."

A pause and then, "I suppose I won't be able to convince you to stay put, will I? Alright, a couple of my men will accompany you."

"General," said Isaac, "Susan ordered me an extra plane on standby in case of an emergency. It should be at Ben Gurion. Brahim can use it."

"Good. Brahim, my people will pick you up in an hour and fly with you. If you need anything, call me. I'll be in touch with you later when you arrive in Switzerland."

The general hung up.

Isaac looked at Brahim. "Are sure you're feeling up to this? You just got home from the hospital and you're recovering from a heart attack. Maybe I should cancel my flight to New York and go with you."

"I'll be fine. The flight is only a few hours and I promise you, I'll take it easy. As soon as I see Abra, I'll feel much better."

An hour later, Brahim was at the door saying good-bye to Isaac and Chava.

"Have you got everything you need?" Isaac asked.

"Yes, my bag is by the door."

"Brahim," said Chava, "you be careful. I pray that Abra will be well. Both of you should come to stay with us for a while when this is all over."

"With the help of Allah, we will. Thank you for your hospitality. *JazakAllahu khair.* May Allah reward you. You and Isaac are the best friends a man can ask for."

Isaac and Chava walked Brahim to the car waiting for him outside. Brahim turned to Isaac, grabbed him, and gave him a hug.

Isaac and Chava stood waving as the car drove away. Isaac turned to Chava.

"You ready to go?"

"I'm almost packed. Just tell me when you're ready."

"I need a couple of hours to tie things up here. I want to make sure Abra is safe before we leave."

As they walked back into the house, arms around each other's waists, Chava said, "Any idea when we're coming back?"

"God willing, right after the symposium. Susan arranged it for July third at the Waldorf."

Chava looked surprised. She didn't think they'd be coming back so soon, but she said nothing. She knew Isaac never said anything he didn't mean.

CHAPTER
84

Sunday, June 8, 2014
Bern-Belp Airport, Switzerland

DR. FARD SAT alongside Abra's stretcher monitoring her blood pressure. Sammi read from Abra's Koran: *"Truly distress has seized me, but You are Most Merciful of those who are merciful..."* (Koran 21:83–84).

The sound of the landing gear being lowered brought Sammi back to reality. A moment later the wheels touched the runway. The landing was extraordinarily soft as the pilot did his best not to disturb the patient. The plane came to a stop, and the staircase was lowered. The two Mossad agents were the first to exit.

A large red ambulance with two blue flashing lights on its roof pulled within a few feet of the staircase. Abra was gently lowered from the plane onto a stretcher and placed directly into the ambulance. Dr. Fard got into the back with her.

Akbar and his guards stepped forward to join the doctor. "We have to be in the ambulance with you," Akbar insisted.

One of the medics attempted to close the doors. "She doesn't have time for this. We have to go."

A moment later the discussion was closed as four unmarked cars pulled up. Sammi moved off to the side with his agents. Something was up.

Eight men emerged from the vehicles, guns drawn, and surrounded Akbar and his guards. One of them said, "You are under arrest for kidnapping Abra Surin, an American citizen, plus money laundering, blackmail, assault and battery, terrorism, and coercion. My agents will assist you in getting into the cars."

Akbar's face turned red. "This is outrageous. I insist on contacting my embassy in Bern. You have no right to hold me. I have diplomatic immunity."

"We have an extradition treaty with Switzerland, and I have a signed document from the Swiss government allowing us to take you and your guards to the United States." The agent addressed his colleagues. "Cuff them and take them to the plane."

Once the Iranians were placed in the back of one of the vehicles, the agent walked over to Sammi. "My name is Jeff Robins. I'm with the NSA. Mike sends his regards."

Sammi shook his hand. "Thank you. Perfect timing."

"Please get into my car. It's the last one. I'll be escorting you to the hospital." Jeff walked over to the car where Akbar and his agents were being held and hit the car roof twice with his fist. "Take him away, boys."

Jeff's mobile rang. "Hello, Mike. Great, it went off as planned. I would give anything to see Akbar's face when he lands in Israel's Hatzerim Airbase in the Negev."

"Great job. I'll meet you back in the States."

CHAPTER
85

Sunday, June 8, 2014
Ben Gurion Airport, Tel Aviv

BACK IN ISRAEL, Mike hung up and dialed General Solomon and Isaac for a conference call.

"General, are you on the line?"

"Yes."

"Isaac, you there?"

"I'm on. Go ahead."

"It's done. The goods are on their way."

"Mike, you did a fantastic job."

"My pleasure, but most of the plan was the general's. Though I did save World a billion bucks in ransom. So now that I'm working for you, make sure I get a big bonus at the end of the year."

"You got it, Mike. I have to tell Brahim the good news."

"Okay," the general chimed in, "but nothing about the plane being diverted to Israel for now. The Swiss will go crazy."

"Okay, talk with you later. I'm about to board my plane. Isaac, I'll see you in New York."

CHAPTER
86

Sunday, June 8, 2014
Green home, Jerusalem

WHEN HE HUNG up with Mike and the general, Isaac turned on his PDA. "Brahim, can you see me?"

"Perfectly."

"Abra is safe. She's still unconscious, but she'll be waking up soon. They're running some blood tests just to make sure everything went alright with the drug Dr. Fard gave her. Sammi is watching her in her room, waiting for you to arrive."

"Thanks. If Abra is capable of traveling, I intend to fly to the States tonight."

"I'll ask Mike to get Dr. Fard a visa so he can come with you and keep an eye on Abra."

"Alright. When I get there and see how Abra is doing for myself, I'll be in contact with you and Susan."

"Have a safe flight. Don't forget that we've rescheduled the symposium for the beginning of July. I'll need you there. Brahim, Susan's calling. Let me take it. Talk to you later."

"Hello, Isaac."

"Yes, Susan what is it?"

"I just wanted to give you an update on the symposium. I've already received acceptances from over eighty-five percent of the guests we invited. Our contact in the White House informed us that the president is clearing his appointments to attend."

"That's good news."

"I checked with your pilot. He said he's ready as soon as you are. When do you expect to leave?"

"We're ready. I just wanted to make sure Abra was safe before we left."

"How is she?" Susan asked.

"She's going to be okay."

"That's good. Now I have to go, Isaac. I'll talk to you when you're in flight."

Chava walked in. "The luggage is in the car. James took it down and I'm ready to go."

James would be flying back to New York with the Greens. Ben was coming in from Paris and would meet them at the airport.

"Alright, let's go."

The car started to pull away when Isaac's mobile rang.

"Hello, Isaac."

"Yes, General."

"Where are you?"

"I'm on my way to the airport."

"Perfect. I need to fly to New York and I thought I could get a ride. The prime minister asked me to meet him there."

"Of course." Isaac checked the time. It was around midnight. "We should be there in about thirty minutes."

CHAPTER
87

Sunday, June 8, 2014
Bern-Belp Airport, Switzerland

THREE HOURS AND forty five minutes after Brahim's plane took off from Israel, he landed at Bern-Belp Airport. As the wheels of his plane touched the runway, he noticed a peculiar sight out of his window: an ambulance and two police cars with flashing lights furiously driving toward his plane. The plane slowed in front of the ambulance and shut down its engines.

A minute later, the stairs were lowered. Brahim descended the staircase to find Sammi waiting impatiently for Brahim's feet to touch the ground.

"Boss, we have her," Sammi said. "She's fine."

Brahim grabbed Sammi and started to cry. "*Alhamdulillah*. Thank Allah, thank Allah. Sammi, get in touch with Fatima right now at the U.S. Embassy in Iran. Tell her to get on a plane and fly to the States. Tell her Abra is fine and we are headed to New York."

"I'll do it, boss. Now we have to go. General Solomon and his people have arranged for another plane to fly all of us to the States. As soon as we're on board, it will take off."

"I want to see Abra."

The ambulance door opened. Dr. Fard was inside with Abra. The doctor stepped out of the ambulance to greet Brahim.

"Mr. Surin, I'm Dr. Fard. Your wife is fine. *Subhaanallah*. Praise Allah."

"Thank you, Doctor, for all you have done."

Brahim climbed inside the ambulance and sat down next to Abra. He took her hand in his. Dr. Fard followed.

Sammi closed the door. "We must go."

Fifteen minutes later, the plane had taken on all its passengers and was airborne. Seats had been removed to make room for Abra and the medical equipment that would monitor her vitals. Special safety belts secured the stretcher. Dr. Fard was sitting next to Abra taking her blood pressure. The NSA security detail and the two Mossad agents sat in the back. Brahim and Sammi sat across from each other.

"Sammi, what the hell went on back there?"

Sammi smiled and thought, *Thank Allah, everything is back to normal.*

"Boss, all I know is what the general's men told me. When the transfer of funds failed to arrive in Iran, they tried to contact Mr. Hussein. There was no response. The NSA had taken him into custody when we arrived in Bern. The president of Iran contacted Ali Banisadr, the head of Vevak, the Ministry of Intelligence and National Security. Banisadr in turn contacted his agents in Bern. They were given orders to kill Abra, Dr. Fard, and me. But General Solomon intercepted the message and arranged for this plane to get us out of here before the Iranian agents could get to us."

Brahim's face was angry. "'Now this is not the end. It is not even the beginning of the end. But it is, perhaps, the end of the beginning.'"

"That's a quote from Winston Churchill, right, boss?"

"Sammi, you know me too well. Let's get some sleep. It's a long flight home."

EPILOGUE

G OOD MORNING, BRAHIM. How are you and Abra doing?"

In his office in his Morristown mansion, Brahim smiled. "Hello, Susan. I thank Allah that she's fine. Dr. Fard has been staying with us until Abra has recovered. We're taking things slowly. We don't want to push her. We're letting her come to her own conclusions."

"She must be in so much pain. To realize that the people she trusted were willing to murder her. And worst of all, that they used Allah as a cover."

"She thought she was one of them, that they cared for her, as I truly do. She feels betrayed. She gave them so much of herself."

"Of course, it makes sense. How did she take it?"

"That she is suffering from acute amphetamine psychosis? I haven't told her yet. I don't want the shock to push her over the edge. It's not an easy thing to explain. It's another betrayal. She loved our maid. She'd been with us for years. I still can't believe she let money be the deciding factor of her loyalty. How am I supposed to tell Abra that the group my wife thought she was working with actually used our maid to slip Lisdexamfetamine into her drinks for the past year, causing her to change into a completely different person?"

"I don't get it. That drug is usually safe."

"It's safe in normal doses. But her blood work came back with a thousand times the normal dose in her system. At that level, it can cause paranoia, aggression, heart problems, uncontrollable anger, even hallucinations. Sound familiar?"

"I'm so proud of you, Brahim. You knew who she really was and you stood by her. When the time is right, tell her the truth. You have to remain the one person in her life who's always completely honest with her."

"You're right, Susan. When the time is right, I'll tell her."

"How'd you figured out she'd been drugged?"

"It was from something Sammi said to Dr. Fard. In the ambulance he mentioned how unreal this all was, that he'd never seen a person change like Abra had over the past year, that she was a completely different person. Dr. Fard picked up on it and ordered a few extra blood tests.

"When he saw the amount of Lisdexamfetamine in her system, it all made sense. We'll get through this. She needs some time to get back to herself and her real life. I plan to spend more time with her. Try to remind her why she fell in love with me."

"Did you play her the tape of the order to kill her by the Ayatollah?"

"Yes, the whole family heard it. Abra couldn't stop crying."

"I'm sorry, Brahim."

Brahim sighed. "Thank you, Susan. But I feel we can finally put this behind us and move on."

"Speaking of moving on, are you all set?"

"More than ready. After everything we've been through, it's clearer than ever that we have to bring the world together to fight terrorism now."

"Isaac asked me to tell everyone that we're starting promptly at twelve o'clock."

"Sammi will be driving me in early. I'll be there on time. Listen, Susan, last night, Isaac, Jim, and I had a conference call. We all agreed that you should be the moderator at the symposium. Arrange it the way you want. We're all wiped out."

"Isaac already informed me. Please give my warmest regards to Abra and the family."

"I will."

Brahim hung up the phone.

SUSAN HAD RESERVED all of the suites in the towers at the Waldorf Astoria on Park Avenue. The Sir Winston Churchill Suite had been ordered for Brahim. Isaac was in the Cole Porter and Jim in the Trianon. The Presidential and Penthouse had also been ordered and held in reserve. The minute Susan heard that General Solomon and Mike were attending, she assigned them the three-bedroom Penthouse suite. Most of the four hundred guests had confirmed their attendance. The John Astor Salon would be filled to capacity.

The Waldorf was busy as guests checked in and out. Taxis lined up waiting for their next fare. When Joe Madino saw Sammi in the limo, he stopped what he was doing to greet Sammi.

"*Holla*, amigo, where have you been?"

"Joe, it's a long story. Some other time I'll tell you all about it. The boss has a very important conference to attend."

"I understand the president is coming. The Secret Service is all over the place. It's been nonstop since last night. People have been checking in for the symposium from all over the world."

Sammi handed Joe twenty dollars. "Keep your eye on the car," Sammi said over his shoulder as he ran to the door, trying to keep up with Brahim.

"I always do," Joe shouted back.

A security detail was waiting for them in the lobby.

"Mr. Surin," said one of the men, "please come with us. Mike has assigned us to you for protection. He is waiting for you with Mr.

Green in the Cole Porter Suite."

Several security personnel stood around talking outside the suite. One of them saw Brahim coming and knocked on the door.

The door was opened by General Solomon. "Brahim, it's nice to see you again."

Brahim smiled. "This is a pleasant surprise. It gives me the opportunity to thank you in person for helping Abra and me through all of this."

"Glad to help. Sammi, you did great. Everyone in the office agrees that you would be an asset to our team at the Tree of Life."

"Thank you, General, but no thanks. I couldn't leave the best boss in the world. No offense, of course."

Mike came to the door. For the last month, Mike had been gathering evidence against the Joint Chief of Staffs for the assassination of the president at the Dorchester. After the symposium, he planned to fly to Washington and make his case. "Brahim, Sammi, how are you both?" he said.

Brahim sighed. "It's an adjustment. Abra is still in shock. But she will pull through."

"I know she will. Why don't you both come inside? Isaac is waiting for you."

When they entered the suite, Isaac greeted them and handed each of them a sheet of paper. "Susan asked me to show you the program to let her know if you want any changes."

Brahim scanned it. "Yes, there is one change. I'm not up to making the opening comments. Isaac, I would like you to do it."

Isaac turned to Jim, who had just walked in from the other room. "Jim, is that okay with you?"

"Sure."

"Susan will explain to our guests that over the Fourth of July weekend she and other members of our staff will be available to meet with individuals and small groups to discuss the implementation of the plan after the close of the speeches."

Isaac's phone buzzed. It was Susan.

"Susan what is it?"

"Most of the guests are being seated by our people. I think you should all come now."

"What about the president?"

"The Secret Service informed me he'll be arriving any minute. One of his aides asked if he could say a few words, before the official opening. I told him that would be fine."

"We're on our way."

Isaac hung up the phone. "We have to go. The president will be arriving shortly, and we should be there to greet him."

Security guards were everywhere. Some of the guests were talking, others smiling while shaking hands. Everyone presented their invitations and identifications at the door. By 11:45 all the seats were full. Standing around the room, Dov's media crews from around the world were poised and ready to cover the event.

Sitting at three VIP tables, close to the podium, were Chava, Jim's wife Mary, General Solomon, Mike, Charlie, Kim Li, Allan, Guy, and Sammi. James stood in the back keeping an eye on the security personnel. Another table was reserved for the president and his staff. The last one was for Isaac's and Brahim's children. Susan stood at the podium. Sitting in chairs to the right of her, facing the guests, were Jim, Brahim, and Isaac. The air was heavy with anticipation as everyone waited for the president to arrive.

One of the president's aides handed Susan a note. She read it, then looked up and addressed the guests. "Ladies and gentlemen, it's my pleasure to welcome the President of the United States."

The cameras went wild and the audience rose to their feet. The president waved and asked everyone to please be seated.

"I have to apologize that I can't stay for the entire symposium. My staff has briefed me on the mission that World Corporation and its principals have undertaken. I want to thank each of you, Jim, Brahim, and Isaac, for your efforts to bring peace to the world. I will do everything in my power to help you succeed."

The president paused and nodded to one of his aides, who came up to the podium holding a green velvet case.

The president took the case and said, "It's my pleasure and honor as president to present each one of you with the Presidential Medal of Freedom. World Corporation has made enormous contributions to the security of the United States, and with your efforts here today to world peace as well. Thank you and God bless America."

The president handed the Medal of Freedom to Isaac, Jim, and Brahim. The photographers clicked away nonstop.

As he left, he took Isaac by the hand and said, "I gave Mike orders to stay close to you." The president didn't know that Isaac had already hired him to do just that. Officially, Mike was still working for the NSA.

Everyone smiled and then the president exited. Susan stood with her hand on the microphone, waiting for everyone to be seated.

"Next to me on this stage," she said, "are three of the most wonderful men I have ever known. Most of you know them from doing business with World. But I know them differently. I have been working for them for almost twenty-five years. You could never work for better bosses, but more than that, you could never ask for better friends. At this time I would like to present to you one of the partners of World, Mr. Isaac Green."

The guests clapped and Isaac stood up to speak.

"Thank you, Susan, for the kind words. We're all here today for the same reason. Because we know the world isn't where we want it to be. We're also here because we know that there's something we can do to bring about the change we want to see. We're all here for the same reason: for peace."

The audience roared with applause. Isaac raised his arm to quiet them.

"Today is a big day for World on lots of levels, and it's about to become an even bigger day for the woman who just spoke to all of you. You wouldn't believe how much she has done to further World and the beliefs our company is trying to uphold. So, Susan, as a small thank-you for all you've done in the pursuit of peace and to help World do what it needs to do, I want to announce that as of today you'll no longer be working for us."

Susan's mouth dropped. *What is he talking about?*

Isaac continued, "As of today, Susan, you're an equal partner with Jim, Brahim, and myself. We hope and pray you will continue with us to build World Corporation."

Susan's eyes filled with tears. As she approached Isaac on the podium, Isaac whispered to her, "We decided in London. You deserve it."

Susan took the microphone. Her words were brief. "Thank you all. I never expected this."

She sat back down in her seat, stunned.

Isaac was standing by the podium adjusting the microphone. He wasn't finished.

"Thank you all for being part of the first World Corporation Symposium against Terrorism. My partner Brahim likes to quote Sir Winston Churchill. This one is for you, brother: 'The short words are best, and the old words are best of all.'

"Terrorism has been eating away at the very foundation of our existence. Over the last month, my partners and I experienced it firsthand. Our families have been personally affected. My wife was in a hostage situation, and Brahim's wife, who couldn't be here tonight, has also faced terrorism, much too close for either of our comforts.

"You may know that Jim is a practicing Catholic, Brahim a devoted Muslim, myself an observant Jew. We are all subject to this plague that has no boundaries. Today no country can escape it. When you open your eyes in the morning and read the newspapers or turn on the TV, death and destruction dominate the headlines. How can we close our eyes to what surrounds us and sleep at night? Terrorist cells are active in many countries around the world. Al-Qaeda is just one of them. The Middle East, Europe, Africa—the whole world is hemorrhaging from terror. And diplomatic band-aids will not stop this. But we can change the world if we keep in mind three things.

"First, passion. All of us have to develop it within our own communities. That's the antidote against this plague. If you want to be successful in business, you must be passionate about what you're doing. If you want to achieve peace, you need that same passion. All of us here understand that.

"The second is people. Who are the most successful people? They are the ones who gather individuals around them with the same passion to succeed.

"The third and final one is perseverance—the dedication and the ability to stay the course.

"We at World are committed to this mission. Each one of you has been presented with an information package on how we are going to accomplish this. Please join us. Susan and our staff will be available to meet with all of you over the next couple of days to answer any questions you may have.

"Sir Winston Churchill said, 'Never give in, never give in, never, never, never, never.' Our slogan will be those short words. God bless you all for coming, and we pray that God should continue to bless America."

Everyone stood up to applaud. Isaac walked over to Susan. "As always, you did a great job. Mazel tov, partner."

Everyone congratulated the partners on the event. Dov was busy with the media, making sure that Isaac's speech made the six p.m. news. Sammi stood next to Brahim and Charlie. Kim Li and Allan stood holding hands and accepting congratulations on their recent engagement, which they had announced right before the symposium. The general and Mike walked off to the side talking.

No one noticed as Chava took Isaac's hand and led him into the lobby. They ended up in front of the famous bronze Waldorf Astoria Clock.

Chava looked into Isaac's eyes and smiled. "You did good, Isaac."

"It was everything I could hope for. And"—he squeezed her hand—"I couldn't have done it without you."

They stood in silence, just enjoying the moment. There would surely be other crises, other concerns that might take them away from each other for a while, but for now they were together and at peace.

"You know, Isaac, I was thinking. You could write a book. Just the events that happened in the last two months would put your book on the *New York Times* bestseller list."

Isaac smiled. "Yeah, but who would play me in the movie?"

Chava leaned over and whispered into Isaac's ear. "Harrison Ford, of course."

ACKNOWLEDGMENTS

The beginning of the journey of writing this book was the birth of a plot conceived by my son Bitzalel. Always a "thinker," his inspired ideas are the basis for the book I chose to write. So kudos to him for getting the journey underway.

The actual form of the book wouldn't have found a cohesive voice without the editing of Shifra Witt. She truly is the book doctor, and her patience working with me was truly remarkable and so much appreciated.

This book and the powerful story it tells needed quite a bit of fine-tuning and tweaking so that the message could be heard. Suri Brand was of invaluable help in the final steps toward bringing the book to fruition.

I would like to thank my granddaughter Nechama Gross for serving as my PA and assisting me with the technical aspects of publishing the book. I look forward to working together with her as we move on to other forms of media.

I was especially excited with the fantastic job my granddaughter Odeya Gross did on the design and graphic of the book's cover. She is a very talented graphic artist and captured my intentions not only for the cover but for the website promoting the book as well.

This book is interwoven with the tale of my life. I would like to thank my children, Yosef, Mindy, and Susan, for sharing in some of the adventures that make this book of fiction what it is.

To all of my family and friends, and in particular to all of my grandchildren and great-grandchildren, I hope this book will give you a glimpse into the journey of my life and an insight into the hopes I have for the ideal world we should all live in, in peace and prosperity.

And, as they say, I saved the best for last. Isaac Green, one of my protagonists, says, "My wife, my life." I actually let him steal my line. There is no one like my wife. Besides the countless hours she sat beside me to make this book possible, her belief in my being able to do whatever I set my mind to do is my greatest inspiration. No words of gratitude suffice.

ABOUT THE AUTHOR

DAVID BROWN is a true renaissance man. During the over forty years that he served as a financial adviser as well as CEO of a public company, he has traveled extensively as a consummate professional, yet always viewed the world through the eyes of a curious child. Life is an adventure, and every person he meets on his travels have become part of an extended family of associates and colleagues that span decades and continents. His worldview finds a voice in his first debut as a novelist. It reveals a deep hope for the future of the world and for his family, who are of paramount importance in his life.

Made in the
USA
Lexington, KY